VORTEX

A TEMPEST NOVEL

DISCARD

JULIE CROSS

THOMAS DUNNE BOOKS
ST. MARTIN'S GRIFFIN
NEW YORK

This is a work of fiction. All of the characters, organizations, and events portrayed in this novel are either products of the author's imagination or are used fictitiously.

THOMAS DUNNE BOOKS.
An imprint of St. Martin's Press.

VORTEX. Copyright © 2012 by Julie Cross. All rights reserved. Printed in the United States of America. For information, address St. Martin's Press, 175 Fifth Avenue, New York, N.Y. 10010.

www.thomasdunnebooks.com
www.stmartins.com

The Library of Congress has cataloged the hardcover edition as follows:

Cross, Julie.
    Vortex : a Tempest novel / Julie Cross.—1st ed.
        p. cm.
    ISBN 978-0-312-56890-0 (hardcover)
    ISBN 978-1-250-02072-7 (e-book)
    1. Time travel—Fiction. 2. Spies—Fiction. 3. Love—Fiction. 4. Science fiction. I. Title.
    PZ7.C88272Vo 2012
    [Fic]—dc23

2012040053

ISBN 978-1-250-04478-5 (trade paperback)

St. Martin's Griffin books may be purchased for educational, business, or promotional use. For information on bulk purchases, please contact Macmillan Corporate and Premium Sales Department at 1-800-221-7945, extension 5442, or write specialmarkets@macmillan.com.

First St. Martin's Griffin Trade Paperback Edition: January 2014

10 9 8 7 6 5 4 3 2 1

TO MY HUSBAND, NICK, WHO
HAS ENDURED THE ENTIRE
PUBLICATION RIDE WITH ME.
I LOVE YOU. THANK YOU FOR
MAKING ME A STRONGER,
BETTER PERSON.

VORTEX

PROLOGUE

The only things that gave me the strength to pull myself off that grassy spot and walk farther from Holly
were the images that flashed through my mind—Holly,
sitting in that orientation, hiding the book in her lap with
her name carefully written inside, her hair twirling
around the pencil she was using to take notes. I had sat
three rows behind her that day...today...and
watched her the whole two hours. And even though
she hadn't once looked back at me, I figured she must
have known I was staring because she rolled her eyes at
me outside the building, just before I got in my car.
There was something both affectionate and challenging
in that look she had given me.

Now, repeating that day, I felt so much relief knowing
I wouldn't be in that room with her, allowing her life to
collide with mine in such a dangerous way. I just had to
keep playing those memories over and over, removing
myself from the picture in my head, and I knew I'd get
through this. I'd live without her as long as I could imagine her life without me. More importantly, her life would
be better without me.

The moment I walked into Dad's place, my arm in a
sling and a whole lot of crap to explain, it was a little
easier to temporarily set my thoughts of Holly aside...
for now.

Dad took one look at my injured shoulder as I leaned my good arm against the door frame of his home office and strode quickly across the room. "What the hell happened to you, Jackson?"

"I got shot." I let out a breath, prepping for his reaction. "In August of this year . . . by Raymond . . . one of the Enemies of Time. He's dead now . . . well, he was dead in August . . . which hasn't happened yet . . . so, I guess I'm not sure . . ."

He froze in his spot, eyes widening. I reached in my pocket and removed the memory card that August 2009 Dad had given me, and offered it to him. "This is yours . . . sort of."

He completely ignored the memory card and moved closer, resting his hands on my face, looking me over carefully. "Are you okay? Tell me you're okay."

And this was the moment when I knew for sure that I could trust any and all versions of my dad.

"Physically, I'm fine." I tugged his hands from my face and placed the memory card in his open palm. "But we have a lot to talk about and we might need Chief Marshall and Dr. Melvin."

He nodded, still half in shock, probably wondering how I knew Chief Marshall, then pointed to a chair for me to sit down in. I waited patiently while he zipped through notes on his computer. I couldn't read any of his code, but I had guessed what he might have read by the time I heard him draw in a breath and rub his hands over his face.

"I'm sorry about Eileen," I said finally.

He closed his eyes for a moment and then turned in his chair to face me. "We aren't going to tell anyone about Holly or this Adam Silverman kid . . . not Chief Marshall or Dr. Melvin. No one."

"Good," I said immediately, glad we were on the same page.

"I have a plan for keeping tabs on them." He stared over my shoulder at the wall, lost in thought. "A reliable source that will make sure everything stays under the radar. But you have to promise me you won't look up their emails or Facebook or anything that's traceable. Understood?"

I swallowed the lump in my throat, feeling the finality in my answer. "Understood."

"And there's no way I'd ever let you join Tempest," he stated flatly, as though he'd read my mind. "I'm not sure what my other self was thinking . . . maybe he took a blow to the head before agreeing to this, but it's not happening."

Didn't he understand why I'd made the choices I'd made? "I have to. I'm not going back to my old life. I can't. I know about Jenni Stewart. I met her in 2007 . . . in that other universe or whatever. She was only my age and Chief Marshall let her join the CIA."

My knee bounced up and down, anticipating his argument. It felt like a clock was ticking inside my chest. If I didn't dive in, headfirst, to something totally new, I would find myself running into that camp counselor orientation, apologizing to Mr. Wellborn for being late and undoing the one unselfish thing I'd managed to do in my life.

Dad's expression faltered, showing early signs of defeat. "You do realize that I've devoted eighteen years of my life to preventing this very thing from happening."

"I know."

"I didn't raise you for this." His eyebrows knitted together. "What I mean is . . . you've had it pretty easy . . . you've never had to worry about anything . . . never had to defend yourself. You aren't ready for this. Maybe we could just—"

"Then I'll get ready," I said firmly, standing up from my chair. I reached for the phone on the desk before Dad could stop me. "Should I call Chief Marshall, or are you going to?"

"Fine." He snatched the receiver from my hand and slammed it back into the cradle. "Do you even know his number?" he asked as he dialed from his own cell phone.

I gave him half a smile. "Uh . . . no."

"If I do the half-jump, I'll still be in this room, but I'll also be somewhere else . . . wherever I jump to," I attempted to explain to Dr. Melvin and Chief Marshall. Their faces both reflected skepticism, like maybe I had just imagined this whole element of time travel. "I can prove it. Give me something to go look up or a question that I can only answer if I've managed to look into the past."

"So, you're totally here in this year, right now?" Dad asked. "You're not sitting in a vegetative state somewhere else in addition to being in this room?"

It was freakin' confusing. I knew that, but I couldn't help getting frustrated trying to explain these weird phenomenons for the millionth time. I plopped down on the living room couch, letting out an exhausted sigh. "I'm not half-here. I'm all the way here. I did a full jump from a different timeline to get here."

"And how can you be sure of this?" Chief Marshall asked.

"I feel different in a half-jump. Sensations are dulled, like hot and cold or pain." As if to emphasize my point, my shoulder started throbbing from beneath the sling. I rubbed it a little with my free hand, which only made it hurt more. "A half-jump is like a shadow of the timeline I'm currently in. That's why nothing changes in my present or home base."

The explanation was stolen from 007 Adam, but I figured it might make me sound like I knew what I was talking about.

"And you view the timelines like worlds running parallel to each other?" Dr. Melvin asked. "Just for clarification . . . to you a full jump is when you travel to a different, parallel, world, not a time jump within the same world?"

"Right . . . and I know for sure there's multiple timelines because I went back to 2007 . . . not in a half-jump, I was all the way there, feeling the pain and the cold and all that," I rattled off. "Then I returned to my original timeline and it was 2009 and those versions of you guys didn't remember anything that happened in the 2007 I had just returned from."

My head was already spinning and I had a feeling we were just getting started.

"Perhaps we should get a look at this skill . . . have him show us the half-jump," Dr. Melvin said. "Though, I don't want to physically put him in jeopardy, with the gunshot wound and all."

Chief Marshall, leaning back against the living room mantel, held up his hands. This was almost like our conversation in 2007, when he knocked me out with the poisonous rag and dragged me to that secret headquarters. "The boy will do no time-traveling unless we order it, understood?"

Dr. Melvin and I both reluctantly nodded.

"I think your excitement, Dr. Melvin, is a bit premature." Marshall folded his arms across his chest, staring me down from his six-and-a-half-foot stature. "He may have gained a few new tricks but he's not mature enough to deal with the repercussions of his actions. So, you say it was Raymond who shot you?"

"Yes," I said through my teeth. This version of Marshall wasn't any better than the other two I had met.

"And Raymond is . . . as you described . . . a short redheaded man . . . a little stocky, blue eyes, spiky hair . . . a shoe print may or may not be permanently etched on his face?" Marshall asked as if this were a police interrogation with an idiot suspect.

Maybe Dad was right. Maybe I didn't need this. My mind drifted to Holly, driving home in her old beat-up Honda . . . then I imagined Adam there with her. I pictured them laughing together, joking about the spoiled kids they'd have to supervise all summer.

I looked up at Marshall and forced the anger from my tone. "Yes, that's Raymond, and he's dead. Dad killed him. But the first time I met him was in October of 2009 and he shot—" I froze for a second, watching Dad shake his head ever so slightly at me, keeping me from mentioning Holly. "He tried to shoot me and . . . and didn't succeed, but then I was stuck in 2007 and who knows what I screwed up with that full jump to the alternate universe or whatever? If I had known some agent stuff, maybe that wouldn't have happened. Don't you want me to have some method of defense? For everyone's sake."

"We aren't a normal division of the CIA," Marshall explained. "Whatever preconceived notions you may have developed from television or spy movies need to be dissolved immediately. Our first priority isn't the U.S. government or even the American people . . . it's humanity in general . . . more specifically, preserving the natural, ethical state of humanity. Tempest spends at least two years training new agents and drilling this into their heads. We can't let you jump in on their game and tell them all you were created in a lab using the genetics of a cloned woman . . . We can't tell them you can time-travel or that the Tempus gene hidden in your physical makeup has allowed you to learn Farsi in a day and memorize step-by-step pictures of self-defense. We can't tell them that, if we want them to continue trusting their leaders . . . such as myself and your father."

"How many agents-in-training are we talking about?" I asked, only because I was curious. The whole division seemed so ambiguous to me. I could hardly wrap my head around the concept.

"Those details are on a need-to-know basis," Marshall said. "Are you understanding what I'm trying to tell you, son?"

It was obvious he'd already planned to let me join. He probably knew I'd ask, somehow. Walking me in circles beforehand must have been part of his mental game.

"Don't call me son." The words snapped out of my mouth before I could stop them. Marshall only narrowed his eyes at me, but said nothing. "Yes, I understand. Don't tell anyone about my superpowers . . . don't use my superpowers . . . and most importantly, don't tell anyone I came from a clone."

Marshall stared at something on his BlackBerry. "So, you're willing to give everything up . . . the freedom we've given you on the government's dollar? According to Agent Stewart, you have a fund-raiser to attend tomorrow night, and the following night, a party at Caleb's house. Sounds like good times."

"I'm ready to get the hell out of New York, if that's what you're asking."

Marshall's lips formed a devious grin that made my stomach do flip-flops. "Great, plane leaves at six tomorrow morning for our next training location."

"Where—" I started to ask, but Marshall held up his hand to stop me.

"Need-to-know basis, kid. Get used to it. And don't expect me or Agent Freeman to treat you any different from the other recruits."

"Agent Freeman?" The man who'd followed me and Courtney to school every day in seventh grade. In the timeline I had just left, he knew about me being able to time-travel. "Are you . . . going to tell him anything? About me?"

"No," Dad and Marshall said together. Marshall strode out of the room, and the second the front door shut, Dr. Melvin's face changed to that of the sympathetic old man I had known my whole life.

"Let me have a look at that shoulder," he said, already pulling the sling over my head. "You'll have to be careful with it for another couple days."

I looked over at Dad. "Do you know where I'm going in the morning?"

He attempted a smile. "You mean where *we're* going . . . and I do know. The desert."

"Like Arizona?" I asked.

"Like the Middle East."

The Middle East? The confidence that had come out in my exchange with Chief Marshall slowly deflated as I realized that I truly had no idea what I was getting myself into.

MARCH 16, 2009, 6:00 A.M.

"Is someone going to tell me what the hell is going on?"

Dad, Marshall, Freeman, and I stood on one of the runways at JFK, staring at a very fancy private government plane. One I had flown in many times, thinking it was Dad's CEO jet.

"Jackson will be joining our squad for the next several weeks," Marshall said.

Freeman stared blankly at him. "What? Is this some kind of school assignment?"

Marshall's smirk was directed at me, as if saying he knew no one would take me seriously. "I'll rephrase my answer. Agent Jackson Meyer will be joining the Tempest Division for training. In fact, I'm assigning him to your group: Advanced Defense. Give him the same tough love you give to the other recruits."

Freeman looked at me. "This is a joke, right?"

Dad clapped him on the back. "Nope. He's all yours. Kind of tradition, don't you think? Your father trained me, I trained you . . . and now you'll train my kid."

Dad and Marshall boarded the plane, leaving me outside with a bewildered Agent Freeman. He finally shook his head and turned to me, speaking low and under his breath. "I'm not sure what stunt Marshall is pulling here, but don't worry . . . I'll make sure you're okay."

"Uh . . . thanks," I said, not knowing how else to respond.

When I stepped onto the plane, I quickly counted heads and came up with eleven unfamiliar faces. All young. Very young. Probably my age or a year or two older. My eyes stopped on Jenni Stewart, waiting for her reaction. How would she differ from the girl who had bailed me out of jail and posed as Dad's secretary in 2007?

Her head snapped around, searching two rows back for Dad like she wasn't sure what role she was about to play. Perhaps secretary? Or something totally new.

Marshall stood behind me, letting a murmur of gossip fill the cabin before speaking. "Many of you know of Agent Meyer's son, Jackson . . . he'll be joining your group for the next expedition. You are to treat him as one of your teammates."

"Wait," a broad-shouldered dude from the back row said. "He's the French poetry major, right?"

"Aren't you supposed to be babysitting little brats or something?" another guy said.

There was a twitter of nervous laughter. I kept my eyes on Jenni Stewart, knowing she'd been fine with helping me learn some stuff in 2007. Her eyes were wide and confused, darting from Marshall to Dad to Freeman, but she said nothing and I could practically hear the theories racing through her mind. Next to her sat a skinny freckle-faced kid who had to be even younger than me.

I slid into the seat in front of them and stuck my hand out to the kid next to Jenni Stewart. "I'm Jackson."

"I know who you are . . . we all do." He didn't shake my hand. Instead, he turned his eyes to the book in his lap. "Mason . . . Mason Sterling."

Jenni Stewart rolled her eyes and elbowed Mason in the side. "This should be a blast . . . Junior playing secret agent. He must have thrown a mighty big tantrum to get his way onto this flight."

"Yep," Mason said under his breath.

I sighed and turned around in my seat, slumping low enough so no one could start throwing stuff at my head. *Fine.* If this was how it had to be, I'd prove my way into this group. Whatever it took. No more wearing my heart on my sleeve. I needed a hard shell, one that kept me from thinking about Holly and wishing I could talk to Adam or half-jump to visit my twin sister Courtney again.

This is my life now.

As the plane took off, I stared out the window and promised myself to stay focused. To do whatever I had to so I could be good at this job. Then I'd learn about the Enemies of Time . . . find out what the hell happened to create that future that little Emily had shown me and why the hell she looked so much like Courtney. And I could do all of it without the risks that came with time travel. That was what had gotten me into trouble in the first place.

"Sorry about that," Dad said, taking the seat beside me. "This is a very tight-knit group and we've taught them to be suspicious of everything."

I glanced at him. "I get it . . . I need to earn my spot . . . earn their respect. I've played this game before." *Yeah, winning over 007 Holly,* I couldn't help thinking.

Dad must have read my mind. "Are you worried . . . about . . . ?" *Holly*. He didn't say it, but I guessed.

"I trust you." My eyes locked with his for a few seconds so he'd know I meant it. It was about the only thing I knew for sure. I turned my eyes back to the window. "I just don't trust myself, but I'm trying."

She'll be okay . . . she'll be happy. I closed my eyes and let my mind drift to Holly, only without me. I smiled to myself. *Her life will be perfect. Just perfect.*

I could survive for a long time just knowing that.

Mason kicked the back of my seat, jerking me out of my daydream. "What happened to your arm, dude?"

I kept my eyes straight ahead, not turning around to look at either of them behind me, but I spoke loud enough for both Jenni Stewart and Mason to hear. "Gunshot wound."

"Cool," Mason said, then he practically yelled, "Ow! Damn, Stewart!"

Dad laughed under his breath and I shrugged my good shoulder, hiding my own grin. At least I had made a good first impression with one person. One down . . . a bunch more to go.

TEMPEST AGENT
TRAINING DIARY

Adam,

I'm still keeping this journal for you even though I'll probably never give it to you. It's better if I don't, but sometimes life doesn't go how I want it to, and if I've learned anything from you, it's to be prepared for the worst. I'm keeping it safe in a lockbox given to me by Dr. Melvin that only opens with my fingerprints.

The desert sucks. Hot as hell during the day, cold at night.

Sharing a tent with a 17-year-old whose own journal contains photos and background reports on every single girl I have ever dated. Apparently this was one of Mason's first training assignments. I can't picture myself with any of them now. It's like a different person lived that part of my life and all I can think about is she-who-must-not-be-named.

Oh, and everyone calls Mason Sterling . . . Mason. Even Dad and Freeman. Which is really weird. Maybe it's because he's so young and Agent Sterling sounds like a middle-aged man on steroids?

Learned the Tempest mission statement today, though I doubt they have a brochure to advertise this on: "Tempest is devoted to protecting the world from the alterations of our past, present, and future through unnatural or unethical methods. When dealing with technological advancements, Tempest is also looking out for the best interest of not only the American people, but the human race."

MARCH 20, 2009
LOCATION: DESERT. STILL

Jenni Stewart! Yeah. Not my favorite person. And yeah, she's the only girl here and that must be hard on her, but that's no excuse to spend every waking moment making my life miserable. Why not Agent Parker? Or Miller? Not that I know either of them very well yet, but both of them are way more chauvinistic than me. Not to mention shamelessly staring at her ass all the time, which I do NOT do. I think what I hate most about her is that I have no idea who she is. Every single day she tries a new cover . . . Ghetto girl from Harlem, or Little Miss Southern Sunshine . . . and then there's the foreign covers . . . she's done them all. I know Foreign Affairs is her specialty in Tempest, but can't she at least be real for five minutes?

Learned proper gun mechanics today despite my still very sore shoulder. Agent Freeman says I'm a natural shooter. Remember, he's the dude that followed the 13-year-old me and Courtney to school every day. Anyway, I was really nervous at first. My previous experiences with guns involve watching Holly get shot and then me killing Raymond, the red-haired EOT (Enemy of Time), in a half-jump when I visited my two-year-old self in 1992. After I got back to home base in 2009, I kept seeing the blood on my hands even though it wasn't there. But here it's just targets or cardboard cutouts. I can deal with that.

Tomorrow's target-shooting test is my first chance to actually be good at something. Agent Stewart, be prepared to get your ass kicked by the new kid.

MARCH 22, 2009
LOCATION: DESERT

    Now that I've had a week to acquire data and experi-
ence, I have a good idea of what a typical training day
looks like:

5:00–6:30 a.m.—PT (5–10 mile run plus additional
    physical torture from Freeman or Dad).
6:30–7:30 a.m.—Shower (only 6 portable shower stalls
    so it's motivation to finish PT first) and breakfast.
7:30–12:30 p.m.—Specialty training. For me and 3
    others this means weapons, hand-to-hand combat
    (more exercise!), and lots of target shooting, both
    close-range and from a scout location.
12:30–1:30 p.m.—Lunch (either MREs, PB&J, or we boil
    hot dogs and beans over a fire, but no one usually
    wants to make a fire or be out in the sun midday).
1:30–3:00 p.m.—Foreign language study (I do mine
    with Dad and sometimes Dr. Melvin, not sure what
    anyone else does).
3:00–6:00 p.m.—Covert operations, some specialize
    in this but we all have to learn how to tail a suspect,
    know you're being tailed, plant listening devices, search
    for devices, recognize explosives . . . stuff like that.
6:00–7:00 p.m.—Dinner, usually cooked outside, and
    we do have Marshall or Dad taking the helicopter into
    cities and bringing back fresh produce and stuff that
    isn't made to survive a nuclear bombing. This is prob-
    ably the high point of the day.
7:00–10:00 p.m.—This varies. We've done role-playing,
    practicing different covers, we've studied for exams on
    geography and history. It's been different every day.

10:00 p.m.—We're supposed to sleep at this time, but I've noticed that pretty much everyone pulls out books and computers to study past Tempest data and prepare for . . . well . . . everything.

MARCH 25, 2009
LOCATION: DESERT

EOT facts: 12 different time travelers have been sighted, dating back to 1983. Memorized all of their photos and basic info today.

EOTs I've encountered:
Thomas (hasn't been seen since 2005, apparently this timeline's data doesn't include my adventures in the 2007 alternate universe or the previous 2009 I left before coming here. More on that later)
Raymond (dead. Shoe-print guy)
Cassidy (biological mother)
Rena (dead. Blond chick from hotel rooftop)
Jacob (just learned his name. Helped crash that wedding in Martha's Vineyard)
Edward (also just learned his name. The dude that showed up when the storm hit on the boat with Holly, Dad, and Adam)
Harold (dead. Dad shot him in the 2007 timeline. Apparently he's a clone made by Dr. Ludwig)
Based on bloodwork drawn from the EOTs Tempest has been able to capture at one point or another, some show strong evidence of the Tempus gene and some have it hidden in their blood, harder or almost impossible

to locate. Mine is hidden. Dr. Melvin suspects they each have different years of origin and therefore are either further or not as far along in the evolution process. Not the monkeys-turning-to-humans evolution, the kind where normal people turn to time travelers. So, does it eventually become harder to detect the Tempus gene in blood or did it start that way?

And do the EOTs, like, have a meeting place . . . or a meeting year? What would that invitation look like?

Dear EOTs,

Let's all gather in 1984 . . . sometime in July. Maybe at the Empire State Building. Bring a future snack to share because McDonald's is frying their food in animal fat in this year and we wouldn't want that type of lard to invade the future. Please check your calendars and make sure you don't have any planned attacks in July 1984. If you do, let me know which day might work best for you.

Love,
Thomas

APRIL 3, 2009

Found a report in the CIA database from October 2005—the last time Thomas was sighted in this time-line. It was Dad that he sought out. Dad recorded a three-minute conversation muffled slightly by the sound of wind and New York City traffic in the background. It went like this:

Thomas: We're sorry to hear about Axelle Product A. Dr. Ludwig thinks he may have a solution to prevent the tumors . . . with the other subject, anyway.

Agent Meyer: I'm not interested in any of Dr. Ludwig's solutions, Thomas. But I think you already know that.

Thomas: His scans show no signs of cancer?

Agent Meyer: His brain function is that of a normal fifteen-year-old boy in the year 2005. Axelle appears to be nothing but several million dollars not worth spending.

Thomas: I see. And your continued interest in the boy is motivated by what, exactly . . . ?

Agent Meyer: Human compassion. Something you know nothing about.

Thomas: I know everything there is to know about human compassion. I just choose not to be trapped by it. But you have nothing to worry about, Agent Meyer. We have no interest in Product B. Not unless things change, and it doesn't look like that will happen.

Agent Meyer: And if it does?

Thomas: Then I suppose we'll be seeing each other again.

The conversation ended there and the report states that Dad fired three shots, but Thomas vanished, leaving him no outcome to record. Obviously Thomas survived, since he found me when things did start changing. I wonder, how soon after my first jump, in November 2008, did they figure out what I could do?

APRIL 9, 2009

The art of time travel. That's what we're studying now. I'm on the edge of my seat memorizing every word that Dad, Marshall, or Dr. Melvin says. Then I have to go back to my journal later and apply the facts to my own experience. Basically, what I learned so far is that half-jumps don't count as anything related to timelines. Actually,

I had to ask Dad this in private because I couldn't exactly raise my hand and say, "Hey Dr. Melvin . . . when I'm time-traveling using my gene from a cloned person . . ." All 12 of my teammates would simultaneously draw their guns and point them at me. Or maybe the idea is so out there that they'd just begin treating me for heat exhaustion.

For some reason, learning that those jumps almost don't count makes me feel a little more grounded to one place. Less lost. From the time I was born—June 20, 1990—to the date I left when I jumped to 2007—October 30, 2009—I had been in one timeline. Just one world. I've been referring to that as World A. I've been calling the 2007 alternate universe World B. This is where I have to stop because I'm still trying to figure out exactly what happened next. More soon . . .

APRIL 12, 2009

It's like Chief Marshall wants me to fail! Like he expects it. This makes me throw everything out of my mind—saving the world, saving Holly, time travel—and the only thing I can focus on is wiping that stupid-ass stoic expression off his face. He's, like, carved in stone or something. Everything I do gets that same look from him. He knew I would do this, or ask a certain question. I hate being predictable to anyone, let alone Marshall. He could at least make an effort to help me feel like I belong here, or get the others to understand this. Oh, well. I'll just have to work harder. I'll just have to beat everyone.

APRIL 15, 2009

Dad and I had an entire conversation today in Farsi. It took me less than eight hours to understand Farsi through Dr. Melvin's method he used on me in 2007—playing the recording in my ear while I slept. But I'm just now getting down the speaking part of it. And I have been practicing constantly for nearly a month. The other trainees are more than surprised with my quick progress. If only they knew how quick it actually was. Only five of us can speak Farsi, of course Stewart is one of those so I don't get to feel all that superior. Mason's another one, but that's no surprise considering he has the highest recorded IQ in all of North America.

Dr. Melvin asked me a few minutes ago which language I wanted to learn next and Marshall answered for me, saying, "Mandarin." Now I'm curious to find out if we're going to China or if maybe there'll be an EOT attack and they'll give important information in Mandarin. Or if Marshall just hates me and so picked one of the hardest languages to learn.

APRIL 18, 2009
LOCATION: UZBEKISTAN, TURKMENISTAN, DESERT

My first field training mission! We took a helicopter to Karshi-Khanabad Air Base in Uzbekistan. Apparently, the U.S. Air Force used this base from 2001–2005 for al-Qaeda missions. They kicked us out in 2005. Anyway, we had to "accidently" land our helicopter there. The cover was Red Cross workers heading for Africa with a malfunctioning aircraft. The military workers weren't exactly happy to see us, but they didn't shoot anyone, which I thought was a plus. Although I might have been willing to sacrifice Stewart for the greater good of the team.

She was sent inside first to communicate with the director of something, and Mason and I had the job of sneaking through a window and planting 5 listening devices. We succeeded with no major problems and Freeman rewarded all of us with a trip to a bar somewhere in Turkmenistan. It was actually air-conditioned. I don't think I've ever appreciated artificially cooled air as much as I did today. Mason, Dad, and I were the only ones brave enough to sample the food. It wasn't bad. Different, but edible.

APRIL 19, 2009
LOCATION: DESERT

We're going to China. I totally called that one. And my Mandarin is coming along nicely. Maybe it won't be hot and dry there. I can deal with anything but desert conditions.

APRIL 20, 2009
LOCATION: XIAMEN, CHINA

We landed in Xiamen today. It's on the coast, not far from Taiwan. Mason, Agent Parker, and I were in the city gathering supplies when I saw this blond girl, just the back of her, and I totally freaked out. I think it was because we were in China and there's not too many blondes here. This girl stood out like a sore thumb. It wasn't Holly. Not that I expected it to be. Of course I didn't. But that didn't keep me from running to Dad and asking him if he'd checked up on her recently. This was the first time I'd asked him for details. I knew he'd tell me if anything was wrong, and I couldn't bear to be reminded of her unless I had to. He told me he has a source . . . a non-Tempest source that's keeping an eye on her, and I have nothing to worry about.

I just want to be able to move on. Not like move on to another girl. That's the last thing on my mind right now. I just want to not want her with me. To not feel like I made a mistake. I know I didn't. Even Dad agrees.

Sometimes I try to imagine what Holly's doing, what she'll look like in ten years, all the amazing things she's bound to accomplish, and I'm grateful for the fact that she doesn't have to miss me like I miss her.

APRIL 24, 2009
LOCATION: XIAMEN

The art of time travel, Part 2—okay, Adam, you're going to love this if you ever get to read it. So, last time I left off trying to figure out what happened after World B (2007 timeline). When I jumped to August 13, 2009, and confirmed that I was not in World B anymore because that Adam said he hadn't met me until March 2009, not September 2007. According to Dr. Melvin's time-travel theories, the ones I'm slowly letting my brain slog through because it's migraine-worthy, I returned to World A. But my steps looked something like this:

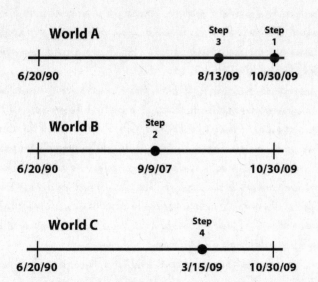

Then the final step includes the introduction of World C . . . or at least I can assume this. Next, I need to tackle the theories on what I'm possibly able to do. Not that I'm going to time-travel, but I need to know what the EOTs might be capable of. The more I learn about time travel, the more sure I am that I never want to do it again.

APRIL 28, 2009
LOCATION: TAIWAN

We're doing a mission here but my part is boring, monotonous surveillance. Which means watching video footage from one of the cameras we planted in a government building. I'm not even close to the mission site, so it's totally boring.

Time travel fact of the day: just learned that a full jump, in the same timeline, like if I did this in World A, is called a complete jump and alterations are possible. Thomas has been known to do this. I can't find any other EOTs listed with this ability.

Tempest fact: When Courtney and I were toddlers, rolling around in sandboxes, the entire Tempest division consisted of: Agent Freeman, Sr., Dr. Melvin, Dad, Chief Marshall, and Eileen. That's it. Only a couple attacks from known time travelers were even reported. There was, however, a division of the CIA that seemed to be against Tempest and especially Axelle. Dad and Agent Freeman, Sr., were constantly creating covers and being chased/followed by them.

I wonder what changed. Why did Tempest decide to start recruiting more agents two years ago? Did Chief Marshall learn something about the future? I've asked Dad and he just said that they've always known the time travel war was coming. Maybe it's the clones?

MAY 5, 2009
LOCATION: BEIJING

Freeman just told us that we'd be getting partners eventually. Tempest agents don't go on missions alone. Plus, we all have such unique backgrounds and abilities, we need to be matched with someone who isn't just like us. That way we have a variety of skills to use in a mission. I'm very concerned that I'm going to get stuck with Stewart or Mason. I can't stand Stewart. Actually it's mutual hate. We can't stand each other. And Mason, well . . . I might just like him a little more than I should. Okay, not like that. Just that he's so young and what if something happened to him, on my watch . . . like with Dad's old partner, Agent Freeman, Sr.? He was killed the same day as Eileen, the woman who carried me and Courtney. The woman who Dad once loved, maybe still does love.

It would be so much easier if I could just work alone. Maybe in another alternate universe, like World D, you're in Tempest with me, Adam. I'm sure Marshall and Freeman would partner us up together. You're the brains, I'm the skilled shooter, and now that I've been forced into top physical shape, I could do the running around and you could do all the boring observation, which I'm sure you'd find way more intriguing than I have. You spent plenty of time watching me while I looked like a vegetable. That had to be boring as hell. We'd make an awesome team. And you could help figure me out. I don't really have anyone to do that with now. Of course, I trust Dad 100% but he's so careful with me. Always worried about giving me too much information. Like I'm going to break down any second and not be able to handle what he's telling me. Maybe it's just out of habit. He kept so many secrets from both me and Courtney for such a long time.

MAY 10, 2009
LOCATION: HONG KONG

Most Important Tempest Lesson thus far: every aspect of training is on a need-to-know basis. We can't talk about what happens in our specialty groups to members outside of it. But Advanced Defense yields no big secrets. Not like Futuristic Technology, which I'm dying to learn about. It sucks. We all have access to each other's agent profiles, but I know what mine says and more importantly what it doesn't say

(Axelle experiment Product B, known time traveler), so I can't really trust anyone's profile in the database. Maybe we're all time travelers and just not telling each other. That would be hilarious. Maybe Eileen gave birth to 13 babies and we're all different versions of the Axelle experiment. Maybe we are the EOTs and we're battling our future selves? Oh, my God, I need a drink.

MAY 11, 2009
LOCATION: BANGKOK

There's one secret, only one, that I've kept from Dad. Emily. Something about that little girl showing up in the storm, following orders from a future version of me, seemed too important to hand over to Dad, knowing he'd do whatever he had to in order to protect me. He would have killed Thomas if he'd had the chance. The fact that a mysterious little girl might cease to exist if he had killed Thomas wouldn't be enough to stop him. But I don't feel the same way. I picked her up, I saw her cry, saw her regretfully leave me and head to somewhere that didn't seem pleasant. She is something important to me. I just haven't gotten to that point in my life yet. Whatever point where she first meets me. Do I have a child in the future? She has my eyes. Or is it like I first thought, on that rooftop with Thomas, some kind of version of Axelle but different? Like maybe instead of a half-breed, she's a ¾ breed?

MAY 15, 2009
LOCATION: IN FLIGHT, HEADING WEST

We are going to Europe! France, more specifically. I can't think of anywhere in France that could possibly be as bad as the desert or rainy part of China with nothing but sea creatures to eat. Apparently, Tempest has headquarters in France now, near the Alps. I heard Parker say it's all underground.

Languages I've mastered and passed exams on: French, Spanish, Farsi, Mandarin, Turkish, Russian, and German. Stewart just passed the Gaelic exam. Seriously. Gaelic. I'm totally doing that next.

MAY 17, 2009

So, I'm not the new kid anymore. The day we got to France, Agent Lily Kendrick showed up. Yes, that's right, another female added to the group. So far Kendrick is kinda squirrelly and nervous. Not sure if she'll hold up with this group. Stewart's not too fond of her, which doesn't mean much because Stewart really only gets along with Mason.

Lily Kendrick's profile from the CIA database:

Gender: Female
Age: 21
Height: 5' 8"
Weight: 125 lbs
PT Exams: all passed
Basic CIA training: Complete
Specialty Field: Biological Advancement
Language exams passed: Farsi, French, Italian, German, Russian, Dutch, Flemish, Spanish, Portuguese, Latin, Turkish, Mandarin, Japanese, Korean

And the past several days, I got the feeling that I would end up with Lily Kendrick as my partner. I was totally right. Marshall and Freeman both had paired us up for a couple of competitions. Which is something we do a TON of here in France.

I don't really know what to think about having Kendrick for a partner. She's sort of nice, but in a way that makes me suspicious. I already know Stewart is out to get me, and that comes with its own built-in security. I don't know anything about Kendrick other than the fact that when she's not nervous she's pretty good at almost everything.

MAY 27, 2009

Adam, I realized today that I haven't done a good job of explaining the different areas Tempest agents specialize in and you are seriously going to find this fascinating. I would love to know where Marshall would have placed you. I could see you in several different specialties. Anyway, here's the 411 on this area of the division:

All Tempest agents specialize in an area where they show unusual aptitude, and it's not just to have experts in different subject matters, it's also to keep any one of us from knowing all the department's secrets. For example, Kendrick studies her specialty with Dr. Melvin— Biological Advancements. Mason specializes in Futuristic Technology (I may have mentioned this in a previous entry). From what I've heard, he can disable bombs with materials that won't even be used by the military for another fifty years. How they get these materials and the information about the future is one of those secrets that only Mason's specialty group is allowed to know. Like I said before, it sucks big time.

Apply this to an actual mission and here's how it would go down: let's say . . . me, Mason, and Kendrick were all in the field on a mission and someone needed to disable a bomb and someone else needed to chase after a potential attacker and possibly fire a shot at him or her. I'd be the man running and Mason would be the man (kid) on the ground, snipping wires and deactivating shit. And Kendrick would be the man (woman) injecting the attacker with anti-time-travel drugs (yes, they actually have those), assuming it was an EOT attacking. Otherwise, she'd dose him or her with something else to knock him or her out.

See why I can't figure out which role you'd play? You could do Kendrick's or Mason's jobs just as well as they can.

MAY 30, 2009

Kendrick and I had a really great competition today. We nearly won. Then, after dinner, she sat by me in the library and tried to start a casual conversation. It was really weird. I just kept picking apart every word she said and trying to figure out her real motives. I've learned too many ways to dissect lies and deception in these past couple months. I don't think I'll ever be able to have a normal conversation with someone again.

CHAPTER ONE

I could hear my heart pounding, even over the volume of the helicopter. Judging distance and memorizing images of our surroundings were skills I'd learned to use to my advantage during the past two and a half months of Tempest training. But today they had taken away my sight. And by "they," I mean Chief Marshall.

After an hour of their obvious diversions and turning the helicopter in circles to confuse us, I was seriously ready for a time jump . . . somewhere calm and on the ground.

"In about sixty seconds," Freeman barked over the noise of the helicopter, "I'll give you the coordinates of our location, the door will open, and both of you will be dangling by those ropes we've attached you to. Your chance of survival will increase greatly if you have an idea of what your feet might land on."

Awesome.

I fought the urge to rip off my blindfold and look down. Without seeing the journey we'd taken, I'd never be able to figure out where they were about to dump us. Agent Kendrick was already shaking beside me. I couldn't see her, but I felt her shoulder trembling as it pressed against mine.

"Calm down," I whispered into her ear. "Or it'll only get worse."

My heart slowed instantly as I used my own advice for Kendrick on myself. Never let anyone see you sweat. Never let them in your head . . . not Chief Marshall, not my partner or any of the Tempest trainees, and especially not the EOTs. This was one of the three most important lessons I'd learned in training. The other two:

Everything is a test.

Everyone is alone.

The sound of the helicopter door being wrenched open caused my stomach to drop. *Calm . . . stay calm.* Noise from the rotors and wind burst in, cold air smacking me in the face.

I barely heard Freeman shout the coordinates, and then I heard Kendrick yell into my ear, "The east side of the French Alps . . . rough surface . . . loose rocks . . . but people climb it."

I swallowed hard. "Great."

And they literally *had* turned us in circles since we'd left this morning, considering Tempest headquarters were at the base of the French Alps.

Ten seconds later, Kendrick and I were being pushed through the open door, each secured to our own rope as we swung back and forth in the wind.

"Jackson!" Kendrick shouted. "Take off your blindfold."

Oh . . . right. But that would require peeling my fingers from the rope. Instead of releasing a hand, I used my forearm to nudge the cloth from my eyes. The sun blinded me at first and then I looked down as the mountain swung in and out of focus. "Holy shit!"

Kendrick's long dark hair whipped in the wind as her eyes scanned the mountainside. She didn't look nearly as petrified as I felt. I had a feeling her genius mind was spinning too fast to let fear distract her. "There's a ledge . . . we're gonna have to jump a little . . . doesn't quite reach the end of the rope . . . but I don't know how long before they cut us off from above."

I glanced up at the helicopter, still hovering ten feet over us, Freeman ready to untie us and slam the door shut any second now. "Okay, ready when you are."

We quickly worked our way down the forty-foot ropes, but even Kendrick hesitated at the end, our feet dangling, trying to reach the small ledge, but coming up short by about five feet. We'd have to unhook the clips securing us to the ropes in order to land on the ledge.

Today's test, in terms of explaining the rules to the trainees, was the most simple we'd had so far—blindfolded journey where we'd be left alone with our partners, and all we had to do was find our way back to headquarters. It was a timed test, of course, but the rules were simple. The execution, however . . . not so simple.

"On the count of three," Kendrick said, her eyes meeting mine.

And for a second I had to wonder if this was a different test. Like maybe I was supposed to con her into going first. Or I'd release myself from the rope and she wouldn't, and then they'd pull her back up to safety and take off without me.

Only one way to find out.

"One, two," I said, gripping the release button on the clip between my fingers. "Three!"

The blur of Kendrick falling beside me obscured my vision, and the surface of the mountain appeared before I was ready for it. The side of my face smacked into a jagged rock, immediately followed by the warm trickle of blood dripping down my cheek. My feet found the flat surface and both Kendrick and I pressed our hips into the mountain, toes turned out.

"We've got pitons . . . in our bags, right?" I asked.

"Yeah," Kendrick said between breaths. "Jackson . . . you're bleeding."

As she reached for my forehead, I shrank away from her hand and quickly wiped the blood with the sleeve of my T-shirt. "It's fine. Forget it."

She pulled her hand back and looked at the large rock in front of us. "Can you reach in your bag and hand me a piton?"

"Don't you have your own?"

She held up the end of a rope, which I hadn't even noticed had been thrown from the helicopter. "They only gave us one rope. We're gonna have to share it."

The challenge in her eyes was too obvious to miss. "Then hand it to me and I'll tie it for both of us."

"On what? You've got nothing but loose rocks in front of you."

I remained silent as I handed her a piton and watched her pound it into the mountain. She tugged hard on the rope and then reached for my harness, clipping me to the rope before I could object.

"This should hold both of us," she said.

My fingers held tightly to the edge of a rock. "You first."

Kendrick shrugged and then started her descent. My eyes dropped to the ground again without permission and Kendrick's face dissolved. A flash of Holly's blond hair flying toward the ground materialized in front of me. Blood pumped in my ears and the air in my lungs seemed to vanish. *Not this. Not now. Focus!*

"Jackson?" Kendrick said from a few feet below me. "You okay?"

No. "I'm fine."

I turned around quickly and stared straight at the slab of rock in front of me, then started to climb down. Kendrick moved in silence below me for the next hour. The effort of securing pitons and retying the rope every twenty feet was exhausting and made conversation difficult.

The valleys below us were still distant green blobs when Kendrick finally spoke again. "I love how you're still trying to hide the fact that you're an acrophobe."

"So it seems," I said, looking down at her. I almost laughed when I saw her eyes roll.

"Anyway, I was just thinking . . . since I don't really have an issue with heights . . . it's good that we've been paired together."

"All right, you got me," I said, keeping my focus straight ahead. "I'm scared of falling off this mountain . . . and it's not like you weren't shaking up there in the helicopter."

"I wasn't worried about the height. I was afraid I wouldn't have the answer, wouldn't have a clue where we were. Being lost freaks me out."

Okay . . . so what? We're gonna get personal now? Talk about our hopes and dreams . . . great fears? Yeah, right.

Finally, after hours of climbing, we reached less vertical terrain. Agent Kendrick and I unhooked our rope and stuffed everything into our backpacks. When I looked around at our surroundings, I could hardly believe my eyes. "This is right near headquarters."

Kendrick nodded, smiling a little.

"Did you know where we'd end up when you picked our landing

spot?" I couldn't help asking, and sounding slightly impressed, which I was.

"Yeah," she admitted. "But not right away. It was a good guess. And now maybe we can pass the test and record the fastest return time. I'd love to win a day off."

"Impressive," I said. "You're not just trying to live through this, but also attempting to win. Did you see anyone else?"

She swept the area with her eyes, then sighed. "We're either way ahead or way behind . . . Damn, this place is beautiful. This is where I want to go for my honeymoon. In one of those little villas right at the base of the Alps."

I nodded in the direction of the underground pathway. "Let's win Marshall's contest first and plan honeymoons later."

Honeymoon? Seriously?

We raced toward the secret entrance and shifted the giant stacks of hay to the side. Both of us grinned, knowing we were most likely the first to come through. It would have been impossible to push the hay back after crawling into the hole.

"I already know what I'm going to do with my day off," Kendrick said. "Eat . . . and eat . . . pastries . . . lots of pastries."

My foot was already feeling around for the ladder, excitement and adrenaline rushing through my veins.

I lifted my eyes to look at my partner and nearly shouted as several figures, blurred by the sun's glare, appeared around us. Kendrick's shout was muffled instantly. A strange, almost metallic-smelling gas filled my nostrils, and then a foot made contact with the side of my head and my vision completely dissolved.

The thud of my head smacking the ground echoed through my ears and all I could think was—he found me.

Thomas.

After my months of obsessing over every ounce of data on this man, we'd finally get to face off again.

CHAPTER TWO

Luckily, the blackout was restricted to my vision only and I remained conscious.

"Don't let them touch you!" I shouted to Kendrick as strong arms wrapped around me.

I tossed the attacker to the ground, then squinted into the sun. My vision started to return, but fused with large blind spots. I counted the enemies in half a second: six blurred bodies, against two. I could make out Kendrick's slim body and long hair. She scrambled to get up from the ground. One of the thicker bodies dove at her. Instinctively, I jumped between them and slammed my foot into the attacker's chest, sending him backward. The groan of a male voice followed my counterattack.

And that smell . . . like rusty metal and copper, so strong I could taste it.

The next thirty seconds consisted of flying elbows and fists. Fast silent hits to various body parts. Luckily, only one of those hits got me. I could already feel a bump forming on my cheekbone.

Kendrick spun around, taking in the surroundings, not sure exactly what to do next, now that we had gotten a few of them down. I grabbed the back of her shirt and pushed her toward the only opening in the fuzz of bodies around us.

"Run!" The word had barely left my mouth when I felt a gun press into the center of my back. The spots in my vision vanished and I took in the man lying on the ground and the other four getting to their feet with reluctant movements.

I recognized every single one of them. All EOTs, but not all men. And their faces had been etched into my mind, but only one mattered right now. Thomas. I could feel him behind me.

"Hands up, kid, you're outnumbered," one of the men beside me said. His red hair caught my attention, even with my current vision issues. *Raymond . . . shoe-print guy?* It looked like him, but wasn't he supposed to be dead?

Slowly, I raised my arms in the air. Kendrick turned back around and lifted her eyebrows for a split second. I shook my head, but it didn't do any good. She whipped out her own gun from the back of her pants, pointing it at the man holding me hostage.

"Drop your weapon!" she said, her voice shaking a little.

"I could do that," the man behind me answered, his voice alone causing my heart to race. It *was* Thomas, and now all I could think about was getting to the top of that mountain and tossing him from it. "Or I could just . . . vanish with your friend here. And I think you know what I mean."

Oh, God . . . it really is them. I held my breath, trying to keep it steady. "Let her go."

"Sorry. Can't do that," the girl who looked like Rena said.

Isn't she dead, too?

And I took notice of the fact that none of the others had drawn weapons . . . which meant they might not have any. I counted to three in my head, planning my movements carefully, then I used my heel to kick Thomas and cause his knee to buckle. At the same time, I twisted his wrist so the gun pointed upward. As expected, a shot fired into the sky. Two seconds later I had Thomas on his back, my foot at his throat, cutting off the air supply to his lungs.

"Go!" I said to Kendrick, not even looking up. Her feet shuffled a bit as she hesitated, but then she took off in a run. She only made it about thirty feet before collapsing onto the grass, screaming and clutching the sides of her head.

I couldn't help her without taking out everyone around me, including the enemy under my foot.

The man's features swam in front of me until I could finally focus on them. It was definitely him . . . Thomas. He looked a little different, but nearly the same. Maybe he was older now? Either way, my blood boiled and my pulse pounded into my finger as it rested on the trigger of the gun. "I never should have let you go the first time."

Memories flicked at high speed . . . Thomas's impassive face as he raised Holly over the ledge of the building. Her scream pierced through my ears all over again and it was all I could hear other than the pounding of blood in my veins. *I can't let him go again.*

He needs to die.

"Jackson!"

The deafening scream inside my head turned down a few decibels, along with the growing fury in my fingertips.

"Stop him!" someone shouted.

"Jackson . . ." A familiar voice.

The tension flooding through my hand loosened a little. "Dad?"

I shook my head, trying to focus on the person who had just spoken to me. He sounded like Dad, but didn't look like him. He moved toward me, placing a hand over the gun I now held loosely. He whispered in my ear, "It's just a test . . . memory gas. What you're seeing is altered."

"But . . ." I stuttered. "I thought . . ."

Strong hands gripped my shoulder, turning me around. "Let's go. The test isn't over yet. In fact, since Dad had to ruin the illusion, I think your final exam is going to be much, much more difficult."

Chief Marshall. I recognized his voice, but he looked different. Like someone else. A bag was placed over my head and my arms were tied with rope behind my back. This time I didn't resist, still stunned from the realization that I *hadn't* just been in the middle of an EOT attack. And I knew the final test was coming up, since we had all nearly reached the end of our training, but I didn't think it would be today, especially after being dropped from a helicopter with only a mountainside to land on. Wasn't that enough drama for one day?

The next phase of the test involved a long walk to an unknown underground location. Headquarters were underground, I was used to that. But this place had metal floors that clanked and an almost hospital-like smell.

Someone pressed me into a large chair and some kind of cuffs encircled my arms, covering them from my wrists all the way to my elbows. The cuffs squeezed against my skin.

The bag was finally yanked from my head and I saw Kendrick beside me, bound by her arms to an identical chair. Her knees were pulled to her chest, face pressed into them as she shook uncontrollably. Her shoulders wiggled back and forth as she tried to free her arms.

"Just . . . please . . . just let me see them," she said with a shaky voice.

See who? Is she hallucinating fake people, too?

Chief Marshall strode in front of us, pacing back and forth. "Agent Meyer," he called to Dad. "Question her while she's still like this . . . since the other subject's data has been invalidated."

He turned to glare at me and then stormed out of the tiny room. On the wall just in front of us a digital clock hung, and when I glanced sideways I realized there were at least eight identical chairs and a clock or timer in front of each. The red numbers on mine flashed and eventually stayed, reading *85*.

Kendrick's numbers were jumping all over the place . . . *120 . . . 152 . . . 165.*

Dad glanced at her clock and his forehead wrinkled. He crouched down beside her and whispered, "Relax, Lily . . . you're okay."

"No . . . no, I'm not!" She shook her head back and forth. "Just let me go and I'll come right back, I swear."

"Kendrick," he said more forcefully. "Can you smell the metal? Think about it . . . you know what this is."

She stiffened and then raised her head slightly, wiping the tears on the shoulder of her sweatshirt. I wasn't sure what to think. I'd never seen any other agent break down like this.

The door opened again and Dad stood up and paced the front of the room, like Marshall had moments ago. "Tell me where you are, Agent Kendrick," he barked.

I barely listened to his questioning because I was distracted watching the other trainees being marched in and strapped down just like us. Stewart ended up right beside me.

"How's it going, Junior?" she whispered to me. "Didn't wet your pants, did you?"

Mason, Stewart's official partner, was on her other side. He didn't look as calm and malicious as Stewart right now, but he didn't seem as freaked out as Kendrick had been seconds ago. *Or me, fifteen minutes ago.*

"So, tell me what you saw," Stewart whispered loudly to me. "Your credit cards stolen?"

I squeezed my fists together and watched the number *85* on my clock change to *90*, then *95*.

"As you may have noticed," Chief Marshall said, walking slowly from the door to the center of the room, "those cuffs around your arms keep a constant measure of each of your pulse rates. In about twenty seconds, a number is going to flash below your current heart rate. That is the average resting heart rate Dr. Melvin has recorded during physical assessments."

I watched my clock, counting down until the number *63* flashed below my *90*. Kendrick's target number was *78* and Stewart had the second lowest at *67*.

"You have exactly one minute to lower that number to no more than ten beats per minute above your individual resting heart rate. Should you fail to do this, a gradual progression of physical punishment in the form of electric shock and heat will be administered through those armbands," Marshall continued with uninterested ease, as though giving a guided tour of a boring landmark.

I closed my eyes and took in slow deep breaths, *feeling* rather than watching my pulse slow. When I opened my eyes again thirty seconds later, my number had dropped to *78*.

Stewart stuck her feet out in front of her, crossing her legs and stretching. Her pulse held steady at *69*. This was why she specialized in both Covert Operations and Foreign Affairs. The girl was comfortable and relaxed in anyone's skin, pretending to be anyone or anything.

Twenty seconds later, my number had dropped to *71*. Chief Marshall turned his eyes on me, narrowing them to slits. "Agent Meyer . . . can you tell me what prevented you and Agent Kendrick from reaching headquarters in the allotted mission time?"

"We were attacked, sir," I said immediately.

"By whom?" Marshall asked, resting his hands on my chair and getting right in my face.

71 . . . 72 . . . 73 . . .

"I'm not . . . I don't know," I said, scrambling to remember which agents, besides Dad, had actually been present. I never got a good look at their real faces after the delusional fog dissolved.

"Think hard, Agent Meyer."

74 . . . 75 . . . heat flowed through my arms, not scalding temperatures, but I knew it would get worse. Kendrick gasped beside me, but when I glanced her way, she bit down on her lower lip and smoothed her expression, faking calm.

Good. She's learning.

Her pulse, however, raced, fluctuating from *105* all the way to *125.*

"If Agent Meyer Senior hadn't stopped you, Agent Freeman might not be alive right now," Marshall said. "How do feel about that? How do you feel about having your environment, your *mind,* altered in such a drastic, consequential way?"

He's exaggerating. I wouldn't have killed Freeman.

My legs were free, so I had to fight the urge to kick him in the stomach. Seriously? How did he think I felt about it? *Yeah, it was a real blast.* Dad's face tightened, probably sensing my anger, and he shook his head ever so slightly at me.

"It wasn't an experience I'd like to have again," I answered finally, biting down the words I really wanted to say.

76 . . . 77 . . . 78.

Beside me, sweat trickled down Kendrick's face and she closed her eyes, letting out short rapid breaths.

Pain shot through my arms, traveling across my entire body. I gritted my teeth, trying not to make any movement to prove my discomfort. A yelp from one of the agents came from several seats away.

"Are you going to tell us what that gas was?" Mason asked from two seats over. There was a definite strain in his voice and I could see from his own clock that he was struggling just as badly as Kendrick to keep calm. They had definitely taken the mind games to a whole new level today.

"Yes," Marshall boomed, tearing his direct attention away from me. "The substance each of you inhaled today contained a chemical that we have yet to fully identify."

That was how Dad was able to lure Kendrick out of her delusion . . . she was specializing in advanced bio. Dr. Melvin probably had her studying the weird chemical.

"Is this the final test?" someone shouted from the last seat to my right. "Is it standard?"

"No, it's not, Agent Miller. In fact, our division needed data to use as a beginning point in our research. The gas is something that exists many, many years from now and its purpose is to alter an environment or situation using an individual's own stored memories. That is the only information Dr. Melvin and I received, and of course we were curious to see how memories were selected and the effect it had on each individual. Can anyone think of a reason this substance could be useful to a government agency?"

"Crime scene investigation," Agent Parker said from Kendrick's other side.

Just hearing about this futuristic weapon had caused my pulse to race again . . . *82 . . . 83 . . . 85,* and the heat reached a nearly unbearable level. Kendrick's face had gone completely white. Her numbers climbed to well over *140* and the wrinkle in her forehead told me she was most likely getting electrical shock as well.

"Yes," Marshall said. "But something even more threatening."

"Assassins," Stewart said. Her number flickered to *70* for a split second and then quickly fell to *68.*

"Very good, Agent Stewart." Marshall paced for several seconds, causing everyone to grow more nervous. He stared right at me. "None of us know how this substance will be used or when exactly, but this is part of our future, that much is guaranteed. Weapons such as these are not ethical or risk-controlled methods of preserving humanity, and as soon as Tempest finds out who the person is behind this invention, the individual will be stopped. That's a risk and an unfortunate loss we must be willing to take."

But, of course, they had no ethical hang-ups about testing it out on unsuspecting trainees.

And I still couldn't believe a gas could work that way . . . that something chemical could just unleash memories I had tried so desperately to hide.

A strange thought occurred to me at probably the worst possible time. If the chemicals made me think Agent Freeman was Thomas and my reaction was deadly, what would I have done if one of them had looked like Holly?

I shook the thought from my head and focused on Agent Freeman, who had just entered the room and stood next to Marshall. "Now that we have the experimental weapon out of the way and all of you are in a compromised position, we figured this might be a good time to test your knowledge."

Everyone's pulse sped, including mine.

"Agent Kendrick," Freeman said right away to my partner. "If you and another one of your teammates here were trapped in a confined space, having no means of communication and no idea when you'd be rescued, which teammate would you prefer to be held with?"

The way he asked this, polite and casual, using the word "prefer" as if we were playing some cheesy board game, made it sound like there wasn't a real right or wrong answer. Which made me nervous for Kendrick, but when I glanced at her again, some color had already flooded back into her cheeks and her pulse slowed to 91.

"What are the dimensions of the space?" she asked.

"You're assuming you can see?" another agent from several seats away said.

"I can measure without seeing," Kendrick responded, still keeping her eyes on Freeman.

He tossed some random numbers at her and she countered with yet another question: "What is the estimated temperature of the space?"

Freeman lifted one eyebrow, sweeping his eyes over her clock, which now held steady at 79. "Eighty-nine degrees."

"Without knowing any potential methods of escape and the skills required to attempt those methods, I'd choose Agent Sterling." Kendrick's response came without hesitation, showing she hadn't been stalling. She really needed that information to form her answer.

"Why is that?" Freeman asked.

"With that tight of an area and the normal temperature already being on the warm side, Mason has the lowest body fat percentage and his entire body mass is nearly the smallest of the group, therefore he'd use the least amount of energy."

"Nearly the smallest," Stewart pointed out before Freeman could respond. Stewart herself was actually the lightest and smallest of all the trainees, maybe of all the Tempest agents.

Freeman turned his eyes to Stewart and back to Kendrick, who looked unbelievably calm compared to ten minutes earlier. "She has a point . . ."

"Yes," Kendrick said, keeping her voice even. "But I had to consider psychological compatibility. Stewart's more likely to create conflict, which would lead to delayed solutions."

"But Agent Stewart tests higher in pressure situations than nearly anyone in the division, as she's proven today. Agent Sterling, however, seemed to struggle the most," Freeman pointed out. "Wouldn't you rather be confined with the agent most likely *not to* panic?"

Yes, Stewart definitely had earned that role in a very scary and intimidating way, but in the past few weeks I'd managed to challenge her on more than one occasion. Sometimes it was easier to let your fears and emotions turn numb and allow your mind to take over and just . . . go through the motions. Apparently the CIA likes those methods very much and rewards them with high test scores.

"Fine," Kendrick said, a trace of annoyance and reluctance leaking into her voice. "I wouldn't pick Stewart because she knows she'll handle it better than I would and it's possible she'd kill me just to have enough oxygen to plan her escape and complete whatever mission had gotten us trapped in the first place. And even though I'd like to put the division first, I'm pretty sure my own self-preservation would kick in and I'd prefer not to be killed for the greater good."

I was slightly shocked by Kendrick's response, but in an almost humorous way. Did she really think Stewart would kill her just to save the world or whatever? Stewart completely infuriated me ninety-nine percent of the time, but I didn't think she'd ever actually kill me.

"Honesty is always appreciated," Freeman said, then his gaze flitted over me, pausing for a split second before moving to Stewart. "Agent Stewart, who would you choose?"

I waited for her comment on Kendrick's answer, but she didn't even look like she cared. "I'd also choose Mason, for pretty much the same reasons."

Freeman continued to ask the same question of the entire group and everyone chose Mason. It was obvious we were being judged on more than our answer, and a couple other agents tried to come up with intelligent questions like Kendrick had, but it was clear the information wasn't important enough to really affect their choice.

"I find it very interesting that none of you chose Agent Stewart—"

"Actually, you didn't ask me," I said, interrupting him. "I'd choose Stewart."

"Why?" Freeman said, immediately shifting his focus.

"Like you said, she's the best under pressure and the smallest and lightest. And she's also . . . also . . ."

"What?" Freeman prompted.

I sat up straighter and made sure my voice would sound firm and direct. "She's the least likely to form an emotional attachment." *Because we don't like each other very much.*

"Interesting," Freeman said, but didn't elaborate further. "Agent Kendrick, your partner is ranked second on his ability to work under pressure and has the fourth-smallest body mass of the group . . . Sterling is just a notch below him. Why not choose Agent Meyer? In fact, why didn't any of you choose Agent Meyer?"

Silence. Dead silence. Several pulses sped up, but mine held steady.

I didn't care that no one had picked me. I liked it better that way, and honestly, if I had to choose, I'd have picked to be trapped alone.

Freeman's eyes swept over the group, and when no one spoke up, he eventually ended the silence. "Fine . . . I'd like for all of you to put your answer in writing by the end of the day. We're done for now, but each of you will return to these lovely chairs and it will be much more threatening next time. Tomorrow, be ready for multiple foreign language exams."

The cuffs loosened and released all of our arms at once. There was a nervous chatter that sprang up among the group as everyone filed out the door. Chief Marshall returned and held me and Kendrick back from the others. "Stay," he commanded.

Kendrick threw me a weary glance, but all I could do was shrug.

"I was listening in on your test," he said. *Of course he was.* "And I'd like to hear your response to Agent Freeman's final question."

He was looking right at Kendrick, who had begun biting her lip nervously. She really needed to work on concealing her feelings.

"Honestly," she said, "I'm not sure exactly why I didn't pick Agent Meyer . . . it might be an issue of trust."

"You don't trust him?"

"I don't think he trusts me," Kendrick said with a sigh.

No surprise there. I didn't trust any of them, but wasn't that the point?

Marshall rocked back on his heels and kept us waiting for a full ten seconds. "Both of you will complete an assignment for me as soon as possible. You are to give each other a task to perform that the other person cannot question or ignore."

"What kind of task?" I asked.

"Something that will challenge the other . . . something that hits on a personal weakness."

"But . . . isn't that a method of dissolving trust? Preying on a teammate's weakness and using it against them?" Kendrick asked.

"Not if the intent is to make them stronger," Marshall answered, and with that, he waved us out of the room.

And somehow I knew I'd be leaping off tall buildings or something just as horrible. The only weakness Kendrick had on me was the height thing, and it was very fresh in her mind.

Both Kendrick and I were shocked to discover that the room we had just spent over an hour in was in headquarters behind a hidden door right outside the dining room.

"Can you believe those torture chambers have been sitting right next to where we eat and sleep and we never knew?" she said.

"And it's only going to get worse." I hesitated for a second and then decided not to bring up the obvious tension-inducing issue of me not trusting her and Marshall's most recent assignment. "Hey, what happened in there? You were so—"

"Out of control?" Kendrick said bitterly. "Totally freaked out?"

"Well, yeah, but then you just . . . recovered . . . like it was nothing . . . If my arms were getting some serious heat, I can't imagine—" I stopped in the hallway and lifted her wrists, flipping them over to examine the insides. "Why . . . how . . . ?"

I dropped her arms. "There's no burns on you. Not a single mark."

"I know." Something danced in her eyes . . . the excitement of a secret discovery?

"Did you figure out how to turn off your chair or something?" I scratched the back of my head as we walked toward the dining room, where the scent of tomato sauce and freshly baked bread wafted into the hall.

"Think about it, Jackson. Everyone walked out of there just fine, and I wasn't the only one struggling in the beginning."

I remembered the yells of pain from some of the other agents. I looked down at my own arms. "It didn't really burn us?"

She held a finger to her lips, but nodded. "All those cuffs did was send a signal to our brains, making us think that we were being burnt or shocked. That's why we had to physically see our own heart rates, so we'd anticipate the consequences."

"Mind over matter," I said, shaking my head.

"I know, right? I'm sure some of the others will figure it out eventually, if they haven't already."

A few minutes later we were in the dining room with plates of pasta and, as the unfortunate result of being the last ones to arrive, we were forced to share a table with Stewart and Mason. "Hey," Mason said with his mouth full of lasagna, "we've got two days of freedom coming to us. You guys got anything planned?"

I had almost forgotten about the forty-eight hours of leave we all received every three months, assuming no major universal threats required our presence.

"Haven't thought about it yet," Kendrick said, "but I have a feeling it'll involve crepes."

"What about you, Jackson?" Mason asked.

I shrugged. "I don't know . . . probably just stick around here and get some studying done for the upcoming exams."

"And I was sure you'd be headed to a wild party," Stewart said, then she turned her eyes on Kendrick. "You know, this one time . . . I came into Agent Meyer's apartment to do the routine nightly surveillance while he was out of town. Junior here was passed out in the hallway, couldn't even make it to his bed . . . and the governor's daughter was out cold on the couch, totally trashed. Can you imagine the scandal we would have had to cover up if it leaked to the public? I had to drag Junior's ass into the shower because he smelled like a beer keg had been dumped over his head."

Summer 2008. I remembered it. Well, not the part after I passed out. And she was basically bringing up a very wild night like it happened every day, when that wasn't the case at all.

Mason laughed a little under his breath and I ran my fingers through my hair and made every attempt to keep my mouth shut.

"How nice of you to hose the poor boy down, *Jenni,*" Kendrick snapped.

I was starting to think Kendrick might be able to tolerate Stewart even less than I was. Maybe because she was the only other chick in this division right now and Kendrick had probably originally hoped that they could form some X chromosome alliance. But not Stewart. No freakin' way.

Stewart smiled. "It was quite a task. Not to mention the fact that I caught a glimpse of a little more of Junior's skin than I wanted. Even the really little Agent Meyer, if you know what I mean."

I groaned and started to get up from my seat. "I'll see you guys later." Footsteps followed behind me out of the dining room.

"We've got thirty seconds before the door closes," Dad said in a low voice.

My heart pounded. We had done this for the first time a week ago, and every day since, and it still freaked me out.

CHAPTER THREE

I made it through the secret exit, completely unnoticed. Dad was wait-ing for me in the tunnel on the other side. It was totally dark.

"You got a flashlight?" I whispered.

A tiny light came from beside me and lit up the dirt ground in front of us. I blew on my hands and rubbed them together as we walked. It was a very chilly fifty-one degrees here.

"What's the matter? Stewart getting to you again?" Dad asked.

"Man, she's driving me nuts. What the hell is her problem?" I kicked a rock in front of me so hard it rolled completely out of sight.

"Sorry, I can't play Dad and get involved. It would only make things worse," he said. "I agree she's given you enough shit to deserve a good ass-kicking, but you have to look at the situation from her per-spective."

"I thought you weren't going to play Dad."

"Not Dad, just experienced agent. She gave up her life as she knew it two years ago and busted her ass while you partied and did whatever the hell you wanted. Which is fine because that was her job, but when you come in here and start outscoring her, of course she's going to be a little ticked."

"I hadn't really thought of it that way. Still, it's so junior high." We stopped walking. "I'll go up first," I said, pointing at the rope that would lead us to ground level.

I started my climb and felt the satisfaction of knowing I never would have been able to do this three months ago. It was a forty-eight-foot rope climb, with one small ledge in the middle if you absolutely had to stop for a break.

This was the emergency exit, should the elevator fail. Then again, we had at least four agents who knew every aspect of elevator repair.

The air turned warmer the closer we came to ground level. Sweat trickled down my face as I neared the top of the rope. I threw myself over the edge and onto solid ground.

My whole body relaxed when I took a deep breath and inhaled the scent of the nearby waterfall. The sun warmed my face instantly. Finally, Dad's dark hair emerged from the small hole in the ground.

"Come on, old man," I said, reaching out a hand to help him over the edge.

He flopped onto the ground, panting a little. "Damn, that gets harder every time."

We always stood next to the waterfall, which ran down the side of the mountain. Maybe in case someone *had* managed to slip a listening device on one of us. The rushing water would interfere. Dad stumbled behind me as I made my way through the trees to a soft patch of grass where the water sprayed just enough to keep us cool.

After we sat down, Dad pulled out his phone, holding it out to me. "I have some pictures . . . if you want to see? I know you were worried about her a few weeks ago."

I lay back in the grass and shook my head. "I don't want to see. Just tell me if there's anything to worry about."

"Okay," he said with a sigh. "If that's what you want."

"You really think she'll stay off the EOT radar? And Adam, too?" I asked.

He stretched out next to me. "Yes, and if not, I'll know immediately because of the precautions we've taken. This is what I do best, Jackson. The same thing I did with you and Courtney almost your entire life. Trust me."

"I do."

Dad glanced sideways at me and I could tell he was debating asking me something or bringing up a sticky topic, but it only lasted a second before he spoke up. "Dr. Melvin's worried about you. He said you did a little too well today . . . regulating your heart rate . . . That was pretty impressive for anyone, let alone someone with only three months' training. Especially after—"

"After I almost killed Agent Freeman," I said right away.

"I wasn't going to bring that up, actually. Just the fact that you performed beyond expectations today, and Dr. Melvin also showed me the results of your emotional readiness test from last week. Second-highest mark in the entire training group . . . ?"

"Who was first?" I asked, then both of us said the answer together: "Stewart."

"So what?" I said with a shrug. "Shouldn't be anything to worry about if I scored well."

"It is if you figured out how to lie your way through it." Dad lifted an eyebrow, X-raying my face the way Chief Marshall always did. "Denial is only the first stage of grieving. If that's where you are right now, then it's gonna be a problem when you get assigned to real missions."

What came after denial?

"Stages of grieving apply to death. It's not like she's dead," I said, a little more defensive than I should have sounded. I took a deep breath to calm myself. "Besides, Dad . . . me and Holly . . . it was like the honeymoon phase for us. A week or two more and we would have been at each other's throats. I had a bad habit of screwing up and she had very high expectations, rightfully so."

He looked at me for a long moment and his face spread into a grin. "Damn . . . you really did lie your way through that test. As your superior officer, I'm very impressed. But as your father, I'm worried about you."

"Don't be," I said firmly. "We all have to learn how to deal with bad stuff and keep going, right?"

It was hard for me to complain to Dad about Holly when I knew she was okay, while he had lost the woman he loved forever. If it weren't for that, I might have opened up to him a little more than I had. Especially considering the fact that we'd spent more time together in the last three months than we had in the last three years combined.

Dad laughed under his breath. "I would have loved to have seen you confessing love to a girl. I honestly didn't think that day would ever come. It's never been a priority for you, to be with someone. Not that there's anything wrong with being independent. I wanted that for you . . . and for Courtney."

"Well, you probably won't ever see me confessing love to anyone again." I had a feeling this statement was true, but I didn't know if it was because I'd never get over Holly or because I *would,* and still choose to be alone, like Dad had.

"I wish Eileen could see you, like this. She just had so many ideas and . . ." He stopped and turned his eyes up toward the sky again. "Anyway . . . she'd be proud of you. That much I know."

"God, this is depressing," I muttered after a long and eerie silence fell between us. Both of us started laughing, slicing through the tension. "Sorry, I had to say it."

"Point taken," Dad said. "Did you and Kendrick have a hard time with the test today? The first part, I mean . . . the rest I know was difficult for most of you."

"Nothing we couldn't handle." I sat up and stretched my arms before lying back again. "How come I've never heard anything about Kendrick? There's not much in her file."

"She's got a different background than the others. She's a med student, you know. That's why she hasn't been with you guys until recently. She had classes."

"How can she be a med student if she's only twenty-one?"

"Agent Kendrick is very smart and extremely creative . . . especially in the areas of medical research and genetics. Chief Marshall and Kendrick both agreed that traditional agent training was the best place for her to start." He averted his eyes from me and scratched his head. "She'll do fine in the field. Not as well as Stewart, but good enough. Dr. Melvin's already got her working on research for some of his upcoming experiments."

"Not clones, I hope."

Dad threw me a sharp look. "You know he's not interested in those types of projects."

"Yeah, yeah, so I've heard . . . like, a thousand times." I rested my arms behind my head and studied the clouds slowly moving over us. "Marshall gave me and Kendrick an assignment. He thinks we need to trust each other more."

"I heard about that." Dad stod up, nodding toward the hole in the ground we had emerged from.

I reluctantly got to my feet too, knowing we would have to head back soon. "Do you have any idea what would challenge Kendrick?"

Dad laughed under his breath. "Surgery, stitching someone up, setting a broken bone, performing an autopsy."

"Is she, like, flunking out of med school or something?" I asked. "Can't Dr. Melvin tutor her?"

"Tutoring wouldn't help. She knows what to do." Dad shrugged and tightened the knot that kept the rope secure to a giant rock. "There have been a few situations where trainees were in need of medical attention and she froze up. Basically panicked. She's textbook-perfect, just has trouble with the application part of her skills."

Okay, so, this was a good challenge for her. At least it wasn't a life-or-death task. More of a phobia.

I started climbing down first and Dad followed. We had nearly made it back through the secret entrance when I heard a voice coming from the other side of the door. Dad froze, listening carefully. The wall slid open and Chief Marshall stood in front of us, arms crossed, the bright lights shining behind him.

"I'd like a word with you, Agent Meyer," Marshall said to Dad.

Dad stepped through the opening and I followed. That was when I noticed Stewart standing right behind Marshall.

That snitch. But how did she know?

"This is my fault," I said immediately. "I snuck off and my dad came to find me."

"Interesting," Marshall said, looking down his nose at me. "That isn't the version I heard."

I glanced at Stewart, who looked at Dad, and the tiniest flicker of worry crossed her expression. Her eyes got wider for a split second, the whites of her eyes a contrast to her caramel-colored skin.

"Obviously there was reason for concern," Marshall said. "Breaking rules costs lives. Your father should know that better than anyone. You can add an extra twenty miles to your PT requirements for this week and next."

"Fine," I said before stepping around Marshall and heading down the hall.

Unfortunately, Stewart had to be a complete bitch and follow me. "I knew you couldn't keep yourself confined. Your dad's probably giving you the details of every test. Cheating asshole."

My hands balled up into tight fists, but I took in a deep breath and shook them out. "Okay, believe whatever you want. I broke the rules, you caught me. The end."

"This is not the end." She jumped in front of me, blocking the way to my room. A huge grin spread across her face. "What the hell are you doing that's so important, anyway? You're trying to get out, aren't you? The CIA's not as glamorous as it seems?"

I shoved her to the side and dove into my room before she could say another word. Then I grabbed a handful of pencils from my desk and launched them across the room.

"What the hell?"

I jumped and banged my head against the shelf next to me. Kendrick was stretched out across my bed, her cell phone pressed to her ear and one arm over her face, probably blocking the flying pencils from jabbing her in the eye.

"Sorry, the maid's in my room," she said.

"The maid" was code for the two lowest-ranked agents following daily competitions, who had to clean everyone's room as a punishment.

I sat down at my desk, resting my head in my hands, trying to take deep breaths. "No, everything's fine," Kendrick said into the phone. "Just a little flying-pencil incident."

I listened in to find out who she was talking to. From what I'd seen, most of the other agents didn't really call anyone, not to chat.

"Hey . . . let me call you back, all right?"

After she hung up the phone, I spun around in my chair to face her.

I preferred that she hear about what had happened with Dad from me instead of Stewart.

"How come you never call anyone?" she asked, still stretched out on my bed.

"Just don't need to, I guess."

"Stewart seems to think you had quite the social life. You must have friends to keep up with, back in New York."

"What's the point? Not like I have time to hang out or I can tell them anything about what I've been doing all these months."

"Still . . . you've got to maintain some grasp on reality. We'll be spending a lot of time blending in with the real world soon." She sighed and shook her head. "Okay, what's the deal with the pencils? Are you practicing for a darts competition or really pissed at someone? Hopefully not me?"

I told her everything that had just happened with Stewart, Dad, and Marshall. I was pretty sure Kendrick would take it better than Stewart had, but her reaction surprised me.

"What an immature bitch. Seriously, is this junior high?"

I threw my hands up. "Exactly what I said."

Kendrick had this look of deep concentration, then she sat up really quick and grinned. "Oh, my God . . . I know what your task is."

I perked up a little, guessing this had nothing to do with more mountain-climbing, which was what I thought she might go for, given our mountainside conversation about acrophobes this morning. "Beat Stewart at a silent defense match? Blindfolded, maybe?"

She shook her head but kept grinning. "You have to kiss her . . . like, in front of everyone. Total hard-core make-out session."

I rolled my eyes. "First of all, she'd kick me in the balls before I could even get close to kissing her, and second, I don't see how this is a challenge. I'm not afraid to kiss people, and it's not going to make me a more trustworthy partner . . . or a better agent."

Kendrick got up and walked behind me, putting her hands on my shoulders. "Someone has got to put this chick in her place. She'll spend the rest of her life dangling every embarrassing moment over your head, like collateral. 'Oh, Junior, when did you get your braces off? Let me tell everyone what your bare ass looks like,'" Kendrick said, mocking Stewart's current French character perfectly.

This sales pitch was getting better and better. "Okay, you've got my attention."

She spun me around to face her. "You've got to walk up to her and just . . . kiss her and show her who's in control. The girl thinks she owns you. Personally, I'm sick and tired of listening to her."

"That's kinda . . . *anti*-girl-power, isn't it?"

She considered this for a minute before answering. "In this case, it's necessary. And you're not a little kid anymore . . . that's how she treats you. It's got nothing to do with gender. She's, what, a year and a half older than you?"

"What's Marshall going to think when you tell him my assigned task is to kiss someone?"

"I don't care what he thinks. It's his fault for leaving it so open-ended." She yanked me up off the chair. "Let's go now before you chicken out."

"Maybe now isn't the best time. I think I'll just end up punching her."

"That's not nearly as interesting as kissing. Come on. She's probably in the workout room." She was already dragging me out the door. We had to go down three hallways to get to the large exercise facility. Stewart *was* in there, practicing self-defense moves on the mats with Agent Parker. I started to walk into the room, but Kendrick held me back. "Wait, you've got to get into character. Be sexy."

Apparently I wasn't that already.

We both looked into the room after hearing a loud thud. Stewart had just thrown Parker, who was way bigger than me, flat onto his back and was laughing at him as he struggled to breathe.

"I can't do this," I mumbled.

"Yes, you can."

I shook my arms out like a fighter entering the ring. *This is a test.* Just another test. Besides, I'd had to flirt with women as part of CIA training. It'd gotten me access to government data I wasn't supposed to have in China, and, once, free ice cream.

Kendrick nodded her encouragement. "You totally got this. Just slip into that character and you'll never have Jenni Stewart bitching at you again."

Now, *that* was a prize worth winning. Assuming it worked. I headed in Stewart's direction, but then froze up and turned around again. "I'm not sure I'll like this enough to fake enjoyment."

"Come on, you're a freakin' guy, pretend it's someone you don't have the urge to vomit all over."

I laughed a little and turned around. *Pretend, pretend, pretend.* Been there, done that. Kendrick slipped in behind me and jumped on a nearby treadmill. Every single trainee was under the age of twenty-three, and never had I seen any attempt to get close to Stewart other than self-defense. Stewart stuck out a hand to help Parker up and then pulled it away at the last second and kicked him right in the stomach. Honestly, I was surprised he fell for that.

She finally noticed my presence. "Junior, did you come for a little match, or do you only release your frustrations by throwing things in your room like a two-year-old?"

I took a deep breath and forced myself to focus on the goal. "Sure, I'll have a go."

"Excellent," she said, with her evil-agent grin.

Kendrick coughed loudly behind me. She must have thought I was deviating or chickening out.

Stewart stood in front of me, her face full of energy. She lunged forward but I got my arms around her and started to lift her off the mat. I put her down seconds later, with a heavy sigh. "Sorry, I can't do this . . . not like this."

"So, I win?" she said.

"Yeah, I guess." Channeling the player guy I used to be, I moved close to her. "I'm sorry . . . for getting pissed off. You did the right thing, turning me in."

"I knew you'd see it my way." She turned a little toward the other agents on the equipment, probably to make sure everyone had heard my fake apology.

I grabbed her hand and tugged. "Wait . . . one more thing."

It's just meaningless kissing. The emotional still-in-love-with-the-girl-I-couldn't-be-with part of my brain stayed shut off, as it had been for weeks now. The agent in me knew Kendrick was right. Revenge came in many different forms.

My hands slid down the sides of her neck and the smallest amount of confusion flickered across her face. "What are you—"

I didn't let her finish. And it wasn't a soft gentle kiss. It was a manly, controlling one. I knew my inner agent was still switched on when I recalled exactly how many seconds we had been kissing: twenty. No punching. No resistance. Her arms stayed completely limp at her sides while mine wrapped tightly around her, and she let me. In fact, she was the one to stick her tongue in my mouth. Seriously?

I waited until forty seconds had passed, then I moved my mouth to the side of her neck and whispered, so only she could hear, "That's what you get for calling me a little boy."

I released her so quickly she nearly fell over, then I strolled out of the room like this was something a badass agent like me did every day. Kendrick was right behind me, along with Parker.

"You are beyond awesome!" Kendrick said, slapping her hand to mine. "Oh, my God, I wish I could have recorded that."

"Dude, you've got balls," Parker said. "And she could have twisted them in a knot."

I groaned, imagining what could have happened as a result of getting that close to her with my eyes closed. "I know, seriously."

"I don't know if you noticed, but she didn't exactly shove you away. It looked mutual to me," Kendrick said. "Maybe all the training and observation skills have kept us from going for the most obvious answer: you like someone, so you act like you hate them."

"I thought that was only grade school kids," Parker said.

Kendrick was right, I did feel like Stewart finally got a little dose of the torture she'd forced on me for months.

Loud sirens boomed from inside the walls and red lights flashed everywhere. The three of us froze in the middle of the hallway. There was only *one* reason for red lights.

CHAPTER FOUR

"We've just intercepted a death threat targeted at the chancellor of Germany," Marshall said, pacing back and forth in the giant common room. "There's reason to believe the EOTs are behind this. We have exactly two hours to prevent the murder of one of the most important political figures in the world."

"Excuse me, Chief," Agent Freeman interrupted. "Can you tell us anything about the source?"

Chief Marshall's eyes rested on Freeman, like they were conversing silently. "I'm sorry, I can't reveal that information at this time."

"Will all of us be in the field?" another trainee asked.

Marshall shook his head, and I could practically hear the silent groans no one dared to utter aloud. Everyone was itching for a real-life assignment, even me.

"Since we've never seen more than three or four EOTs at any given time and because this mission should be fairly simple, we don't plan to complicate things further by charging in with the entire division. Agent Meyer Senior and Agent Freeman will each lead a team of two," Marshall said, and a few agents did groan out loud this time. There were fourteen of us. Most likely my incident from earlier would eliminate my participation, but a lot of others would be left out, too.

I relaxed a little, letting my heart slow down. No reason to panic if I'd just be sitting on my ass looking up shit in the Communications Room. I leaned back against the wall and Kendrick did the same, then whispered to me, "Look at the bright side, I saw that guitar in your room . . . You can entertain me while I record data. Maybe we can write a depressing song about secret agents who never get picked."

I rolled my eyes at her, but attempted to smile, since she was obviously just trying to be nice.

Marshall turned to us, scanning his eyes over the group. "Agent Freeman will take Stewart and Parker," Marshall said.

More groans.

"Shouldn't I be going with my partner?" Mason asked. "What about the potential for explosives in this situation? I have the highest marks on all the deactivation tests—"

"Not this time," Dad said.

Mason's freckled face turned a little red, but he didn't give up. "But what if—"

"Sorry, Mason," Dad interrupted, more firmly this time, ending the conversation.

"Agent Meyer Senior will take Agent Kendrick . . ." Marshall hesitated and turned to stare at my partner. She straightened up immediately, her jaw practically dropping. "And the other Agent Meyer."

Now my heart had returned to pounding. More like beating its way out of my chest. *Good thing we aren't hooked up to the torture chair anymore.* The first person I looked at was Dad. He didn't even make eye contact and his face was completely unreadable.

"The rest of you will remain here doing routine surveillance and monitoring the mission's progress."

The groans came out louder this time because the decision had been made. They didn't have anything to lose. I was still holding my breath and Kendrick wiped her sweaty hands off on her pants. Parker and Stewart, however, looked excited and confident. The complete polar opposite of Dad's team. *Poor Dad.*

Dad turned to the four trainees assigned to the field. "Change into something that blends in with typical tourists. You've got three minutes."

This was really happening. Not the fake staged missions I had participated in over the last three months. But the real question was, why did Marshall choose me and Kendrick over some of the others who had more well-rounded skills? I knew he had a very specific reason. I just didn't know what that was.

One thing I had learned after three months of training was that almost every task or assignment revolved around mind games. Question everything and everyone.

Kendrick and I stared at the beautiful castle in front of us, lit up for the nighttime crowds.

"My first trip to Heidelberg, and of course I'm working," she said with a sigh.

The Heidelberg Castle sat up on the side of a hill, and the majority of it was open on top. Several sections had been destroyed and rebuilt after being set on fire during a war and then hit with lightning on a completely separate occasion. Today wasn't the first time this landmark had been part of a war zone.

We both moved so we were on either side of Dad. I could see Freeman leading his team to the opposite end of the castle.

"The chancellor and her family arrive in exactly twenty minutes. They'll head to the northeast corner and work their way west," Dad said. "No guns unless it's the last straw. Our goal is to tiptoe in and out completely unnoticed. Got it?"

"Yep," we both said.

"Good, now get to your first positions and don't move a muscle unless I give you direct orders, understood?" Dad's eyes paused on mine. A warning.

"He doesn't want you here," Kendrick said as we walked away. "I can tell."

"Yeah, I figured. Marshall's probably punishing him for helping me sneak out earlier," I said. "And he knows all the agents left behind will be pissed at me for getting picked." Kendrick and I paid the entrance fee to get inside the castle and took our time, drifting casually to the assigned location.

"What about you? Are you glad you're here?" I asked her.

"Honestly, I feel like I'm gonna barf," she admitted.

The hardest part about these assignments was that we couldn't just call up the chancellor's office and tell them it wasn't safe to come here, because then the EOTs wouldn't show up, either. Which would mean we wouldn't know where to find them and they'd just plan another attack on the same person and we wouldn't know about it. It was more effective to let them get as close to success as possible, then stop them. But also more risky.

Both of us leaned against the castle wall, breathing heavy, waiting as the light drizzle of evening rain began to fall. We kept perfectly still as Freeman reported to everyone that the chancellor had arrived with her crew. A few minutes later they drifted past us. Eight subjects altogether. And there were only six of us to protect them.

Kendrick stuck her hand out, feeling the raindrops hit more frequently. "I think they're here."

"The EOTs?" I asked. "How do you know?"

Her eyes were focused on the sky now. "The rain, you know—" Her head snapped forward and she stared right at me, eyes huge, then she looked away, mumbling, "Shit . . ."

I remembered the storm that had hit so suddenly when Dad, Holly, Adam, and I were on the boat before I left that other timeline.

"Wait a minute," I said, grabbing her arm. "What about the rain? Is this something from your specialty classes?"

She looked at me again with fear in her eyes. "Jackson . . . please don't—"

I shook my head, turning my focus back to the area we were supposed to be monitoring. "Forget it . . . don't tell me."

And I'll just figure it out later when I have time to think. There must be a reason they were trying to keep this from me.

Stewart was next to shout through our earpieces, in muffled French. Water had run into my ear and I couldn't tell what she was saying, but I could hear the slight panic in her voice.

"What did she say?" I asked Kendrick.

"There's an explosive . . . on the north end . . . something she's never seen before."

My eyes met Kendrick's and I knew there was no avoiding it. Dad couldn't leave us pressed against this wall any longer. Sure enough, he ran up behind us and didn't even stop, just called over his shoulder, "Go . . . both of you."

He didn't need to tell me twice. The rain fell in giant sheets as we tore through the outdoor corridors.

"Okay, so I guess they should have picked Mason," Kendrick shouted over her shoulder.

"If you can figure out that torture chair, I have a feeling you can deactivate bombs just fine."

As we ran north, Stewart's face came into view as she flew toward us. "What the hell are you doing?" I asked her. "Who's working on the weapon?"

"No one, I followed—" she started to answer, her face flushed with fear.

Freeman, Dad, and Parker came up behind us. "Who's with the explosive?" Freeman asked immediately.

"I followed protocol and waited ninety seconds. No one responded. The fucking thing is made of some weird shit!"

Dad raised his hand to stop her and swept the area with his eyes. "All right . . . Kendrick, go with Stewart and get Mason on the phone if you have to . . . Jackson and I will head west, and Freeman and Parker will stick with the chancellor."

It was both amazing and a relief to see my dad in action . . . the leader. "How did it get here? Didn't someone sweep the entire place an hour ago?" I asked.

"It wasn't here an hour ago," a familiar voice spoke from behind us.

All six of us spun around to face the large brick wall, drawing our guns in a swift mechanical motion. But my grip on my pistol slipped as I stared through the rain at Thomas and about eight others beside him. My eyes fell on the red-haired woman to his right.

"Cassidy," I mumbled under my breath. I felt Dad's eyes on the side of my face for a second, and then he moved closer to me. I wanted to look at this woman and not feel anything. No connection. Because

I had a feeling that was what Dad wanted. But she looked so much like Courtney . . . it was hard not to feel anything.

"Why are there so many of them?" I whispered to Kendrick. She shook her head, and her hands held steady on her gun. "And they're not all in the database."

Thomas turned his eyes on me and gave a stiff nod. "Jackson, nice to see you again. I had hoped it wouldn't be under these conditions, but . . . it's always fascinating to see how Agent Meyer's only *son* is turning out."

He put a slight emphasis on the word "son" that only Dad and I would pick up on.

"Quite a large group you've brought," Agent Freeman said, then he turned his attention to the chancellor and her crew, who I just noticed were standing behind us, recognizing the threat but unsure what to do. Before anyone could move again, a bolt of lightning crashed down onto a nearby tree and the thud of a heavy branch falling onto a piece of the castle momentarily jolted our attention from the scene.

My heart pounded and I could hardly breathe, knowing we were outnumbered and this was obviously a bigger deal than Chief Marshall had speculated.

"Don't move unless I tell you," Dad hissed into my ear.

Thomas held his hands up and walked closer to us. "We understand why you're here, and I say this with the utmost respect for your dedication, but you need to leave and let this happen. The future will be better for everyone. I promise."

"Why here . . . why her?" Dad asked Thomas, nodding toward the chancellor.

I couldn't look at the group behind us, but I could hear them mumbling in German, the two bodyguards holding out their weapons.

"She's at the beginning of a complicated chain of events and we are morally obligated to fix it. To shape the world ahead," Thomas said, then his eyes burned into Dad's. "This was a direct mission from Eyewall."

Dad sucked in a breath as if this meant something, but I had no idea what. *Eyewall?* None of us moved, and that must have been enough of an answer. Half of the EOTs in front of us vanished.

Kendrick gasped beside me and when I turned my head, Cassidy was right behind her, her elbow hooked around Kendrick's throat. I didn't even get a chance to attack because my partner had her on the ground in seconds and quickly jabbed Cassidy in the neck with the medication us nonmedical people referred to as "anti-time-travel drugs." Cassidy's eyes fluttered shut and Kendrick looked up at me with panic on her face.

Thomas still stood in front of us as the others jumped to different locations. I knew most of them wouldn't be able to jump out of here and back again more than a couple times before the heavy fatigue set in. Or at least I hoped they wouldn't. Then again, we all had thought there wouldn't be more than four of them. That obviously wasn't true.

A gap opened up in the line of defense and I took my chance and tore away from the group to try to get to the explosive. Kendrick was right at my heels, probably knowing I'd need her help.

"Jackson!" Dad shouted, but an EOT with dark hair popped up behind him and Dad had to throw him to the ground while ducking under Parker's line of fire. Stewart took off from her attacker and ran ahead of us, toward the tower where the explosive must have been. Screams erupted from the chancellor's group as Freeman and Parker dove around, trying to cover all of them.

Thomas's eyes followed Stewart, and suddenly he was gone. Maybe going after her?

"Get out!" Freeman shouted to all of us. I almost followed him and Dad.

From over Kendrick's shoulder I saw a tiny person with red hair running toward the tower where the explosive was.

It couldn't be her . . . could it?

I shoved Kendrick in the direction of the exit where Freeman and Dad were headed. "Go!"

She hesitated, then gave me one last fleeting look before running. I sped through the long corridor and charged up two flights of stairs. I could hear Dad and Freeman shouting at me, but I couldn't leave. The second I reached the tower, I saw her. Emily.

Unfortunately, I was interrupted by the appearance of another EOT. A tall man with blond hair. He landed on the step in front of me and reached for me so quick, I flung myself sideways without thinking about the consequences. The man tumbled down the stairs, finally reaching a flat surface, groaning and looking up at the sky.

I leaped down the stairs and retrieved one of the injections we all had to cart around during a mission, hoping I could stab him in the correct location. I mimicked Kendrick's movement from a few minutes ago and stuck the needle into the throbbing vein in his neck.

The man let out a half groan, half laugh and shook his head. "You can fight as hard as you want this way, Jackson, but it'll never be enough. You have to use it . . . your abilities."

I pressed my foot to his chest, planning to hold him down until the drugs kicked in and he passed out. "Why? So I can blow up the world? It's not like I can change anything. Only one person can do that."

The man shook his head vigorously. "No, no . . . you're wrong. There are others like Thomas and there are also other ways to alter the future. Think about it . . . you've already done it."

His eyes fluttered shut and I felt my head pounding so hard I couldn't think for several seconds. What did he mean? *You've already done it.* The imaginary clock counting down for the explosive practically ticked inside my head, jolting me back to reality. I charged up the stairs to the tower and she was still there. Definitely not a figment of my imagination.

The little eleven-year-old girl was busy leaning over this complex and massive explosive. "Emily!" I had to step over one of the fallen branches just to get to where Emily sat.

She looked up at me for a second and then her hands were moving fast, pulling pieces apart. Stewart was right. This explosive was weird, made of glass, with clear tubes and vials of colored liquids running in all directions. Maybe Mason got to study these in his specialty training in Futuristic Technology, but I had never seen anything like it before. No wires. Nothing familiar from the basic deactivation training I'd been given.

She mumbled to herself and I could see her hands shaking as more tubes ended up beside her, outside of the massive glass case. Finally, she let out a breath and sank back onto her heels, one hand clutching her chest. "Twenty seconds to spare."

I knelt down across from her and reached for one of the tubes with a light blue liquid sloshing back and forth. She grabbed my hand to stop me. "Don't touch anything . . . trust me."

"What are you doing here? And how did you know how to do . . . *that*?" I asked.

She stood up and dusted off the knees of her jeans. "We have to destroy this, we can't let anyone see it. The technology is too . . . advanced."

"How do we destroy it?" I asked frantically.

Then I saw another victim of the sudden lightning storm lying at the bottom of the steps I had just come up to get to this section of the tower. Not a human victim. Another thick branch, like the one I had just stepped over to get to Emily, this one with tons of smaller branches and bright green leaves stemming from it. I could clearly see sparks and the first sign of fire near the end of the branch.

I jumped over the branch again and yelled to Emily, "Pull this right over the explosive . . . and put as many leaves in the center as you can."

After racing down the steps, hurdling over the EOT's body, I carefully extracted the piece of tree on fire, holding my hand in front to block the wind and rain from putting it out. It was possible this was a very bad idea and I should have just handed over the bomb to Dad and Freeman so we could study it, but I had to trust her at least a little. She might have been taking orders from another me.

The second we had some good-sized flames going, Emily and I raced down the stairs and clear to the other side of the castle. She leaned against a wall, catching her breath. "Jackson . . . I don't know what's happening, but things keep changing."

"In the future?" I pressed.

She nodded. "Just be careful . . . about jumping . . . I think someone has already changed things since your last jump."

"What things?"

A pained look crossed her face and then disappeared right away. "Just stay in this timeline, okay? Promise? No matter what you find out?"

"I'll try," I said. "I promise I'll try."

She gave me a quick squeeze around the waist and whispered, "I'm sorry . . . that I can't tell you more . . . but I have to go."

Her hands dropped to her sides and she was gone. Like a figment of my imagination. I heard Dad's voice coming through my earpiece. "Jackson! Where the hell are you?"

"West tower, Dad," I answered, speaking directly into my wristwatch.

"We think the explosive might be inactive now. Apparently Thomas has decided to set an entire section of the castle on fire."

An entire section? It hadn't looked *that* bad a few minutes ago.

Sure enough, when I looked over at the farthest end of the castle, black smoke drifted toward the sky. It was going to take a lot more than this rain to put out that fire.

"What's the new cover story? Are we drugging the witnesses?"

"We've already gotten the chancellor out safely. Freeman's taking the whole delegation to our third command center. Hopefully in twelve hours they won't remember a damn thing."

I spun around in a circle, looking at the flames and the perimeters. Dad was nowhere in sight. However, I could see the back of Thomas's head as he ran after Parker. Blood pumped twice as fast through my veins. The urge to kill him that I'd had earlier today, after the memory gas, returned with a vengeance. The image of him tossing Holly off the six-story-high roof flashed through my head and I shook it out. *Focus. She's not here.*

I ran fast, gaining ground on him, but just as I got about three feet from Thomas, he was gone.

"Damn!" I spun around, looking for any others. The wind picked up and blew the thick black smoke directly in my face. Tears streamed down my cheeks and I coughed out the smoke.

I almost retreated, but Stewart's voice came through my earpiece.

She was giving her coordinates and requesting backup. And of course she was right in the middle of the flames.

Why the hell did she go in there? Did someone tell her to get the explosive out? None of us had come equipped for fire.

I pulled my shirt over my face and ran into the fire. I expected to see Thomas, but it was just Stewart tied to a pole.

Someone tied her to a pole with a rope?

I could barely see in the midst of all the smoke and flames. Stewart's head bobbed around as she lost consciousness. I snatched the pocketknife from her hands and started on the section of the rope that she had already begun sawing apart. Water streamed out of my eyes and I could hardly breathe. Finally the rope dropped to the floor and I picked Stewart up before she fell over, then I charged up the nearest staircase, hoping that a helicopter was on its way.

I had to admit, I was glad Stewart needed rescuing instead of Kendrick because she's four inches shorter than my partner. With my lungs ready to collapse and three flights of stairs to climb, those four inches and fifteen fewer pounds made a big difference.

"Where the hell are you?" I shouted to Dad through my coms unit.

"We can see you. We'll be right there. Helicopter's on its way."

Magic words.

I reached the top of the final staircase and put Stewart on the floor and collapsed next to her. Her eyes were still closed, but she continued to cough. Parker was the first to reach us.

"What the fuck happened to you guys?" he said, dropping beside her, loosening the buttons on her shirt.

"She got tied up, literally, in the fire," I said between coughs. "I don't know how long she was down there."

Feet pounded against the stairs next to us and then Dad and Kendrick appeared. Parker and I both looked up at the sky where the helicopter hovered nearby. It turned sharply and headed in our direction.

Dad pulled me off the floor, his hands clutched around the front of my shirt. "Don't ever go against my orders . . . understood?"

He didn't sound angry. He sounded like me after 007 Holly had climbed across that swing set and flipped off of it. Only worse.

"I'm sorry," I said. But I wasn't, and I couldn't tell him that because I'd never told anyone about Emily. Not even Dad.

"The fire must have deactivated the bomb," Kendrick shouted over the approaching helicopter. "Otherwise it would have exploded by now?"

All of us stared at each other, and it was obvious we were thinking the same thing: *What the fuck just happened and why did Marshall throw us to the wolves tonight?* Nobody said a word, but it was a mutual, silent question.

I picked up Stewart again and got her in a seat first before digging for an oxygen mask. Her head fell against the window and Kendrick handed me a mask to slip around her face. Her eyes barely opened.

"You're all right," I shouted to her over all the noise. "It's over."

"We'll head back to headquarters. Have Dr. Melvin meet us on the ground," Dad yelled to the pilot.

Medical attention was a must for this group right now. Dad had a cut across his forehead that would probably need stitches, and Parker was pulling off his shoe, revealing a very swollen ankle. I had several cuts and scrapes on my face and arms, but nothing else.

Kendrick sat in front of us and started removing the streaks of black from Stewart's face with alcohol wipes. "Her breathing doesn't sound too labored."

I decided now might be the time to break the news to her. I pointed at Dad's now-oozing cut. "You have to stitch that up. It's your task."

She looked up at me and her eyes were huge. "No . . . please . . . anything but that."

"I can't take it back now that I've told you," I said.

She glanced quickly at Dad and then back at me. "I can't . . . I'm sorry. I just can't."

"You'll be fine. Seriously, how hard can it be?" I said, wishing I hadn't picked this moment to spring it on her after all.

She shook her head again and I thought there were tears in her eyes, but with all the smoke, it was hard to be sure of the cause.

The helicopter lifted up and made a sharp right turn. Flames were still rising despite the emergency personnel now on site. I hoped they would be able to stop it before it spread to the surrounding trees. Looking at this destruction and remembering how the hotel at the beach had also been nearly demolished made my stomach tie in knots.

The future that Emily had shown me, that horrible version of New York, didn't seem so impossible anymore. But who really caused it? Did it happen before the perfect future that Thomas had shown me? Or maybe they were in completely different timelines, and if so, I had no idea which one I was living in.

CHAPTER FIVE

The many questions surrounding last night's mission weighed on my mind all through the morning's training. Even Stewart showing up at the Advanced Defense group's target practice in a very tight red dress couldn't distract me from finding answers. Apparently she'd had some kind of training mission in a local town, but wouldn't tell any of us what exactly she'd had to do that required this particular attire. Of course, Freeman had no problem letting Stewart barge in on our training time and possibly show up most of these guys. Except me. I could beat Stewart in accuracy with target shooting. But sometimes just the sound of the gun brought back the memory of Holly falling to the floor, blood seeping through her robe, and I wondered if I would actually be able to kill anything that wasn't cardboard. Luckily, no one knew I had these kinds of doubts.

Stewart found a new cardboard cutout behind a tree and set it up on my side of the field, while Freeman ran through a skills test that I had already mastered with some of the other agents in my group. "Give me your gun, Junior."

I almost didn't loan her my weapon, but then I got an idea and handed it over. She aimed for her fake person, knocking a hole right through its forehead.

"Nice shot." I stood beside her, keeping my eyes on the side of her face. "Too bad you didn't get here about twenty minutes ago . . . Freeman was telling us about Eyewall—"

She laughed. "Nice try, Junior. *My* specialty studies organized opposing forces, not yours. Your little robot Advanced Defense buddies couldn't process that information if their lives depended on it."

I took note of the fact that she only said my group members couldn't handle it, but left me out of that accusation. I wondered if it was intentional or not. Did she think I was more skilled than the others in my group?

"So you know what Thomas was talking about?" I pressed, having nothing to lose at this point.

"It's possible."

"Is it another name for the EOTs? Or another CIA organization?"

She glanced at me, raising her eyebrows. "Give it up, Junior. You know the rules . . . Don't go digging for shit you're not supposed to know."

"Tomorrow," Freeman said, gathering everyone together, "we're going to practice this again, but with a few altered variables. All of you need to be prepared for changes in a mission's plan that happen on the spot. I'm sure everyone's looked over the reports from Heidelberg . . . Many unexpected changes occurred and we had to think on our feet."

"Yeah . . . what was up with that?" Agent Miller asked. "All of us were here sitting around doing nothing."

"We should have been there," someone else said. "Both teams could have been wiped out if it weren't for that fire."

Freeman's eyes bounced among all of us. Even Stewart lowered my gun and turned her attention to Freeman. "I don't think the chief expected—"

"Why were there so many of them?" a trainee named Agent Prescott interrupted. "We've never had more than four time travelers present at any attack . . . There were nine of them last night."

So I wasn't the only one with questions on my mind after yesterday.

"True . . ." Freeman's face stayed completely impassive, but I could almost see his struggle to find a response . . . probably to figure out a lie to tell us.

"How do we know fifty of them aren't going to show up at the next mission?" Agent Miller asked. "We don't even have fifty agents in our division."

Freeman let out a sigh and leaned the bundle of cardboard people he'd been carrying against a tree. "Look . . . this group covers Advanced Defense and *only* Advanced Defense. Other than basic information all agents are given, I can't go into specifics about the mission unless you want to review guns or hand-to-hand combat from last night—"

"What about that bomb? No one got a picture of it?" Agent Prescott asked.

None of us had ever bombarded Freeman like this and I knew there must have been a lot of fear and curiosity flowing through the entire division. It wasn't just me.

"Taking a photograph for you to study wasn't exactly a priority," Stewart snapped.

"Tell that to the Futuristic Technology guys," Agent Miller said, glaring in her direction. "That gas yesterday was weird enough. I'd like to know what we're up against, numbers and weapons, and I don't give a damn what you are or aren't supposed to tell us."

Whoa.

"That's enough, Agent Miller," a voice boomed.

Marshall. Of course. He always found a way to sneak up on us at the worst possible time.

"Freeman, take your entire crew to classroom six and wait for me there," Marshall said.

Freeman tensed up and then shook his head at all of us. "Let's go. Stow your weapons out of sight, please."

Stewart dropped my gun into my palm. "What did I tell you? I knew this would happen."

"Hey, I asked you, not Freeman . . . and you can't tell me you weren't wondering the same thing about the EOT numbers last night." I paused, studying her face carefully. "Or do you know the answer to that, too? Is that part of Covert Ops?"

"No." She turned her back to me. "That would be Lily Kendrick's field of expertise, and I can guarantee she'll be a little easier to manipulate than me . . . Maybe try kissing her."

Yeah, because that won't make our partnership awkward.

"Nice dress, Stewart," Agent Parker said as we all filed into underground classroom six. "I'll let you interrogate me if you promise to wear that."

Kendrick breezed past me, taking in the Parker/Stewart moment.

"Brace yourself," I whispered to her.

Kendrick didn't look at me. She just stepped around the scene in the doorway and picked a seat all the way across the room. The way she slammed her notebook onto the desk, I could only assume she was pissed at me. But why?

I started to walk over and sit beside her, but Chief Marshall stormed into the room, breaking up Parker and Stewart's soon-to-be brawl. Dad, Freeman, and Dr. Melvin trailed behind Marshall. All fourteen of us dove into our seats, not wanting to add fuel to whatever fire we had started this morning.

"Since it's obvious all of you feel the need to gossip like a bunch of fifteen-year-old girls," Marshall said, "I'm going to address everyone at once, with the correct information."

Dad stood in a far corner of the front of the room, leaning against the wall. He glanced at me for a second and then looked away.

"Our division is under serious attack," Marshall said. "All training exercises are ceased at this time . . . indefinitely. The information we received during last night's mission confirmed what we've feared for some time now. The Enemies of Time have grown substantially in numbers—"

"But isn't that what you've been preparing for?" someone asked from behind me. "That's why you've taken on so many new recruits in the past two years."

Marshall nodded. "Yes, but this is far worse than we ever anticipated. And now they've built a present-day army, another CIA division, with the sole purpose of finding us and wiping us out, one by one."

My stomach turned over and over, but curiosity won and I had to ask more questions. "Wait, can this group . . . I mean . . . are they—"

"Time travelers?" Marshall finished, and I nodded. "No, and from what we have gathered, Eyewall has no knowledge of the existence of time travel."

"Eyewall?" Mason and I said at the exact same time. He continued before I could. "But . . . didn't Thomas say something about a direct order from Eyewall? That was a time-travel mission."

"That's right, Agent Sterling," Marshall said. "Eyewall also exists many, many years from now. They're responsible for creating products such as the memory gas we used on all of you. The organization today has no knowledge of these future developments. In fact, we have reason to believe they might be working under the assumption that Tempest supports unethical medical and scientific developments."

"Why would they assume that?" Kendrick asked.

"In this year, it's a lot more difficult to convince a group of agents to kill another group of agents out of nobility when the ideas for the future are so foreign and far-fetched . . . and time travel is both a physical risk to the individual and a risk to humanity. Having someone fighting their battles right now makes the EOTs' job much easier."

"So what's our plan?" Agent Miller asked. "Offense or defense?"

"Both," Marshall said immediately. "Senator Healy's ball in New York next week is an international event, raising money for cancer research and other medical advancements. Scientists and politicians from around the world will be present at the event. We believe Eyewall will be there and they'll be expecting a few of us to show."

New York? Did he just say New York?

"All of you will be leaving tomorrow and will spend the week conducting searches throughout the Plaza and attempting to identify any and all of these Eyewall agents." Marshall sat down on the desk in front of us and I could hardly listen to him, my heart was pounding so loud. *I can't go back there.* "Even though this isn't how we usually do things . . . even though you've been told otherwise, it's important that we take out these agents before they get to us. If we don't kill them first, we'll be chased forever . . . all of us."

Silence fell over the entire room. The dive-in-with-both-feet attitude that most of us usually had was gone today. We had never been told to kill anyone . . . Yeah, out of self-defense, like in a fight or something, but really all we'd ever been taught was defense against EOTs, and that always involved anti-time-travel drugs. We had to interrogate them later for information and we needed them alive. This plan left me feeling more conflicted than ever.

And I did *not* want to go to New York.

"Do you need a few agents to stay back here and keep watch?" I said suddenly. "I'll volunteer."

Marshall glared at me. "If I needed that, Agent Meyer, I would have asked for it. You will go with your team to New York. Agent Freeman will work with the substitute chief to lead the mission."

"Agent Freeman? What about Agent Meyer? What about you?" Mason asked.

Marshall looked over at Dad and then back at us. "Agent Meyer and I will be conducting a separate mission and won't be traveling to New York."

What?

"We have a substitute chief?" Stewart asked.

"Who?" someone else asked.

"Yes, we have a back-up leader and you will find out who when you get to New York," Marshall said.

The second Marshall dismissed us to pack our bags, I headed straight for Dad. We had to get out of this. He had to let me go on whatever mission he was going on or at least find a way to go to New York with me.

Unfortunately, Marshall jumped right in my path. "You wanted to be a big boy and play secret agent, so that's what you're going to do. Dad can't follow you everywhere."

I glanced at Dad, his face revealing more anger than I'd ever seen before. Marshall was testing us . . . both of us. He was testing our commitment to Tempest and also punishing us for running off by ourselves so many times. I let most of my fury out in one long breath, knowing I was risking more than just my own punishment. He'd take it out on Dad. "I was just going to ask where we'd be staying."

"At your home, I presumed," Marshall said, looking bored with the question.

"I'd rather not, sir, if that's okay."

"Fine. We own an apartment down the hall from Agent Kendrick's," Marshall said, surprising me. "You can stay there for the week."

Marshall waved Kendrick over and told her about the housing plan, then his eyes narrowed at her. "I understand you were given a task by your partner that you did not complete. Is this true?"

Her eyes dropped to the floor. "Yes."

"You've earned twelve hours of stitching up cadavers in the morgue," he snapped. "Dr. Melvin will supervise."

The color completely drained from Kendrick's face and I felt like the biggest ass in the world. Kendrick kept her eyes on the floor and mumbled, "Yes, sir."

The second Marshall had walked away from us, I tugged on Kendrick's sleeve. "You have an apartment in New York? You live there?"

"Yeah."

"Where? Why didn't you ever tell me?"

"Because you never asked." She sighed and looked away from me. "East Village . . . that's where I live."

"East Village?"

She rolled her eyes. "I'm a med student at NYU . . . obviously you knew that."

Yeah, I did. And now she had to sew up dead people, all because Dad gave me that little piece of information. I shut up then to avoid making her even more pissed off at me. As I walked out the door, I heard Dad say, "Jackson?"

I turned around, but Chief Marshall stood between us, arms folded across his chest. The pained expression Dad wore made my stomach feel even sicker than earlier.

"Yeah, Dad?"

"Be careful."

"I will." I left and caught up with Kendrick, deciding to drag one more answer out of her. "Aren't you worried . . . about going home? Running into people you know while you're doing secret-agent stuff?"

"I'm a lot more worried about getting through the seven-hour flight." She flung the door open to her room and went inside, leaving me to guess what she meant.

CHAPTER SIX

It took an hour and a half of the seven-hour flight for me to see what Kendrick meant. Honestly, I'd never seen anyone with such terrible motion sickness.

"We've ridden in helicopters dozens of times, how is this different?" I asked her as she leaned over the garbage can I had just swiped from the bathroom a few minutes ago.

"I'm fine for an hour or so . . . and then this . . . happens." Her face was buried deep in the garbage can now as she heaved out whatever was left in her stomach.

Luckily, this was a private government flight. I waved Dr. Melvin over despite Kendrick's protests. She wiped her face with a tissue and leaned back against the chair, closing her eyes.

"You've got to give her something. She's been barfing for two hours straight . . . started about ninety minutes into the flight," I said to him.

"I can knock her out with antinausea drugs."

Kendrick shook her head vigorously. "The second I'm unconscious, one of those evil time-traveling bastards is going to pop up on this plane and kill me."

"Do you have any documentation of EOT attacks while in flight?" I asked Melvin.

He looked like he was trying not to laugh. "None at all, Agent Meyer."

"Yet," Kendrick said, reaching for the trash can again.

I pulled her hair off her face. "I think you've suffered enough."

I nodded to Melvin and he retreated down the aisle and then returned with a syringe full of something. He jabbed her in the arm with the needle and her eyes closed seconds later. I got up from my seat and lifted the armrest so she could be stretched out across both seats.

Melvin tossed a blanket over her and smiled. "This will probably be the most peaceful rest she's had in over a month."

I stumbled into the aisle and took the only empty seat left, next to Stewart. Then I leaned back and closed my eyes, knowing I wouldn't sleep. How long had it been since I'd slept soundly, like Kendrick? It felt like, by now, my body had been trained to survive on very little rest.

"Jackson? Wake up," Stewart said, nudging my shoulder. "ETA is five minutes."

Did she just call me Jackson and not Junior?

I rubbed my eyes and stretched my arms over my head. "Wow, I can't believe I fell asleep. Any EOTs show up?"

Stewart pushed her lap tray up and snapped it into place. "Yeah, about ten of them. None of us wanted to get up, so we sent Dr. Melvin to deal with it."

I laughed and yawned at the same time. "He probably bribed them with candy."

Both of us looked out the window and watched the New York skyline get bigger as we dropped toward the ground.

"Are you glad to be home?" she asked.

"Not really," I said.

Her eyes met mine and I could tell she was searching for meaning in my answer. Why wouldn't I want to be back here in my comfortable life?

"What about you?" I pressed. "What's your New York cover? You were here for two years, right?"

She grinned maliciously at me. "It turns out I'm from your neighborhood . . . well, not *really*, but that's been my cover on occasion. Spoiled daughter of an Irishman. I have my own Upper East Side apartment, a couple buildings away from yours. And that little test mission I did yesterday won me a very fast car."

Isn't she a little dark to be Irish?

"Great," I mumbled. *So I get my Dad shipped off somewhere unknown and Stewart gets a car.* And I had a feeling as soon as we landed I'd be forced to listen to her speak with an Irish accent for the next week. Maybe that was better than the French character she'd been maintaining for the last three weeks.

Kendrick was still passed out cold when we landed. Melvin said she would be loopy for a couple more hours. We stuffed her in the back of a car and she slept all the way to her building. Even just the twenty-minute drive from the airport to her apartment was enough for me to feel a strange sense of freedom, except it wasn't the comforting kind. More like wide-open exposure. My senses were a little too alert as we drove through the streets of New York.

The driver took the bags up to the door outside and I still hadn't gotten Kendrick to wake up. I had to yank her from the backseat and then toss her over my shoulder. I could feel her head swinging back and forth behind me. Her long hair nearly touched the sidewalk. While I stood in front of her apartment door, digging for the keys in her purse, I heard a noise coming from inside.

My heart started thudding, but I clicked into agent mode and held tight to the back of Kendrick's legs while drawing my gun and holding it at my side. I turned the doorknob slowly and heard someone shuffling inside.

"Whoever you are, don't move!" I yelled.

I pointed my gun in the direction of the kitchen and a tall guy with blond hair came running into the living room with a huge knife in one hand.

I immediately raised my gun and moved my finger over the trigger. "Drop the knife, now!"

"Oh, God." The dude's eyes completely bugged out. "Okay . . . just put her down and you can have my wallet . . . whatever you want."

I lowered my gun after hearing the panic in his voice. Then I noticed he was wearing a pink apron and something was cooking. Something that smelled like stewed tomatoes and onions. "Um . . . sorry, I think I have the wrong apartment."

"Wait! This is Lily's place," he said. "I'm Michael . . ."

"Michael?"

"Her fiancé."

Fiancé? As in getting married? Kendrick is getting married? And to a guy who obviously hadn't had a single self-defense lesson in his life? Talk about fifteen-year-old-girl gossip . . . this would make Tempest headlines, for sure.

I tucked my gun away, deciding to fall into step with whatever cover Kendrick had created until she woke up and could fill me in. "Sorry, I thought you were an intruder or . . . *something.*"

I tossed Kendrick onto the couch and Michael set the knife on the coffee table and leaned over her. "Lily, you okay?"

"She had some issues on the flight. The doctor knocked her out with something so she could sleep." He was still looking at me like I might shoot him. "We work together," I added.

"Do all CDC employees carry a weapon?"

CDC? Not sure I could fake this cover job. *Let's just hope Michael knows as much about the Centers for Disease Control as he does about self-defense.*

"Brand-new standard protocol," I said.

His face relaxed and then he jumped up. "Are the bags still outside? Let me run and get them, you must be ready to pass out after carrying her up the stairs."

I made another attempt to wake Kendrick while Michael went to get her suitcases. She stirred a little and finally opened her eyes. "God, are we home already?"

"Yep, safe and sound." I helped her sit up and then looked around the room for the first time. Everything was pink and flowery. Wedding-planner books were strewn across the coffee table. This was the most girlie, anti-secret-agent apartment ever.

Good cover, I guess.

"And I've already had the pleasure of meeting your soon-to-be spouse."

She rubbed her temples and groaned. "Oh, God . . ."

"You couldn't have warned me? Seriously, I pulled a gun on the guy, thinking he was an Eyewall agent or an EOT."

Her eyes widened. "Shit . . . tell me you're kidding . . . ?"

I shook my head just as Michael came banging through the door, lugging two suitcases. "Lil, you're awake."

She sprang up from the couch and practically jumped over the coffee table before wrapping herself around him. "I knew you were here, I smelled my favorite dinner."

"Well . . . I'm going to go check out my place," I said, stepping around the hugging couple.

"Wait, you have to stay for dinner," Michael said. "You deserve a good meal after putting up with Lily for weeks."

"Please, Jackson," Kendrick said, lifting an eyebrow.

Was dinner a bribe to keep me quiet about the fiancé thing? Guess I'd have to find out.

"All right, if you insist."

"This is seriously the best coq au vin I've ever had," I said to Michael during dinner.

"It's soaked in a wine sauce for twenty-four hours and the tomatoes and onions add the final touch," he said.

"Michael's going to culinary school," Kendrick told me. "He's almost done and already has a ton of job offers from some of the best restaurants in New York."

So badass CIA agent Lily Kendrick was going to marry a chef. This gossip got better and better by the minute.

"I can totally see why."

Michael grinned at me and refilled my wineglass. "So, how did you end up working for the CDC and going to med school? You barely look old enough to be out of high school."

I wiped my face with a napkin, giving me a second to think. "I'm not really a med student." Kendrick coughed into her napkin, but I ignored her. I couldn't pull off being a pretend soon-to-be doctor. It just wasn't within my abilities. "I'm mostly doing data entry for the CDC and really basic intern-type stuff. Unfortunately, I'm not a science genius like some people." I rolled my eyes toward Kendrick. "And my dad's in the pharmaceutical business . . . so *he's* really the one that got me into the CDC.

Lots of corporate and government connections. You know how that goes."

"The family business," Michael said. "My parents own a restaurant in Jersey. More like a diner. But I was always creating new meals and sometimes they'd even put one on the menu."

Michael was a tall, slim, average guy who probably would have had no idea what to do with that knife he'd tried to threaten me with earlier, other than dicing onions. How did he end up crossing paths with a CIA agent and then hooking up with her?

After dinner, Kendrick walked me to the door while Michael was cleaning up the kitchen. "Thanks for . . . going along with my story. I should have told you. It's just—"

"That's what we do, right? Lie to civilians?" *Forget who we are . . . who we were.* I opened the door and looked out into the hallway. "See you in the morning."

"You know where your place is?" she asked.

"Well, you're twenty B and I'm twenty F. I think I can find it." I only had to walk about forty feet down the hall to find my new apartment. I pulled out the key Marshall had given me and opened the door and then shut it behind me. The smell of mildew and dust filled my nostrils as I searched for a light switch.

"Somebody must have died in here," I mumbled to myself.

"Just needs a little cleaning," a voice said from behind me.

I turned around instantly, whipping my gun out and pointing it toward the farthest corner of the apartment, where I could just barely make out the shadow of a man.

"Relax, Jackson. I'm just here to deliver a message from your boss," the man said.

My feet moved on their own, toward him. "What's the verification code?" I demanded, following standard protocol.

He recited this week's code words perfectly, then took a step closer to me. Headlights drifted past the window and I got a one-second glimpse of his face. I lowered my gun and fumbled around for a light switch. There was one on the wall by the front door.

A single light filled the whole apartment. An old man with gray hair grinned at me.

"Uh . . . Senator Healy?"

"So, you *do* recognize me," he said.

Only because we're planning on crashing your ball next week.

"Yeah, from TV and the newspaper," I stuttered. "What . . . what are you doing here?"

And why do you know our top-secret verification code?

"Months of training have gotten you wound a little tight. You'll have to loosen up and slip into the real world again." He unbuttoned the front of his suit jacket and slipped it off, tossing it over one arm. "I know everything about you, Jackson. No secrets between the two of us, understood?"

Yeah, right, maybe if I was five I'd fall for that. "Sure."

He smirked at me, like he knew what I was thinking. "You have no idea how excited I am to see you reaching this amazing potential."

Okay, I'm in the CIA and even I think this is super-creepy. "You said you had a message for me?"

He nodded. "Just a few items that Chief Marshall couldn't tell you in such close proximity to the others . . . Very good work you did in Heidelberg, by the way. I hear Agent Stewart has taken a liking to you."

"I wouldn't exactly say that." *He's not the substitute chief, is he?*

He drifted into the very small kitchen area and ran a finger over the countertop. "We'd like for you to pursue that. Stay on her good side. Maybe even take things a little further if you feel the urge."

Now I was just confused. "Um . . . are you trying to tell me Chief Marshall wants me to hook up with Agent Stewart?"

He shrugged. "Do what you can with that one. We'll understand either way."

Obviously he's met her.

"Is that all you . . . wanted?"

"No, there's more." Senator Healy turned to look at me and the casual expression dropped from his face. "Lily Kendrick is very important to this project, to this division, and we can't have her . . . *distracted.*"

"She's a fantastic agent. I don't think you have anything to worry about." The words came out firm and straightforward, but I had a feeling we weren't on the same page.

"Great. But keep in mind, so are you, and even more gifted than the others. Whatever assignments you're given, don't lose sight of who you are. More importantly, don't forget what you can do. What you were *made* to do. I have a feeling you haven't even come close to reaching *that* potential."

Was he telling me not to stop time-traveling? It sounded that way. Marshall had basically forbidden me from even thinking about jumping without his approval. "But why do it if I don't need to? Aren't there risks?"

"Yes," he said. "You can't screw around anymore, but I can guarantee you'll find yourself in a situation where it's the right thing to do. Perhaps you know exactly what I'm talking about . . . ?"

That might have been his way of trying to find out if I'd been to the future. Maybe he already knew something about his future and wanted to make sure I saved his ass even if it meant time travel?

He was already heading for the door while I was still trying to catch up. "Don't worry about Kendrick, we'll take care of that situation. You just work on Stewart."

I put my hand on the door, preventing him from going out. "Wait, what are you going to do to Kendrick?"

"Don't worry. I already told you, Lily is very important to this division. As is her safety." He pulled the door open the second I released my hand from it. "We'll see each other again soon. You'll be a very important guest at my party."

"Guest?" I thought this was a mission. Wouldn't I be dressed in black, lurking in the shadows of the Plaza Ballroom?

"You'll be attending as a guest on behalf of your father's company . . . in his absence, of course," he said before ducking out the door.

I bolted the door shut and let my eyes sweep over the studio apartment that smelled like death. Kendrick had two bedrooms in her place.

And she had furniture. Which I didn't have, other than a bed that pulled down from the wall.

No wonder Marshall was so quick to comply with my request for an alternative place to stay. I could go home, but then he'd win this game that I didn't even know we were playing.

I yanked the frame of the bed to lower it and got one glimpse of the mildew-covered, cat-piss-smelling mattress and immediately slammed it shut again.

Instead, I threw my backpack on the hardwood floor and laid my head on it. I wanted to call my dad and tell him about Senator Healy, but I knew he was already off on his mission with Marshall.

I spent at least an hour tossing around on the hard floor, going over and over the implications the senator had made. And why the hell did he bring up Stewart? Maybe he knew something about the future, like we get in a fight and cause some major disruption. Didn't seem that unlikely. This was the most alone I'd been in months. The stringent training schedule and the closeness of our rooms in the underground headquarters kept me so exhausted, I hadn't thought about much else. Eventually I forced myself to fall asleep because the irrational thoughts were increasing and I needed to stay on top of my game. Always.

CHAPTER SEVEN

"Dang, Jackson. What kind of shithole place did they give you?"

My eyes weren't even open yet, but I could already see the sun shining through the uncovered windows. "How did you get in?" I asked Kendrick.

She reached out a hand to help me up and wrinkled her nose in disgust. "I picked the lock. You should consider getting a better deadbolt. I can't believe you slept here."

"I think Marshall is still punishing me." I brushed the dust off my clothes and started digging through my suitcase. "I don't suppose you have soap at your place?"

She nodded toward the door. "Come on. You should bring the whole suitcase, otherwise rats might crawl in while you're gone."

Twenty minutes later I came out of Kendrick's shower smelling more fruity than I would have liked, but it was better than having bacteria crawling all over me. Kendrick was in the kitchen, wiping the counters down.

"Where's Michael?" I asked her.

"He went to help his dad with something at the restaurant."

"How come you didn't tell me that you lived with someone?"

"It's sort of his unofficial residence. He goes to school here and was commuting from his parents' house in Jersey . . . he stayed over a couple times and eventually I told him to leave some of his stuff here. It's no big deal, and it's not like I'm here all the time anyway."

"Does Chief Marshall know about Michael?" I asked.

She eyed me warily. "Not that I know of . . . I haven't lied or anything . . . It just never came up."

"So, what . . . you're just gonna ask Marshall for time off so you can get married? And you think he's actually gonna go for that?"

"I don't know!" She tossed the sponge into the sink and gripped the countertop with her hands so tightly her knuckles turned white. "Doesn't matter now, does it? You're going to tell him, just like you told him about the helicopter when I wouldn't stitch up your dad . . . and the rain thing . . . when I slipped up."

So that's why she was so pissed at me a couple days ago.

"I didn't tell Marshall anything . . . Someone else must have."

She shook her head, looking defeated. "What do you want, Jackson? What'll keep you quiet?"

"Answer a few questions for me." I knew very few things about my partner. Before, it didn't bother me too much, but now, after Senator Healy's little visit last night, I wanted to know why she was so important. "How long were you training . . . before France?"

"Six months with Tempest," she said immediately. "But most of it was here and some in D.C. last winter during break. I joined the CIA two years ago. That's when I moved to New York and started med school."

So, she joined at nineteen, too. I slid a chair out from the dining room table and sat down. "Where did you live before New York?"

The smile dropped from her face. "Chicago . . . but not in the city. The north suburbs. Is that all?"

"One more question." I hesitated for a second. "It's weather, isn't it? It's altered by time travel?"

She leaned against the counter, taking in a deep breath before finally nodding. "That's how we track them . . . weather patterns changing. Think about it . . . Tempest . . . Eyewall?"

"A storm . . . that's what Tempest means . . . a strong and violent storm. And Eyewall—"

"A ring of towering thunderstorms, the most severe part of a cyclone," she said.

I swallowed back my fear. "Eyewall . . . as in Tempest has finally met its match."

"Let's hope not," Kendrick said.

Why wouldn't Dad or Marshall want me to know about the weather changes? What if I time-traveled by accident? Shouldn't I know these things just in case? Or was Dad afraid I'd start studying weather-pattern changes and go on suicide missions alone, hunting down EOTs? And maybe Marshall didn't trust me not to find them and decide to join up with the opposition.

"Are we cool, then?" Kendrick asked.

I shook off the shock of this new information and focused on the here and now. "Yeah, we're cool."

Relief washed over her and she even smiled. "We've got a few hours before we meet up at the Plaza. I think we should clean your new apartment this morning. And I also need to pick up some books from the NYU Bookstore. Maybe you should get some stuff, too, just to keep in your apartment as a student cover or whatever."

"You want to clean the apartment?"

"You have cleaned before, haven't you?"

"Are you going to start with the rich-kid jokes, too, like Stewart?" I swatted her in the head with an envelope lying on the table. "For your information, I do have experience in the custodial arts."

She tossed me a pair of rubber gloves. "I'll believe it when I see it."

I clapped my hands together, inhaling the scent of new books. "Okay, what should I get to fill my borrowed apartment with studentlike evidence?"

"Textbooks, lab coat, flash cards," Kendrick listed off.

"So, I should follow in your footsteps, Dr. Kendrick? Pretend to be a med student?"

"That or the Unabomber."

We wandered the store for a good twenty minutes, forming a large stack of supplies. I tossed them on the counter and handed the girl at the register a credit card. "You don't think this will look too staged? . . . We're only here for a week, right?" I asked Kendrick, speaking in whispered Russian to avoid listening ears.

Kendrick opened her mouth to respond, but I tuned her out immediately. I had just heard a very familiar voice coming from behind a shelf in front of us. A voice that sent my heart racing.

Holly . . . my Holly . . . 009 Holly.

"I just like to look at the required reading and see what might be interesting."

"That's a unique way to choose a course," a male voice said.

I leaned against the counter for support and took a deep breath, trying to figure out why Holly Flynn was in the NYU Bookstore at the same time as me.

She doesn't know me. She isn't my Holly. Not anymore.

I just had to hold it together and not run over and kiss her or something else completely idiotic. I'd survived this in 2007. I could do it again now. I didn't want to see her—not now, after I'd endured three months of reprogramming. But it would be very irresponsible to leave without at least seeing with my own eyes that she was all right.

"I'll be right back, okay?" I said to Kendrick, who nodded, her nose stuffed in an advanced biochemistry book.

I felt more nervous and sick at that moment than I had standing in front of the line of EOTs in Heidelberg a few days earlier. I peered around the aisle where Holly stood next to a sales guy. I thought my heart would stop beating completely. I hadn't seen her in months and nothing had faded. I wanted to run away, but at the same time, I couldn't. I spun around so my back was to her, concealing my face. A few seconds later, someone bumped into me from behind and a pile of books tumbled off the shelf onto the floor.

"Oh, damn, I'm sorry," the sales guy said.

I bent over to help him pick up the books, and seconds later Holly's feet were right in front of me, and then we were reaching for the same book. I knew what would happen next and I didn't stop it.

I couldn't.

Her eyes lifted to meet mine and she drew her hand back from the book and grabbed another one. "This goes on the shelf right behind you."

I opened my mouth to answer, but no sound came out, and I was sure my staring had to be a little on the creepy side. "Uh . . . yeah."

From the corner of my eye, I saw Kendrick approach us. A giant bag swung back and forth in front of her legs. "Ready, Jackson?"

I stood up slowly and Holly did the same, dropping the book in my hands. I continued to stare.

And so did she.

"Do I know you? You look . . . familiar," she said.

A long moment of silence followed her question, and finally Kendrick waved a hand in front of my face. "Hello? Jackson Meyer?"

I can do this. Stick to my cover. It's simple. I shoved my mind into agent mode and took on my role. "I don't think so."

Holly's cheeks turned a little pink. "Oh . . . sorry. That's so weird, because there's a Jackson Meyer in my Modern Lit class."

There is? And she's taking a summer class? I don't remember her doing that before. This was what I got for telling Dad not to give me too many details.

"It's a fairly common name," Kendrick said.

"Or I paid someone to take it for me and now my cover's blown," I answered with a grin that I hoped was fairly convincing.

Holly laughed. "Well, you should get your money back because he looks nothing like you."

"Hopefully I still have the receipt." My voice was the perfect casual tone, but I was sure my face wasn't equally calm.

Holly glanced toward the door, where a buff, jock-looking guy with dark curly hair grinned when he spotted her. My heart beat twice as fast as he walked closer, then stood behind her and kissed her on the cheek. I stuffed my hands in my pockets to keep from clenching my fists.

Who is this guy? What the hell happened to David?

"I'll be looking at the T-shirts, Hol," he said before walking away again.

"Who's that?" I blurted out. And yeah, I sounded exactly like a raging jealous boyfriend.

Holly looked confused for a second and then smiled. "You've probably seen him on TV, right?"

"Brian Belmont," Kendrick said with a little bit of a girlie squeal I had never heard from her before. "Starting quarterback for UCLA.

Broke the record yards thrown by any UCLA player in history during his freshman year."

Holly nodded, but put a finger to her lips. "He's not up for football talk right now." She pointed to her shoulder. "Just had surgery and he's out for an entire season."

"I heard about that," Kendrick said with a sympathetic nod. She must have misinterpreted the shock on my face, because she nudged me in the shoulder. "I'm an obsessive college football fan. No making fun of me."

"Yeah, I guess I have seen him before," I said, staring at Brian sifting through a rack of NYU T-shirts. The original 009 Holly and I had run into him at a carnival in Jersey. He was with David and they caught us making out on a bench right after their big breakup. Brian went to her high school. But he was a year ahead of her, like me.

Now she's dating him? How the hell did that happen?

"I'm sure he won't drop-kick you or anything if you really want to say hi," Holly said to Kendrick.

She nodded eagerly and started to follow Holly. I grabbed her arm and pulled her in the other direction. "Sorry, we have to go."

"No, we don't," Kendrick said.

I groaned and followed behind both of them. My eyes moved up and down Holly's back, searching for something familiar, the same purse or key chain, anything that made her Holly. Right now she had a different boyfriend and a different schedule, since she was taking an early college course.

"Hey, Brian. Apparently you have fans on both sides of the country," Holly said, pointing at Kendrick.

Brian stuck a T-shirt back on the rack and gave Kendrick a half smile. "Really? I didn't know NYU students cared about UCLA football."

"I'm a med student. We're a completely different breed," Kendrick said.

"Well, then spend your time getting to know the replacement starting quarterback, because I doubt I'll be on the field much next season," Brian said.

Too bad. Poor Brian Belmont.

"I've studied a ton of physical therapy. What kind of post-op rehab program are you on?" Kendrick asked.

Brian answered her question in detail, but I couldn't hear a word of the conversation. All I could do was stare at his good arm snaking around Holly's waist. I immediately formed a mental list of ten different and very painful ways I could remove his hand from her body. It took every ounce of energy I had to grind my teeth and maintain the three feet of distance separating me from Mr. Football God.

Why was I okay with David, but not this dude?

Because I knew she only had lukewarm feelings for David. I knew he wasn't an asshole. I didn't know anything about this guy. He could be a major sleazeball.

Cover . . . you're undercover.

Not only was I undercover, I was preventing Holly from being thrown off a roof by Thomas a couple months from now.

"I can't believe no one has even suggested that surgery. The research shows unbelievable results. I actually know the doctor who performs it here in New York. I could probably get you a free consult," Kendrick said.

Wait, don't help him. Actually, no, we should do everything we can to heal him up ASAP so he'll go back to L.A.

"Seriously?" Brian said. "That would be . . . awesome. I knew there had to be some crazy procedure that no one wanted to tell me about."

Kendrick smiled and shrugged. "Great, give me your number and I'll have him call you."

I waited while they exchanged numbers. The jealousy had mostly faded and was replaced with a deeper loneliness than I'd ever felt. I barely noticed Kendrick a minute later, tugging my arm and leading me out of the store and in the opposite direction of the other two.

"How cool was that?" she said.

"Amazing," I mumbled.

She stopped and turned to face me. "What's with you?"

"I'm just hungry. You're delaying my snack time."

She rolled her eyes at me. "Are you worried because that girl met someone with your name? That your cover may be blown?"

"Yep, that's it," I lied.

"We're supposed to meet Freeman at the Plaza in an hour," Kendrick said. "Wanna head over early? Maybe walk around Central Park?"

"Sure." This should be a blast. A walk down memory lane, the very last thing I needed right now. But in a week I would be back in France with Dad and I could push this out of my head and just keep working.

JUNE 11, 2009
LOCATION: PLAZA HOTEL IN MANHATTAN

Adam,

I almost called you this afternoon. Mostly to convince myself that you are in fact a real living person and I'm not writing to imaginary people.

Seeing Holly was too much. Way too much. And four hours of the most boring surveillance of my entire life didn't help to keep my mind busy. The only highlight of this New York City mission so far was Freeman showing us the underground tunnels and CIA stations below the hotel. It's like an entire village down there. There's even a lab. Kendrick spent an hour in it with Dr. Melvin.

The biggest moment of drama came at the very end of the workday when all fourteen of us were shuffled into a classroom underground, and in walked Senator Healy. Let's just say, my shock last night was nothing compared to the rest of the group's. No one seemed to have any idea of Healy's involvement let alone him being the substitute chief.

Dad hasn't answered any of my texts, which isn't too big of a surprise since he's on a mission, too, but it still leaves me on edge. So much that I might do something *stupid tonight like walk by your house just to see if you're home. I know Holly didn't recognize me, but something tells me you might. There's no logic to back this up, just a gut feeling. Or maybe it's what I want to believe. I really need to find something to keep my mind occupied tonight so I don't do anything stupid.*

Jackson

"I can't believe Senator Healy is part of Tempest! And Marshall's backup . . . that's just crazy."

"Will you stop saying that?" Stewart said to Kendrick.

Stewart, Mason, Kendrick, and I were all eating Thai food at a restaurant not far from the Plaza.

"There's a lot of shit we don't know about our organization," I said. "We're on the lowest end of the information chain."

"Freeman looked just as shocked as the rest of us," Kendrick said. "Do you think he knew?"

We all fell silent for a few minutes. None of us had an answer, or at least nothing anyone was willing to share. But it was a very good question.

"Real work sucks," Mason said, changing the subject. "I can't believe we came all the way to New York to do some stupid inspections any halfway competent FBI agent could do."

"FBI agents are far from competent," Stewart said.

"We're like medical interns," Kendrick said. "The guys who've already put in a few years will always be called first. But they're not going to let us all rot into fat loser agents, right?"

"Hopefully not," Mason added. "Agent Meyer is probably knee-deep in some awesome mission, laughing at how pathetic we all are."

Just the thought of my dad on a dangerous mission sent my heart racing.

"Maybe we should get a new mattress for that disgusting bed," Kendrick said, distracting me from dwelling on Dad's whereabouts. "Make life a little more comfortable for the next CIA agent to use that apartment . . . though I've never seen anyone come out of there before. Michael said he thought he might have—"

"Michael?" Stewart asked, looking extremely curious and amused as Kendrick's eyes grew wide with the realization of what she'd just done.

Kendrick glanced at me and let out a breath. "Michael . . . my fiancé."

I dropped my fork and it clattered against the glass plate. *She just told them?* After all that stress this morning?

"What?" Mason and Stewart both said.

"I'm getting married . . . you know, a wedding. I'm not sure exactly when . . . Probably whenever we get through with training and have our permanent assignments," Kendrick said.

Permanent assignments were not very common in the CIA. Dad's situation was unique, and he *still* had to travel all the time. What fantasy world was Lily Kendrick living in? I always pictured her as more of a realist.

"That's . . . *different,*" Stewart said, as if she were completely thrown by this information. "I guess, with mind-numbing missions like this one, we'll all have time to get married and have a couple babies. Personally, I'd rather shoot myself, but whatever floats your boat."

"You're such a bitch," Kendrick said. "Has anyone ever told you that before?"

I fought off the urge to laugh, because Kendrick looked dead serious, like she was actually trying to help Stewart.

Mason's eyes darted between the two girls, but Stewart just smiled and waved her hand. "Almost everyone has told me I'm a bitch, but I really don't give a shit. At least my life won't be full of disappointment."

Kendrick looked a little confused, but I knew exactly what Stewart meant. Not that I ever wanted to come close to agreeing with Jenni Stewart over Kendrick.

If Dad was here, he'd tell me to keep working, find a new distraction. I stared at Stewart still shaking her head with disbelief and I got up from my seat. "Let's get a drink at the bar before you start a fight and get us all arrested."

She groaned, but followed me anyway. We slid into stools right in the center and the bartender looked at us expectantly. I ordered two beers and he immediately asked for IDs. Even Stewart wasn't twenty-one yet, but we had at least a dozen fake IDs, making us range in age from sixteen to twenty-six. Which, according to the CIA software program, were all believable ages for us with some tweaking needed on the higher and lower ends.

"What are you up to, Junior?" Stewart asked.

"Nothing. Just saving Kendrick from you. She's nice. You're not. Seemed like the right thing to do." I picked up my beer and took a drink, waiting for her to get pissed off at me.

"Being nice isn't going to get you anywhere in this job," Stewart said. "Someone needs to tell her that."

I lifted my eyebrows. "She's not the one who got herself tied up and nearly died in Heidelberg."

As predicted, Stewart's face twisted with anger. "It's not my fault that Thomas popped up in front of me and then behind me. You think I wanted you to be the one hauling my ass out of there? I'm sure you would have rather saved Kendrick than me."

I picked at the label of my beer bottle and started laughing, even though she was about two seconds from nailing me in the groin.

"What?"

I kept my eyes on the bottle, still laughing. "Nothing, really. I just remember thinking that I was glad it was you . . . because Kendrick would have been a hell of a lot heavier to cart up three flights of stairs."

Stewart barely cracked a smile. "At least there's one advantage to being short in this job."

"You want another drink?" I asked, pointing to her near-empty bottle.

"I don't really derserve the calories after the boring-ass day we've had," she said with a sigh.

I leaned on my elbow, staring at her halfway tolerable expression. "I'll tell you what. We have one more beer and then you and I can do a six-mile jog in the morning."

"Assuming the world doesn't get attacked between now and then," Stewart said. "And it should be ten, not six."

"Of course," I said, waving at the bartender.

Stewart stared at me while we waited for the drinks. There was something challenging in her expression, and yet she hesitated before saying, "You should come see my apartment . . . like tonight."

"Okay," I said, surprising her and myself.

I wasn't sure what made me say yes. It may have been Senator Healy's request for me to spend more time with Stewart, or it might have been running into Holly with Brian earlier. Even Dad agreed I had made the right decision with Holly, and today she had looked . . . *happy*.

I needed to get her out of my head, and fast. I needed to keep myself from calling or, worse—visiting—Adam.

"Seriously? You're willingly going to spend time alone with Jenni Stewart? By choice?" Kendrick asked. She had cornered me after the second beer, shoving me into the women's restroom, and I had to tell her why I wasn't taking the subway home with her tonight.

"Come on, Jackson. You've got some plan cooked up and I want in on it," Kendrick begged. "Or you're actually into Stewart, and if that's the case, I'm going to talk you out of it."

I rolled my eyes. "I am not *in* to Stewart."

"Why won't you tell me your motives?"

I couldn't answer that, so I had to quickly change the subject. "Why did you tell them about Michael? After throwing a bribe at me this morning . . ."

"Because I knew they wouldn't believe me. Telling them straight up was the best way to guarantee it," she said without hesitation.

I didn't really have a response to that. There was certainly some logic to her answer, but now I wasn't sure I believed her story. Maybe that was also in her plan. Maybe Michael pretended to be a chef and he really worked for Eyewall? *Who the hell knows?*

CHAPTER EIGHT

Everything in Stewart's apartment looked brand-new and void of any kind of personal touch. I wandered around the living room, looking at the generic pictures on the wall.

Stewart leaned against the mantel and watched me. When I finally turned around to face her, the reality of why she asked me here, why I came over, hit me all at once as if I hadn't let myself absorb it until that very second.

I picked up an inhaler lying on the coffee table. It was the only personal item in the room. "I didn't know you had asthma. It's not in your profile."

She walked over and took the inhaler from my hand and stuffed it in her purse, which still hung on her shoulder. "I don't have asthma. Just temporary lung damage due to smoke inhalation."

"I guess I didn't get to you fast enough in Germany?"

"Actually, that's kind of why I asked you over." She let out an exasperated breath and stepped closer to me. "Freeman told me not to follow Thomas and I did it anyway. That's why I ended up there. I left Parker alone with two EOTs."

My jaw practically fell open. "Freeman didn't put that in the report. He said you ended up alone because his coms unit had too much static and he couldn't hear you—"

She held up her hand. "I know what it says. I've read it, like, a million times."

For once, I was close enough to really see her and not so pissed off that I couldn't pay attention to small details. It was almost like her spirit had dimmed compared to that girl I'd spent just a little bit of time with in 2007. That girl was witty and eager to tell me everything she knew, but not in the bitter way she was doing it now.

"Do you know how many times I've gone against orders?" I pointed out.

"Yeah, I know. That's why I told you. It's not like you can turn me in without a lot of shit coming your way. Blackmail is a specialty of mine."

She was so close now, I could see right down the front of her dress. I lifted my eyes to avoid the distraction. "I wouldn't turn you in, even without the blackmail attempt."

Her constant flip-flop in moods was wearing me out. Senator Healy's message wasn't the only reason I wanted to attempt to crack Stewart's shell. Part of me had to know if there was actually a real person in there. I let out an exhausted sigh and backed away from her. "I don't get you. I know that's your goal, but it kinda sucks to be around you. Like this, anyway."

She looked a little shocked, but it only lasted a second. "I'm not that much different from you. Think about it. You can be just as impersonal."

"Why did you really want me to come over, Stewart?"

Her fingers glided across the mantel, like she was checking for dust. "Parker thinks I'm denying my feelings for you, and now he's got Mason on board, and it's not true. I don't like you . . . Sometimes I even hate you."

"I never thought you liked me," I admitted. "Parker's just screwing with you."

"So, we're clear on that?" she asked.

I shrugged. "Yeah, totally."

Then, in about two seconds, she closed the gap between us and kissed me. Like, really kissed me. I immediately pushed her away without even thinking about it. "What are you doing?"

"You don't like me, I don't like you," Stewart said casually. "That's why this will work out perfect for both of us."

"Try not to take this personally, being the sensitive woman that you are, but I'm having a lot of trouble picturing you and me doing anything remotely romantic together."

"Okay," she said slowly, looking completely off her game. "Maybe that's my fault. All my covers lately have been on the abrasive side. I could work on something a little softer or seductive."

I shook my head immediately. The last thing I needed was a seductive Stewart screwing with my head. Ninety percent of me was ready to walk out the door. This had been a big mistake. But then I remembered the aching need I'd had earlier to call Adam and the fact that it hadn't faded one bit. *Just stay . . . distract yourself.* "Why don't you try telling me something that's actually true? No cover."

"I hate black-eyed peas." She walked away from me, into the kitchen, and returned a minute later with a bottle of vodka, orange juice, and two glasses. "Secret number two—I'm a lot more honest while intoxicated. And I'm not quite there yet."

She set the bottle and glasses down on the coffee table. We both plopped down on opposite ends of the couch. She nodded toward the coffee table—*an invitation.* I hesitated before picking up the bottle. I hadn't had hard alcohol in a very long time and I'd been careful not to overindulge on European beer since the training schedules were so demanding. The lack of control while being drunk scared me. It did now, anyway.

Stewart watched me closely as I filled both our glasses and then took a big gulp from mine. She did the same, making a face as she swallowed.

"My parents kicked me out when I was sixteen," she said, looking down at her hands. "Actually, they forced me to go to college early."

"Where did you go to college?" I asked.

"Columbia, then NYU." She drank an even bigger gulp. "I made it two years and then I got arrested and sent to prison."

I groaned and rubbed the blurriness out of my eyes. Now I needed to get drunk just so I could put up with her bullshit. Assuming I was going to force myself to stay in her company for a while longer. "I don't think I've heard your prisoner cover yet. Is that like the ghetto girl?"

"You're such an ass. You wouldn't know the truth if it hit you in the face," she snapped. "I created a few extra identities at both colleges. Then I messed with the computer system and made sure the other versions of me had their tuition paid in full. Apparently, that's a federal offense, and since I was eighteen . . ."

"You went to prison," I finished. "How many identities are we talking about?"

"Ten." She laughed at the expression on my face. "I did everything right. Went to all their classes, joined a few campus groups. I just had one minor screwup and the FBI was able to trace the false tuition payments. Everything happened really quick after that. My parents wouldn't respond to any of my calls and I was basically raked over the coals and thrown in a women's prison in Virginia. After two months, I met your dad."

I sat up straighter. "You met my dad in prison?"

"He came to see me. Said he heard I pulled off quite a stunt. Then he offered to get me out . . . give me a spot as an agent, but there was a catch."

"What?"

She polished off her drink and sank farther into the couch. "I had to change my name, everything about me. No family contact . . . ever. I didn't even think twice about it. I think that's why Marshall left me in prison for two months. He was probably watching even before I got caught."

"Yeah, I bet."

I had no idea if she was telling the truth, but the story made sense, in its own unbelievable way. It explained a lot about how she joined so young, but finding out she was a freak who liked to pretend she was different people most of her life was a little disturbing. Mostly that she was undercover before she had to be . . . before it became her job. "What was your name, before they changed it?"

"Kathleen Goldman. My mom is very Irish and my dad is half Jewish, half African-American." She laughed under her breath. "I have no idea what that makes me."

"Like every other American, pretty much," I said with a shrug. "Also, diverse enough to pull off a lot of different ethnicities as covers . . . also useful to the CIA."

She poured herself another glass and refilled mine, which I hadn't even noticed was empty. "You just got way more than five minutes, so I'm done for now."

"Fair enough," I said before standing up and watching the room spin. I had expected to feel something more from hearing these personal details, but none of it proved she was a decent person . . . except for maybe one thing. "Did you hate my dad for sentencing you to this life?"

She stood up and adjusted the cushion on the back of the couch. "No, not at all. Since I know for a fact you've never been to prison, you'll have to take my word for it, two months in the slammer felt like a decade. I never would have survived without—"

She turned around abruptly, but didn't finish her sentence.

"Without what?"

"Without being allowed to shoot someone or do something illegal." She took another large swig of vodka, straight from the bottle, even though her glass had just been filled.

I didn't know what to say. She'd changed her answer. It was obvious. And come to think of it, Jenni Stewart had never said anything bad about my dad. Never. And I could see the fear in her eyes. She didn't want me to figure it out. That there was at least one person she *didn't* hate. And I got it . . . of course I got it. The way Dad had spoken to Kendrick after the memory gas test . . . the kindness in his voice . . . he let himself care about Stewart the same way he let himself care about me and Courtney. He couldn't really help it. *Human compassion* . . . that was what he had told Thomas in that conversation from 2005.

The awkward silence was way too much for either of us to handle. She stepped closer, stumbling a little, revealing her already drunken state, and kissed me again. This time it was slow, giving me a chance to back out, but I didn't. Hashing out her past was almost as difficult for me as it was for her. Her hands rested on my face, lightly. Nothing about her was forceful this time. My heart immediately sped up, but I wasn't sure if that was a good thing or . . . a warning.

It took me a second to realize she was dragging me toward her room. Or at least I assumed it was her room. The cool air that filled the space between us forced me to focus despite the spinning in my head, the lack of worry. Right after we stepped into the bedroom, I stopped moving. "This is a bad idea."

"Why?"

"It just is. Trust me."

"I don't trust you," she said with a grin. "Tell me why it's bad."

Because I don't love you. I don't even like you. "Work . . . you know? Everything will be really weird and . . ."

Her hands slid under the back of my shirt and she started lifting it over my head. I watched the shirt fall to the floor . . . a symbolic message. *Distractions.* I needed distractions . . . and if I needed them, maybe she did, too?

Lips were moving up and down my neck and didn't feel bad. Quite the opposite. "Wait. Just . . . stop for a second."

She dropped her arms and stepped backward, but kept a tight grip on my hand. "What's the problem, Jackson?"

"First of all, you're drunk and I think I might be, too." I sat down on the side of the bed and took a deep breath. "This is just another method of manipulation, isn't it?"

She shrugged. "What's the difference? What could I possibly be trying to achieve beyond tonight? Breaking your heart? Fooling you into a one-night stand?"

Good point. "Good point."

She pressed her hands against my chest until I was lying all the way back. A million doubts were flying through my head, but then she said something that hit me right in the gut.

"You could always go back to your smelly, empty place . . . *alone.*"

Just the thought of lying in my bed with Holly memories stuck in my head, worrying about where my dad was right now. *Holly with Brian* . . . his hands all over her . . . I didn't want to deal with it. Not tonight.

It's just sex . . . meaningless sex. It wasn't like I hadn't done this whole casual thing before. I grabbed Stewart's hand and pulled her down next to me before old memories could invade my thoughts. We both stared at each other for a long moment and then, eventually, I leaned in, closing the space between us. I didn't think about anything but this simple formula:

Hot chick + Guy trying to forget someone else + No future plans = The perfect hookup

It was just science. Science and sex . . .

Her dress fell to the floor beside my shirt and then she crawled on top of me, kissing my neck, my hands feeling their way around her with much less hesitation.

"I actually thought you would be easier than this," she said, speaking with her mouth against my neck. "I know what you have, and more importantly what you *haven't*, been doing these past three months . . . Seriously, how long has it been—"

I didn't even hear the rest of her sentence. With those few words, she had just unlocked a compartment of my mind I had worked so hard to keep hidden from everyone, including myself. Unleashing those memories was far more dangerous than the memory gas . . . and I could feel it coming like a tidal wave—unstoppable and relentless.

"Just so you know . . . I haven't done this in a while." I dropped Holly onto the bed and lay down beside her.

"What crazy world are you living in . . . it's only been—"

I touched my fingers to her lips. "Let's pretend it's been a while . . . like weeks."

"Like you were lost at sea?"

"Exactly."

She stared down at me as she removed her swimsuit top. She was giving me a nice show of skin, but I couldn't take my eyes off her face, her smile. That perfect combination of sweet and bold. I reached out and touched her, traced my fingers over her soft curves, raising goose bumps on her skin.

"Why are you looking so serious?" she asked.

"Just enjoying looking at you." I wanted to say so much, tell her what

I was feeling, but I couldn't form the right words. What else was there to say besides, I love you?

I slid my hands onto her hips and rolled her to the right, until I was now the one looking down at her. If I couldn't say it, I could at least show it. I kicked off my shorts and leaned down to kiss Holly, letting my weight drop onto her. Her arms were tight around me, fingers pressed into my skin. Time seemed to slow and it was just Holly and me with nothing between us. Exactly how it should be. Always.

A while later, we were stretched out sideways on the bed, both of us still a little breathless and too hot and tired to turn around and get under the covers. She rolled on her side to face me, a few inches now separating our bodies.

I stared at her for a long moment, unable to move. Her unyielding trust, the openness in her expression, it was almost too much. Surely no one was allowed to feel this happy and complete. It had to be a crime. Finally, she reached over and touched my hair, breaking the trance I'd been in. "What's on your mind?"

"I was just thinking how perfect this is. Let's just stay here forever . . . move into the hotel . . . forget school and everything else. We shouldn't ever get dressed, either."

Holly laughed, then placed her hand on the back of my neck, tugging me closer to her. "Ask me that right now and I'd probably say yes."

I propped myself up on one elbow, suddenly finding the words I had been searching for earlier. My fingers slowly trailed up and down her back. "I have a great secret for you."

"And I didn't even ask for one . . . This is new."

"A lot of things are new." I moved my hand to her hair and twirled a long strand around my finger. "You know the first time we did this . . . when we were in the shower, after . . . ?"

"I remember."

I tried to look right in her eyes, so she'd know it was the truth. "I almost said it then . . . I love you . . . but I wasn't sure because I've never said that to anyone. I've never felt like this with anyone else." The words nearly *caught in my throat as they tumbled out. "That sounds really cheesy and cliché, doesn't it?"*

She shook her head but didn't say anything. For some reason, her lack of words made me nervous and unsure.

"What about you?" I asked.

She kissed me quickly, then pulled away, just enough so I could see her face. "I couldn't have slept with you if I didn't love you. Not that I expected it to be the same for you . . . I didn't . . . I don't. It isn't like some rule of mine or anything. It's just that I know I won't go through with it . . . unless I love someone. But that's just me."

My arms circled around her, pulling her closer, not caring about the sticky sweat sliding between us. "It's me, too . . . I mean, it is now. There's no going back."

She laughed. "Are you always going to be this sappy?"

I wanted to think of a clever comeback . . . to redeem my manhood, but all I could think about was the fact that she knew . . . before our first time, she knew she loved me, and that's why it was so great.

I was jolted back to reality as quickly as I had left it. My sudden, acute awareness of the nearly naked girl on top of me caused a slight over-reaction on my part. I shoved Stewart to the side, sliding farther away from her.

"What—?"

The confusion on her face was so rare for Stewart that it threw me off even more. "Um . . . I . . . just give me a minute."

I spun around and spotted the bathroom, then dove inside, locking the door behind me. I leaned over the sink, splashing cold water on my face, a poor attempt to wash the memory from my thoughts. My heart pounded and my mind was tackled in this bizarre combination of lust, warmth, and the horrible, painful ache of losing Holly all over again. I lifted my eyes, staring at myself in the bathroom mirror, and I knew this no-strings-attached thing with Stewart wasn't going to happen.

I had said those words to Holly that night . . . *There's no going back.* And unlike then, now it felt like a curse. I'd been damaged beyond repair and was no longer capable of one-night stands or even looking at someone as beautiful as Stewart and feeling a significant amount of attraction.

God, this sucked.

When I finally talked myself into leaving the bathroom and facing Stewart, she was sound asleep, curled up on her side in the middle of the bed. I pulled the comforter up to her shoulders, covering all the exposed skin. A bottle of pills on the nightstand caught my eye and I quietly picked them up to read the label.

And just like that, I had a way to get through the night without doing something stupid. *Sleeping pills.* Without making a sound, I took two from the bottle and swallowed them dry, then I went into the living room and collapsed on Stewart's couch. Within twenty minutes I was out cold, in a heavy dreamless sleep.

CHAPTER NINE

After orienting myself in the morning, remembering that I had crashed on Stewart's couch, I lay there staring at the ceiling, trying to figure out what I felt in this moment. I thought it would be guilt I'd wake up to in the morning. Guilt for cheating on Holly. But the logical part of my brain dominated and I knew there was no reason to feel guilty. Not because we hadn't had sex . . . We *had* done other stuff that would be classified as cheating under normal circumstances. What I felt was worse than guilt. Complete emptiness.

Maybe this was how the EOTs felt? Or maybe the logical part of their brain dominated even more and they didn't have to worry about irrational things like love or revenge. Wasn't that what Dr. Melvin had told me?

I heard the shower turn off down the hall, in Stewart's bedroom, and I got up to retrieve my shirt from her floor. The bathroom door was slightly open. I could see in through the crack. Stewart stood facing the door, just a towel covering her. I nearly turned around and left her alone to get dressed, but she wasn't moving, just staring into space. And I could tell something wasn't right.

I kept watching her as I moved closer, and eventually opened the door all the way and walked in. "Stewart?" I said, snapping my fingers in front of her face.

She shook her head and finally focused on my eyes. "Huh?"

"Are you okay?"

"Um . . . yeah, it's nothing, I just . . . remembered something," she mumbled, still half in a trance.

I only knew she was out of it because the tone of her voice was completely calm, free of the usual attitude. "What did you remember?"

She stepped around me and walked back into the bedroom and she flung open a drawer.

"I think you found out a long time ago . . . about your dad . . . the CIA," she said.

My heart threatened to beat out of my chest, but I forced it to slow down. "It was a few months ago. You know that."

She shook her head right away. I turned my back to her while she got dressed, which provided me an opportunity to compose myself before she caught on to my near-panicked reaction. "I can't put my finger on it . . . not yet. I just have this feeling that you knew and I knew that you knew . . . but then it's blank after that."

I prepared myself for the human lie detector test she would probably give me. And what the hell was she talking about anyway? Maybe Kendrick was right to question her mental stability, especially now that I had heard what she'd done before the CIA.

"I'm not sure what you mean," I said, trying to stall until I could calm myself down.

Her head emerged from the shirt she had just pulled on. "Don't you get it? We were drugged . . . memory-modification drugs!"

Okay, maybe she isn't accusing me of lying.

But was she having some kind of episode of paranoia or something? Well . . . I knew one thing for sure. There was no way in hell I'd be the one to tell her she might be crazy. Like, *actually* crazy. Leave it to Chief Marshall to recruit a complete nutcase right out of prison.

And leave it to me to almost share a bed with the nutcase.

"I never thought your dad would do something like that, to either of us," she said.

I totally wanted out of there, fast, but I couldn't just leave her in this moment of distress. "Maybe you can ask him about it . . . when he gets back?"

She looked at me and took a deep breath and nodded. "Yeah, that's probably the best plan. I have to go . . . meet Mason somewhere."

I sighed with relief. "Me, too. I mean, I have somewhere to go."

She slipped on a pair of shoes and headed down the hallway, but just before reaching the front door she glanced over her shoulder at me.

"And quit acting so fucking weird, Junior. I told you this was no big deal. In fact, I've already forgotten every detail about last night."

I let out a breath. "Okay, so we're cool?"

Before Holly, I had asked that question of a few girls and they always said they were okay, and then I'd get bitched out by their friends for hooking up and then never calling. But this was Stewart . . . She didn't have any friends.

"We're no different from yesterday, if that's what you mean."

I snatched my shirt from the floor and tossed it over my head. "That's good . . . I guess."

During the elevator ride, I racked my brain for a plan. If Marshall and Dad were unreachable, who could I tell about Stewart's lack of mental stability or whatever just happened? I could tell Kendrick, of course, but she had no authority to do anything. The thing with Senator Healy was too weird for me to feel comfortable giving him any inside information. Freeman would just say he had to wait and see what Dad or Marshall thought.

The only person left was Dr. Melvin.

I paused in front of the door to Dr. Melvin's office. The last time I'd been here, Adam and I had stolen information from his computer. Adam . . . he'd know what to do. If Dr. Melvin couldn't help me, I might have to break my rule and pay him a little visit.

No! Ever since I ran into Holly yesterday, the hard agent shell I'd worked so hard to build around me had slowly been chipping away. *Pretty soon I'll be following her around and trying to ask her out.*

I knocked lightly and heard the chair roll across the floor. Dr. Melvin opened the door while still seated in his chair, laughing. "Jackson, how are you?"

"I'm okay." I closed the door behind me.

Dr. Melvin turned off his computer monitor and pointed to the exam table.

I could never get away with visiting him and not at least have my vital signs checked. I waited for him to wrap the blood pressure thing around my arm before speaking. "I've always wanted to ask this: Do you have other patients? Like, regular people?"

He smiled and put the stethoscope in his ears. "I have plenty of patients, and they're quite convincing at being regular people."

"So, it's just the Tempest agents?" I concluded. "What about Stewart? Do you ever see her?"

He shook his head. "No, she's been cleared to see a regular physician as needed, assuming she's somewhere with access to another doctor besides myself. I've never had any reason to study her medically."

"Just me," I said. "Because I'm a freak of nature."

He chuckled lightly, pressing the end of the stethoscope to my back. "If by freak you mean one-of-a-kind, then yes. But I monitor almost everyone else."

"Except Stewart?" I pressed.

He stuffed the stethoscope into the pocket of his white lab coat and sat down on his chair. "Is this why you're here? To talk about Agent Stewart?"

"Yeah . . . I would have asked my dad, but he's on that mission with Marshall." I paused and watched Dr. Melvin's face tighten for a second. He was too readable. Too easy to get information out of, and I had to be very careful what I revealed, because there was no guarantee it wouldn't get unintentionally passed along. "She was acting really weird this morning. Weirder than usual, anyway. She kinda freaked out about something she remembered. Basically, she thinks I found out about the CIA a long time ago and both of us were given memory-modification drugs."

The way Dr. Melvin shot up from his chair sent butterflies flapping in my stomach. "Did she remember a specific event . . . or conversation?"

My heart pounded and I ignored it because there was no reason to hide anything when Dr. Melvin looked just as worried. "So, it's true? She was drugged . . . or *we* were drugged?"

"No," he said right away. "It's worse than that . . . maybe . . . I can't be sure."

"Is it true about her being in prison and everything?" I asked.

"Yes, but I'm surprised she told you that." He flipped through folders in his file cabinet until his fingers rested on one and it was removed from the drawer.

"I was just wondering if . . . well . . . maybe she's not mentally right?"

Dr. Melvin shrugged, with his nose buried in the folder full of papers. "I'll admit that her behavior was a bit extreme in her teen years, but she was bored and underchallenged. Never given a creative outlet. And lately . . . well, she's showing some signs of depression . . . mild ones, which isn't uncommon in her line of work, but it was concern enough that Marshall asked that she attempt to form some real companions."

"Marshall wanted her to make friends?"

Maybe that was what Senator Healy intended when he asked me to spend more time with her? The message *was supposedly* from Marshall.

The old doctor plopped down in his chair, and, the way he stared at me, the intensity in his face, I knew the subject was about to change to something much more serious than Jenni Stewart making friends. "Do you remember the first time you told me how you could time-travel? The very first time."

"You mean in 2007? That other timeline?"

He nodded. "Did I ever ask you if you saw yourself during a jump?"

I was totally confused. He already knew this. Dad and I had told him everything back in March. "Yeah, but you know exactly how it works."

"I was sitting on the edge of a coffee table . . . in the secret headquarters. You were on the couch, wearing a blue shirt," he recited, looking over my shoulder. "Is that correct?"

"Uh-huh, but why—"

"You and your dad would have never bothered telling me what color shirt you were wearing. The two of you gave me all the information in a ten-minute cram session." His eyes widened to the size of hail, like his giant brain had just provided him with an answer. "I'm remembering events from another timeline . . . and so is Stewart."

"What? How?"

"I had this vision two days ago and I just brushed it off, thinking either you or your dad had told me the story . . . but I think part of my mind wouldn't let it go and I've been analyzing these half-jumps. The ones the others can't do."

Except Emily. She could do a half-jump.

"Yeah?"

"Well, you understand how a true full jump works, right? A complete jump. The kind where you don't create a new timeline or jump to a former timeline."

"I think so . . . things can change . . . instantly, right?"

"Your father and Marshall have been concerned with giving you too much information—for your own well-being, of course." *Of course.* "Thomas is the only one we know who can do it without it killing him. If you were able to do this, like Thomas, maybe jump five years in the past . . . you would see yourself."

"I thought the other me disappeared in a full jump."

"Correct."

"Wow, so it *is* like Hollywood . . . if you do it that way," I muttered.

"When you do these half-jumps, I think you're very close to doing what Thomas does," he said quietly, almost like he didn't believe it himself. "It's possible your abilities are evolving and these timelines you've made are merging."

"Does that mean my brain is going to explode or the world is gonna end or something?"

"I don't think so and it's possible nothing more will happen . . . That little snippet of 2007 I saw, and Stewart's behavior this morning, may be related to the fact that we have well above average intelligence. Our minds are trained to be alert to even the smallest detail or vision. I doubt that it would affect a normal person, and there's a good chance that's all we'll see."

"Are you just saying that so I don't completely flip out?"

"No, but that's what I would tell you either way." He shook his head a little.

If there was ever a good time to ask Dr. Melvin some of the questions I'd had ever since Heidelberg, it was now. I hopped off the table and scrambled for a piece of paper and a pen from the desk.

I drew the timeline diagram I had put in my journal.

Dr. Melvin rolled his chair over and watched me. "World A? World B?"

"It's just names I made for the different timelines I've been to."

He laughed under his breath. "Reminds me of that video game you and Courtney used to play all the time . . . what was that called?" He moved his thumbs as if playing a handheld game.

"Super Mario Brothers." I slid the paper toward him. "Okay, so . . . if I left World A and created World B . . . then returned to World A, but not on the exact date I left . . . instead it was a couple months before October thirtieth, 2009 . . . then I've technically altered the future, right?"

He nodded slowly. "Yes, that's true. Even the slightest change in the date you landed in in World A the second time would forever change the future."

I pulled the extra chair over and sank into it. The answers were already falling into place . . . *Thomas-jumps aren't the only way to alter things* . . . The EOT guy in Heidelberg wasn't lying. "Let's say, hypothetically, at this very moment I decided to do a full jump back to World B . . . maybe to October 2007 . . . then I come right back to here—"

"World C," Dr. Melvin said, humoring me.

"Except it's two hours ago and instead of coming to your office I decide to go to . . ." I paused for a second. "I don't know . . . Starbucks . . . and this conversation never happened. I've changed the future, right? It's not that much different than a Thomas-jump. The full jump in the same timeline."

The weary expression that consumed him now made it more urgent to push him for answers. "Jackson—"

"And then, if I wanted to get back to where I left . . . I jump back to World B . . . for a few seconds . . . then I can come back to World C, but two hours further in the future from the last time I left, so it would be this exact second—"

"You can't," he said firmly.

"It's just hypothetical . . . I know Marshall said not to—"

"I mean you *can't*." He pulled the pen from my hand and flipped the paper over to the blank side, drawing his own diagram. "Let's go back to what you've actually done . . . leaving World A, jumping to World B, and then returning to World A, but not to October thirtieth . . . to August thirteenth. Once you make that mark, coming from the other timeline, there's only one way to go further forward . . . no matter how many times you bounce off World B, August thirteenth will be the present for you. I think you might refer to that as your home base?"

I let out a breath, sinking back into the chair. "I have to live it . . . stay . . . September and October would be different from the first time around but the change isn't instant."

"Correct."

"Thomas-jumps work like that, too? Complete jumps, I mean."

"Correct. Think of it like half-jumps . . . you return at almost the exact moment you left. But of course alterations aren't possible with half-jumps."

"Wait . . . then how did Thomas take me—" I stopped abruptly, realizing I'd just told him about my jump to that freakishly perfect future with Thomas. I hadn't told anyone about that. Not even Dad, because it would have meant telling him about Emily, and I couldn't do that.

Dr. Melvin's eyebrows lifted. "Take you where? When did Thomas jump with you, Jackson?"

My heart pounded so fast. "Before . . . the last timeline I left . . . World A . . . it was way, way far ahead . . . it had to be . . ." Another answer also came to me, and it completely blew my mind. "If he was from *that* year . . . if he'd lived it, then he could do it, right?"

"Right." Dr. Melvin held perfectly still, waiting for me to draw the conclusion out loud. Based on her recent slipups, I could almost guarantee that this was what Kendrick spent all her time studying in her specialty. It appeared that Biological Advancements was a very loose term in Tempest. "The EOTs are from the future? Marshall was lying when he told me . . . in World B, in 2007 . . . that the Tempus gene evolved naturally over time . . . and it's been traced throughout history or whatever bullshit he fed me that day?"

"He wasn't lying. The Tempus gene does evolve naturally over time. It just hasn't started yet. And for someone like Thomas, the Tempus gene can be traced throughout history. *His* history is *your* future."

"So the EOTs are up there." For some reason, I'd always envisioned the future as above me, like Canada. "Teleporting, taking vitamins, and having babies that climb around like mini-superheroes, and then they just decide it might be fun to do this time-travel thing and kill the . . . chancellor of Germany or someone equally as important so they can legally make clones or super babies or something two hundred years from now?"

I was fully aware of how ridiculous my examples were, but dumbing it down for myself was how I came up with these answers in the first place. And two hundred years? I just made that up, and honestly, I wasn't really sure all that crazy future stuff Thomas had shown me could happen in just two hundred years.

"It's not quite that simple—"

"That's why you couldn't really give me a straight answer . . . the other you . . . when I asked if someone was going to stop Dr. Ludwig and his clone-making habit. He's probably not even born yet. Won't be for who knows how long. I could be his great-great-great-grandfather, for all we know."

I wasn't sure why, but these revelations about Enemies from the very distant future was actually somewhat reassuring. Sure, it made the world seem much bigger . . . like way higher up than Canada . . . but all this crazy shit like time travel and cloning wasn't naturally part of my world, or at least it wasn't supposed to be. I could believe it and accept it as something that happens around the same time cars start flying and driving themselves.

"Jackson!"

My mind forced itself back to Dr. Melvin's office after the impulsive diversion my imagination had just taken. He had his hands on my shoulders, shaking me gently.

"Jackson? We test agents . . . CIA, FBI . . . We take them through a battery of testing to see who is mentally capable of handling this information . . . knowledge about the future and what is to come." Dr. Melvin dropped his hands from my shoulders and continued to watch my face carefully, maybe looking for signs of insanity. "Obviously, every agent in Tempest is able to deal with the concept of time travel, but not everyone can work properly and effectively knowing too many details. You're one of those."

I laughed even though it really wasn't funny. "I can *actually* time-travel, therefore I'm totally capable of dealing with it."

He shook his head immediately. "It's not just insanity we're concerned with. We need individuals who we're certain won't get impulsive or power-hungry, knowing what is to come. You aren't supposed to know any of this, Jackson." He rubbed his temples, briefly closing his eyes. "I'm not sure what to tell your father or Marshall. If I were following the rules, I'd tell Healy and Freeman right away. They'd pull you from this mission. But perhaps that's for the best. At least until we can be sure—"

"Sure of what?" Blood pumped furiously through my veins. "Sure I'll do what I'm told without asking questions? Sure I won't suddenly decide that I really *need* to take over the world?"

"Jackson, calm down. This isn't your fault."

I shoved the chair back and headed for the door. I'd already heard enough of this bullshit for one day. "No test will ever tell you what a person can and can't deal with. And you . . . *you* have no idea what I'm capable of handling."

I left him sitting there, stunned to silence. I knew he wasn't going to tell Senator Healy about Stewart, because Dr. Melvin had looked just as surprised as the rest of us about Senator Healy's sudden appearance as a Tempest leader. He'd never throw something like this at him without running it by Marshall or Dad first. Plus, he hadn't told Healy about his own weird, merging timeline déjà vu. And now I knew I was right when I assumed Marshall had me specialize in Advanced Defense because he was afraid of me turning against Tempest . . . getting power-hungry, as Dr. Melvin had said.

Dad withholding information like this didn't really bother me in the same infuriating way. I knew his intentions were always to make my life easier. He didn't want me to have too much responsibility or be forced into anything. But on the other hand, his choice to keep stuff from me also proved he didn't know what I was capable of, either. If I could deal with my girlfriend getting thrown from a roof, I could easily absorb—without going crazy—the fact that the EOTs are from the future and that some of them, if their abilities were strong enough, might be able to alter time by bouncing off another world and coming back. Maybe more of them could "Thomas-jump," but I wasn't allowed to know that.

Maybe I can Thomas-jump?

Because of my chat with Dr. Melvin all the way across town, and my wandering through Central Park for nearly an hour trying to fill in the dozens of holes that this morning's information had created, I was late meeting Kendrick at the Plaza for our assigned observation hours.

Kendrick eyed me up and down with a look of disgust. "That's classic. Showing up late in yesterday's clothes."

"Sorry. I had a crazy morning and didn't have time to go home."

"Yeah, spare me the details."

Kendrick didn't say another word to me all morning other than work-related exchanges when she needed my data to record.

When our four hours were up, we walked together without speaking and I could tell she was trying to keep up her silent treatment, but eventually she gave in and blurted out, "I can't believe you spent the night with Stewart! Weren't you afraid of being attacked in your sleep or something?"

"It was no big deal, seriously. We didn't even—"

She spun around to face me in the middle of the sidewalk. "No big deal? Are you really that dense? She's got issues. You can't take advantage of people like that!"

She thought I was taking advantage of Stewart? The tiny little possibility that she might be right made me angry enough to redirect the conversation. "What about you? You're stringing Michael along . . . for what? He doesn't even know you."

Her face took on this horrible mixture of hurt and rage. She ground her teeth together and turned around and continued walking toward the bus stop. On the ride home, I tried to figure out my motivation for lashing out at her. I think the idea that I may be as impersonal as Stewart bothered me more than I cared to admit.

And then I remembered Kendrick's face yesterday when I asked her where she lived before moving to New York. Her secrets lay in that answer. I just knew they did.

When we got back to our building, I followed Kendrick into her apartment and closed the door behind us. "Tell me what happened to your parents . . . your family."

She brushed the hair off her face and stood in front of me, arms crossed. "What happened to *your* parents?"

I must have looked confused, because she rolled her eyes and elaborated on her question. "One of my first tests, when I got to France, was to analyze the DNA of every member of Tempest without their knowledge. I know your dad isn't your dad . . . in a biological sense."

I held my breath for a second as theories spun through my brain. *Does she know that I'm half EOT?* Marshall never would have let her test me if he thought she could figure it out. And another thought occurred to me . . . She told me confidential information related to her specialty . . . again. We were fighting . . . again. What did this mean? Sharing secrets, getting pissed off at each other, her suddenly protecting Stewart. Was Lily Kendrick becoming my *friend*? That was never part of the plan.

"I just found out about my dad not too long before you did," I admitted, finally.

Some of the anger immediately faded from her expression. "I'm sorry."

"He's still my dad. It doesn't really change much."

She took a deep breath and closed her eyes for a second. "My parents and my younger brother died two years ago, and it's the reason I'm here, in the CIA . . . more specifically, the reason I'm in this division. That's all you're going to get from me, okay?"

"Okay," I said quietly.

"You and Stewart . . . that's just none of my business. I won't mention it again."

"Great."

"So, did you and Stewart really—"

I put a hand over her mouth. "You just said it wasn't any of your business. You're such a hypocrite."

She barely cracked a smile and then moved so fast. She had my arm twisted behind my back in half a second. "I take name-calling very seriously. You better say something nice to make up for it."

Kendrick tugged harder on my arm and I faked a moan. "I think you dislocated my shoulder . . . seriously, let go!"

She released me immediately. "Just don't move it—"

"Sucker," I said, then I took off and jumped over the back of the couch before she could make another move. I landed on the other side and turned around, the protection of furniture between us. "Now, let's see you try that again."

She grinned at me. "There's only one way out of here."

Both of us were dancing back and forth, waiting for the other one to make a move, when Michael walked in the door, taking in the odd situation.

"Um . . . hey. What's going on?"

Kendrick kept her eyes on me. "Just settling an argument about which flu vaccine has been the least effective."

"Okay . . . I will *definitely* be staying out of this one." He walked behind her and she turned around to kiss him.

I quickly jumped back over the couch and had my hand on the doorknob in no time. "See ya later, *Lily*."

"Damn," she muttered as I shut the door behind me.

CHAPTER TEN

JUNE 16, 2009, 7:30 A.M.

    Senator Healy gave me the final mission instructions today: be a guest at the party and nothing more. Kendrick is also playing the guest role, since she is currently enrolled as a med student and has even interned for some of the doctors that will be attending.

    I have a confession to make. Late last night, in a desperate sleepless moment, I took a train to Jersey and walked by Adam's house. I didn't see him or anything and all the lights were out, but his car was unlocked. I got in, sat in the driver's seat, looked through his CD collection, and then when I uncovered Jeff Buckley's album, Grace, I found myself stuffing it in my pocket and taking off. It's Adam's favorite. I knew that. And I couldn't put my finger on why I needed to have it, but it was triggering a memory that wasn't yet concrete. Or maybe I just needed to leave my mark in this Adam's life.

JUNE 16, 2009, 7:49 P.M.

Kendrick and I walked into the ballroom at the Plaza Hotel in our formal attire, a tux for me and a pink dress for her, but we both had concealed weapons, earpieces, anti-time-travel injections, and cell phones. So, yeah, tonight wasn't exactly the relax-and-have-fun kind of experience.

Both of us were getting anxious because our lives had suddenly turned so boring and uneventful. Not that we wanted danger every waking moment, but the lack of threat seemed to make the anxiety build.

It's coming, and in a big way. That was what it seemed like to me anyway.

"There's the honorable man of the night," Kendrick said, nodding toward the long table where Senator Healy sat with several of the invited international political figures. "So, who do you want to put your money on? The Chinese ambassador is pretty important. I doubt anyone's trying to take out the Lithuanian dude."

I pulled a chair out for Kendrick and scanned the long table. "My money is on the host."

"That would be a big splash, wouldn't it?" she said with a smile.

Several of the members of the important table were looking in our direction, speaking to others seated next to them in their native language. I put my arm around the back of Kendrick's chair and leaned in close to her ear to whisper, "So, do you think you can read lips and translate into English at the same time?"

She smiled but kept her head forward. "I'll start with the right end and you start with the left."

"Russian, my favorite," I said. I watched the middle-aged man fiddling with his bow tie and grumbling to the woman next him. All I had to do was watch closely and then replay it back over and over until I could translate. "The Russian dude said he hates that they keep putting ice in his drink. It tastes like water and he'll never get drunk."

Kendrick laughed with her eyes on the Frenchwoman. "She's just telling the Italian man about her children. Nothing too useful."

"Practicing your international spy skills, I see," Senator Healy's voice came from behind us.

Kendrick and I both turned quickly.

He chuckled again. "Just kidding. Jackson, please introduce me to this lovely young woman you've brought." He turned to Kendrick and rested a hand on her back. He was testing our ability to remain undercover. "I've known Jackson's father for years. He's been very agreeable when it comes to FDA policy. His company donated over a hundred grand to this event."

"Oh . . . well, that's very generous," Kendrick said.

"Yes, he's a great man. I'm disappointed he couldn't make it tonight." His eyes froze on mine, waiting.

I cleared my throat. "Oh, right . . . Senator Healy, this is Lily Kendrick."

"Perhaps you two would like to meet some of our guests of honor?" he asked with a grin.

We both stood up and I could practically hear Kendrick running through the names and basic info on all the international crew in her head.

Senator Healy grabbed the back of my jacket, holding me back and letting Kendrick walk ahead. "I thought we agreed you would spend time with Agent Stewart," he hissed into my ear.

Was I supposed to invite her? He told Kendrick to come as a guest. We both thought that meant to come with me.

"I have, sir," I said quietly. "I didn't realize you meant tonight."

He let out an exasperated sigh and then said, "I guess that leaves plan B."

Plan B?

When we reached the table, the senator leaned close to me and said, "Feel free to show off a little, greet them in their native language."

I had no idea why he suggested that when I was being presented as the son of a CEO, a native of New York City. Not some CIA agent who could process foreign language better than most geniuses. Kendrick and I made our way down the table, and I did as the senator instructed and baffled the translators. When I reached the Russian man at the far end, I only shook his hand for a second and said hello in Russian. I didn't remember any of the words that followed because my eyes froze on another girl in a pink dress, clear across the ballroom.

"Oh, God, this can't be happening," I muttered.

Kendrick said a quick good-bye to the Russian man and steered me away from the table. "What can't be happening?"

I couldn't answer her. All I could do was stare at Holly, who was standing next to that Brian guy across the room. I had never been more disappointed to see her than I was right now. And it had nothing to do with Brian, the jock strap. It couldn't be a coincidence that she was here and so was I. This was another attack. Thomas's work, maybe? He must have found out about her.

"Something bad is going to happen tonight," I mumbled to Kendrick. "Trust me."

I could feel her eyes fixated on my face, then they traveled across the room. I watched her face break into a grin. "Oh . . . so you saw my surprise?"

"What?"

She nudged me in the shoulder. "Quit staring! I saw how you looked at that girl the other day. Why do you think I offered to hook up her date with that orthopedic surgeon?"

"What?" I said again. I had just been standing there imagining all the buildings Thomas could toss Holly from right here in New York, and Kendrick was telling me this was some kind of elaborate blind date, with Holly's new boyfriend? "Why are they here?"

She pointed to a short bald man standing next to Brian. "That's the doctor who's going to heal that kid's injury so he goes back to California and scores a bunch of touchdowns. I did rotations with him last year. He's amazing. And this place is full of doctors, if you haven't noticed. It is a fund-raiser for cancer research."

"So that automatically means every physician in the area will be here?" I asked, not feeling in the least bit guilty about drilling her with a full-force CIA interrogation. "We didn't get our assignments to be party guests until after you made friends with Mr. Football God."

"I was just trying to make a connection and maybe get him across the country again." She gave me a sheepish grin. "I decided to hack into the senator's email and get a copy of the guest list. I saw my favorite orthopedic surgeon on the list and sent him an email suggesting he invite his newest patient, who I assumed would bring the blond girl you're drooling over."

I let out the biggest breath of relief. "That's seriously true? Promise you're not lying?"

She smirked at me. "Do you know how much planning I put into this? This was the only way. It's not like you can just keep showing up in random places that she happens to be. Way too creepy. But med students . . . mixing with this crowd, and she's not even on the guest list, *he* is."

"Oh, so I'm a med student now?"

Kendrick shrugged. "Just say we had a class together . . . Organic Chemistry. She did see us in the NYU Bookstore, so . . ."

I ran my fingers through my hair and wasn't surprised to discover that my hands were shaking. When would I ever stop worrying about Holly's life being threatened? "I need to sit down."

I headed toward our table and Kendrick followed close behind me. "Aren't you going to go talk to her?"

"No, thanks." I dropped into the seat. My legs were shaking too much to stand any longer. I was so relieved that I didn't even have a chance to be upset about seeing Holly again. *With another guy.*

"Come on, Jackson," Kendrick whined. "I'm trying to fix you up with someone so you don't have to continue the random hookups with Stewart."

"That was one time," I reminded her. *And we didn't even make it past second base.* But for some reason, I hadn't exactly corrected what I knew Kendrick had assumed. Maybe because the outcome wasn't any different. I didn't feel heroic or like a classy guy for not going through with it with Stewart, I just felt alone. Either way. Because I didn't even have anyone to hurt if I had slept with Stewart, and that was the worst feeling of all.

And this was exactly why it sucked to love someone.

Kendrick sat down next to me and smiled. "Well, in case you're wondering . . . her name is Holly and she has no criminal record, not even a speeding ticket."

"She already has a date," I said, trying to close the door on this hookup that was *not* going to happen.

She grinned this devious grin and stood up. "Fine. You can sit here and be pathetic and lonely while I go mingle, maybe snag a dance partner or two."

"Have fun." I rested my head in my hands and was thankful the lights were turned down and music started playing. All the spotlights were pointed at the dance floor, leaving me in a dark shadow. Exactly where I needed to be at the moment.

I only had a couple minutes of peace and quiet before I felt the two bodies slide in on either side of me. "Stewart, Mason, how's it going?"

I took a second to glance right and then left. Mason was dressed as a parking attendant and Stewart had a tray of crab cakes in front of her and wore a waitress uniform. She slipped an earpiece in my ear, the one that didn't already have one.

"We put a bug on Dr. Melvin," she whispered. "I've tried to talk to him about my recent issue and he's acting really weird about it. I think he knows something."

I nodded and carefully scanned the room, looking for the old doctor. He must have just arrived, because I would have noticed him earlier.

"We're headed out back, by the Dumpsters," Mason whispered. "We're not supposed to be in the ballroom. Freeman's letting us check for explosives later, though."

They both dissolved into the crowd, leaving me alone again. I was too busy scanning the room and mentally recording notes to notice the main fund-raising events for tonight had begun. Not until the announcer started calling off table numbers for the $50,000 dance.

If I had been noticing normal stuff, rather than watching for potential Eyewall agents and death threats to the international diplomats, then I might have predicted Kendrick's cheesy attempt to join me and the one person I needed more than anything to avoid tonight.

I had to squint when a spotlight landed on my table and then another on Holly's table as they announced her name. Kendrick slid in behind me and laughed this almost evil cackle. "Try and get out of this one, Jackson."

I groaned and hid my face. The two old ladies at our table squealed and clapped when they figured out it was my name that got picked in the drawing. I did glance in Brian and Holly's direction when they announced her name. Her eyes were wide and I knew for a fact that this wasn't the sort of attention she usually welcomed.

"Now our two single winners need to come up to the front and have a dance. Just one little tango, and fifty thousand dollars gets donated to the Make-a-Wish Foundation on behalf of Target stores."

Kendrick pinched my arm until I stood up. Then fingers wrapped around my other arm and Senator Healy appeared on my other side. He had this fake politician's grin on his face as he waved to the roomful of people, and it suddenly occurred to me that CIA agents would make very good politicians. Lots of practice lying to people.

"What's the matter with you?" he said through his teeth. "Quit standing there like an idiot."

Yeah, he was totally not my favorite person right now. I shook my arm from his grip.

"While you're in the middle of the dance floor, I want you to tell me what the Chinese ambassador and his *friend* are discussing, understood?"

"Yes, sir," I grumbled. I could feel him stiffen with anger beside me, and then he strolled up to the announcer and stood in his spot to make the next drawing of table and seat numbers. I had no choice but to keep moving forward. No hiding out now.

As I walked to the dance floor, surrounded by the smiling, clapping roomful of clueless people, I noticed the receiver on my sleeve had been switched off.

Senator Healy.

How did he do that right under my nose? Because I was too distracted by Holly. But seriously, the guy was getting creepier by the minute. And more suspicious. He reminded me a lot of Chief Marshall.

Holly looked completely humiliated when she stood next to me in the center of the glass dance floor.

"How did we get picked for this?" she whispered.

Lily Kendrick, my idiot partner. "Random drawing."

"This would be much easier if we weren't the only ones dancing," she said with a nervous laugh.

Nope. Wouldn't change a thing. I forced a smile and held out my hand for her. "It's for a good cause, right?"

Her arms went around me tentatively, and then she laughed again once the music started. "I guess they really con you into it, don't they? Either dance with a stranger or some kid doesn't get their dying wish to go to SeaWorld."

"Exactly. Only a complete asshole would say no." I laughed with her and tried to act cool . . . or at least halfway normal. But without even thinking about it, I pulled her closer and tightened my fingers around her hand. "So, have you seen any other Jackson Meyers lately?" I asked.

She glanced up at me and smiled. "Nope, but I know why you looked familiar . . . the other day."

Now, *that* sent my heart racing, and I had to slow it down right away because she was pressed up against my chest. "Oh, yeah?"

"Your picture's up in the boardroom at the Ninety-second Street Y." She grinned sheepishly. "On behalf of your family's very large donation to the after-school programs."

I sighed with relief. It wasn't some weird flash of 007 Holly's memories like Stewart and Melvin had. "Yeah, I've spent a lot of time there."

"I interviewed for a job as camp counselor," she said. "Went to training for a couple weeks . . ."

"You mean you don't work there?" I pulled myself together, letting out a slow careful breath. Obviously I'd changed my life, so Holly's could have been altered as well. "I mean . . . how did that work out for you?"

"It sounded great, but an opportunity came up for me to start classes this summer, so . . ."

"Oh . . . right." All the agent training in the world couldn't keep me from slipping out of cover tonight.

Being officially (and mutually) in love with someone for a few days hardly makes me an expert on the subject, but I knew one thing for sure. Standing here with Holly, I felt the complete opposite of empty.

I brushed my fingers over her cheek, feeling the heat as pink crept up from her neck. Just one more inch closer and I could touch my nose to the top of her hair. My eyes immediately closed and I inhaled deeply. I would have paid a hundred times the donation to feel this good forever. Even with my eyes shut tight, I knew my fingers could find their way to the tiny mole on her lower back and if I touched the bare skin on her right side, I'd run into the light pink, smooth-as-silk scar. There wasn't an inch of Holly that didn't feel familiar to me, etched into my memory. I just never realized how much I'd enjoy knowing this stuff and how much I hated the idea of someone else knowing.

I felt myself leaning farther forward. She was staring at me now, eyes locked with mine, and I forgot what I was doing. Forgot she didn't know me. Forgot everything. My mouth moved closer to hers, my fingers glided up and down her back. My chin tilted downward a little bit more and my heart pounded with anticipation, this perfect rhythm that lurched me forward until only a thin sheet of air separated my mouth from hers.

That was exactly when reality smacked me right in the face. Holly's entire body stiffened. Her eyes darted awkwardly around the room, like she needed someone to come rescue her.

From me.

The final notes of the song played and I dropped my arms, absorbing the icy air that blew right between us. She didn't back up at first, so I stuttered out an apology: "Um . . . sorry . . . that was . . . Never mind," I said finally, and then turned my back on her before it got any worse. From the corner of my eye, I saw Senator Healy move toward her and whisper something.

Probably apologizing or explaining my obvious insanity.

My chest felt so tight, but I wasn't sure if it was grief or a panic attack on the rise. Either way, I had to get out of there, fast.

I darted around people left and right until I could push through the exit door and lean against the wall in the hotel lobby.

Oh, God, this is bad. Very bad. All those witnesses seeing me and Holly together. The Tempest and Eyewall agents . . . Senator Healy. I closed my eyes and tried to breathe and think of an explanation. A cover, maybe?

"Dude, who's the blond chick?" Mason asked.

I opened my eyes. He was right beside me, leaning against the wall. "Um . . . no one. It was just some stupid drawing and I got roped into it."

Mason's eyes moved around the room, scanning, inspecting, like the agent he truly was. "Stewart kinda freaked about it. You think she's jealous?"

I barely had a second to roll my eyes before he snorted loudly and then explained. "The girl is *gifted*. She just said 'fuck you' in four different languages."

He wiggled his ear, and I had to assume Stewart must have been shouting into her communications unit.

"It's not like that with Stewart. Not for either of us," I told him, hoping he'd believe me, but guessing he wouldn't.

He pressed his finger over the tiny piece of metal under his shirt collar and whispered, "But you . . . you know . . . hooked up with her, right?"

I rubbed my hands over my face and sighed. "Can we talk about this later?"

He shrugged. "No big deal."

Mason started to walk away, but I stopped him and grinned, attempting to look sane and unaffected by tonight's drama. "How'd it go with that girl the other day?"

The other day, I had helped Mason talk to this girl we met doing surveillance outside the hotel. He ended up asking her out and I hadn't heard the outcome of his date yet.

His face broke into a grin. "Not bad. Not bad at all." He pulled a tiny bottle of Jack Daniel's out of his jacket pocket and tossed it to me. "I swiped this from a minibar on the fifth floor. You look like you could use a drink."

I stared down at the bottle of liquid courage. I should have started drinking the second I saw Holly. Everyone expected me to play the part of "party guest" tonight. Could I help it if that included alcohol consumption? It wasn't like they were giving me anything important to do, other than waltz around with my hidden cameras and recording devices for someone to review later on. "Thanks, man."

"No problem. I owed you one."

The ballroom doors opened and music flooded into the lobby. Mason disappeared within seconds and I quickly drank the whiskey in two large gulps. Senator Healy strode through the doors, eyes moving around until they rested on mine. He pointed silently into the ballroom. When I walked past him, he muttered under his breath, "What the hell is wrong with you? We've got a room full of potential Eyewall agents and international terrorists and you're out here playing around."

My fists balled up, but I forced them open again and pressed the empty bottle into his palm. "Throw this away for me, would you?"

Kendrick was all the way across the room, sitting alone at the bar. I slid into a seat next to her and ordered another drink. "Tell me the truth, okay? I looked like an asshole, didn't I?"

She wrapped both her fingers around the glass of wine in front of her and kept her eyes focused on the counter. "You know how everyone likes to joke about you being the average guy turned secret agent?"

"Yep," I said, gulping my drink quickly and enjoying the burn of alcohol running down my throat.

"Well . . . I'm one of the few who didn't know of you before you became . . . this." She gestured at me as if I had *Secret Agent* written across my forehead. "But I did guess something about you."

"What's that?"

She stared at me. "There's only one thing that would make someone go from your life to *this* life."

"Stock market crash?"

She dropped her eyes again. "Revenge."

That was when I remembered the dark look that had crossed her face when she told me her family had lived in Chicago . . . and the other day, when she said her parents and younger brother were dead. "Like you, right?"

She nodded. "But it doesn't work. Not for long, anyway. Eventually all that sad stuff turns to anger and then you just don't feel much of anything."

It was like she took every fear and worry from the back of my mind and waved them in front of my face, and I didn't want to hear it. Not now. I polished off my drink and started to get up. "I'm gonna go . . . look around."

Kendrick shook her head and waved to the bartender to bring me another drink. "I'm done with my lecture, so you can quit squirming. I just wanted you to know . . . it was Michael who brought me back to life. I didn't want to feel that way, either. Didn't want to give in. But I'm a better agent this way. He can't be wrong for me. Not when being with him makes me better at saving other people . . . doing all this crazy shit we do."

I relaxed into my seat and drank in silence for a few minutes and then she started laughing. "What's so funny?"

"I totally went all Oprah on you, didn't I?"

I smiled a little. "More like Dr. Phil . . . except much prettier."

She held out her arms. "So sweet. Do I get a hug?"

I glanced around the room with mock embarrassment. "Not in public. I've got a rep to protect."

She gave me a devious grin and leaned over and kissed my cheek. I could feel the lipstick that lingered on my skin. "Now you're wearing pink like you were supposed to."

I spun around on my stool so I could keep an eye on the room. "You think a little lipstick will help me pick up a hot chick tonight?"

"Assuming you don't chase them away," she teased, nodding toward Holly, who was now chatting with Brian and the doctor who was supposed to fix his shoulder.

"Believe it or not, I have a history of striking out at very important moments," I admitted.

I looked at my watch and groaned, realizing only an hour and a half had passed. Still four more to go. It felt like an eternity. I couldn't wait to get back on that plane to France or wherever we had to go next. New York wasn't my favorite city anymore. Not when being here caused insanity.

The view from my barstool allowed me to see everything at once and gave me a good excuse to stay put and drink more. Kendrick shuffled around the room engaging in charming conversation, while I sat on my ass and got a little drunk. *Okay, more than a little drunk.* I started out doing a good job of scanning every small detail throughout the room. Calculating. Memorizing. All while trying to make sense of Kendrick's mini-psych session. It reminded me of the time 007 Adam pointed out that I didn't really act like I was serious about Holly.

Now it was just the opposite. Being without her out of guilt.

But after a few more drinks I stopped thinking about what Kendrick said and slacked a little on watching the so-called potential international terrorists because Holly was dancing with Brian and I had the perfect view of her back. I rested my elbows on the bar countertop and let my gaze fall on Holly and her sexy swaying hips. It was actually nice to just be a typical guy again, staring at a girl's ass and not really thinking about anything else. None of that life-or-death shit.

"Which one have you got your eye on?" the bartender asked from over my shoulder.

I pointed the end of my beer bottle at Holly. "The blonde in the middle, the short one with five-inch heels."

The bartender chuckled and clasped my shoulder with his hand. "No wonder you're all the way over here. Her boyfriend looks like he could crush you with one hand."

I snorted into my beer. "I can take him."

"Keep dreaming, kid, keep dreaming," he said, shaking his head.

Unfortunately, I was drunk enough to consider proving him wrong. Just for fun. But after a couple minutes of watching Kendrick chatting with the Russian dude, hoping she'd wrap it up soon enough so I could get her opinion, someone slid right beside me and spoke to the bartender. "What do you have on tap?"

I spun around in my seat again and saw Holly standing there, glancing hopefully at the bartender, who crossed his arms and said, "For you, Coke or water."

Even in my drunken state, I was ready for her to start twisting her hands nervously or scoot away from me after our awkward almost-kiss. Her eyes fell on mine for a second and she smiled (without blushing). "I thought you left."

I returned the smile and then glanced at the bartender again. "She's a special guest of Senator Healy. I'm sure he won't mind."

"Bud Light?" Holly asked with a little more confidence.

"Of course," he said, and left to retrieve her drink.

I was still waiting for nervous Holly to emerge, but she sat right next to me and even turned to face me. "Pretty smooth. You've done this before? The intimidation factor . . . name-dropping?"

The alcohol, mixed with Holly's familiar scent and the images of her dancing just seconds ago, didn't leave any room for worry or apprehension. *Or logical thought.* I hoped an Eyewall agent wouldn't choose this moment to come out of nowhere and assassinate me.

"What do you think?" I asked as the bartender slid the drink in front of her.

She took a long sip before answering. "I'll guess that you've been to a fair share of fancy parties."

"You guessed right," I admitted, and then added, "But tonight was my first fifty-thousand-dollar dance."

She laughed and had the smallest hint of nerves in her voice, but she kept her eyes on mine. "You sure know how to invade a girl's personal space."

Not wanting to look at her, I tilted my empty bottle and watched a few drops of beer fall onto the counter. "Yeah . . . sorry about that."

She shrugged. "You're forgiven."

Her eyes were so confidently staying on mine that I started to shift uncomfortably under the weight of her gaze. She was too calm. Too sure of herself. Or maybe I was comparing her to 007 Holly, because that was the last time I had to meet her for the first time . . . again. This was 009 Holly. The nearly nineteen-year-old girl. Suddenly I had this intense desire to start all over again. The blissful memories that I had with this girl when we first met . . . the way I kept catching my thoughts drifting to her . . . finding a way to end up in the same place at the same time.

So this *could* be part of my cover tonight? Blending in, chatting up girls. It was what the son of CEO Kevin Meyer would do. I'd be conducting an investigation. Holly could be a teenage terrorist, for all they knew. Someone had to get close enough to find out.

I'll take one for the team.

"So, where are you from, Holly Flynn?" I asked, because it sounded like the thing to say to spark conversation.

"New Jersey."

"I went to a party in New Jersey once . . . a while back." I nodded toward the crystal chandelier. "A little different from this place, but overall a great night."

Her eyebrows arched up. "You went to a party in Jersey? Why?"

I scooted my stool a little closer to her, making room for someone to slide behind me. "Mostly I went to hang out with a girl I liked. It was outside, in the woods, we had a bonfire and everything."

"Beer kegs?" she asked, and then continued after I nodded. "I've been to a few of those. How'd it work out for you . . . with the girl you liked?"

I thought about it for a second and then smiled. "It was nice. Very nice . . . Of course, I'd been hoping for wild sex on a bed of leaves in the woods, but that was more of a poison ivy issue than me striking out. Plus, she had a boyfriend. Big ugly hairy dude."

"Oh, I bet." She scanned the room for a second and her eyes stopped on Kendrick, now chatting with Brian. "You've been sitting here for an hour. Don't you think your date might be a little bored . . . or lonely?"

"She's just my partner . . . I mean, lab partner . . . for med school."

She smiled, and this time it was laced with intentions. "Good to know."

I immediately leaned back, away from her, shocked by the way she was flirting with me. Definitely something I hadn't seen from Holly before. Not quite that forward. "What about your boyfriend? Is he okay with you flirting with strangers?"

She leaned closer to me and her hair brushed against my arm. "Brian flirts better than he plays football. Besides, he can't hear me."

"You sure about that?"

"I'll prove it," she said, then raised her voice. "Ohio State is awesome!"

"Go, Buckeyes!" I added, then we both turned our eyes in Brian's direction. He didn't falter in his charismatic conversation with Kendrick, and she winked at me from over his shoulder. "Okay, I believe you."

"Good," she said, then hopped down from the barstool. "I think you should dance with me."

Now, *that* shocked the hell out me, but I was drunkenly happy and well trained at concealing almost everything. I knew this was a very bad idea, and yet . . . so appealing. Dancing with Holly, for me, had always been this amazingly hot vertical foreplay.

I started to reach for her hand and then hesitated. Something about her behavior was off. Her attitude. Even with the beer swimming through my veins, I wondered if this was some very elaborate practical joke. Like an evil Stewart kind of joke. Except . . . if Stewart knew why this would be worthy of an evil prank, we'd have a completely different problem right now. If she knew what I really am.

"Are you coming or not?" she asked me, with eyes that were a little too innocent. "It's a great song."

My suspicion doubled, but there was no logic behind it except the fact that there wasn't any possible way *this* Holly was just going to give me exactly what I wanted from her without me even asking. Instead of answering, I kept my eyes on hers and she pulled me by the hand toward the dance floor. Just as we reached the center, I had the most crazy, irrational, drunken thought ever. Actually, it was just one word floating around in my head like an annoying bug in a glass of water.

Clones.

I shook the idea from my head, but it didn't disappear completely. I'd know if this wasn't really her, wouldn't I?

The song filled my head and her hands slipped inside my jacket and all I could think was, *This looks like Holly. Smells like her. Feels like her.* I wrapped my arms around her waist and yanked her closer until she was pressed against me. I smiled with satisfaction when I felt her suck in a breath, like I had caught her off guard, finally.

Senator Healy's eyes were on the back of my head. I could feel them. So I leaned closer and whispered, "I'm pretty drunk, so you're gonna have to tell me if I'm . . . invading your personal space."

Her shoulders tensed a little but she smiled. "Well . . . at least there's no poison ivy around."

I laughed really hard and then loosened my hold on her, allowing a little breathing room. I tried desperately to keep my mind here, in the moment, observing this slightly bolder Holly, but the song blaring through the room had quite a history with us. One that involved a very drunk girl who, not so wisely, had decided to do shots with my idiot roommates because I was late and she was bored and pissed off at me.

Then, as a punishment, I got to sit on the end of my dorm room bed and watch her dance to this same Journey song while tossing her clothes to various corners of the room. Not a bad way to end an argument.

I focused on her every move while keeping myself in the game. She'd come closer and then stiffen a little and then force herself to re-lax, then she'd do something with her hands, like touching the back of my hair or resting on my chest. It was all very calculated. Planned. And that was driving me nuts. In a bad way. This was my one impulsive moment. I wanted to do something that would blow her mind. Make her want nothing more than to follow me home and throw her clothes around my borrowed CIA apartment.

Not that I'd actually let that happen.

I spun her around so her back pressed up against me and lifted her arms around my neck again. My fingers rested on her stomach and I barely brushed my nose along the side of her face and then down her neck. This only lasted a couple seconds before I started kissing her neck. My focus flew right out of the room and I could feel her heart pounding, her breath quickening as my mouth sank more firmly into her skin.

"You smell like vanilla," I mumbled against her ear.

She rested the back of her head on my shoulder and closed her eyes. "You said that already," she whispered.

"When?" I asked, lifting my head from her neck.

She spun around again, looking dazed. "I don't know . . . earlier." Her arms dropped to my waist and she pulled until nothing was left between us except our clothes. Blood literally dropped from my head toward my feet. And then my hands were drifting below her waist, trying to wander where they shouldn't, but she let me. For a second, at least.

The song suddenly ended and Holly's eyes focused on mine again and she took a deep breath and stepped back. "I think . . . I need another drink."

"Sure," I said, confused by the quick shift in gears. The heat that radiated off of us didn't help my focus at all.

"That was . . ." Holly said as she sat down. "A good song."

I laughed. "Yep, a very good song."

The bartender brought me another beer and offered one to Holly, but she asked for water instead, which made me laugh again.

"I bet you get a little wild if you're drunk," I teased.

"I bet you won't find out," she said with a grin. "Unless . . ."

I nearly dropped my glass bottle onto the floor. "Unless what?"

"So, where did you say you lived?"

Then I did drop the glass bottle, but caught it right after it slipped through my fingers. "Far . . . very far from here, and it's a total dump . . . I mean, I'd never take a girl there, and besides, you don't even know me."

The cocky smile had dropped and she was staring at me with a more curious expression. "Sure . . . I guess you're right."

It didn't bother me in the least that she'd want to follow me home, but it bothered me that I might not be the only one. Last time, it took me until our fourth date to talk 009 Holly into seeing my apartment, and my dad was home and all we did was walk around for about twenty minutes.

Where was this coming from? I'd practically violated her earlier, and now she wanted to get me alone?

"Or you could just . . . give me your number?" she asked.

No, not going to happen.

An awkward silence fell and I wanted to fill it with something meaningful even if it didn't make any sense to her. What I didn't want was for my fellow teammates to hear me. I picked up a pen from behind the counter and jotted something down on a napkin.

What's past is prologue.

Her eyes dropped to the napkin and she read what I wrote, then glanced up at me with a confused expression. "Not a phone number . . . Shakespeare?"

"Yeah, it was in my fortune cookie at lunch today. Figured I should share the wisdom."

Her eyes froze on mine for several seconds and then she said, "Let's hear another one."

I pulled my chair closer to her and wrote right on the napkin still sitting in front of her.

Misery acquaints a man with strange bedfellows.

She laughed quietly. "Is that why you won't give me your number?"

"Something like that." I leaned my chin on her shoulder for a second as I scribbled the next line. "This one's my favorite."

He that dies, pays all debts.

"Something to look forward to when I max out my credit cards." She reached for another napkin and jotted down a sentence. "Let's see if you know this one."

Then tell the wind and fire where to stop, but don't tell me.

"Dickens?" It was moments like this when I'd be happy for time to move twice as slow. "Let me guess . . . that was the inspiration for your body art."

Her mouth opened, but it took a second for any words to tumble out. "Not exactly, but sort of . . . How did you know?"

I had a clear view of the tattoo on her shoulder blade. I touched it lightly with one finger. "Lucky guess . . . or maybe you're just extremely predictable."

I watched her expression as I wrote down a few more words.

Would you ever kiss a stranger?

"I'm not predict—" she started to say, and then changed courses when she read the napkin. "Would you?" she asked.

"No," I said, before touching my lips to the corner of her mouth. She didn't stiffen this time, but I felt her stop breathing. I started to move over toward her lips, but two very loud, excited men sat on Holly's other side and we both jumped apart.

"That was pretty smooth." Now she was blushing, but laughing at the same time. "Can I ask you something?"

"You can try . . ."

She leaned in, closing most of the gap between us. "Okay . . . so . . . have you noticed that Senator Healy has been watching us?"

I sat up straighter, catching the slight formality that had returned to her voice. "No . . . not really," I lied. "Have you?"

"Totally," she whispered, sounding even more scripted than before. "He's walked behind you, like, five times."

"Four," I answered immediately from the weird part of my brain that stored all this shit. My defenses were up and agent mode had just switched back on. "Not that I'm counting."

"I have a confession to make," she said, dropping her eyes to her hands. "We sort of have this . . . bet going."

My eyebrows lifted up. "You and the senator? How do you know him?"

She shook her head. "I don't really know him. I just met him to-night . . . I mean, he's the one who awards the scholarship that I got for college, but it's coincidental that we're both here."

Not exactly coincidental. And I didn't remember her mentioning anything about Senator Healy and her scholarship before . . . or maybe I never actually asked where it came from?

"Okay . . . so what was the bet?" I asked.

Holly reached out and placed her hands on my face, holding tight. "You can't move your head . . . and you have to close your eyes."

"Um . . . this is weird." I shut my eyes anyway, just to see where this was going.

"What color eyes do I have?" she asked.

"Blue . . . light blue."

"All right . . . what about my date?"

"Brown. Why—"

"The Russian ambassador?"

Hazel . . . with a little bit of blue on the inside. "I don't know."

I opened my eyes and saw that her expression was more serious. She dropped her hands to her lap and forced a smile. "That's good enough. Thanks."

I ran my fingers through my hair, trying to catch up. "Seriously? That's not much of a bet."

She grinned. "Actually, there were two tasks, and I went for the most difficult one first."

"And what was that?"

She turned her eyes away. "To get you to kiss me."

I felt my mouth drop open a little and my stomach twisted, like someone had just punched me in the gut. I forced myself to stay cool. "I hope you won something amazing."

"*Wicked*." She reached in her purse and removed what looked like two tickets. "That's what I won. Front-row seats."

I turned my shoulders forward and picked at the label on the empty bottle in front of me. I shouldn't have been disappointed. This was my decision. Making out with Stewart or having a few drinks and grinding with a girl at a party was one thing, but the second you leap off a roof to save someone . . . you've just exposed your greatest weakness, and I couldn't let that happen again. Not ever. Because eventually there would be a time when I didn't jump soon enough.

I turned my head to the left and caught Senator Healy's eye. He didn't look angry anymore, just gave me a tiny nod of approval. But for what? Maybe he was trying to prove a point? That I could still watch, even when I thought I was slacking?

I needed to be watching now, figuring out why no one knew where my dad or Chief Marshall were. Figuring out why I needed to befriend Stewart and what the hell was so important about Kendrick's focus.

"Another drink?" the bartender asked both of us.

I turned to him first. "Nothing for me." Then I took a deep breath before facing Holly. "Have fun at *Wicked*. I've heard it's a great show."

The first sign of guilt crossed her face as I stood up. She grabbed my arm and held it. "It was fun . . . really."

"Winning is always fun, right?" I stepped closer and smiled before touching my index finger under her chin and rubbing the skin and sighing with relief when I felt the familiar scar. I dropped my hands and walked away. She wasn't exactly my Holly, but I didn't think she could be a clone, either—but I didn't really know how that worked.

I only got a few steps away when Kendrick came over and swept me toward the dance floor. "That little bitch. I could totally kick her ass right now."

The irony of that statement was almost funny. "Don't sweat it . . . seriously."

"Just a warning, I'm not such a good dance partner," she said, putting an arm around my waist.

I pulled Kendrick close enough so I didn't have to look her in the eye. Other than fighting in self-defense practice, I had never been this close to Kendrick, and I wondered if this was more evidence that the two of us were becoming friends. "Any updates?"

She shook her head. "Just keep your eyes open."

That was exactly what I did as we swayed in the middle of the dance floor to a song I'd never heard before. I reverted to lip-reading because it was the most distracting, but after a little while Brian's voice emerged though my earpiece. I realized, within seconds, that Stewart was standing right next to them with another tray of food.

"You wanna stay a little longer or . . . leave early?" Brian asked Holly, and the suggestive tone to his voice made my stomach turn over and over.

She laughed and then said, "Leave early . . . totally."

Now I had to look. I couldn't help it. And the first thing I noticed was Brian's hands resting on her ass and his tongue being shoved down her throat. I groaned to myself, but not so loud that I missed him mumble, "Don't worry, I came prepared."

I spun Kendrick around to face the other way and closed my eyes, absorbing the weight of his words. It was like four fists punching me all at once. *He's sleeping with her?* He stole my moment. One of my favorite Holly memories.

And now I'd have to figure out how to keep from killing him.

"I think you're gonna dig a hole through my hand," Kendrick whispered. I loosened my fingers and then wiped my sweaty palm on my pants. "Sorry."

I watched Holly retreat with Brian and felt a mixture of relief and emptiness. At least I could focus the rest of the night. Drunkenly focus.

Just as I was about to scan the room again, I felt the vibration of my cell phone.

"Is this right?" Kendrick mumbled, now looking at her own vibrating phone. "Freeman wants all of us?"

I shook my head. "That's what it says . . . but why?"

"Let's not make a scene leaving," Kendrick whispered.

I nodded my silent agreement and we waited an agonizing thirty seconds for the song to end before drifting casually out of the spotlight and over to a dark corner. My heart raced with anticipation. Something big had to be happening if they were pulling all of us away right in the middle of a mission.

CHAPTER ELEVEN

We sped up our pace once we were in the lobby and far away from the front desk. "Any idea how they want us to get underground?"

I felt someone brush up behind me and saw that it was Stewart. "Yep. And we don't even have to go outside."

Kendrick and I followed her to an elevator at the end of a long hallway. As the doors opened, Mason was right next to us, slipping in first.

"How do you do that, man?" I asked him. "I never see you."

He smiled at me for a second and then nodded to Kendrick as the doors shut. "All right, Doctor, you and I have to rewire this thing."

I was sure my face reflected the confusion I felt, because Stewart explained. "You need a key to go to the basement level . . . where the laundry room is."

"Right . . . isn't there a staircase?" I asked.

"God, Junior, when are you going to grow a brain?" she said, tossing her jacket onto the floor. "The stairs also require a key, except there's no electrical system we can fool, like with the elevator."

Mason and Kendrick were ignoring us. They already had the cover off the control panel and were now sifting through wires.

"So steal a key from a maid. Seriously, it's not rocket science," I snapped.

"This is less risky. No outsiders involved," Mason mumbled, with his eyes still focused on the wires.

"I don't buy that at all. Admit you just like taking shit apart," I said.

Even though my stomach was fluttering with nerves, I had to smile at the image of Kendrick, in her long pink dress and heels, ripping through wires like the freakin' bomb squad. The confidence was the complete polar opposite of Kendrick trying to stitch a dead body. I wondered what Michael would think if he saw her like this. In her element.

"Hook the red to the orange," she told Mason.

"Got it," he said, and then the elevator jolted downward.

"Nice work, Dr. Kendrick," I said.

She smiled at me and then removed her shoes and held them in one hand. As the elevator doors opened, Stewart and I both drew our pistols at the exact same time. If there was one thing I could contribute to this team, it was a damn good shot . . . although I'd never done any target-shooting while completely wasted. My aim might be a little different.

We dodged several bins of white towels to get to a small opening in the floor. Well . . . actually it was a manhole concealed by a small brown rug. I climbed the ladder first, aiming my gun below, just in case. The second I landed on the ground, Agent Parker and Agent Freeman walked right past me.

"Hey! What's going on?" I asked. "Why are we crawling through the sewers to get to the classrooms?"

Freeman glanced up and down the tunnels as more of us flooded through. "I got a page from Healy who said to round all of you up. He must know something, if we're aborting the mission like this."

I squinted, trying to see down the semidark tunnel. "Who are those two . . . up ahead?"

Freeman said the name of two of the agents who had also just completed their training in France.

Kendrick, Stewart, and Mason had all touched ground by this point and were listening carefully to Freeman. I couldn't ignore the uneasy feeling that came over me. Something wasn't right. I had just been practically standing next to Healy . . . only minutes before getting called.

"Why would he call everyone at once? Don't some of us have posts to guard . . . or something?" I asked Freeman.

"I'm not sure, Jackson. This wasn't part of the original plan, but missions change . . . you know that." He glanced down the tunnel and then back at Parker. "Why don't we run ahead and check?"

"Sure," Parker said, then he called over his shoulder, "See you guys in a few minutes."

Kendrick walked next to me, still holding her shoes in one hand. "What's on your mind?"

"I don't know," I said in low voice. "Something about this seems bad . . . really bad. And Healy told me to—"

I froze in my spot, searching my memory for the assignment that Healy had given me.

Tell me what the Chinese ambassador and his friend are discussing.

I had been distracted by my spotlight dance with Holly, but my mind didn't fail me. After playing the moment in my head over and over, I came up with one complete sentence straight from the mouth of the Chinese ambassador.

"The children will be occupied." Children . . . as in baby agents . . . which was the majority of us . . . And Freeman was a baby leader . . . usually that job fell to Dad or Marshall.

"I think we're being set up," I said immediately. My heart was racing, and even Stewart's attitude wouldn't shake me from this new discovery.

"What are you talking about?" Stewart said with a groan.

"Something's going to happen while all of us are being dragged away from the scene . . . Think about it," I insisted.

"It doesn't matter," Stewart said. "We do what we're told."

"You heard Freeman, this wasn't part of the plan," Kendrick said.

I glanced at Kendrick and then back at Stewart. "I'm going back."

"Fucking idiot," Stewart mumbled under her breath.

"I'm going with you," Kendrick said.

I nodded, then we both turned around.

"Jackson, wait!" Mason said before trotting up beside me. "I'm coming, too."

"Mason! What the hell are you doing?" Stewart shouted at him.

"I'm sorry," he said, not turning around to face her.

"Whatever," she grumbled. "Fucking traitor."

Kendrick started to climb the ladder again and I looked over my shoulder at Mason, his eyes on Stewart's retreating form. "You can go with her. It's okay, man," I told him.

He stared at me and shook his head. "Healy asked me to search the basement for explosives an hour ago . . . me, as the expert in Futuristic Technology . . ."

I swallowed hard and forced down the very bad feeling. "Yeah, that is a little suspicious."

After ten minutes of combing the basement for clues of any kind of attack, we were all starting to feel a little stupid for going against orders.

All three of us turned a corner and walked down a narrow corridor, the hum of the utility room coming from the right side. Mason suddenly skidded to a stop and Kendrick and I smacked into him.

"Mason?" Kendrick said.

He put his hand on the doorknob to the utility room and then pressed his ear to it. "Something's different . . ."

He opened the door and Kendrick and I both looked over his shoulder.

"What the hell is *that*?" Kendrick said.

I followed her eyes to the floor in front of the water heater. "Oh, damn . . ."

The giant glass case lying on the floor with clear tubes of liquid running through it was identical to the explosive we had encountered in Heidelberg. The one Emily disabled.

"Is this . . . oh, God, it is, isn't it?" Mason muttered.

"If you mean the weird-ass explosive Stewart found in Germany, then yes, it looks the same," I said, and then covered my tracks when he shot a glance at me. "Based on her description anyway. I read the report a few times."

Blood rushed to my face. My heart pounded at twice the pace of the tiny clock ticking against the front of the bomb. Kendrick and Mason dropped down to their knees, eyeing the foreign and most likely futuristic object from every angle. This was what they did best. It wasn't my territory, and yet most of Emily's steps of disabling it had stayed etched in my mind.

"There's fourteen minutes left on this timer," Kendrick said.

"This has to be a test," Mason said. "If it were a real threat, why the hell would the EOTs leave a clock counting down the minutes for us? To be polite?"

"I don't know," I said, slowly trying to put the logic together. He had a point, and yet I'd seen this thing before and the EOTs *were* behind it.

"Just be careful, Mace," Kendrick said, holding her breath as he removed the glass cover.

Mason set the glass top beside him and brushed his fingers over a clear tube on the outside. A pale yellow liquid floated inside it. "This one's cold . . . could be—"

"Nitroglycerin," Kendrick finished for him.

"As in dynamite?" I asked.

"In simple terms, yes," Mason answered.

He touched the tube closest to him, with bright blue liquid inside it. I watched his fingers wrap around it and start to tug. "If I just take this one off, I can get a better look at the rest of it."

"Wait!" I said, kneeling down beside Kendrick. Emily hadn't done that first. Maybe there was a reason. "Hold up, okay?"

They both looked at me, waiting to hear my not-so-brilliant plan. "I think you should pull the pink one off first."

"Why?" Kendrick asked.

Because a pint-sized time traveler did it that way.

"It's just a guess. But I have good instincts with this kind of stuff."

"Yeah, and what's your specialty again?" Mason laughed derisively. "Seriously, Jackson. Are you out of your mind? I'm not taking anything apart until I know for sure it won't blow us to pieces."

"He's right." Kendrick pulled out her phone from her pocket and started punching in buttons. "I'm calling Dr. Melvin."

My stomach twisted in knots with every second that ticked down on that clock. Mason's eyes darted fast from one end of the bomb to the other, trying to find something he could use. Sweat trickled down his forehead, causing his glasses to slide down his nose.

I played Emily's exact moves over and over in my mind while

Kendrick mumbled descriptions to Melvin on the phone. I could hear the frantic tone in his responses. He didn't have the answers.

"Nine minutes," I said, throwing a panicked glance sideways at Kendrick.

Mason's hands started to tremble and his breathing grew more and more ragged. "Dude, keep your hands back," he snapped at me.

"Yeah, Jackson's here," Kendrick said to Dr. Melvin, followed by a long moment of silence. She covered the phone with one hand and turned to look at both of us. "He says when it gets to six minutes, we have to get out. It's protocol, if we aren't able to disable it."

My first panicked thought was of Holly, but then I sighed with relief, remembering that she had left a while ago. "Look, Mason. It's more than a guess, okay? You gotta let me take this thing apart."

I reached for the pink tube and Mason stared at me with crazed eyes. His fingers locked tighter around the blue tube. "Don't move! You touch that other tube and I'm pulling this one off!" He ran his free hand through his hair, making it stick up straight in all directions. "I just need more time! I can figure this out."

"Calm down, Mason," Kendrick said, leaning closer to him. "Take a deep breath and try to relax. We both know you're brilliant and you *can* do this."

His shoulders relaxed just a little and he inhaled heavily, letting it out slowly and closing his eyes for a second.

I, on the other hand, was having a hard time not shoving the kid aside. "Seven fucking minutes! Mason, I'm not kidding. Let me help."

"Shut up!"

The sounds of the party above us—music, laughing, glasses clinking—seemed to fill the small space the three of us sat in. None of them had any clue how close they were to taking their last breaths.

"Oh, God . . . this won't be easy," Kendrick mumbled into the phone. She tugged on my shirt and whispered, "Dr. Melvin says grab Mason and get out, now. He's panicking and none of us know what's in this."

"I am not panicking!" Mason shouted back at her.

"Kendrick, I know how to turn this off, trust me, please," I said.

She shook her head immediately. "No one expects you to be the hero right now, Jackson. You're not trained to do this. Forget it. Let's go! We've been given orders."

Yeah . . . orders. From Dr. Melvin, who was practically a second father to both Mason and me. Not exactly an impartial leader, looking out for the good of everyone involved.

I made a quick decision and glanced up at Kendrick first before saying, "I'm sorry. Don't hate me, okay?"

My fingers found the pistol in the back of my pants, and even the whiskey and beer in my blood wouldn't keep me from being sharp right now. In one swift motion, I had the gun pressed to Mason's temple. Kendrick gasped beside me and scooted back.

"Jackson . . . don't," she whispered, like I'd betrayed her.

Mason's face twisted with anger. He knew I had him.

"Mason, get your hands off the explosive, back up, and let me take this thing apart," I said.

"No way. You'll kill everyone in this building . . . maybe the entire block."

"Six minutes," Kendrick said. "Come on, Jackson. Let's just go." Tears trembled in her voice and it hit me right in the gut. Harder than I would have expected.

"I'm counting to five, and if you don't back the hell away I'll shoot you and then I'll take the damn thing apart," I snapped at Mason. "One . . . two . . ."

"Fuck you!" he said, throwing his hands up in defeat before sliding backward, away from the bomb.

I let out a breath of relief, but didn't lower the gun, just in case. My stomach turned over and over and suddenly I wasn't as sure as I'd thought. Or maybe I hadn't thought beyond convincing Mason to hand over the reins. "Get out, both of you—now!" I said.

She shook her head, fighting back the tears that threatened to fall. "If you're staying—"

"Yeah, that's a brilliant idea, Kendrick. Stick around so the CIA can deliver your remains in an envelope to Michael!" I shouted, not caring if I hurt her, so long as she left in the next thirty seconds. "You, too, Mason. Get as far away as you can."

Kendrick still had the phone to her ear, with Dr. Melvin listening in, probably yelling at her to drag me out of here. Ten more seconds of intense stares passed, and she finally stood up and grabbed Mason by the arm.

The second I heard the door slam shut and the pounding of their running footsteps, I set my gun on the floor. My brain went into machine mode and piece after piece was removed exactly how Emily had done it. My heart thudded so loud, I couldn't hear any other sound. I wiped my sweaty hands off on my pants and reached for the last piece of the giant bomb.

My breath got stuck in my throat and I held it there as the time clicked from two minutes to one minute.

No turning back now.

My fingers clutched the tube of green liquid, squeezing it while I drew in a deep breath. Maybe this would work . . . but maybe it wouldn't. The glow at the bottom of the explosive was still shining bright and I could only assume that it needed to turn off.

I closed my eyes, taking in several slow, deep breaths. The clock ticked in time with the pulse of blood pumping in my fingertips. Holly's voice filled my head for the three fleeting seconds it took me to yank off the last piece.

I opened my eyes and slid out the green tube. My heart nearly stopped as the light in the bottom flickered. Just as it turned all the way off, a loud boom erupted from behind me.

A gunshot.

In about two seconds the green tube was set on the floor and I was on my feet, charging out the door. The utility room opened to a long semidark hallway. I could hear voices farther down the hall, and as I started to run, Stewart came barreling into me from another corridor.

"Did you fire your gun?" I asked her frantically.

"No, I just got here." Her eyes met mine for a second and there was just a hint of guilt. "I should have trusted Mason . . . figured that he probably had a good reason if he chose to follow your ass back here."

I pressed my back against the wall and held my gun out in front of me. "I made them leave. We found an explosive and Mason kinda freaked. Don't worry, I already defused it."

Another shot rang through the basement and Stewart and I both jumped into action, walking quickly toward the sound. The hall opened to a large room where two elevators sat in the center. Stewart nodded toward an older lady in a maid's uniform with wild gray hair sticking up everywhere. She was huddled in a corner, shaking, tears streaming down her face. A tiny scream escaped her lips when she saw us with our guns pointing around the room.

I took a few steps toward her and put a hand over her mouth. "Do you have a key . . . to go upstairs?"

Stewart threw me an exasperated look. "We can't evacuate the whole damn building, Jackson. Just help me figure out who's down here."

Loud running footsteps came closer and closer. Stewart and I both froze. Kendrick flew past us . . . and an EOT I recognized from Germany charged after her.

I could practically hear Stewart's thoughts, her calculations. She turned her gun toward the EOT and fired perfectly at his right shoulder and then his left leg. The man collapsed in a heap right in front of the elevator. Kendrick turned around and sighed with relief, then ran back toward us.

I grabbed the maid by the arm and tugged her toward the elevator. "Do you have a key?" I asked again.

"No! No!" she said in a panic.

"Where's Mason?" Stewart asked Kendrick.

Her eyes darted down the three corridors. "I don't know . . ."

I shook the locked door leading to the stairwell, trying to force it open. "Damn it!"

"Forget about it, Jackson. We need to find Mason," Stewart said, heading for one of the corridors.

My arms were now gripping this woman's shoulders as her legs threatened to give out. "Don't scream, okay?" I said to her.

I couldn't see her face, but she nodded her head. Kendrick's eyes widened, staring at something over my shoulder. I knew what it had to be and I released the woman and snapped around quickly, not even looking at my attacker before sending a hard kick to his face. The man stumbled backward and a stream of blood flooded out of his nose onto the white tile floor.

Kendrick gasped when he vanished. I turned in a circle, waiting for him to return. This time he caught me. Right around the waist, throwing me to the ground. My head slammed onto the tile floor, but the look of utter panic on the innocent woman's face distracted me. I aimed my gun at the door to the stairwell and fired a shot at the glass panel above the doorknob. It shattered with a loud crack.

I wrestled with my attacker, not able to pull off a good shot with him behind me. As I was trying to pin him to the floor underneath me, I saw Kendrick reach her hand through the broken panel and open the door, shoving the woman up the first step.

My head hit the floor again and the middle-aged man with brown hair like mine stared right at my face, his eyes, his expression . . . all perfectly calm.

"Thomas said I'd never stand a chance against you," the man said, not taking his eyes off mine. "I'm not sure he's right. I haven't seen you pull any tricks yet."

"That's because he's got us to clean up his mess," Stewart said, curling her elbow around the man's neck.

Red crept up to his face almost immediately and his grip loosened on me. Stewart continued to apply pressure until the guy lost consciousness. His body went limp on top of me and I shoved him over onto the hard floor.

"Thanks," I mumbled to Stewart.

"We need to find Mason," she said.

Kendrick and I stood on either side of Stewart and all three of us stared down the three corridors.

"We'll each take one," I said.

They nodded their agreement and I took off down the hallway to the right. Another gunshot halted me and then soft fingers curled around my wrist, only touching me lightly. My first thought was Mason. He could sneak up on you better than anyone I'd ever seen. My eyes traveled down my arm, taking in the smaller, feminine hand, and then the flash of red hair falling in front of my face distracted me. The room spun and I felt it. Familiar as ever, even though it had been months.

I was jumping, and Cassidy . . . my biological mother . . . was dragging me to some unknown location and time . . .

My defensive move was a couple seconds late, but I tried anyway and focused my mind on something . . . something buried in my subconscious beyond reach.

Until now.

CHAPTER TWELVE

The first sound I heard was Cassidy's loud holler. She released her hand from my wrist and sank to the floor on her knees. Her eyes bugged out, wide as golf balls.

Where are we?

I took a half second to glance around and was shocked to see the familiar sight of my dad's kitchen. *My* kitchen. But it was different.

Cassidy dropped her eyes to her arms and I did the same. Blue and purple streaks ran up them, like instant bruises. Nausea swept over me, and it had nothing to do with jumping.

Had I done that? When I pulled the jump here instead of wherever the hell she was trying to take me? I heard a new voice gasp and glanced up to see a brown-haired woman standing in the doorway, eyes almost as big as Cassidy's.

Eileen. Did that mean this was before 1992? Or maybe if it was a different timeline . . . something changed . . . maybe Eileen lived past October 1992 in a different universe. It was definitely a full jump. But how would I know if it was a *Thomas*-jump?

Cassidy let out another loud holler and I dropped down beside her. "What the hell happened? What's wrong with you?" I almost wished I had more of a grudge against her so her screams wouldn't affect me like this, but they did. Then, before she could answer, before I could attempt to help, she vanished.

I stood there, trying to catch my breath, to let my heart slow down, while Eileen stared openmouthed at me.

My legs shook as I walked closer to her. I'd never seen her up close. Not when I was old enough to really remember.

I shouldn't be doing this. I knew that. I really did, but something took over and one foot stepped in front of the other and my rational mind surrendered control of the situation.

She was holding her breath . . . hands slowly lifting up as if I were a police officer ordering her to do this. "Wait . . . please just—"

I stopped right in front of her, only twelve inches from her face. "I wish I could remember . . . something," I whispered, more to myself than to her.

Eileen lowered her hands, eying me curiously. "Remember what?" she asked, the Scottish accent leaking through.

She was stalling. Had she called for someone? Used some emergency signal or something? "What year is it?"

She deliberated for a minute, then finally said, "1992."

The year she died.

"What month?" I asked, a little more urgently.

"July . . . July thirteenth," she croaked.

And I knew instantly how I could tell if this was a *Thomas*-jump. Before she could stop me, I tore down the hall, opening three bedroom doors before finding the right one. Classical music played softly through a cassette player on the dresser next to a Winnie-the-Pooh lamp.

Air failed to move through my lungs as I stared at the little boy asleep in a tiny bed. He was lying on his back, hair sweaty and blankets balled up at the foot of the bed, blue one-piece pajamas zipped up to his neck.

The agent in me didn't turn off, even with the shock of what I'd just done. I took two seconds to allow my eyes to scroll over the contents of the room: two dressers . . . a changing table . . . another tiny bed with a little redheaded figure in light purple pajamas curled up in a ball, a doll tucked under her arm . . . *Courtney*.

Then I was back to staring at my younger self, Dr. Melvin's words from the other day, in his office, repeating in my head over and over: *If you were able to do this, like Thomas, maybe jump five years in the past . . . you would see yourself.*

And I was definitely seeing my other self . . . while feeling the weight and presence of my entire body here and now. Not a half-jump.

"Wait!" Eileen said, running up behind me. "Please, don't hurt them . . ."

"Oh, God . . . I *can* do it. Shit." I reached my hand out, holding the wall for support. "And 1992 . . . ? Two, then . . . I'm two. *He's* two . . ."

Eileen drew in a quick breath and I realized right away what I'd done. The fear dropped from her face and was replaced with shock and disbelief. "Oh, God, it can't be . . . you can't be . . ." She stepped closer, wrapping her fingers around my chin, turning my head one way and then the other. "Jackson?"

I nodded slowly, waiting for her reaction. *Everything I do here is changing the future. This is real.*

Both of her hands were on my face now, studying every inch of it. "This is unbelievable. Are you . . . are you okay?"

"Yeah." I stood perfectly still, not sure how to feel or what to think. I glanced down the hallway. "Should I . . . go?"

"No," she said quickly. "Not yet. Please. But maybe you should sit down?"

I should have been thinking, *I can Thomas-jump.* But instead, my focus switched to, *This is my mother . . .*

I nodded again and followed her into the living room. Both of us sat at opposite ends of the couch. It wasn't until she reached over and took it from my hand that I realized a gun was still clutched between my fingers. No wonder she had freaked out when I stormed into the younger me and Courtney's room like it was an assassination mission. She rested the gun on the table and then picked up my wrist, pressing her fingers to it and staring at the clock on the wall.

Checking my pulse.

I didn't know what to say to her, but I couldn't stop staring and I had no desire to leave. I guess it wasn't all that strange to be curious about the woman who had given birth to me . . . raised me for the first two years of my life. Let the two-year-old me dump sand over her head.

And she was Dad's Holly.

Eileen took a deep breath. "Do you know who that woman is? The one who just disappeared?"

"Yeah . . . Dr. Melvin told me."

Her eyes were brown. A light caramel color. And she had freckles running across her nose. Just a few.

She rested her hands on my face again and smiled. "You look so . . . handsome . . . grown up . . . How old are you?"

I felt my forehead wrinkle—a post-drinking pain shooting right between my eyes. More proof that this wasn't a half-jump. "Well . . . somewhere between nineteen and twenty . . . sort of . . . It's kind of a hard question for me to answer."

She dropped her hands and her eyes to her lap. "Probably not as hard to answer as other questions. Like, why you're looking at me like that?"

"Like what?"

The second I saw her face again, I knew.

Like why it looks like I don't know you . . . not in the future.

I opened my mouth, trying to come up with some explanation, some kind of cover story, like I had done those times I'd visited Courtney in a half-jump.

Eileen shook her head and held up a hand to stop me. "It's okay, Jackson. You shouldn't have to be the one to deliver that kind of news to me."

Did she know she was going to die? Did she know when?

I leaned my head back on the couch and closed my eyes for a second. "I don't know what to do . . . I've never been able to change anything. What if this makes everything worse . . . what if it fixes everything? What if I can't ever do it again?"

The responsibility was heavier than I'd ever expected. So heavy that I almost didn't want it, even though I knew what it could mean for me and my life.

Her fingers closed around my left hand and she squeezed it. "Why don't you tell me the whole story? Start with the first time you jumped. How old were you?"

"Eighteen," I said, opening my eyes. "But it's a long story . . . and there's parts that I can't tell you." *I don't want to tell you.*

She smiled at me and said, "I've got time, and feel free to edit as needed."

I drank the last swallow from the mug of coffee Eileen had given me and returned it to the table. After two hours, I'd had time to sober up, which was probably a good thing if I planned to jump back to the middle of our battle in 2009. Or whatever the hell was going on at Senator Healy's ball.

So far, Eileen and I had been through my first jump, my experiments with Adam (the half-jumps fascinated her, just like they had with Dr. Melvin), Holly getting shot, me jumping to 2007 and getting stuck, then my trip back to 2009 and the jump that followed a few days later, taking me to the timeline I had just left from. I hadn't told her anything about herself or Courtney, and she didn't ask. Which made me wonder if she already knew.

"We're still alone. Why hasn't anyone else come to check out the situation?" I watched her write notes with such intensity. She reminded me a little of Adam during one of our experiments.

"It's the middle of the night, remember?" she replied.

"Yeah, but I thought you guys were all about constant security. Keeping the future Tempest weapons alive." The sarcasm leaked out without permission.

Her face pinched with worry. "Jackson . . . is that what you think?"

"I'm sorry. That came out wrong." I tugged at the collar of my dress shirt and unfastened another button.

Eileen started laughing, and then scribbled something in the notebook resting on her lap. "You have the same mannerisms as your two-year-old self. It's quite amazing, actually."

"That's a comforting thought."

She laughed again. "Sorry, *that* came out wrong. It's just . . . you're quite impulsive, even for a toddler. And very gifted at charming apologies. You hate being told what to do . . . conforming. Especially when the orders are coming from Courtney."

I suddenly became very interested in the pictures on the mantel. My sister's name had just been dropped into the conversation for the first time and I didn't want to go there.

"It's okay, Jackson," she said. The amusement had dropped from her voice and I could feel her stare beaming into the side of my face. "I know about Courtney."

I shot a glance at her. "How?"

She swallowed hard and her eyes filled with tears. "I've known for a long time now."

"But Dr. Melvin told me they didn't catch it fast enough. That her getting sick was a complete shock," I practically shouted.

Eileen kept her eyes on mine. "He doesn't know. I acquired the information in a situation similar to this one."

I wasn't sure why, but this really pissed me off. The end of her life should have been devoted to fixing Courtney. *She's a fucking doctor . . .* a brilliant one, supposedly. I let out a breath and bit down hard on the inside of my cheek. It was difficult to throw angry words at someone who you knew was going to die in a few months.

"So, what about Cassidy?" I asked, changing the subject. "What was up with the bruises on her arms? Did I do that?"

She quickly followed my lead and snapped back into scientific mode. "Well . . . I don't think you intentionally caused harm to her, but you redirected the jump, and this distance . . . this type of jump, might have been more than she could handle. How do you feel right now? You mentioned you've had quite extreme physical symptoms in the past."

I nodded. "I feel fine, which is exactly what happened when they dragged me along on some of those jumps before, but I don't get why."

She set the notebook on the table and turned toward me. "You're using the other time traveler. Your mind is protecting itself by shutting down when someone else has similar powers. And it's also possible you've gained strength in these last few months. Perhaps from growth or simply because you haven't been jumping. I think Cassidy's power combined with yours is the reason you were able to do the complete jump."

"So . . . I might not be able to do the Thomas-jump on my own, and . . . and I might have done that to her . . . hurt her?" I hated the idea that Cassidy's pain, the disgusting bruises, might have been caused by me. I sighed and then sat up straighter. "I won't do it anymore, then . . . I'm valuable enough to Tempest without time travel."

"Maybe," she conceded. "But I also believe, now that you know the risk of hurting someone else, your mind will act accordingly. Keep it from happening, if possible."

"Assuming I don't turn into a robotic freak of nature that doesn't care about anything."

She smiled a little. "Jackson, think about it. When you jumped off that roof and took an ordinary mind with you, she was okay, right?"

I thought about this for a second and remembered Holly, helping me climb that roof, diving behind poles. "I think she was fine, but I didn't stick around very long."

"The effects, the symptoms, would have been immediate." Her face turned more serious than it had been all night and she sucked in a deep breath as if giving me a warning that bigger news was coming. "There's something else you need to know . . . but I'm afraid telling you will make things worse for you. You're already allowing yourself to feel responsible for events beyond your control." Her face grew weary and tired. "I don't see any other option, though."

"Okay . . . ?" I said, already fidgeting with nerves.

"Well, what you said about the timelines and making new ones, that's all true. It's very dangerous. In fact, the results could be catastrophic. I have a source who confirmed this and I've tried to tell Chief Marshall and Dr. Melvin my solution, but I can't explain how I know."

"You can't rat out your source?" I asked, even though it seemed ridiculous to protect anyone when we were talking about the end of the world or whatever.

"Yes," she said with a nod. "Revealing the source may prevent their existence."

Wait a minute. *It couldn't be . . . could it?*

"Did you think she was Courtney?" I whispered, and was surprised at how eerie my voice sounded.

Eileen's eyes widened. "I . . . yes . . . yes, I did. But just for a minute. Her eyes are blue . . . not green." Panic filled her expression. "Please tell me you haven't said anything?"

So Eileen knew Emily. Who *was* this kid? Some kind of all-powerful god? Or was she just a time-traveling puppet, and if so, who was pulling the strings?

"I haven't told anyone. Not even my dad . . . I mean, Kevin," I stuttered, remembering that two-year-old Courtney had called him Kevin that day in the sandbox.

Eileen let out a huge breath of relief and sank back into the cushions. "I'm glad you call him Dad, Jackson. It makes everything seem better."

"You haven't told him any of this?" I asked. "He doesn't know about Courtney or anything . . . ?"

She shook her head sadly. "That's what I was getting to. I thought about telling him so many times. The hints I gave him, the bits and pieces . . . He didn't take it well."

"What's that? What *does* he know?"

Eileen scooted closer and picked up one of my hands. "I told him that I believed you and Courtney were born to make sacrifices . . . leaps so giant most people couldn't fathom it. And when the time comes, you'll step up without question."

My stomach twisted in knots. This was worse than one of Chief Marshall's cryptic speeches he had given almost daily to all the trainees. "But it's more than a belief, right?"

Her eyes locked with mine. "Yes, it is. I think Kevin believes me, he's probably guessed that I've acquired unreported information, but he hasn't asked. He always has the same defensive answer . . . You and Courtney won't have to do anything. Won't have to make any sacrifices because he'll fill that role for you. He's quite determined."

In that moment, I felt closer to my dad than I ever had, even though we were very far apart. "That's exactly what he did. He made every effort to give me virtually no responsibility. Nothing to worry about or fear. At least he did . . . until recently. But that was more my fault than his. Where is he right now? I mean, in this year."

She rubbed her eyes with the back of her hands. "I'm not sure. Actually, that's the reason I couldn't sleep. He hasn't called for five days. He almost always finds a way to contact me sooner than that."

"Well, I guess now you don't have to worry. You know how it turns out."

"That's true," she said.

Exhaustion started to creep up. I leaned forward and rested my head in my hands for a second, rubbing the blurriness from my eyes. "Damn," I muttered.

Eileen rested a hand on my back. "I shouldn't have told you all this. It's too much, isn't it?" She paused for a second before answering her own question. "Of course it's too much."

"No, it's not what you said . . . it's just . . ." I lifted my head and looked at her again. "I don't really think I'm that person. The self-sacrificing type. I know it seems like that because of what I told you about Holly, but I've been having a lot of weak moments lately. Especially tonight. And I keep having to leave everyone."

"What do you mean?" she asked. "Holly has no memories of you leaving her. It was quite brilliant, actually."

"Yeah, *that* version of her. What about the one I lured into a relationship and then left in 2007? And what about the 009 Holly, sitting at home waiting for me to come over? The guy who asked her to marry him and jumped off a roof to save her? She's still there, and does that mean, when I vanished, the asshole version of me reappeared? That'll go over real well." Once I started my guilt-ridden rambling, it was hard to stop. "And what about Adam? . . . I left a bunch of different Adams with some scary information and no way to get answers."

Sympathy filled her eyes. "I think you're going to have to explore the possibility that maybe . . . maybe you've done the complete jump before? I'm just not sure . . ."

"What? Not sure about what?"

"This is one of the things I was trying to tell you a minute ago," she said. "I'm not sure you can create multiple timelines . . . One other timeline, maybe . . . but two . . . ? I think it's more likely you've done complete jumps without realizing it. But if you did this the last time, then where—"

"Is the other me?" I finished for her. "What do you mean, I can't make more timelines? I thought that was what all the EOTs were doing all the time . . . except a few of the exceptional ones. So, they can make dozens of alternate worlds and I can only make one? And sometimes . . . I don't really understand the threat from the Enemies of Time. If they all jump around to these different timelines, then why are they so determined to alter the world I came from . . . in 2009? Why don't they just jump back to the dinosaur age and fix everything?"

"Jackson, do you understand what my contribution to Axelle was?"

I shook my head. The only part I had heard was the giving-birth part. This must be the big information she'd been afraid to tell me a few minutes ago.

"Right now, in this year . . . very few time travelers have been seen. As a teenager, I studied Dr. Melvin's research, which dated back to the 1950s. We understood how time travel worked, how the gene showed up in random people, and that actually being able to jump through time and survive it was truly rare. But making a new timeline, an alternate universe . . . that was my theory, except it wasn't possible." Her face lit up with a strange excitement only a brilliant and slightly mad scientist could pull off. "In fact, it's still not possible in this year."

Huh? "Huh?"

"You thought the half-jumps were what made you different, but that's just your body's way of protecting itself when you attempt the complete jump and fail. At least I'm assuming that." She paused for several seconds. "*You* are the only one who can make a new timeline. Not Thomas . . . not any of the others. It was a gut feeling I had. If I mixed the cloned time traveler with a normal man, we'd have branches splitting from our main world. A way out . . . if you needed it."

I tried to swallow this new information, but it just got stuck in my head. "Wait. So, all the stuff everyone else in Tempest believes, about the EOTs making new timelines constantly because they can't do complete jumps . . . it's not true?"

"Think about it, Jackson. Suddenly the EOTs are everywhere, when before we had only seen a few, and rarely at that. Maybe you haven't been given that data, but from what you've told me, the world has changed a lot since you took that jump back to 2007. Like you opened a door and they can go through it now. All the ones with the Tempus gene that weren't strong enough, skilled enough to do the complete jump, didn't even know they could time-travel and suddenly they can. It's like a crutch you've provided."

The vision of the line of EOTs in Heidelberg, appearing out of nowhere, sprang into my mind. Everyone was shocked by the increase in numbers. I opened the door . . . They were bouncing off the world (or worlds?) I created.

That was when I remembered Dad, Dr. Melvin, and Chief Marshall scrambling to answer my questions in that 2007 timeline. They were seeing Eileen's theory come alive for the first time.

"But why would you want that?" I couldn't help asking.

"I didn't exactly plan for the others to be able to follow you, but now I'm seeing that it's possible. I thought it would be a way for you to escape them, if needed. Go somewhere that they couldn't." Her eyes started to tear up again and she covered her face for a second with her hands. "I never wanted you to be a weapon, Jackson. Never wanted Courtney to get sick . . . but when Emily came to tell me you would be a part of this and possibly a part of the solution, I knew that I'd have to accept it. Let it happen. Do everything I could to make you the kind of person who wouldn't stop searching for the right answer."

As crazy as this information seemed, it almost made sense. She knew Courtney and I would be surrounded by people who could take control, try to use us. So she gave us a way out. A choice. A little bit of free will.

We were interrupted by the phone ringing. At three in the morning. Eileen jumped, looking startled, and then said, "I'm sorry, I have to get that."

She took off for the kitchen and I could hear her say, "Kevin!"

I stood up, shaking out my stiff legs, then walked over to the patio door. Rain pounded against the balcony outside. Rain that I might have caused with my last jump. I closed the blinds, feeling way too exposed, and moved toward the fireplace. It was lined with pictures I'd never seen before. Dad holding me on his lap, playing the piano. Dad asleep in a rocking chair with Courtney snoozing in his arms. She looked so little, maybe a year old.

"Yes, the kids are fine," Eileen said, still on the phone with the younger version of Dad.

I knelt down and picked up a puzzle from a stack on the floor. These toys were proof of my childhood with her. Evidence that I had a mother. At least for a little while. A wave of sadness suddenly hit me, knowing that the only memories I had of Eileen were five minutes in a sandbox and a few puzzles.

And tonight. I had tonight.

"Jackson's been wearing your tool belt around night and day," Eileen said. "He can't wait for you to come back." She paused for a long minute. "No . . . no, everything's fine . . . I'm just a little tired . . . and I miss you."

Tears trembled in her voice. I wondered how the dad on the phone would handle that. Then a weird idea formed in my head, probably because I hadn't seen him for so long. And I really wanted to . . . or at least hear his voice. I tried to remember when, exactly, Eileen had said he'd left. And when I couldn't recall, I just picked a random date in the past. Then I closed my eyes and focused on that day. I nearly yelled out loud when I felt the splitting-apart feeling. It had been a long time since I'd done a half-jump and it seemed worse than I remembered it.

OCTOBER 5, 1991

My reward for withstanding that awful sensation was the wonderful, blissful feeling of not feeling that pounding headache or the results of the mild beating I had taken before jumping to 1992. I was in the kitchen again and I could hear music.

A Billy Joel song.

I crept slowly out of the kitchen and into the hallway. I couldn't hear any talking, but when I peeked around the corner into the living room, Dad was there.

A very young Dad. Like my age now. He was lying on the carpet right in front of a blazing fireplace, his eyes closed, but he was tapping his fingers to the music. I remembered the way he seemed to know I had been hiding in that coat closet the time I jumped to 2003 and ended up in his office. I'd have to be careful here if I wanted to observe for any length of time.

A bedroom door opened down the hall and I sprang back into the kitchen, pressing myself up against the counters as Eileen breezed past, not even glancing in my direction. I returned to the hallway, listening in.

"Sleeping on the job," I heard Eileen say.

Then Dad spoke. "If I lie here and close my eyes, it almost feels like . . . like I could be anywhere."

"Anywhere? Like forty years in the past?" Eileen asked softly.

Was that totally random, or were they talking about time travel?

"Maybe," Dad said.

The song stopped and I held my breath, wondering if he'd heard me or something. A few seconds later he said, "I like this one." And another song started.

More Billy Joel.

Their voices got softer and the music louder. I crawled on all fours behind the couch and peered around the end of it. I could see both of them now, lying on the carpet side by side. Then Dad rolled onto his side and propped himself up on his elbow. I held my breath again, sure that he must have seen me. But his eyes were focused on Eileen.

"What is it?" he asked her suddenly.

"You," she said with a smile. "You confuse me . . . maybe because I know your secret now. I just don't know what to do."

Secret? What secret?

"About what?" Dad asked, and I could hear the alarm in his voice.

Then Eileen whispered something I couldn't hear, but it made Dad's face change from worried to amused. He leaned down and kissed her. "So, you're worried that I'm just an innocent boy that can't handle being seduced by a beautiful woman."

Oh, God . . . I know exactly where this is headed. Now I'd have to figure out a way to erase that image from my memory.

Eileen laughed and then Dad was kissing her, his face buried in her neck, mumbling things I couldn't hear. I fought the urge to slap a hand over my eyes when he started fiddling with the buttons on her shirt. It was hard not to be creeped out and slightly offended watching your "parents" about to *get it on,* regardless of the circumstances.

I took a chance and emerged a little more from behind my hiding place, to get a better look at Dad's face before jumping back. It felt like an eternity since I'd seen him in France last week. He lifted his head for a second and stared at her, both their faces gleaming with the light from the fire. And I knew my assumption was right.

She really was Dad's Holly. And it really was a beautiful moment to see up close . . . creepy . . . but still beautiful.

But this was the nightmare every teenager fears. Watching their parents have sex. If I stayed any longer, I'd be scarred for life.

I closed my eyes and felt myself pulling back together. Joining the part of my body that had remained in 1992.

"Jackson?" I heard Eileen call from behind me.

I shook my head, feeling all the fatigue and pain hit me at once. "Uh . . . yeah . . . I'm here."

When I turned around to face her, she had her arms crossed, eyebrows lifted. "Did you just do something? . . . The half-jump, right?"

"No," I lied.

She rolled her eyes. "Nice try. Want to tell me what you just *had* to see?"

I shrugged. "Nothing important . . . you and him. It was only a couple minutes. I left before it got R-rated."

She blushed a little but held my gaze. "Is he . . . okay? I mean, in the future?"

A whole new idea took over. A brilliant plan. I straightened up and my voice came out louder than I had planned. "I can take you! Why the hell didn't I think of that hours ago?"

Her eyes were suddenly huge and she shook her head. "No, Jackson . . . we can't do that. It's too dangerous."

But you're going to die anyway, I wanted to say, but I didn't. "You said my mind would keep from hurting someone . . . that I'd control it."

"This isn't a situation of great need," she said. "Plus, think about how that would work . . . I disappear from this date and reappear in the future. Your memories and life will be altered. We don't know the effects it will have."

I reached for her hand, but she pulled it behind her. "He needs you. I know he does."

"Jackson, think about what you're saying." Her tone had changed, like she was trying to talk a suicidal man down from a ledge.

"But you love him and he doesn't have anyone now," I said, moving closer.

For some reason, I wanted this so much. For Dad, for me. This was something I could fix. And she knew things Dr. Melvin, Dad, and Marshall didn't know. I grabbed her hand and held it tight.

For the first time since my gun had been placed on the table, Eileen looked scared. Very scared of me. "Please don't do this, Jackson."

We stared at each other for several seconds while I spun the idea through my head. Wasn't this a benefit of my superpower? I should be able to get something I want from this, right?

Eileen spoke again, softer, less afraid. "It's not meant to be . . . Trust me."

And for some reason, I did trust her. But it totally sucked. My heart sank to the pit of my stomach, knowing the brilliant plan wouldn't be played out. I dropped her hand and let out a frustrated breath. "Fine . . . whatever."

"Jackson, it's not that I don't want to be with Kevin." She reached up to touch my face again. "I love him . . . more than you could ever know. I hope you believe that. But all you can do . . . all anyone can do . . . is love who you want to love, while they're here. Whatever obstacles come with that. Even if you know what happens in the future. Take the time that you're given and enjoy it."

"That's it?" I said almost sarcastically. "Not exactly very scientific."

"Most things don't need to be analyzed or put under a microscope. Either it is . . . or it isn't."

Another, less desperate idea formed. "Let me tell you how it happens and then . . . you can stop it . . . you can survive."

She nodded slowly. "Okay, tell me. Tell me what happens that day."

That was too easy . . . way too easy. "You're not going to stop it, though, are you? But how could you just . . . if you knew . . . There's no way you wouldn't avoid the situation—"

I stopped suddenly, running through the details of tonight. A sadness and frustration cold as ice washed over me. "You wrote things down. Someone like you would easily remember the conversation without taking notes."

She dropped her hands from my face and sighed. "Yes, I'd remember."

"You're gonna take something," I concluded. "Memory-modification drugs. You've got the details you absolutely need, and the rest . . . me . . . you're just going to erase it."

"Yes," she said, wiping a tear from the corner of her eye. A beeping sound rang through the quiet living room. Both of us glanced at the front door. "It's Agent Freeman. You should go . . . *now.*"

I nodded and watched the door as it started to slide open. I snatched my gun from the table and closed my eyes to jump back.

What kind of side effects would I have from this return to the future alone? Without the use of another time traveler's mind to protect my own . . . ?

CHAPTER THIRTEEN

I was in the exact same corridor that I'd left and I felt like hell. Times two. My wobbly legs trudged back down toward the main room. Stewart screeched to a halt at the end of my path.

"Did you find him?" she asked.

It took me a second to realize what she was talking about . . . that only minutes had passed for her. "Uh . . . no . . . what about Kendrick?"

"That little fucker, where the hell did he go?"

I shook my head, fighting the usual time-travel nausea and fatigue. Both of us had about a second to contemplate this before Kendrick, Mason, and some dude I'd never seen before came barreling down Kendrick's path. I had to assume the guy they were running from was an EOT.

Two more guys popped up right behind Stewart and both of us spun into action, pointing our guns at the newcomers. Stewart's face twisted with anger when a guy suddenly appeared behind her. She tucked the gun away and tackled the man to the floor.

The dude chasing after Mason and Kendrick reached for the hood of Mason's sweatshirt. I dove forward, grabbing him around the ankles, causing him to fall flat on his back, and just like the other guy earlier, his face filled with excitement when he realized who had just attacked him.

"Perfect," he said. "I've got something to show you."

I could feel him trying to jump, like Cassidy, but this time I was ready. I pulled every piece of my mind to this moment, right here. He hollered loudly, pressing his hands to the sides of his face.

My mind was slipping, fighting his efforts with every ounce of energy I had left.

"Stop! Stop!" he screamed.

Mason spun around and took in the situation. I released the man and left him writhing in agony on the floor. He curled into a ball, clutching his ears.

"Dude, what the hell did you just do?" Mason asked, staring at the man in disbelief.

I slowly sat up and could barely focus my eyes on anything. I didn't miss this aspect of time travel at all. "I . . . I don't know. He just—"

The man suddenly went still and I felt my pulse speed up with fear. *Please don't be dead.*

Mason reached down to check for a pulse and the color drained from his face. He lifted a hand from the man's head and blood gushed from his ear.

"Oh, God," I mumbled before glancing around the room desperately. "Kendrick! Get over here!"

My eyes returned to the bleeding man and I continued to stare until I heard footsteps behind me.

"It's from his last jump . . . must have been too far or too quick . . ." Kendrick said, and then her eyes met mine.

Do something, I tried to say without words. She sank down beside me and touched her fingers to the man's neck.

"Faint pulse," she muttered to herself. Her hands shook as she turned his head side to side and then she gasped when the other bloody ear was exposed. "His brain's bleeding, and . . . we have to relieve the pressure."

I could hear her starting to panic. The idea of slicing him open or doing anything other than basic first aid was more than she could handle. Blood covered her hands and stained her dress.

Mason stood over us and Stewart ran up behind him, a hand covering one of her eyes. "I injected my guy with the anti-time-travel drugs." She skidded to a stop. "Oh, man, what the fuck is going on here?"

"We don't know!" Kendrick hissed at her.

Stewart groaned and walked toward the man's legs, and before anyone could stop her she stabbed him in the thigh with a syringe. "There. He's not going anywhere. Now, if you guys could finish this little memorial service, we can retrieve the pieces of the explosive Junior took apart before something happens."

"She's right," Mason said. "We gotta do that."

Kendrick pressed her fingers harder against the man's neck. "He's gone . . . no pulse."

I felt sicker than ever as I peeled myself from the floor with great effort. The four of us headed toward the main opening where the elevators were and were finally joined by Parker and Freeman.

"It's about fucking time," Mason mumbled beside me.

I nodded my agreement. Freeman's eyes moved over us, one at a time. "You guys all right?"

Stewart was on my other side, still covering one eye. I turned to face her and pulled her hand away. Her eye was already swelling and she had a cut that had a steady stream of blood flowing from it. I pressed my fingers over the cut, trying to stop the bleeding.

She flinched and slapped my hand away. "Cut it out. I'm fine."

I wiped my bloody fingers on my pants. "So, what's the plan?" I asked, looking right at Freeman. He was the oldest, most experienced agent here. He should be telling the rest of us what to do.

"Is anyone still here?" he asked immediately. "By anyone, I mean EOTs."

Kendrick pointed down an empty hallway. "The one that just chased me disappeared over there. I think that's everyone." She turned her eyes on me and then back to Freeman. "Um . . . one is dead . . . just behind us. Nothing we did . . . From his last jump, most likely."

The nausea returned in one hard hit and Freeman's face blurred and then doubled.

"Jackson?" he said. "You okay?"

Mason rested a hand on my shoulder to steady me, but I hadn't even realized I needed it.

"Wait!" Stewart said, pointing a finger at me. "What happened to the chick with red hair? Isn't that the same one we caught in Heidelberg?"

She was right. I'd totally forgotten that Cassidy had been captured weeks ago. "Um . . . yeah . . . I think that was her, but she just left. I couldn't inject her fast enough."

"Don't forget, she might be a copy," Freeman said, as if we were talking about a painting in an art museum or something. "The rest of the group is evacuating the building above us. I'm not sure what the cover story is, so go with your best judgment if anyone approaches you. Dr. Melvin's going to freak out if we don't get him whatever's left of that explosive. He's positive it's the same one that we saw in Germany."

Stewart nodded toward the hallway behind Freeman and Parker. "It's this way."

Everyone began to walk quickly in the direction of the utility room. Mason lagged behind, still gripping my arm as I stumbled forward.

"Are you all right?" he asked, looking extremely worried.

"Yeah, I got hit on the head or something . . . probably a mild concussion." I held him back for a second and made sure the others couldn't hear us. "Hey, I'm sorry . . . about earlier."

His face reddened and he looked at the floor and nodded, like maybe he was embarrassed about his reaction. "It's fine."

"It's not that I doubted your skill. It's just that . . . it's okay to not always have the answers."

"Yeah . . . maybe," he said.

And when he looked at me again, all I could see was the scared freckle-faced kid, hiding behind the brainy, extremely stubborn agent.

As soon as we started walking again, Mason snorted loudly. "You would have never shot me, anyway."

I glanced at him and smiled. "You never know, man."

Even though my legs were about to collapse, I stumbled up toward Freeman and tapped him on the shoulder. "I'm guessing you didn't run into my dad or Marshall?"

He gave me a long hard look, then shook his head.

"Did Dr. Melvin tell you they put a timer on the bomb? It's totally weird . . . this and Heidelberg. Thomas had said in Germany they had some change or alteration in mind and then they just gave up. Why the big production?"

"Exactly what we were just talking about," Parker chimed in from Freeman's other side. "It's almost like they want to tell us something or—"

"Test us," Kendrick added. "We actually thought it might be Marshall testing us . . . with the whole ticking-time-bomb thing."

"Test you? Interesting theory," a deep voice spoke from farther down the hall.

All six of us stopped and turned to face twenty EOTs, all in one hallway. Thomas was front and center, the unwelcome answer to Kendrick's question.

"Holy shit," Stewart mumbled behind me.

Freeman stepped out in front of us, taking on his role of senior Tempest agent. "Wow, Thomas, this is quite an army you've brought."

Thomas stood with his arms crossed, wearing the ultimate poker face. "Well . . . things have changed a little recently."

Was he talking about me, opening up the alternate universe or whatever the hell Eileen had meant when she told me it was my fault so many of them could time-travel now? Or was it Dr. Ludwig's clones? Or both?

"Do you really think it's morally right to threaten the lives of all these innocent people?" Freeman said. "Are you aware of the amazing men and women gathered here tonight? Surely some of them will have a positive impact on the future."

Freeman was following the negotiation protocol exactly by the book. Talk first . . . then attack if needed. But twenty of them, against six of us—not great odds.

"Where is everyone else?" I muttered to Parker under my breath.

He pointed a finger toward the ceiling. "There's more EOTs upstairs."

More?

"Actually," Thomas said, "we believe there is far too much talent in your organization to go to waste. But we had to see for ourselves . . . test the waters a bit."

I could feel the tension building, could feel that all of us were just seconds from drawing our guns and waiting for the order to attack.

Thomas reached in his jacket pocket and pulled out a clear tube with blue liquid flowing from one end to the other. "This is what you wanted to retrieve, the remains of the explosive, correct?"

Freeman reached for his pistol, and the rest of us did the same.

Thomas and his cronies didn't even flinch at the sight of the six of us with guns pointed at them. "I imagine you're all curious about this substance," he continued with an eerie calm. "The blue liquid turns into a gas when released. It paralyzes everyone within ten feet for about an hour. It won't be discovered until the year 2200 and not widely used until the year 2210. Police, in that year, never carry a gun or harmful weapon. They release the gas on the suspect and he or she is detained without any harm to themselves or others. This is the kind of world we're trying to create for all of you . . . a peaceful place in which no one lives in fear."

I remembered the perfect future Thomas had shown me. It looked like the goal had already been met. But him "sacrificing" Holly had left me unable to trust him—ever. Feet shuffled around behind me. Everyone was getting restless, waiting for whatever would happen next. The previous encounters had all been much less personal.

"We have to stand by what we've been taught," Freeman said. "Surely you can understand that, Thomas."

"Of course . . . but I'm sure you have doubts." Thomas's gaze fell on me. "I know some of you must feel trapped in this position. Obligated to sacrifice everything, and for what, exactly?"

Now it was my turn to shift uncomfortably. Of course I had doubts. Lots of doubts. And this was the ultimate intimidation, because none of us had expected it.

"I think it's time we join forces," Thomas said. "It's inevitable, actually, and things will be much better if we can make this truce sooner."

"I'm sorry," Freeman said. "Even *I'm* not authorized to make those kinds of decisions."

No one was authorized for that because it was never an option . . . ever. You could hear the fear and confusion leaking into Freeman's voice.

"All right . . . I understand, and I'm sorry to hear that free will isn't something any of you practice," Thomas said.

Free will. There was that term again invading my thoughts for the second time tonight. And what did Thomas mean when he said we'd join forces eventually?

There was no time to think about it. Suddenly EOTs vanished from down the hall and jumped between us. Everywhere.

I knew I couldn't force them in or out of a jump. I was too beaten up already. Too weak. Bodies flew all around me, like a video in high-speed motion. I tossed someone over my back, then kicked another EOT in the face. My only goal at the moment was to keep them from jumping with me.

A foot came at me, hitting me hard in the side, slamming me against the wall. My vision blurred, but through the haze I saw a slight figure tearing away from the fight, diving under people, hurdling over them.

Once I realized it was Mason, I felt relieved at first, thinking he was running away . . . then I saw where he was headed and the EOT running after him, a tube of pink liquid sloshing in the EOT's right hand.

"Mason, no!" Stewart shouted. "Forget about the bomb!"

Both of us fought our way around the crowd and Thomas called out to the EOT trailing Mason. "Don't let him get to the weapon!"

"Mason! Get the hell out of there!" I yelled.

The EOT behind him glanced at Thomas and then tossed the pink tube into the utility room Mason had just entered.

"No!" I shouted at the same time Stewart shouted, "Mason!"

Simultaneously, we both drew our guns and fired a shot right at the EOTs back. He fell to the floor in a slump. The sound of shattering glass rang through the hallway just after the gunshot. My eyes zoomed in on

Thomas, who was running from the utility room that held the remaining bomb fragments, and then on Stewart, who was running toward the utility room, hurdling over the fallen EOT.

I grabbed her around the waist and tackled her to the floor. She only had about half a second to fight me, and then the loudest explosion I'd ever heard in my life filled the small space.

The sound echoed in my ears and I couldn't hear anything else. Instinctively, I threw an arm over my head and one over Stewart's. Tiny pieces of wood and plaster flew at us from every direction. I squeezed my eyes shut and tried to jump, but my mind couldn't focus on anything but here . . . right now.

The ringing in my ears quieted and voices shouted all around me.

"Oh, God . . . Mason," Kendrick said.

"Jackson!" Freeman called.

I rolled off Stewart, who sat up, looking stunned. We were both covered in dust and debris from the explosion. She glanced at me wide-eyed and then sprang to her feet. I watched as she ran in the direction of the explosion and then screeched to a stop, staring at the hole in the wall that used to be the utility room.

The reality must have hit me at the same time as it hit Stewart.

Mason is in there . . . was in there.

I peeled myself off the floor and walked up next to Stewart. She was shaking her head . . . eyes still huge.

"No . . . no way. He got out. I know he did. There's got to be some escape or . . ." My voice trailed off and both of us continued to stare.

"Jackson!" I heard Dr. Melvin shout.

I spun around and saw him and Senator Healy sifting through the mess to get to us. But it was Healy who reached me first and placed both his hands on my shoulders. "Are you okay, son?"

His tone was completely different than earlier. This was genuine concern.

"Mason . . . he's . . ." I couldn't say it out loud.

Stewart swallowed hard and then spun around to face Healy. "He's dead . . . blown up into tiny bits."

The anger in her voice was so thick it hit me like a punch in the stomach. This was the most emotion I'd ever seen her show. I reached out and touched her shoulder. "Stewart . . ."

She slid away from me, holding both hands up in front of my face. "Don't . . . just shut the hell up—all of you."

Freeman tried to stop her from walking away, but she shoved him against the wall and took off running. I was still weak and frozen to my spot, but I didn't miss the complete devastation on Dr. Melvin's face and the long look he gave me, and maybe I was imagining it, but it seemed like he was asking me to fix it. Or just wishing I could.

But it didn't work like that, did it?

Kendrick stared at me for a second, her eyes filling with tears, and then she ran after Stewart, but I knew she'd be right back. If Stewart wanted to be alone, she would be alone.

I leaned against the wall and closed my eyes, hoping everything would be different when I opened them.

"Get him some water," I heard Healy shout to someone. Then cold fingers touched a tender spot on my cheek. "What happened, Jackson? Did someone take you with them? It's okay to tell me. All the EOTs are gone," Healy said.

I opened my eyes again and glanced past Healy to see Dr. Melvin still staring at me. "I'm sorry," I said to him. "We tried to stop him, I swear."

He nodded his head slowly and then walked closer, jumping into doctor mode. "Let me check your pulse. And yes, you should have some water, Jackson."

Healy backed away and let Dr. Melvin take my wrist.

"I'm sorry," I said again to Dr. Melvin. "He just went in there and . . . I don't know . . ."

"I know . . . *I know*," he said, but his voice cracked.

The nausea from my earlier jumps, and from all the drinking, hit me at once, and next thing I knew, my head was hanging over a white porcelain sink and I was staring down at my own vomit. I barely noticed Senator Healy handing me a bottle of water in the bathroom or him asking me if I was all right. All I could manage to do was try and shake the blurriness from my head and stay on my feet. Nothing else mattered at the moment.

An hour later, the mission group was in the underground classrooms. Stewart was nowhere to be found and none of us wanted to talk about it. Most of us were sure that Freeman would have us on a flight back to France within the hour, and honestly, I couldn't wait to get out of here.

I slumped farther down in the chair I had fallen into the second we entered the room. Freeman and Parker sat on either side of me, upright and alert, instead of leaning on their desks for support like I was.

"Though many of you may have just learned this information in the past week," Senator Healy said, pacing in front of the fourteen Tempest agents, "my position in this agency is meant to be a silent one. However, in both Chief Marshall and Agent Meyer Senior's absence, I'm left with no choice but to take over as your commanding officer."

"What the hell happened tonight? Obviously someone wanted to lock us all up together so we couldn't do a damn thing about the EOT attack," Parker blurted out. "Who infiltrated our alert system? I didn't think that was possible."

Senator Healy glanced at Dr. Melvin, who sat at the desk in the front of the room, leaning on his elbows. He pulled himself up straighter and nodded before saying, "There are always ways around our security. The Tech Support Team is already working on identifying the source."

"Tonight's event . . . the loss of a very valuable agent . . . is going to be difficult for all of us to deal with," Healy said. "I encourage each and every one of you to offer support to your teammates and take some time to rest and recover so we can be strong and prepared for next time."

This speech was already the complete opposite of Chief Marshall's usual suck-it-up-and-move-on lectures.

"Where is Marshall, anyway?" an agent from across the room asked. "And Agent Meyer? Why did we do this mission without them if it was going to be so difficult?"

More sounds of frustration followed his question, as if everyone were thinking the same thing. Including me.

"Unfortunately, I have some more bad news." Healy shook his head, looking grim. I held my breath, feeling my heart thud with renewed fear despite my exhaustion. "We lost contact with Agent Meyer and Chief Marshall three days ago."

Silence fell over the entire room. After several long seconds, I found my voice and managed to croak out a couple words. "Three days?"

Healy and Dr. Melvin exchanged a look, and then Healy said with a sigh, "I think all of us are going to have to accept the possibility, given certain evidence, that Agent Meyer may have accepted a bribe from Eyewall—not the group you all were hunting tonight, but the people responsible for that group's presence in this year."

Future Eyewall. The clone makers.

But Healy was wrong. Dad would never take a bribe from them . . . *ever*. He'd never leave me alone unless he absolutely had to.

"What about Chief Marshall?" someone asked. "Did he take a bribe, too? Maybe he handed them Agent Meyer to get himself out of a bind."

Okay, another Dad fan. Good to know.

"Agent Meyer has a very specific motive for accepting help from the EOTs," Healy said immediately. "One I can't share with any of you at this time, but it makes the evidence a bit more concrete."

I could feel all eyes on me, as if I had the answer to this unspoken question. As if I knew what would be more important to Dad than staying with me. I didn't know. I had no idea. And I really needed to find him and to tell him that I'd done a Thomas-jump. I needed his help more than ever right now.

"But he's alive?" I blurted out.

Healy's face tightened. "We believe so."

"Are we going back to France or what?" Agent Parker asked.

It was Freeman who spoke this time. "We did manage to gain some insight into Eyewall during tonight's mission. There's a lot of data to review and it's worth sticking around for at least forty-eight hours."

I sighed and forced my heart to slow back down to a normal pace. *It's only two more days.* I just needed to focus on finding a way to contact Dad. This would be considered a situation of great need and might call for a time jump . . . assuming I could even manage it.

It was nearly two in the morning by the time everyone started to file out, slowly, like stepping back into the real world would force us to think about Thomas's speech . . . about Mason.

"Jackson?" Senator Healy called to me before I stepped out the door. "Can I have a word with you?"

I glanced at Kendrick, who I assumed would want to ride home together.

"Dr. Melvin wants me to help him with something in the lab," she said, exhaustion filling her voice. "It's just down the hall. I'll wait for you."

I nodded to her and Healy closed the door after the last agent walked out. He gestured for me to sit down again and I did, mostly because standing was difficult. The old man slid behind the desk across from me, angling his chair slightly so we were facing each other.

"I just wanted to see how you were doing," he said gently. "You can't let yourself feel responsible for what's happened tonight. No one expects you to be able to fix this. I hope you know that . . . ?"

I shrugged but didn't say anything. It wasn't that simple. *And it never will be.*

He sighed like he could read my thoughts. "We aren't going to give up trying to contact your dad. No matter what the protocol tells us, I won't stop searching. He's a good man. No matter what any of the other agents tell you, don't doubt what you know to be true."

I didn't want Healy to know how close Dad and I were, so I shifted the subject. "I'm having trouble thinking about anything except all those EOTs. Do they have, like, a dozen cloning machines in the future or something?"

Healy scrutinized my face, maybe checking to see if I had gone into shock yet, but shock seemed to come a lot slower for me these days. "Dr. Melvin is very ashamed of his years spent trying to make cloning a real process, attempting to get government funding for such projects. Without his research, we might not have many enemies to battle. It was a foolish boy's dream. But it takes age and experience to fully comprehend the weight of one's actions."

Poor Dr. Melvin. And I thought I was living with guilt. "Why did you tell me that Kendrick was important to this division? Are you related or something?"

"No, nothing like that, Jackson," he said with a slight smile. "I don't know all the details, Marshall told me as little as possible, but she is supposed to discover a cure for a deadly epidemic that will plague the future. I believe that's one reason the EOTs may spare her life."

"Seriously? Does Dr. Melvin know this? And won't the EOTs know whatever magic medicine she's destined to make and they can just make it themselves?"

He shrugged. "Apparently they prefer not to adjust events that don't need adjusting. Mess with as little as possible and hope to shape everything perfectly. And Dr. Melvin doesn't know any of this and you aren't going to tell him. He'd spend the rest of his life trying to discover something he was never meant to find . . . He'd kill himself trying."

I let out a frustrated breath. "Okay, but why does she have to be in Tempest? Can't she just work in some lab and keep out of the way of explosions and whatever else we have to put up with?"

"First of all, she *wants* to be here. For reasons I don't understand." His face turned more serious. "But your idea was the exact option I presented to Chief Marshall. However, he felt her skills were too valuable to not use her as an agent . . . and now she'll never be allowed out. Not alive, anyway. But if she continues to study medicine and stays free of distraction, she can still make her discovery."

The not-allowed-out part wasn't a surprise. I had already assumed that for all of us, but it didn't make it any easier to swallow. I leaned my head against my hands and rubbed the blurriness from my eyes.

I felt Healy rest a hand on my shoulder. "Jackson, you should go and get some rest. I've already said too much. I'm truly sorry for everything you've been through tonight."

"It's all part of the job, right?" I slowly stood up before retreating down the hall to find the lab Kendrick had mentioned.

Kendrick was already slipping out the door as I walked up. We both looked at each other for a long moment. Neither of us knew what to say. Her hair had slipped out of the careful updo from earlier tonight and her hands and face had traces of blood and dirt. She looked like hell and I'm sure I did, too.

"Ready to go?" I asked her.

She nodded, and both of us headed out in silence. There was nothing to say. Not tonight.

Kendrick's hands shook so badly, she couldn't get the key into the lock of her apartment door. I slowly took it from her hand and opened the door. The gust of air-conditioning hit us and her eyes lifted to meet mine.

"Thanks," she said.

"Lily!"

We both stepped through the door, surprised to see Michael up and dressed, the TV blaring. He was supposed to be out of town. "Thank God! I've been watching the news for hours. I came back from Long Island as soon as I heard about the accident at the Plaza. I've been calling your cell all night . . . I was sure . . ." His voice cracked and he stopped talking and looked at me, then at Kendrick. "What happened to you? Is that . . . *blood*?"

Senator Healy had told us there was no hiding the explosion from the media, but to the public, the EOTs' weird bomb was actually an electrical explosion in the boiler room. I had no clue how many memories had been modified tonight and I couldn't think about it now.

Kendrick glanced at me and her eyes widened like it had just occurred to her that she couldn't be the shocked agent in the presence of her unsuspecting fiancé. "Well . . . it's just . . . well . . . first we went . . ."

I jumped in to help her because the stuttering was too much to handle. "Luckily, we weren't anywhere near the explosion, but this little kid and his mom were hurt and Kendrick . . . I mean, Lily tried to . . . you know—"

"Stop the bleeding," she finished for me.

Michael flopped down onto the couch with a huge sigh of relief. "God, Lil, that must have been awful. I don't think I've ever been so worried in my entire life. What happened with the kid?"

She looked at me again for a second, tears already falling, then she walked across the room and curled up next to Michael, hiding her face in his shirt. He wrapped an arm around her and reached his other hand down to pull off her shoes.

I knew she was thinking about Mason right now and that she didn't want to fall apart in front of me. But Michael didn't expect her to be tough. He was okay with this softer, less confident version of Kendrick. I turned around and left them alone, heading toward my still-nearly-empty apartment.

The first thing I did was take a long hot shower and wash the grime and guilt off of me. Then I lay in bed and dialed Stewart's number half a dozen times but got no answer. It wasn't that I really wanted to be around her, but everything basically sucked for her tonight and I was afraid she might get a little crazy or something . . .

After only a few minutes, the weight of Mason being gone and Stewart's reaction overwhelmed me so much that I time-jumped out of instinct . . . The need to do *something* was too strong to ignore. I had to try, knowing Thomas-jumps might not be out of my ability range. Could I save Mason? Could I change what happened? Just a few hours. That was all I'd need. And then after this, whether it worked or not, I'd have to shut down again. Turn off that part of me that was becoming attached to people I'd never wanted to let in.

CHAPTER FOURTEEN

"Damn!" *Dad's voice.*

"This is your fault, Agent Meyer!" *Chief Marshall.*

Chief Marshall stood beside Dad, his hands raised in the air. Dr. Melvin stared at the empty space on the other side of the room. No one even noticed me.

That was when I saw him. Lying at their feet. The man named Harold . . . supposedly one of Dr. Ludwig's clones. I couldn't be *here*, could I? My eyes traveled to the couch, and sure enough, she was there. Passed out. Hair falling around her face.

007 Holly.

The empty space Dr. Melvin stared at . . . that was where the other me had vanished . . . the exact moment I'd left 2007 and finally made it back to 2009.

I barely heard Dr. Melvin clear his throat, trying to get Dad and Marshall to notice me. This moment, the fact that I abandoned *this* Holly, had never left my mind. Everything was exactly how I'd envisioned it: Holly still lying here, waiting for me to come back.

"Jackson?" Dad said.

I looked up at him absentmindedly, before remembering how much I'd wanted to see him. All the days that had passed with virtually no contact. The only problem was, based on the events from this version of 2007, I knew I had landed in a different timeline. Not what I'd intended to do at all. But it wasn't much different than seeing him in a half-jump.

"His clothes are different," Chief Marshall said, scrutinizing my face with his X-ray vision.

"Uh . . . yeah," I muttered, then walked closer to Holly.

"Jackson, you need to give us some time to explain everything before you try to do anything else," Dad said, moving toward me. "I promise Dr. Melvin will tell you all about Axelle."

I looked at Dad again and then at Dr. Melvin, trying to figure out what he meant. "I already know about Axelle. Why—" *Oh, wait. Now I get it.* They were under the impression that I was both scared and not trusting any of them. Hadn't I done a half-jump out of this exact moment with Chief Marshall's hands around my throat? *The jump that led me to that hospital room with Courtney.* Seemed like years ago. "It's fine, Dad. I understand."

"You do?" Marshall asked.

"Yep." I knelt down in front of Holly. "Dr. Melvin, how long is she going to be out?"

He gaped at me, his mouth hanging open. "Uh . . . a couple hours, probably . . . are you *all right*?"

"I'm fine." I shook her shoulders a little. "Holly? Hol?"

She mumbled something incoherent and rolled toward me, but her eyes stayed closed. I wasn't sure what, exactly, I wanted to tell her, but I hated the idea of this moment being suspended. Hanging by a thread while I lived a different life in another timeline.

I shouldn't be forced to choose . . . or maybe I shouldn't be allowed to choose.

Dad knelt beside me. "Jackson . . . where did you come from . . . just now?"

"2009."

"Again? Or for the first time?" Dr. Melvin asked.

I sat down on the floor in front of the couch. "Again, but I've already been here . . . I mean, a lot of stuff has happened *since* I've been here."

"Like what?" Dad asked.

I laughed under my breath. "Like me being a Tempest agent."

Dad and Dr. Melvin started to talk at the same time, but Marshall held up a hand to stop them. "Don't tell us any more. You need to return to that other timeline. It's the best way to ensure everyone's safety."

I stood up and nodded. "I know how it works . . . I was actually trying to do something else . . ." I glanced at Dr. Melvin again. "The complete jump, or whatever you call it . . . Obviously it didn't work."

"So your mission wasn't to end up here?" Marshall asked.

I shook my head. "No. Am I allowed to ask questions?"

Marshall raised his eyebrows, but Dad nodded.

"What if . . . hypothetically, I haven't seen you in a while? Like if Freeman lost contact with you. Should I be worried?"

Dad's and Dr. Melvin's faces tightened, then Dad said, "No, never worry about me until there's something to worry about." He faked a smile. "No news is good news, right?"

"Right." Clearly, he didn't realize I'd been trained as a human lie detector for the past three months. "When did Senator Healy become a Tempest agent?"

"Senator Healy?" Chief Marshall said. "No, not possible."

"He's not the backup chief? Not even in a different timeline?" I asked desperately. How could they not know this? "And it's two years in the future."

"I suppose it's possible," Dad answered slowly, but all of them looked doubtful.

Maybe this alternate world was *really* different than the one I came from. Maybe Thomas had been fooling around with that other timeline.

I knew Marshall was right. I needed to go, because the side effects of time travel would hit me hard after last night. Except Dad was here. And one of my Hollys . . . a version of her that actually liked me . . . was here.

Dad rested a hand on my shoulder. "I'm sorry, Jackson . . . about everything. Your life is complicated, but that doesn't mean I don't care."

"I know, Dad. Really, I do." I wanted to ask him about the bribe or whatever Healy had mentioned in 2009, but not in front of Chief Marshall.

Then I did something I hadn't done in years . . . I hugged my dad. And a small part of me expected him to be defensive or reluctant, but he hugged me back without asking any questions.

"Take care of Holly . . . and Adam," I whispered to him before letting go. "Just in case I have to come back here or . . . Just because . . . okay?"

He let go of me and stepped back. "I will."

The dead guy on the floor caught my attention again and then I looked down at Holly, before deciding to move her somewhere else. "I'm going to get her out of here . . . in case she wakes up soon." Her head hung limply over my arm after I picked her up and I had to be careful not to ram her into a wall. None of them said anything or even followed me as I walked to my room.

Adam was out cold, lying sideways across the bed. I set Holly down by the pillows and covered her with a blanket. She'd wake up next to Adam, who would know exactly how to explain the situation to her, except she wouldn't know why I'd kissed her . . . and let her read my letter to Courtney and then abandoned her, leaving her to go hook up with David or Brian "the jock strap" in a few months.

It doesn't matter. It didn't matter. What I needed to do right now was to be an agent on a mission. Hold it together and not let myself sink into the reality of this timeline. *It's not personal, it's business.*

And the memory of Courtney's letter gave me an idea. I grabbed some paper and a pen and sat down at my desk. I could at least leave Holly with something.

"Oh, God . . . who hit me over the head?"

I jumped and then sighed with relief when I saw Adam attempting to sit up, squinting from the bright desk lamp. It wasn't until he was completely upright, staring at me, that I realized how long it had been since I'd seen him. Much longer than Holly.

Don't do it, Jackson. Don't get sucked into this world where you have friends and people who might have to die for you.

"How do you feel?"

"Like shit," he mumbled. "Fucking hell. Did I really drink *that* much?"

I couldn't remember. "Well, I think the CIA may have drugged you. They gave Holly something."

He crawled toward the other end of the bed and picked up her foot, tapping it lightly. "She's got no reflexes . . . What the hell happened? Another attack, like Friday?"

I turned to face him and took a deep breath. "Sort of, but for me, last night was a really long time ago . . . months, actually."

Adam shook his head and banged it lightly against the back of his hand. "Damn . . . is this a half-jump? I'm really getting sick of hearing about these and not remembering anything."

"No, it's real. You'll remember it. But when I leave and go back to that other timeline, none of this will have happened there."

He straightened up. Comprehension seemed to hit him all at once. "What about the other you? The one that I partied with last night. Did you . . . live through that already?"

"Yeah, but I don't think that me is coming back—"

"Hold up a sec," he said, jumping off the bed.

I waited while he walked into the bathroom and splashed water on his face. "Okay, I'm awake. Now tell me everything."

Just leave. Leave now before this gets harder. But I couldn't. Not yet.

It didn't take as long as I had anticipated to explain the very basic events of the last few months. Adam hadn't taken a handful of caffeine pills this time, either, so he wasn't constantly interrupting with more questions. And I left out a lot of details.

"I can't believe you're working for them . . . And this experiment is totally creepy. How do you know for sure they're not—"

"I just know, okay?" I interrupted. "Trust me."

"Are you sure you have to go back?" he asked.

"Pretty sure." I stared down at the blank page in front of me. "Do you think the other me, the one that disappeared from Spain, will just appear again?"

"That's the most logical answer. . . except a few weeks have gone by. Will your other self wonder what happened to all those days?" Adam asked.

"Yes."

We both turned around and saw Dad standing in the doorway. "Really?" I asked.

Dad walked in the room slowly and sat down on the couch. "Dr. Melvin and I were just discussing how to handle this situation. We have a few options. One, we create a cover story for the seventeen-year-old Jackson. An accident that resulted in a three-week coma with memory loss. Or two, we tell him everything about Axelle, about his future abilities. I feel a little more confident presenting this option now that I've seen how well you've handled the information."

"But if Jackson doesn't know he can time-travel, or that he'll be able to time-travel," Adam protested, obviously not trusting Dad or the CIA, "that might be pretty hard to believe."

Dad continued to watch my face carefully. "There *is* an option three . . . You could just stay here."

The idea was appealing in a way that I knew wasn't right. Holly and Adam were at risk around me. They needed to go back to their lives and forget about me. And I had too many puzzles to solve in 2009.

I already let her go. If I stay, I'll have to go through all that again . . . eventually.

I was still deep in thought when I realized Dad was looking at me expectantly. "You want my opinion?" I asked.

He smiled a little. "I figured you'd know yourself better than we would."

Adam snorted really loud. "Uh . . . no, he doesn't. Given the fact that you lied to him his entire life."

So true. Seventeen-year-old me had no idea what was coming a year from now . . . that first time jump . . . but Dad and Dr. Melvin had some idea, even before I landed in 2007 for the second time. "Go with the accident story," I said reluctantly. "But tell the truth after it happens . . . the first time jump . . . and maybe some of that other stuff we've talked about."

The lines on Dad's face deepened, but he nodded and I knew he understood what I meant: talk to me about Courtney . . . maybe Eileen. Don't let two years go by with a wall between us.

"Wait . . . we're friends, right? In that other timeline? You updated *that* me and everything?" Adam asked, panic rising in his voice.

I could feel my heart race and I tried to slow it down. Dad would notice, but I doubted he'd say anything. I faked a grin, raising my head to look Adam in the eye. "Yeah, of course. That's the deal, right?"

To my relief, he returned the grin, looking even younger than I remembered. *He's only sixteen . . . a year younger than Mason in 2009.* I got up and sat beside Holly, picking up one of her hands and squeezing it.

"What should I tell her?" Adam asked quietly.

His words hung thick in the air, and the thought of him telling Holly I was gone hurt so much that I forced myself to shut down again, to rationalize, like I had done these past three months—until the mission in New York. "You'll tell her that I took off . . . maybe to Spain or somewhere else across the world to comfort a dying relative. She'll be upset . . . She'll probably cry and get pissed at you for not waking her up." I swallowed hard and kept my voice perfectly even. "Then she'll get over it."

And then she'll go out with David or Brian . . . go to college . . .

"Just like that," Adam said, shaking his head in disbelief.

"Yep. Just like that . . . It's statistically proven. The CIA collects this type of data all the time. When an agent builds a relationship with a potential source and then abandons them, eighty-five percent of sources show no signs of grieving or change in emotional behavior beyond two weeks." I went back to the desk and picked up the pen again. "I'll even write a note, help with the cover story."

Dad stood up and walked toward the door. "I'll let Dr. Melvin and Chief Marshall know what the plan is. Come see me before you—"

"Sure," I said, cutting him off. "If that's what you want."

Adam's eyes were clearly fixated on me as I began to write. "Dude, what's going on with you?"

"You mean, besides the obvious," I said, not looking up from the paper. The flat emotionless tone that came out of my mouth surprised even me.

"Fine . . . whatever," he grumbled, flopping back onto the bed. "It's not like I could ever *help* you with anything."

His sarcasm really pissed me off. This was hard enough without Adam making me feel guilty. He had other friends besides me. He'd be fine. I was going back to a place where I didn't trust *anyone*. Even that version of Holly had been playing mind games with me at Healy's ball.

I knew that was different than having a highly trained agent screwing with my head, but still . . . it was *Holly*.

"Everything's gonna be fine. You have nothing to worry about. Both of you will be placed under the best protection the CIA can offer," I recited mechanically.

"Great. A real comfort . . . especially after witnessing your transformation from my friend to some order-following robot."

I ground my teeth together and reached for a new piece of paper. He wasn't going to get to me. Not here in this timeline where I knew I couldn't stay.

He walked closer and started reading over my shoulder. "*Dear Holly. I apologize for leaving so abruptly. A lot of things in my life are complicated right now. This wasn't an easy decision for me* . . . You forgot to say, *It's not you, it's me.*"

I covered the paper with my arm and looked up at him, keeping my face as calm as possible. "This is personal."

He groaned and shook his head. "No, it's not, man . . . not even a little."

Ouch. I ignored him and went back to writing, but a couple seconds later he pulled the paper right out from under my hand. I stood up, reaching for the letter. "Seriously, cut it out."

Adam's face twisted with anger and he ripped the page in half before I could stop him. "She loves you!"

"Don't—"

"Holly loves you and you expect me to give her this bullshit letter and wait for her to just forgive and forget . . . That's the most demented thing I've ever heard." He dropped the pieces onto the floor and threw me a disgusted look. "I told you not to mess around with her . . . but that's all right . . . You can go back to whatever version of Holly you've got waiting for you and I'll take care of this one."

He was so close, staring right at me, and I couldn't cover it up. My heart sank and the grief was all over my face. Adam's anger dissolved in about two seconds. "What happened . . . ? Did she get shot again, or . . . ?"

I shook my head but didn't say anything else.

"Come on . . . you gotta tell me. Is something going to happen here, like, in the future?" He grasped my arm, forcing me to stay right in front of him.

"The only thing you need to do is keep her away from the other me," I said a little too forcefully.

Adam stepped back and dropped his hand. "I just don't get it. You were so pissed that your dad lied to you . . . and you just told him to keep you in the dark until the time travel starts. How do you know telling the other you about what you'll be able to do in the future won't help it to happen earlier . . . or maybe you *won't* think it's that crazy? And maybe I could help that version of you, and tell Holly about some of it. She could at least see the other you that way."

"No!" I said. "Do you know what that version of me would do to Holly? Because I have a pretty good idea. He has no reason to talk to you, either."

Adam's arms folded over his chest. "So *that's* what you really think . . . that if you weren't trying to figure out why you could time-travel in 2009, you would have never become friends with someone like me? You talk about that guy like he's a different person. It's still *you,* Jackson."

I didn't know if he was right about the reasoning behind our friendship. There was no way to repeat that process and find out for sure. But I couldn't even attempt to swallow the idea of 007 Holly hooking up with the seventeen-year-old me. I knew *exactly* what went on in *his* head.

"Don't do it, Adam," I pleaded. "Promise me you'll let it go."

"Okay, fine . . . so you're not with Holly in the future alternate universe or whatever. I get it," he said, more exasperated now than angry. "But you're alive. You can keep jumping. How do you know there's not some tiny sliver of hope that it'll work out? Don't you want to leave her with something better than that garbage you wrote, just in case you come back?"

Hadn't I just said that to Dad a few minutes ago, when I told him to take care of Adam and Holly?

I sighed and rested a hand on her cheek. "I don't know. I just don't know what's better," I admitted.

"She won't hate you for leaving. Neither will I," he said. "Do you ever think maybe it's just meant to be . . . that Holly's always going to love you . . . all those versions of her . . . and even someone with super-powers like you can't keep it from happening?"

The way he said this wasn't manipulative or a guilt trip, it was a real question, so I allowed myself to process it. "The timeline I just came from . . . that Holly . . . doesn't like me at all, and she's got someone else. And the first Holly I met . . . she really didn't have the best im-pression of me." I shrugged, like it didn't matter, like it didn't hurt. "So, there's your answer, I guess."

He shocked me by laughing. "Well, all the versions of me have liked you, so at least you have that."

"Gee, I wonder why," I joked. "The dimples, right? Not the fascinating-freak-of-nature part."

He gave my shoulder a hard shove, but he was still laughing. "Fi-nally, the robot's gone. Now write a decent love letter, asshole."

It only took about half a second to decide what to write. Five words . . . that was all I needed to say. I quickly folded the paper and stuffed it inside her purse. I heard Dad call my name from the other room.

"Can you tell him I'll be right there?" I asked Adam.

"Yeah, sure," he said, walking out the door and shutting it behind him.

I lay down beside Holly again and rolled her on her side to face me. "Holly? Wake up . . ."

Her eyelids fluttered a little and opened halfway.

"Holly?" I tried again.

"Does my mom know you're in my bed?" she mumbled.

I smiled at her even though she couldn't see me. The second my arm draped over her waist, she scooted closer and curled up against me. "Actually, you're in my bed."

"Yeah," she said with a sigh. "It smells like you."

I had to get away from here . . . or else I wouldn't. I kissed her cheek and spoke right in her ear, "Don't fall in love with any football players."

Her eyes flew open and she shot up, nearly banging her head into mine. "Did I . . . did I drink a lot of champagne or something . . . ?"

I sat up, too, and smoothed her hair down with my hand. "Um . . . you might have. I'm not sure."

She glanced around my bedroom and I just stared at her, letting a million different emotions flood over me and bury me . . . Then my hands were on her face. Just as she opened her mouth to speak again, my lips were on hers.

Her response was immediate. She had her hands on the back of my neck, fingers in my hair, then under my shirt.

"I have to tell you something," I mumbled against her mouth.

"Yeah?" She pressed her mouth harder against mine and then pulled back a little. She lay down on the pillow again and I could see her eyelids fluttering as if she couldn't hold them open.

"I just . . . it's just . . ." I rested my head beside hers and felt around for her hand before squeezing it. "Nothing is easy for me. Being here with you . . . being without you . . . it's all so hard, and it feels like I'll never be able to breathe again . . ."

She kissed me once more, pressing her whole body against mine. After several long seconds, she pulled away, but kept her arms around me as if she knew I was about to leave her. "You love me," she said.

"Yes, but—"

"That's why it's hard. I know what you mean . . . I didn't want to love you . . . I didn't even want to like you, but I do." She smiled as if she were joking, but I knew she was just playing it cool, in case she revealed more than I had. "This would be much easier if your Dad really was a janitor."

Oh right . . . I almost forgot the lie I originally told about my family to 007 Holly.

I'd have to be a complete idiot to leave this girl. An absolute moron. I buried my face in her hair, holding on to her for a long time, and then I kissed her cheek before letting go.

She was breathing deep again, eyes sealed shut in a drug-induced sleep. I slid off the bed and gave her one more kiss on the cheek. It took every ounce of willpower I had to not crawl under the covers with her and fall asleep . . .

I stepped into the hallway and immediately felt the presence of someone. The slightest shuffle of feet . . . the almost-silent breath that was just drawn in. I flung the hall closet door open and reached blindly into the dark for something to grab. My fingers wrapped around a shirt and I yanked the owner out, surprised by the lack of weight. I pressed the person against the wall and finally got a good look at the scrawny freckle-faced kid.

"Mason!" My hands were already shaking. Images of his body dissolving to bits reeled through my mind and I couldn't push them out.

"Jackson, it's okay, he's one of us!" Dad said from the other end of the hall.

I came here to save Mason, to fix him . . . I had almost forgotten. Maybe I needed to know more or something, so I could jump more purposefully. "Mason, you gotta tell me something . . . some personal info . . . something that will help me—"

"Let go of me!"

"Jackson?" Dr. Melvin said. "Is this why you're here?"

Mason lifted his foot and gave me a hard kick in the stomach before I could stop him. I stumbled back into the wall, clutching my midsection. Mason's eyes darted between me and Dr. Melvin and Dad . . . Comprehension came quicker than I thought it would, and his entire face filled with panic. Fifteen-year-old agent-in-training Mason drew a gun and pointed it right at me. "It's you, isn't it? You're the experiment. I heard you talking to your friend about Axelle."

"Mason . . ." Dr. Melvin said.

I lifted my hands up in front of me, not able to hide the shaking fear in my voice. "I really have to help you . . . Not here . . . Maybe I just need to know things about you . . . anything."

Maybe, if I could get a better feel for Mason's life before I knew him, I'd be able to do the Thomas-jump to help him. Strong emotional memories always seemed to take my power to a higher level.

He lowered the gun, his eyes locked with mine. "What happens to me? What's going to happen?"

"Do not tell him anything!" Marshall boomed, fighting his way into the hall. "Agent Sterling, you will hand over your gun and leave immediately."

Mason didn't budge and I wasn't all that surprised by his stubbornness. I'd seen it before many times. "Tell me what happened!"

"No!" Dad and Marshall said together.

Then everything that followed happened in a five-second blur. Mason pointed his gun down the hall and fired straight over everyone's head. They dove down anyway and he came charging at me full-speed.

He threw a hard punch right at my jaw. "I fucking hate you! If you weren't around, they wouldn't even come after me . . . or any of us . . . It's because of you!"

His anger hit me so hard, I couldn't even fight back. "I'm sorry, Mason . . . I'll fix it . . . I'll fix everything . . . I swear."

"Jackson, go . . . get out of here!" Adam shouted, but I couldn't even see him.

I caught Dad's eye from the opposite end of the hall. He gave me a tiny nod, just as another one of Mason's blows hit me right in the temple.

I shoved Mason off me and dove into the bathroom, but I only waited a second before jumping back to 2009.

CHAPTER FIFTEEN

I must have fallen asleep right after jumping back to 2009, because when I finally opened my eyes and took in the borrowed CIA apartment, light was streaming through the windows.

And there was an intruder sitting on the end of my bed.

I leaped up, tossing blankets aside and nearly tripping over Mason's duffel bag . . . the one I had brought with me last night from his locker in the underground lab. The intruder sat with an eerie calm as I caught my breath and prevented my own heart attack.

Jenni Stewart.

Not the usual Agent Stewart, this was the train-wreck version. She still wore her clothes from last night, dried blood, grime, and all, her hair flying in a dozen directions. She looked absolutely demented. I kept one hand wrapped around my phone, which I must have fallen asleep holding on to.

"Stewart . . . I've been trying to call you?" I said, walking back toward the bed.

She lifted up a pink notebook, covering her face with it. "Recognize this?"

"No," I said right away, and then looked closer. It was just some kind of journal or diary. Actually, Holly had one like that . . . 009 Holly. So, this 009 Holly would probably have the same notebook. But where was Stewart going with this? She saw us dancing last night, maybe? Or overheard some of the conversation? It didn't matter. I'd lie and deny anything more than what she'd seen.

She slowly opened the notebook and read a little yellow Post-it pressed to the inside cover. "*Jackson, this was left in my hands and you should have it. It might help.*" She looked up at me, raising her eyebrows. "This is your dad's writing . . ."

My heart raced. "Is he here? Have you talked to him?"

"No," she said quietly, and I could see that her disappointment reflected mine.

"I have no idea why he left that for me. And *me* is the key word here . . . not *you*."

She laughed a slightly insane cackle. "Right . . . it happens to belong to the girl you danced with last night. Short . . . blond hair—"

"I know what she looks like," I snapped. "Again . . . I don't know her and I have no business reading any of her personal belongings, and neither do you."

"Really? That's funny, because you're all over this thing." She flipped to the middle of the book and I held my breath, waiting. "June twenty-third, 2009. *When I get to camp this morning, I have no idea what to expect from Jackson. I almost feel more nervous than last night. We kissed. One incredibly hot, amazing kiss last night. We established nothing. Decided nothing. So, yeah, today's weird.*"

Oh, God . . . it can't be . . . can it? Something from another timeline that I hadn't brought myself? Did that mean that I had definitely created another timeline when I left Holly in August 2009? Eileen seemed to think I may have done the Thomas-jump, but I doubted that. Especially after my failed attempt last night.

Spots appeared in front of my face and I was nearly positive I'd pass out any second so I sank down onto the bed. "No . . . no it's not—"

"Not what, Jackson?" Stewart prodded with a scary edge to her voice. "Not a journal documenting months of make-out sessions and some seriously fucked-up angst? You know, she's even got me in this thing? Oh . . . and then there's the fact that pages and pages have been devoted to August, September, October . . . 2009. As in *the future . . .*"

She got up and stood across from me. All I could do was wait and be ready for what would inevitably come. There was no way she didn't know about me now.

I didn't expect the derisive laughter that followed. "All these fucking months I was trying to figure you out! Do you know how crazy it's been for me? I've known you since you were seventeen. Knew everything about you . . . and then suddenly you're an agent and speak every fucking language in the goddamn universe. It all makes sense now . . . perfect sense."

Okay, here we go. I moved my hand from the cell to the gun tucked under my pillow.

She tossed the diary onto the couch. "Displacement! That's what fucking happened to you, isn't it?"

Huh? "Huh?"

"Don't look at me like that . . . You came from another timeline, didn't you?"

Yeah . . . or at least I'd thought so until Eileen . . . "Uh . . ."

Stewart stopped staring at me and started pacing across the floor. "So, something happened to you or whatever . . . And they made one of the EOTs move you." She froze in place. "Or did they do it on their own . . . like as a threat to your dad, and now you're stuck here 'cause your brain might explode if you get moved back?"

My mouth hung open. I had no idea what to say or how the hell I had managed to keep my secret a secret. She thought an EOT had changed my timeline . . . not that I *was* an EOT. Dr. Melvin told me about Displacement when I had jumped off the roof with Holly that one time.

Go with it, I told myself. "Um . . . yeah, something happened . . . and, well . . . it needed to not happen again. So, yeah, you're basically right. But I promised my dad I wouldn't give all the details. You know how it works. It's not healthy for any of us to know too much about the future."

Now it was Stewart's turn to let her jaw drop. "Damn . . . how far ahead were you? I mean, you don't look much older. Did you already start agent training? Because that would explain the rapid progress." She sighed, looking disappointed. "I guess you don't have to tell me if your dad said not to."

"What if I just say it was less than a year in the future, and yes, I had some training?" My heart still pounded and sweat dripped from everywhere, but Stewart was too fascinated by the discovery to even notice these obvious signs of lying or concealing things. Although most of it was true. Sort of.

She suddenly dove for the pink notebook again, flipping frantically. "Wait . . . I think I know why you left that other timeline. The day before I found out you were our newest recruit, I was assigned to follow you to work. But you weren't there." She stopped on a page closer to the front and placed the notebook in my lap. "Here, read this."

I looked down at the page and recognized Holly's handwriting immediately.

MARCH 15TH, 2009

I work on Mars or maybe Jupiter. Seriously. It's that weird. I've been to Manhattan plenty of times, but mostly tourist places where normal middle-class people, like myself, gather to look at something. Or whatever.

But people actually live on the Upper East Side. That's just nuts. Oh and I made a great first impression. Remind me not to walk and read at the same time because accidental collision with very cute boy (I almost don't want to write "boy," but "man" sounds creepy and "young man" sounds dorky) may occur. And if you're really stupid and decide to read, walk, and carry big strawberry smoothie at the same time, you may ruin the cute boy's shoes.

I was like, OMG!! But I'll admit, he took it well. Actually, he laughed then saved my book from the smoothie, which was awesome because I would have had nothing to read on the way home.

For the rest of this month, it's just training two nights a week, so no real work yet. However, I did something really cool today when Mr. Wellborn, our camp director, mentioned that his computer lab instructor for the camp took another job and he was looking for someone with extensive computer knowledge. I got brave and raised my hand and was like, "One of my good friends is going to MIT *and just won the National Science Fair. He's awesome with kids and is looking for a job."*

Mr. Wellborn was really impressed and took Adam's info. Adam will flip when he finds out the pay and I know he'd like to get out of Jersey just as much as me. We've always had that in common.

When I was leaving, the same guy I had run into earlier and ruined his shoes, walked out the door, right in front of me. I watched him get into this long black car, waiting for him out front. The driver (wearing a black suit and some kind of earpiece) even ran around and opened the door for him. Seriously.

I rolled my eyes and I think he saw me because he smiled. Obviously he's an Upper East Side product, but why the hell does he need a job? Maybe court-appointed community service? Wouldn't really make sense given the pay rate for the job and all the applicants. He should have been assigned to a camp for disadvantaged children in Harlem or something.

That's all for now.

Love,

Holly

"That was you, wasn't it?" Stewart asked, yanking the notebook from my lap. "The ruined-shoe guy? That's the day you met her . . . and the day you became a member of Tempest." Stewart looked at me and rolled her eyes. "And, what? She walked into the building, smoothie still intact . . . so dramatic . . . and tragic. Did you pick the date? 'Cause that's really corny."

"Yes," I managed to say. This notebook was harder to swallow than any of the pictures Dad had of her from his "source."

"God, you're such a pathetic loser," she said with a groan.

I glared at her, and she looked slightly guilty. "Sorry, I'm sure it was heartbreaking . . . but damn . . . how weird is it to, like, do the same day again?" she asked.

I let out a breath I'd been holding for I didn't know how long. "You have no idea how weird it is."

She narrowed her eyes at me, looking more serious and businesslike.

"You're gonna have to tell Kendrick. She's all girlie and in love and I wouldn't be surprised if she plans another matchmaking session between you and Blondie. Obviously, whatever made you need to be out of this girl's life was too important to get screwed up with another fifty-thousand-dollar dance."

"Damn," I muttered under my breath. "Was that really just last night . . . as in less than twenty-four hours ago?"

Just the mention of last night caused Stewart's face to darken, and I remembered how angry she was, how she stormed off and no one heard from her. "Hey—where were you, anyway?"

I stood up and she did the same, making a great effort out of closing Holly's diary and placing it in my hands. "Here . . . you should keep this."

I set it on the counter and stepped closer to Stewart. "Come on . . . just tell me where you went last night. No offense, but you look like hell."

She moved toward me so quick, I was nearly positive it was an attack. But then she kissed me . . . like she had a few days ago, except more urgent. I let it go for about ten seconds, trying to rationalize the situation. It was obvious she wanted a distraction, like I had the last time. I gently pried her off of me and grasped her shoulders firmly with both hands.

"This is a bad idea."

Her hands slipped into the front pocket of my shorts. "I think it's a great idea."

I shook my head right away. "Stewart, I know what you're trying to do . . . I saw it happen, too . . . I kept seeing it . . . seeing him . . . every time I closed my eyes last night—"

"Stop! Just shut up." She tried to wiggle out of my grip, but I held on tighter.

"I'm not letting you run off again. Look at you. You still haven't changed your clothes, and . . . and . . ."

"And I'm wearing him, right? He exploded into bits and I'm just leaving him here . . . splattered all over me." Her voice cracked and a single tear ran down her cheek, washing away some of the dirt.

I stared at her face, shocked by her tears, hating that I had to be caught up in someone else's grief. But it was almost easier to have this moment with Stewart than with anyone else because she didn't expect me to say something wise or brilliant. She wouldn't want me to say sorry or that everything would be okay . . . We could bypass all of that bullshit.

I grabbed her and pulled her into a tight hug before she could run off. Her face pressed against my shoulder and I could feel her whole body shaking. She went from pulling away from me to clinging to me like I was a lifeline. After a couple minutes she mumbled into my shoulder, "If you tell anyone, I'll kill you."

"I won't," I promised. "In fact, I've already forgotten."

She let go of me and sat down on the couch, leaning her head back and closing her eyes. "I wish I were a fucking idiot so I could believe good things happen to people after they die."

No one had ever said more accurate and truthful words than those. It was the reason I sucked at dealing with death. I could never get past the still, cold bodies . . . being locked in a coffin . . . trapped . . . buried underground alone. Why couldn't I have been brainwashed by some religious cult? Forced into a belief system that included a happy afterlife?

"I know what you mean. I'd gladly welcome a dose of blind faith right now." I reached down and grabbed Stewart's hands, pulling her up so she was standing. "Come on. I'll turn on the shower for you. You can't go back to your place looking like this."

Or anywhere in public.

She nodded, and I watched her carefully as she moved toward Mason's bag and started riffling through it, removing a Snow Patrol T-shirt and a pair of gray sweatpants. Just by the way she walked toward the bathroom I got the impression that Stewart must have been up all night. And she took quite a few hard hits during yesterday's fight.

I steered her by the shoulders and turned on the water, waiting for it to heat up. Stewart leaned against the wall, closing her eyes.

"I remembered something else, too," she mumbled sleepily. "Something about me and you . . . and a jail cell."

More 007 memories.

I kept my face as calm as possible in case her eyes opened again. "Huh . . . maybe we got in a bar fight and the CIA didn't want us to remember."

She laughed. "If we did, I bet we kicked everybody's ass."

I lifted her shirt over her head and tossed it onto the floor. My eyes stayed focused on the wall behind her. Even though I'd seen Stewart nearly naked the other night and the following morning, it just didn't feel right to look now. Maybe that meant we didn't hate each other anymore . . . like we'd formed some kind of friendship.

She left the rest of her clothes on the floor and I opened the shower door for her and waited in the bathroom to make sure she didn't fall over.

"Hey, Stewart?" I asked after a few minutes.

"Yeah?"

"My dad was giving me information . . . about Holly . . . in France. That's why we snuck out sometimes."

She fumbled with the knob, so I reached in to turn off the water and handed her a towel. "So, he was keeping it from everyone . . . not just the trainees?"

"No one else knew about Holly . . . until now, anyway," I answered, the nerves leaking into my voice.

Stewart threw on Mason's clothes in silence and then stumbled out of the bathroom. "I'm not gonna tell anyone about you and Blondie, if that's what you're wondering. Kendrick won't, either."

"Right."

"Okay, don't believe me, Junior. But the way I see it, you don't have anything to lose trusting me, trusting Kendrick. Either do it, or don't. Quit being such an indecisive girl." She rubbed her eyes and sighed. "Is she home? Kendrick? I gotta get her help with something."

"Yeah, I think so." I grabbed the pink notebook and Stewart headed out the door in front of me.

The second Kendrick let us in, Stewart said, "Sleep . . . I need to sleep. Give me whatever you got."

Kendrick glanced over Stewart's shoulder at me as if asking for my approval. I just shrugged, not really seeing a problem with this plan. Stewart did need to rest if she'd been up all night. Kendrick provided her with some little white pills and a bed much more comfortable than mine.

Kendrick gestured toward the patio, asking if I wanted to sit outside. I sat in one of the two chairs and Kendrick set some kind of pink dip and crackers on the table along with a bottle of wine and some glasses. "It's salmon dip. Michael made it."

I took advantage of the moment alone to follow Stewart's advice. "You know that girl you tried to hook me up with last night . . ."

"Yes . . ."

The pink notebook rested beside my elbow and I carefully slid it across the table toward Kendrick. "This is hers. Well, not exactly hers . . . a different version of her, actually."

Kendrick's hand froze on top of the journal and she lifted her eyes to meet mine. "Okay, you've got my attention."

I reached for a couple crackers and ate them slowly while Kendrick poured two glasses of wine. "I'm really hesitant to tell you the details—"

"Whatever shit you've got going on, that's your business. I'm not going to investigate, analyze, spy on you. Nothing. Tell me whatever you want to tell me . . . or don't."

I kept my eyes on the street out in front of us. "Fine. And I'll do the same for you. I won't start digging for your secrets."

She shot a glance at me, lifting one eyebrow. "Oh, really? Then what was poker night about a couple days ago? You weren't trying to get information out of Michael?"

She was right. I had tried to worm information out of Michael the other night after agreeing to play poker with some of his friends.

My stomach twisted with guilt. "Well—"

"That's exactly how you become one of them," she interrupted.

"One of who?"

"Stewart, Freeman, Parker, Marshall." She waved her hand as if to say, *The list goes on.* "They've all adopted the CIA's favorite rule: It's not personal, it's business, and they live it twenty-four/seven."

I set my wineglass on the table and sighed. "I'm sorry about Michael. Seriously."

She turned her whole body around to face me and stared hard, looking more intimidating than ever. "You can screw with my head all you want, I'm trained to deal with that . . . to expect it . . . but don't ever mess with Michael. Don't pretend to be his friend or any of that shit. Understood?"

Kendrick was right, I really did have trouble trusting her, even more than I thought. But seriously, what other choice did I have except to "trust no one," as 007 Adam had once told me? This noble speech of Kendrick's could all be an act. But if it wasn't, then she might understand why I needed to keep Holly a secret. Michael might be enough for her to get how important this information was to me.

I leaned back in my chair and folded my arms across my chest. "Do you swear on your life . . . and on his life . . . that Michael isn't just some cover Chief Marshall gave you?"

The anger dropped from her face and she looked completely appalled. "No . . . no, he's not. How could you even think that?"

"How could I *not* think that?" I said. "You're keeping secrets from him, why not me, too?"

She let out a breath and nodded. "Okay . . . you're right. There's a lot of red flags with us."

Even though we were supposed to be turning off our inner agents right now to establish trust or whatever this talk was, suddenly I had a strong urge to hear her story . . . her secret. Like we could just blackmail each other for information.

And I thought she wanted to tell me.

"My life is a lot more exposed than any other agent's . . . and I'm not totally ignorant on the subject of dead family members, you know," I said, throwing a sharp look in her direction.

Pink crept up to her cheeks. "Right . . . I know . . . I mean, yes . . . that's true, but . . . ."

"But what?" I asked, lifting one eyebrow, challenging her to tell me it was different. It might be, but she'd never use that as an excuse.

Kendrick finished her glass of wine and poured another, like maybe she was getting up the nerve to tell me. She knew exactly what I wanted to know. Her family . . . what happened to them . . . ? "Remember what you said the other day? About Michael not knowing me."

"Yeah, I remember," I said.

"You're right . . . but you're also wrong. I *am* the girl that he knows. The one who loves to look at baby furniture just for fun and cries at stupid romantic comedies. I'm other things, too, the person *you* know, but that's because I can do stuff most people can't. Not by choice. But none of it's fake . . . Does that make sense?"

"I think so." Both of us were completely silent, and I knew it was coming . . . She was about to tell me.

Then I could tell her about Holly . . . at least the Displacement theory Stewart already knew about.

"My parents and my brother were murdered almost three years ago . . . by EOTs."

I held my breath, waiting for her to say more, watching her chug wine like water.

"I came home from a friend's house and . . . walked in the living room." Her voice started to shake and a single tear trickled down her cheek. "The TV was on and my parents were stretched out on the couch asleep . . . I always told them when I got home so they wouldn't worry. I shook my mom first and she didn't respond . . . That's when I realized she wasn't breathing. Neither was my dad. But they looked . . . totally fine."

"Damn," I muttered, but Kendrick didn't hear me. Her eyes were fixated on something over my shoulder.

"I called an ambulance right away and then I just stood there, not knowing what to do. I mean, I knew CPR and all that, but I couldn't move . . . until I remembered Carson." She paused to take a breath and wiped her eyes on her sleeve again. "He was tucked into his bed, the TV off, his school bag hanging on the door. And for a second I thought he was okay."

She stopped talking and just sat there, staring down at the table. Already I wanted her to shut up, to not tell me the rest. But I focused on the goal of gaining information because I knew if I stayed in agent mode it wouldn't hurt as much. "Do you know what happened?"

She nodded. "The autopsy said carbon monoxide . . . but Chief Marshall changed it. He said it was an untraceable poison."

"Marshall?" I asked, trying to figure out when he entered the story.

"He showed up while I was in Carson's room. He dragged me out of there and into a car. I woke up in a place that looked like someone's house. Marshall was there . . . said I could never go back home or . . . or the EOTs would kill me, too."

"Don't you have other family?" I asked. "An aunt or a grandparent?"

"They think I'm dead," she whispered. "Everything about me was changed. My birthday changed from November fifth to the seventh. My hair used to be a much lighter brown. My Social Security number, school records . . . all of it changed, but I wouldn't change my name. Your dad said it didn't matter. He was there, too . . . the night they died."

I swallowed hard. The connection between her family and mine made agent mode more difficult. *It's not personal, it's business.* "He was?"

"Yeah. He brought me my mother's necklace. It was her mom's . . . one of those family heirlooms. He took my dad's pocketknife, too, and a picture that Carson made for me. It was hanging in my room . . . right above my dresser." She drew in a deep shaky breath and let it out slowly. "God, it's just so fucked-up. My brother wasn't even halfway through third grade. Why would anyone want to kill him?"

"I don't know," I said, but my brain reeled with theories.

"It's because of me," she said with a flat tone. "They know something about me . . . the EOTs . . . in the future. Maybe I kill off a whole swarm of them or something." She smiled just a little. A pathetic attempt to lighten the mood.

"Do you ever wish you could go back to your house or . . . see some of your other family?" I asked.

"I'm not really close with anyone else. Half live in Canada and the other half northern California . . . I'd love to have my mother's wedding ring . . . Maybe if she was here I wouldn't be as interested in something used, but now I kinda love that idea."

No wonder Michael had said she had a lot of shit to deal with. Maybe even worse than me. Kendrick, Stewart, Mason—all of them had crazy tragic events that led to them being here. Maybe that was a prerequisite for Tempest agents. Most of us didn't have anything left to lose. Except Kendrick had Michael . . .

"All right," Kendrick said, more businesslike. "I told you . . . Now it's your turn."

"Yeah . . . okay." And just like that, I spilled everything about Holly . . . me and Holly. For the first time in months, I felt a little bit lighter, like maybe I had someone to share this great big burden with. Someone to tell me I did the right thing.

"Damn . . . how long was I out?" Stewart came stumbling into the living room six hours after crashing in Kendrick's bed. We had moved from the patio to the living room and Michael was here, hanging out with us, which meant we'd had to change our conversation to normal topics.

"A while," Kendrick said, eyeing Stewart's crazy hair. "You okay?"

"Yeah, just totally starving."

It was decided that Michael would cook and I would run to the store to retrieve missing ingredients.

When I returned to the apartment building, lugging several sacks of groceries, about halfway up the stairs I heard a sound coming from my borrowed apartment. Very quiet movements an amateur wouldn't take notice of. Instead of heading to Kendrick's place and possibly getting my partner and Stewart to use as backup, I put the groceries on the landing and crept toward my front door. My heart thudded as I leaned against the wall beside the door, listening.

My gun was now at the ready and my free hand texted a 911 to Stewart and Kendrick, since they were just down the hall . . . even though I might be taking the risk of creating a scene in front of Michael for nothing.

I took a deep breath and unlocked the dead bolt, then turned the doorknob quickly.

The first thing that came into view was the glow of a tiny flashlight, then the quick intake of breath from its owner. The light clicked off immediately.

"Drop the flashlight and put your hands up!" I shouted, pointing my pistol into the dark.

Nothing. No one. No sound.

I flipped the main light on and scanned the room. There were very few hiding places in this tiny apartment.

I nearly dropped my gun when I spotted a petite figure hiding under the table.

"Holly?"

CHAPTER SIXTEEN

She didn't answer me, but she did crawl out of her hiding spot now that I'd seen her.

"What are you doing here?" I asked. Her eyes followed my hands as I lowered the gun and set it on the kitchen counter. "Sorry if I scared you. I heard something from outside . . ."

She rolled the tiny flashlight between her fingers, eyes darting around the room. I could tell she was holding her breath. Her silence worried me and I started to walk closer, and when only three feet separated us, she reached one hand behind her back and quickly drew a pistol, pointing it right at me.

My hands shot up in the air. "Hey! What the hell are you doing with a gun?"

A lock of hair fell over her eyes but she left it there, focusing on my face. "I really didn't think it was you . . . I was so sure you weren't the one . . . just a quick look around, and then . . ."

"Then what, Hol? What's going on? And when did you start carrying a weapon besides pepper spray?"

Sweat formed on her forehead and when I glanced at the barrel of her gun, I could see her hands trembling. Her voice shook as she spoke. "Your fingerprints . . . they're all over Adam's car. You were in there . . . I know you were. But why Adam? What did he ever do to you?"

My heart beat at race-car pace and my stomach turned over and over, fighting the urge to vomit. I could barely spit out the words, "What happened to Adam?"

"Like you don't know. How do you do it . . . pretend like that . . . all the time?"

The fear in me took over and I needed answers, fast. In one quick motion, I snatched the gun from her hand and turned her around, wrapping my arms around her from behind, restricting her movement. "Tell me what happened to Adam. And *when* . . . when did it happen?"

She jabbed me with an elbow and attempted to throw me over her shoulder, but the size difference was too much for her to fight. "Tell me the date!"

"Stop acting like you don't know!" Her nails dug into my arm, every muscle in her body straining to break free. "I was so ready to defend you . . . so ready . . . You've even got his stuff . . . his CD."

The rage building up in me was too much to control. She had information I needed and I had to get it. The gun pressed into her back, causing her to gasp. "Holly!"

"May nineteenth."

"What time?" I demanded.

"Afternoon . . . three . . . no, four." Her body relaxed and a couple tears dropped onto my arm. "I should have brought another agent with me and . . . God, this sucks."

Agent? Oh, no. No fucking way. "What kind of agent? Do the police know you're here?"

She laughed darkly, but I could feel her shaking. "Yeah, right, the police? Seriously? Why don't you tell me who you work for, and I'll do the same?"

I felt the wind whoosh right out of my lungs. What the fuck was going on? *Adam's dead and Holly's some kind of secret agent?* "So the whole story about the bet . . . at Senator Healy's ball . . . that was just you spying on me?"

"Like you weren't there to spy on me," she snapped, then she tilted her head up, looking right at me for the first time since I'd snatched her gun. "You're going to kill me, too, aren't you?"

Her eyes, her voice, those words . . . In an instant the agent in me dissolved. The narrow-minded rage had dissipated, bringing more clarity than I wanted right now. I released her immediately and backed away, feeling my knees go weak. Dad had a source . . . He was checking up on Holly and Adam for me . . . He would have told me if something had happened . . . unless . . . Hadn't Emily said things kept changing . . . ? "How did this happen?"

"You killed one of my best friends." She turned around to face me, her eyes pleading with mine, but for what? "This is how it goes, right? Nobody gets caught and gets away with it."

"I don't know," I stuttered, trying to keep up with this crazy turn of events. This wasn't in the training manual. There was no protocol to follow.

She took a deep breath, closing her eyes tight. A few more tears tumbled out. "Can I please call my mother? I need to hear her voice . . . just for a second . . ."

It felt like someone had ripped my heart right out of my body, that was how much her words hurt me. *She thinks I want to kill her* . . . How could this happen? Who would put Holly in the FBI or the CIA or whatever the hell organization gave her a gun and an assignment?

The floor creaked loudly as I approached her again. Her chest stopped moving and she held her breath, squeezing her eyes shut even tighter.

I picked up her hand and turned it palm up, placing her gun on top. My fingers lingered over hers and I whispered, "I would never hurt you, Holly . . . ever. Just leave . . . It's okay."

Her eyes flew open, staring straight into mine. She tightened her hands around the gun and knocked me out of the way. It was a very predictable move, but I let myself fall down, for her benefit. I stayed sitting on the hardwood floor, while she pointed the gun at me again and backed up slowly toward the front door. I could see the confusion and relief flickering in her eyes, and then pain clouding everything. "He was a really amazing person . . . I can't believe you—"

"I know," I said, choking back my own tears. "I know he was."

My face had dropped to my hands and I didn't even see her leave, but I heard the door shut quietly. The first thought to come to mind was, *I can't have her back*. Not the girl I loved in the future. Those timelines were gone, leaving me only with a version of Holly whose life had taken some serious turns for the worse. Someone was doing this. It wasn't a coincidence. It couldn't be.

Thomas trying to screw with my head again.

And Adam . . . What had I done to get him killed? It hurt too much to even contemplate tonight. I just wanted to crawl under my bed and hide out until someone told me what to do . . . who to save, where to go. If only I could flip a switch and go into mechanical mode so I didn't have to feel any of it. Just work . . . nothing else.

I lifted myself off the floor and collapsed onto my bed, but the second my eyes drifted shut, Adam's voice invaded my thoughts. Had I ever even told him . . . how cool it was to have one person in my life whom I could tell everything? This was completely true. I kept secrets from my dad, from Holly, but Adam knew all of it.

He's gone.

He was gone the second I jumped to this timeline because I erased him, like I'd erased my Holly. Except I always had a method of convincing him. *His code.* That had stayed in the back of my mind, like a favorite place you could keep coming back to.

May nineteenth . . . *May 19, 2009 . . . afternoon.*

That was the only nudge I needed to jump back. Thomas-jump, Thomas-jump . . . *Please be a Thomas-jump.* But my insides burned and ripped to pieces immediately. A half-jump . . . which meant . . . failure. Complete and utter failure.

CHAPTER SEVENTEEN

Holly hadn't misled me. This was the right date. Adam was alone in his house when I found him. The front door unlocked. The neighbors' kids splashing around in their pool next door. And Adam, sprawled out on his living room floor, blood seeping through his pant leg.

"Fuck!" he said when he heard me walking across the floor. "Not another one."

I could see his head rising, and eventually he sat all the way up. I ran over to him, dropping to the floor beside his leg. "Adam! You're okay . . . I mean, it's just your leg."

His mouth dropped open and his eyes widened. "Jackson! What the hell are you doing here?"

I had just started applying pressure to his leg wound with a dust cloth that was lying on the coffee table, but I froze when he said my name. "You know who I am?" This version of Adam shouldn't know me any more than Agent Holly knew me.

He pressed his hands to the side of his head, wincing and squeezing his eyes shut. "Yeah . . . I mean, in theory . . . sort of. Oh, no—you aren't here to change this, right? You can't!"

"No," I said bitterly. "This won't change a thing . . . unfortunately."

"Good." His breathing had become labored, but he opened his eyes, looking at me intensely. "I have a source . . . a great source. Just let this go. Let me go."

"Adam, it's just your leg," I said, pressing harder on his bloody jeans. Why was I even trying? Obviously it wasn't just his leg.

He shook his head, as if reading my thoughts. "I saw things . . . I time-traveled and . . . oh, damn, my head is fucking killing me."

My eyes traveled from the bleeding leg to his face, and it was like everything moved in slow motion and I already knew what was coming. He lifted a hand from the side of his face and both of us stared, horror-stricken. Sticky red blood covered his palm and dripped between his fingers. I couldn't breathe or move. He collapsed onto his back, giving me a clear view of the dark red, almost purple oozing from his ear.

My hands no longer pressed on the leg wound. The panic had left, leaving only grief. I was here to watch him die. Or just leave him, and I knew what that would do to me. Tears fell from my eyes and I didn't try to stop them.

"There's surveillance cameras . . . CIA-planted devices," he croaked. "The corner of Lexington and Ninety-second Street . . . find the pictures . . . hack into the system . . . whatever you can do . . . two months ago . . . March fifteenth . . ."

"What? What are you talking about?" I leaned in closer. "Adam . . . who did this to you?"

He closed his eyes again, his breathing jagged and inconsistent. "It was just . . . an accident . . . accident."

Oh, God . . . no. "Was it me? Did I do this?"

He didn't answer, and I reached out desperately and shook him. "Adam! Was it me? Did I try and take you somewhere?"

"No," he gasped. "It wasn't you."

My fingers were still tangled around the front of his shirt and I couldn't bring myself to let go. Why let go? Why hold on? Any gains I ever made would end up like this. Where was *my* end, and could I just jump there and get it over with?

I wiped my eyes with my sleeve and noticed Adam had gone completely still. Adam . . . my best friend . . . gone. All logic disappeared and I shook him again, harder this time. "Please wake up! Please! I can't fix this . . . I can't do anything right."

His hand opened as his entire body relaxed. A wad of paper fell from his palm and somehow I managed to open it, recognizing his writing immediately.

JACKSON,

Something's happening to the world right now and I can't figure it out. Agent Collins and I are doing everything we can to solve the puzzle. I remember pieces of meeting you, as if it happened in a dream or a retelling of a story I was too young to remember. But that part doesn't matter, only that I know who you are...I know you're not bad. I know Tempest isn't bad. But Eyewall...I don't know much about them. Even though I thought I did.

Keep looking for clues. Keep asking questions and whatever you do, DO NOT fix this!

ADAM

It took me only about two seconds to figure out why Holly thought I'd done this to him. An EOT found this note . . . They knew Adam was figuring things out . . . They knew they needed to frame me to add fuel to the fire. To keep Eyewall wanting to hunt us down.

I folded the note and stuffed it back into Adam's hand, wishing I could take it with me.

"I'm so sorry," I whispered to him before jumping back to my present day and time.

CHAPTER EIGHTEEN

"It's completely clean in here," Kendrick said, crawling out from underneath my bed.

"Check under the sink with the metal detector . . . run it over the pipes," Stewart said from behind my laptop.

I'd been sitting on my bed, leaning against the wall, staring at the TV for almost two hours. Complete numbness . . . that was all I felt at the moment and I was afraid if I moved, even just a little, that would change.

"Blondie's not in any of the recent surveillance photos taken of Eyewall agents," Stewart said.

Obviously. No way would I have missed that.

"Would she really be working for Eyewall?" Kendrick asked from under the sink. "I thought she was just some average girl."

"Probably not, but that doesn't mean she isn't," Stewart said. "Think about it . . . Jackson left her in another timeline to keep her safe. Her diary's floating around . . . Obviously, he's been set up for this. The diary was in Agent Meyer Senior's place. Someone meant for Jackson to find it. Not only is he trying to avoid contact with her, she's been brainwashed to hate his guts."

I inhaled slowly, focusing on the Mets game on the TV in front of me.

Kendrick came out from under the sink and adjusted her dress. "You're right, she could just be a pawn . . . and Adam Silverman, too, although it sounds like he's got some useful skills."

Had some useful skills.

"So, do you think Agent Meyer knew? That she was involved in the CIA?" Kendrick asked, tentatively because she knew how Stewart and I might react.

"No," Stewart said firmly, closing that door quicker than it had been opened. "Let's not forget that Blondie was at Healy's event . . . even though you manipulated that situation. She acted really bizarre. I listened in on most of her chat with Jackson."

They had stopped including me in the conversation over an hour ago when I'd stopped answering questions. Once I heard the details— Adam Silverman, senior at George Washington High School in Newark, New Jersey . . . soon-to-be MIT freshman . . . died May 19, 2009 . . . cause of death . . . accident in the home.

Right. An accident.

"Holy fuck!" Stewart shouted, jumping up from the couch. "Why didn't I remember this?"

From the corner of my eye, I saw her open the closet door and pull out the big bag of Mason's stuff, the one she hadn't touched since taking the T-shirt and sweatpants from it this morning. When she removed his laptop, I could sense the reluctance as she carried it over to the couch like it might explode or shatter any second.

"Mason did some crazy computer-geek shit and if she had an earpiece in or any communication device that night, it should be recorded here."

"How is that possible?" Kendrick sat down next to Stewart, leaning close to the computer screen. "He would have had to stream it through the Internet and that would make it available to anyone."

Stewart let out a deep breath and turned the computer toward Kendrick. "Yep . . . he streamed all the radio communications within a half mile of the area and had it encrypted to the hard drive. Only someone as smart as you and him would be able to unscramble it and sort through the hours of data."

"Right, I'm on it," Kendrick said with a sigh.

Personally, I didn't need to hear anything from that night. What I needed to do was decide if I was going to leave. Get the hell out of this nightmare universe. I could go back to that 2007 timeline. Adam and Mason were alive in that year. 007 Holly hadn't accused me of murder. That was another plus.

I didn't even remember closing my eyes, but I must have.

"Five minutes," Kendrick said. "I'm moving it to my iPod and we can listen through our earpieces."

The sun streaming through the blinds surprised me and I jerked upright, rubbing my eyes. "It's morning?"

"Guess he's not deaf and mute after all," Stewart said.

I swept the room in one quick glance and saw they both were wearing sweats and there were crumbs and napkins all over the kitchen counter . . . and coffee . . . I smelled coffee. I got up from the bed and walked into the bathroom, turning on the shower to avoid communication.

"He's totally bonkers right now. What are we supposed to do with him?" Stewart asked, loud enough for me to hear.

"Just let it go for now," Kendrick said. "I'm sure the six hours of sleep must have helped."

Six hours? That had to be a new record for me. Actually, I'd hoped to feel some sense of purpose or determination to fix this year . . . this universe, when I woke. But I just wanted out. Maybe I'd talk to Dr. Melvin first, if I could get him alone.

When I was in the kitchen a few minutes later, pouring a cup of coffee, Kendrick came up to me and stuck an earpiece in my ear. "You okay?"

"Not really."

"We've unscrambled several CIA agents' conversations from the night of Healy's event. We were surrounded by agents. The three we identified as Eyewall were in some remote location, giving directions. That's why we didn't have any pictures."

"Great."

Kendrick sighed and left me alone in the kitchen. I didn't think she had any idea what to say, which was good, because I didn't need her giving me some reason to stay. I leaned my head on the counter, burying my face in my arms as the recording started.

"Flynn . . . what part of 'keep your eyes open from a distance' do you not understand?"

"That's Agent Collins," Stewart said. "He's in Eyewall."

"And how do you know that?" Kendrick asked, pausing the recording.

"I just do," Stewart said firmly.

I took a second to glance at Kendrick and we both exchanged a look, knowing Stewart had just given us information only her specialty was allowed to have. *She must really trust us now.*

My face was buried again as Kendrick restarted the recording.

"What the hell was I supposed to do?" Holly's voice emerged in a muffled, breathless whisper. *"They called my number. Brian practically shoved me out there."*

The $50,000 dance. I heard Kendrick groan from the couch . . . She had set it up. Set us up. The sound of running water came through the earpiece. Holly must have walked into the restroom.

"Lewis is all ready to go. She's been prepping for days on every detail of this kid's life and now it's gonna have to be you," Agent Collins snapped.

"No . . . I'm not ready for this," Holly said.

"I'm not ready for a five-foot-nothing trainee to screw up my mission, but I guess we'll just have to deal with it."

A whole lot of static followed Agent Collins's foreboding message, then his voice returned. *"All right, Flynn. Suspect number twenty-two has an estimated blood alcohol level well above the legally drunk limit. You're on . . . but do exactly what I tell you. Exactly. He's not expendable like the others . . . not yet. We need him."*

Expendable? They really were in this until death. Chief Marshall hadn't been kidding about that.

I could hear the music, feet shuffling against the dance floor. The whole scene played itself clearly in my mind.

"He's been shamelessly staring at your ass for twenty minutes. I've got the geek squad sifting through old girlfriend photos to see if you remind him of someone, but it really doesn't matter. You've got him hooked, somehow. That's all we need to know."

"Or he's playing us and we're falling right into the trap," Holly mumbled.

"Exactly why we have backup for you," Collins said. *"Go order a drink and don't make a big deal out of the incident earlier."*

"Right," Holly said. *" 'Cause that wasn't even a little bit creepy."*

"I don't know, Flynn . . . Maybe he's on something . . . opiates or whatever fancy drugs rich kids like him can get their hands on," Collins said.

"What do you have on tap?" Holly said.

"Wishful thinking, Flynn," Collins said with a groan. *"Now say something to him."*

The bartender replied with his sarcastic offer of "water."

"I thought you left," Holly said.

Then I heard my own voice, talking the bartender into giving her a real drink and Holly ordering her Bud Light.

"Sit down next to him and do not drink more than one beer . . . in fact, don't even drink half of it," Agent Collins said.

"Pretty smooth. You've done this before? The intimidation factor . . . name-dropping?" Holly asked.

A few more exchanges of words between Holly and me, and finally Agent Collins spoke again. *"Okay, he knows it was an awkward moment earlier, so go ahead and acknowledge it. Maybe it'll break the ice."*

"You sure know how to invade a girl's personal space," Holly said.

I heard myself apologize and then the change in tone when I had decided to pursue this one evening of guilty pleasure.

"So, where are you from, Holly Flynn?" I asked.

"Tell him the truth," Collins said. *"If he's working for Tempest, he'll be able to find out anyway. If he's not . . . he won't care or even remember."*

Agent Collins was quiet all through the conversation about Jersey and parties in the woods and beer kegs. But when Holly said, *"You've been sitting here for an hour. Don't you think your date might be a little bored . . . or lonely?"* And then I said, *"She's just my partner . . . I mean, lab partner . . . for med school."*

Agent Collins laughed and said, *"I love those drunken slipups, don't you? Lab partner, my ass."*

"What about your boyfriend? Is he okay with you, flirting with strangers?" I asked.

"*Go ahead, Flynn . . . level the playing field, but nothing too definite,*" Collins said.

"*Brian flirts better than he plays football. Besides, he can't hear me,*" Holly said.

"*Good. Very good,*" Collins said. "*Now ask him to dance . . . Carter and Lewis are out there. She'll jump in when he gets bored with you. This job is yours to keep if you want it, but just between you and me, Lewis is dying for you to screw up. She just told me that you don't have the balls to get any closer to the subject.*" He laughed again, like he knew this would set Holly off. She didn't like to be told what she couldn't do.

A few more words between me and Holly . . . She asked me to dance . . . The Journey song played, getting louder and louder. And I remembered her carefully calculated movements. She wanted to prove them wrong, but she wasn't as comfortable as the character she had played that night. Except . . . there *were* a few minutes when I felt like she got lost in the moment . . . or maybe she was just lost in her role.

Or maybe I was lost in mine.

"*I bet you get a little wild if you're drunk,*" I heard myself say.

"*I bet you won't find out,*" Holly said.

"*Get him to invite you over, Flynn. We need to search his place,*" Agent Collins said.

"*Unless . . .*" Holly said.

"*Don't go overboard, you can always slip something in his drink. No seduction needed,*" Collins said.

"*So, where did you say you lived?*" Holly asked.

I heard myself turning down her open-ended invite and then we must have started writing on napkins at that point. I barely listened to the next couple minutes. Instead, I thought about what Holly had written on that napkin: *Tell the wind and fire where to stop, but don't tell me.* Was she trying to tell me something? The quote was just so . . . *Holly*. Inside and out. That made it a lot harder to separate that girl from the one in the diary.

The part where I kissed her followed and then Agent Collins spoke again. "*Okay, he's obviously not inviting you over. Let's go with the fall-*

back plan. Prove he's an agent and close the door on this interaction between the two of you, at least for now."

That would explain the weird questions about people's eye color. The fallback plan involved Senator Healy's made-up bet, *Wicked* tickets, and me trying not to be completely crushed. After the part where I had walked away, Holly started speaking to Agent Collins in muffled whispers.

"*I don't think it's him. He's just so . . . vulnerable, but guarded,*" Holly said. "*He can't have anything to do with Adam . . . I don't know . . . He just doesn't seem like the assassin type. This is harder than I thought it would be.*"

"*No one is asking you to be Freud,*" Agent Collins said in a much gentler tone than he had used all night. "*You just follow orders and let us figure out the rest. You did well tonight. For a rookie.*"

"*What now?*" Holly asked.

"*I don't think it would hurt for you to make suspect number twenty-two a little jealous. Plant a seed for future use,*" Collins said.

I could hear Holly sigh. "*Sure.*"

"*All right, I get it . . . you need a break. Grab Brian and make sure our guy sees you leaving early . . . together. That'll be good enough. And, Flynn?*"

"*Yeah?*"

"*Get some sleep . . . eat something . . . call your mother . . . whatever you need to do to get your ass in gear. I want you healthy. At one hundred percent for the next mission. We can't change what happened to Adam, but we can keep it from happening to you and find out who did it,*" Collins said.

There was a long moment of silence before Holly spoke again, saying, "*Okay . . . I'll try.*"

"*Carter?*" Collins said after another brief pause.

Carter was the guy on the dance floor. I had already pulled up images in my mind of that night and was nearly positive I could identify this guy. That was more info about Eyewall than we had two days ago.

"*Yeah, boss?*" Agent Carter said.

Now I had the name, face, and voice.

"*Flynn's heading out . . . We'll revisit suspect twenty-two after tonight,*" Collins said.

Agent Carter laughed. *"She's gonna have to sleep with a suspect eventually. What else is she good for? You're too easy on her. Lewis would have never gotten away with that."*

The recording stopped and I stayed there, leaning against the counter, taking deep breaths, trying to keep myself from flinging a chair out the window. Finally, I stood up and walked over to the couch. Kendrick sat frozen and wide-eyed, while Stewart chewed on a fingernail, avoiding my stare.

"Did you guys have to do that?" I asked.

"What?" Kendrick asked, looking surprised by the question. "Go undercover? Flirt with a suspect?"

"Not flirting," I said firmly.

Stewart finally looked at me. "He's asking if we've slept with someone as an assignment."

"No," Kendrick said right away, then she let out a breath and added, "But close."

"Seriously?" I said. "Like you really felt like you had to do it . . . or was it your idea?"

Stewart laughed and then her face turned completely serious. "Yeah, she did it because it sounded fun . . . Are you on something? We do what we have to do. If Kendrick was fat and ugly she wouldn't have to worry about any of that. Neither would I. But power is power in whatever form we can get it."

My eyes bored in to Stewart's and I had to ask. I *had* to know. "Is that what it was . . . with me? Did someone make you do it?"

She stared right back, waiting a long time before answering. "No. It wasn't an assignment. Your dad would have never . . . I mean . . . I couldn't . . ."

"How did you know about Agent Collins?" I asked, changing the subject quickly while she was being honest.

She let out a breath, shaking her head in frustration. "Agent Collins offered me a job."

"When?" Kendrick asked.

"Two years ago . . . right after I started training."

"Does he know which division you work for?" I asked, and even though I wanted to not think like an agent, I couldn't help it. Stewart was offered a position by the division trying to take us down. How did we know she hadn't accepted that position, but stayed in Tempest as a—

"He knows now . . . but then, I'm not sure," Stewart answered, her eyes bouncing between us, probably weighing our suspicion.

"Well, maybe you'll remember more about the EOTs or some details to help us take them down," I said, thinking that might be the only way to free Holly.

Her face changed to stiff and formal. "I'm not going to *remember* anything else, so you might as well just forget about telling anyone."

I crossed my arms and stared her down. "What's the deal? Did you *want* to join Eyewall? You heard what they think about us."

"Forget it," she said, shaking her head. "I just thought you, of all people, might understand."

Kendrick kept her eyes on us, but stayed silent.

"Why me? I haven't been invited to their secret society, if that's what you think. Agent Collins hasn't offered me a job," I said.

"Did you listen to anything Thomas said the other night?" Stewart asked. "He said things none of us have ever heard before. And it didn't really sound like they wanted us dead. I know we should assume he's being manipulative, but what if he's not? We don't even know what the hell we're fighting. All we know is what we're told by Marshall and now Healy. I'm not taking down any Eyewall people without a damn good reason."

Both Stewart and I turned toward Kendrick, who was now staring at her hands. She took a deep breath before looking up at us and saying, "Stewart's right. Everything about the other night had me shook up but I couldn't place where my fear was coming from . . . and now this thing with Holly . . ."

"We don't know anything," I conceded. The uncertainty should have made everything feel worse, and maybe I was still in shock, but the fact that the three of us had just agreed to doubt the people we worked for created this bond I'd never wanted to form, and yet . . . it was nice. My heart sped up as an idea formed, and I let it spill out before I could second-guess myself. "I need you guys to look up something. It's really important, but I can't tell you why just yet."

"Okay . . . ?" both of them said together.

"Surveillance photos . . . from March fifteenth of this year . . . around five in the afternoon until six." I waited for them to shake their heads or show some kind of reluctance, but neither did. "The camera on Ninety-second Street . . . right in front of the Y."

Stewart grabbed the laptop from Kendrick and set it on the kitchen counter, already typing superfast. "I think I know how to find those."

Kendrick rushed behind her, watching over her shoulder. I glanced down at the coffee table and saw they had Holly's diary out, along with a few pictures of Adam and me that Holly took and taped to various pages. I picked up the pink notebook and the pictures and sat down on my bed, flipping through the pages.

SEPTEMBER 27, 2009

> *I'm so, so confused. Now would be a great time to have a parental figure truly lay down the law. Or just tell me what to do. I made plans with Jackson tonight that started with me meeting him at his dorm and then me breaking up with him (of course he only knew the first part). Well, I show up a few minutes before seven and his roommates, Jake and Danny, let me in.*
>
> *Because he's not back from class yet.*
>
> *Seriously? It's seven o'clock. What the hell has he been doing for the last five hours? Some kind of mysterious activity. Like always.*
>
> *By seven-thirty, I'm completely pissed off and he doesn't answer his phone. I decide not to leave because I'll lose my nerve and I won't be able to say what I need to say tomorrow.*

I knew I had avoided reading this last night for a reason. My eyes drifted from the notebook page to the picture of Adam and me at the zoo . . . an elephant's ass positioned right between us. I turned a bunch of pages, choosing one closer to the front of the notebook. There was another picture of me and Adam at an overnight campout, Holly seated between us, sharing a blanket.

Holly knew the answer to 007 Adam's question: he was my friend, even without the time travel. I think I had never actually come up with concrete reasons why he and I connected so well right after we met, but looking back on it now, *that* me was probably very desperate for someone to see through all my bullshit and not make a big deal out of it.

And he was Holly's friend, someone who shared her restless desire to avoid ordinary life.

And he was gone.

"Jackson?" Kendrick said, while Stewart continued her search for the photos. "While you were asleep, we came up with a couple different strategies for making sure Holly's safe and not in the line of fire between Tempest and Eyewall."

I heard her words, but I couldn't let them sink in. My eyes bounced between Stewart and Kendrick, then down at Holly's diary and Adam's picture. And the idea that Stewart and Kendrick had spent all of last night helping me. Now they had a plan to protect a complete stranger . . . *for me*. It was risky and against CIA orders and neither of them looked even the least bit doubtful.

And I've been lying to them all this time.

It was too much to handle . . . too much to keep to myself and still be open about everything else. *Adam's gone . . . Mason's gone . . . Dad's MIA . . . Holly's brainwashed.* This was my family now, or as close as I'd get in this timeline.

"Junior?" Stewart abandoned the laptop and walked toward me, snapping her fingers in front of my face. "Did you hear anything Kendrick just said?"

I grabbed her arm and held on to it to keep her from snapping. "I'm not sure you guys should help me."

"Why not?" they both said together.

"No one in Tempest is going to kill me or throw me to the wolves . . . The EOTs aren't going to kill me," I said, feeling my breath quicken with panic, knowing it would all tumble out. I couldn't stop it. "But you guys—especially Stewart—are disposable."

"Because of your dad?" Kendrick asked. "I don't think that really gives you a big advantage. He's just as replaceable as us."

"No, nothing to do with my dad," I said slowly, trying to figure out why they hadn't caught on to my hints.

"He's just fucking with us," Stewart said, shaking her head.

"I'm not fucking with you!" I took a deep breath, lowering my voice. "They won't kill me because I'm too valuable . . . An EOT didn't bring me to this timeline, I brought myself here."

CHAPTER NINETEEN

Stewart leaned her face very close to mine, then threw a worried glance in Kendrick's direction. "Do you think it's just shock?"

"Most likely," Kendrick said, walking closer to us.

I gave Stewart a light shove out of my way and went straight for the closet, digging up my lockbox with all my notes. "I'm only telling you guys all this because I probably won't stay here very long. So it really doesn't matter."

"We should call Dr. Melvin," Kendrick muttered under her breath.

I found the page and slammed it onto the bed. "In 1989, Dr. Melvin and Tempest used the eggs of an EOT and joined them with an average Joe's sperm and stuck them in a woman named Eileen Covington's uterus, and nine months later a pair of half-EOTs were born."

"Wait . . . are you talking about Axelle?" Kendrick asked.

I gaped at her. "You know about it?"

Stewart looked back and forth between the two of us, confused.

"Yeah, I know about it . . . but not much. I don't know what happened to products or the subject," Kendrick said. "I thought it hadn't happened yet."

"The subject was shot by an EOT named Raymond in October of 1992. The female product of Axelle died of brain cancer in April of 2005," I said, all in one long breath. "And the male product of Axelle . . . well . . . you're looking at him."

"Uh-uh," Kendrick said.

"No way," Stewart said, shaking her head.

Okay, so they weren't going to try and attack like I had thought, but they might check me into the mental ward. I hadn't really considered that outcome. "If you guys would just sit and think about it for a few minutes—" I stopped suddenly, not having the patience to wait for them to think it through. Blood was pumping too fast through my veins. Despite Emily's warnings and everything else, I took the impulsive route. "I'll just show you."

"Show us?" Kendrick and Stewart said together.

"Yep." I took a step back, away from both of them. "Don't blink."

Half a second passed and I stood in the exact same spot in my apartment. But Stewart and Kendrick were gone, all the papers and cups strewn across the coffee table were gone. I turned on my computer monitor and clicked on the date: June 16, 2009, 12:22 P.M.

It was two days ago . . . I had focused on that date, but it felt more forced . . . or just heavier, and I was sure I had jumped further back in another timeline, unless . . .

Frantically, I grabbed a knife from a kitchen drawer and shoved the bed aside, then slowly lifted a floorboard with the aid of the knife blade. I flipped the jagged piece of wood upward and carved the words: *Jackson was here.*

I made sure the board was smoothed down flat and the bed returned to its original position before jumping back.

JUNE 18, 2009, 7:32 A.M.

I ended up landing so close to Kendrick I knocked her back onto the couch and fell right on top of her. She just looked up at me, eyes wide with shock, and said, "Holy shit!"

"Oh, my God," Stewart said from behind us.

I swallowed hard, waiting for either a million questions at once or an attack.

"But you don't have it," Kendrick argued from underneath me. "The Tempus gene . . . you don't have it . . . I'd know."

"Maybe because I'm only a half-breed?" I rolled off Kendrick and onto the floor, then lifted the bed up toward the wall. My fingers searched frantically for the almost-invisible crease where I had pulled up the wooden floorboard. My hand froze, feeling it . . . just like I had left it a few minutes ago. My heart raced as I pried it up and stared at the carving, now two days old.

"Holy fuck!" I shook my head in disbelief. "I actually did it. I mean, I've done it before, but this time I actually tried to do it . . . I altered the past. I did a Thomas-jump."

The grin on my face must have looked totally creepy, because Kendrick and Stewart slid closer to each other, as if preparing to converse quietly, but probably neither knew what to say.

For me, I had just realized that maybe I didn't have to leave after all. Didn't have to take the risk of making new timelines. I could actually alter the past. Fix it. Everything.

"Let's make some more coffee," I said finally. "This is gonna take a long time to explain."

"Oh . . . kay," Kendrick said, moving toward the kitchen.

Stewart sighed and sank onto the couch. "I'm all ears . . . This is gonna be good, isn't it?"

"If crazy is your definition of good, then yeah. It's gonna be great."

CHAPTER TWENTY

"It's not working!" Pain shot through my head and all I could do was lie facedown on the wood floor, panting and waiting for even ten percent relief.

"Maybe you're focusing on the wrong moment?" Kendrick suggested.

We had spent the last eight hours talking time travel and experimenting. Kendrick knew a lot more than I ever could have imagined and was almost as helpful as Eileen had been. It was now even more obvious why she was in this division.

But none of her knowledge or research could help me actually succeed in doing the Thomas-jump again. I totally sucked at it and the half-jumps were wearing me thin.

"Let's take a break . . . please?" she said, pointing to the couch. "We can review the timeline data again. Maybe that'll help you get a grasp on what you're trying to do."

I sighed with frustration but couldn't really argue when I had zero energy left. I pried myself from the floor and rubbed the blurriness from my eyes. "You know when I jumped off the roof . . . in August 2009 . . . before I came here . . ."

"Yeah?"

"I keep forgetting about this question, but I've been wondering ever since it happened, and something always prevents me from asking Dr. Melvin or my dad." I leaned back against the couch, closing my eyes and breathing slowly to fight off the nausea. "There were two Hollys . . . It was weird, because I assumed it was the 2007 timeline—"

"World B," Kendrick added.

"Yeah . . . World B . . . but, you know . . . in 2009 . . . like I fast-forwarded a couple years *and* jumped sideways . . ."

"You couldn't have jumped past—"

"The last date I left in 2007," I finished, nodding without opening my eyes. "I know. Dr. Melvin explained all that. But then it had to have been a Thomas-jump, right? But it couldn't be, because she would have remembered seeing me and herself when we fast-forwarded again."

Kendrick's forehead wrinkled as she flipped through pages of notes. "What was the date for that jump?"

"It was 2009 . . . the second time, after I returned from World B. We jumped from August fifteenth and landed on August twelfth . . . I have no idea of the time."

"What was your source?"

"Some woman's newspaper," I said.

"That was the only source you checked?" Kendrick asked, and I nodded. "Well . . . from my research on complete jumps, the memory could have come on slowly. Tempest doesn't have a lot of data recorded from actual subjects affected by a complete jump. It was only, what, like fourteen or so hours before you jumped back to March fifteenth?"

"Yeah, that's right." I opened my eyes and looked over the paper in front of me again. "So what you're saying is . . . if I'd stuck around, she might have remembered seeing another version of herself three days in the past?"

"She already did remember seeing two of herself . . . She was there," Kendrick said. "The only memory she may have acquired would be the memory of that other version of herself getting to Central Park with Raymond and whichever EOTs were around. Some people are just built to handle shock better than others. Maybe Holly is like that. Instead of crawling into a shell and shaking with fear when she gets thrown off a roof and sent through her boyfriend's time portal, she just stows it away . . . doesn't absorb the impact of that moment until much later."

"That sounds like an agent skill," I said dryly, hating that Holly had anything to offer the CIA. I wanted her out of there . . . back to her normal life, worrying about which classes to take and whether or not her old clunker of a car would start in the morning.

"You know the future that Emily took you to see?" Kendrick asked, pulling me from my thoughts of Holly.

"The shitty one that looked like the Zombie Apocalypse had just happened?"

"Uh-huh." She thumbed through her notes for a minute then finally glanced over at me. "I think I know what happened. It's a term I stumbled on in the Tempest database while I was studying everything ever written on time travel. A Vortex. That's what it's called when the frequency of time travel increases. It supposedly can cause earthquakes, tsunamis, hurricanes . . ."

I gaped at her with my mouth half open. "What . . . ? I mean, why wouldn't anyone have told me about that? Or told me not to time-travel because it may cause an earthquake in the future? That seems like an important detail to not keep secret, even if Marshall and Dr. Melvin were trying to hide things from me."

"Probably because it would take a lot of time travel to do this. By 'a lot,' I mean hundreds of people . . . maybe thousands . . . jumping all over the place." She leaned back against the couch and diverted her eyes from mine. "It's possible . . . I don't know for sure . . . but this might be Eileen's data." She let out a breath and rushed to get the rest of her words out. "It goes with her theory of you somehow opening up World B and allowing the EOTs to bounce off of it, thus increasing the number of time travelers, and as a result, a Vortex was created. Or will be created. I'm not sure which it is."

Her words hung in the silence that followed this revelation. So, basically it was my fault the future crumbled to bits. I started the Vortex.

"Wow . . . that's a fun bit of info to carry around. So glad we had this chat." I smiled at her to show I wasn't blaming her, but the timing was a little bad. I had enough shit to deal with right now.

Michael knocked on the door before Kendrick could respond, and after watching her face light up when she saw him, I had to tell her to go. Healy would most likely be sending us all back to France anytime now and she'd have to leave him again and I knew it was on her mind even though she had devoted all her energy to helping me these past two days.

I had about five minutes to myself before Stewart burst in like she lived here. "They're gone!"

I jumped up from the couch. "Who's gone? What happened?"

"Not who," she said. "The photos you told me to find. I got my hands on everything up until four fifty-nine in the afternoon on March fifteenth . . . and then I found all the photos beginning with six thirteen in the evening—"

"But nothing in between?"

"Correct."

"So then, Adam was on to something. Those pictures are important." I sank back into the couch and had to lean forward and put my head between my knees for a few seconds. It hurt to say his name . . . to remember him bleeding . . . dying.

"What's wrong with you?" Stewart asked, flicking the top of my head.

"Time travel . . . lots of it."

"And . . . ?"

I lifted my head, slowly sitting up again. "And I suck at it."

Stewart tried to hide the disappointment on her face, but I saw it. She wanted me to save Mason. I knew she'd been thinking that ever since I'd told her what I could do this morning, but she'd never say it out loud. She'd never ask me to do it because that would mean admitting how much she cared. "I bet you don't suck at it . . . You're just a little too pampered. Not enough experience with mental toughness. The rest of them are full-bloods, so they don't have the average-Joe genes in them. Probably lowers your IQ about two hundred points."

"Thanks," I said, rolling my eyes.

She sank down beside me and turned her head, showing off the dark circles under her own eyes. Holly's diary rested in her hand and she passed it back and forth between her hands several times. "Maybe if we got someone to throw me off this building you'd have more success . . . ?"

"I've thought about it."

Her expression faltered for a second and I snorted back a laugh.

Catching Jenni Stewart off guard was a rare occurrence and I had to appreciate it. Of course, that cost me a hard punch in the shoulder. I got up from the couch and stretched out across my bed, already feeling like I was half asleep. My bones ached and my teeth had started chattering as if I had a fever or chills. I wrestled myself under the blanket, knowing I'd have to rest before anything else could be fixed or figured out.

"Hey," I said, remembering where the conversation with Kendrick had left off. "Have you heard of this Vortex theory?"

Stewart shook her head so I explained what Kendrick had just revealed and that it was possibly from Eileen's notes.

"I think we should talk to Dr. Melvin." Stewart fell next to me on the bed, shaking the mattress and causing another wave of nausea to hit me hard.

"I figured," I mumbled. "But I need to think about the best approach. He's easily scared off, and then he shuts down and won't tell us anything."

"Yeah, I know." She rested her head on the pillow next to me.

"What are you doing . . . ?"

"Sleeping. Something I haven't done in twenty-four hours." Her voice already sounded muffled and sleepy. "I've been too busy helping you with all your issues. If you get to sleep, so do I. We'll be better prepared for Dr. Melvin."

"Or Eyewall trying to kill us," I added.

"That, too." Stewart scooted closer to me, and the warmth of her body kept me from protesting. My blanket wasn't nearly big enough to stop my teeth from chattering.

"What's it feel like?" she asked after a couple minutes of silence.

"Like the worst kind of flu . . . like I have a fever of a hundred and five," I said, closing my eyes again.

"No, I mean time travel . . . the actual jumping part. What does that feel like?"

The warmth of her body heat continued to fill the space under the covers and my teeth finally stopped chattering. "The half-jumps feel like everything is being tugged in two . . . and then when I come back, it's like the worst kind of jet lag. All this time has passed for me, but not for anyone else in home base."

"I don't know if it will ever stop sounding crazy to me . . . unbelievable might be a better word."

I laughed. "Yeah, me either."

She scooted even closer, barely resting her cheek against my chest. "Mason and your dad and I had this really long debate one night . . . I think it was last year and we were doing fourth-line surveillance for a mission in Costa Rica. Mason was going on and on about some wacko paradox theory and was convinced it wasn't possible to survive seeing your other self in a complete jump . . . that the shock alone would kill the person, both of them. Your dad said something and I didn't think much about it then, but now . . ."

"What?" I asked, feeling my eyelids getting heavier.

"He said people can handle much more than anyone ever thinks . . . not in a cheesy perseverance kind of way, but just that we're made to adapt to our environment. Humans are survivors. I know it seems like basic secret-agent pep-talk stuff, but I got this feeling like he knew from experience, like maybe he had to face himself at some point." She yawned and leaned against me even more. "Never mind. I'll explain it better after I get some sleep."

The mention of my dad seeing another version of himself made me think again of Holly staring at another Holly. She had indicated a possible need for therapy, but other than that she was okay.

"We're both probably doing the exact same thing—analyzing everything he's ever told us, like the words are pieces to a big giant puzzle we need to solve." Without thinking, I draped my arm around her waist, then laughed under my breath when I realized what I had just done. "Are we cuddling? I figured if you ever got this close to me again, I'd either be severely injured or naked."

"It's a rare moment of weakness. Pity, that's all." She relaxed her muscles, letting out a deep exhausted breath. "You act like I never touch anyone without either abuse or seduction."

"Were any of your college student characters stable and affectionate?"

I joked, but really I wanted to know how far she took those roles. I'd actually wanted to know this since right after she told me her story.

"Not really. I dated a lot of different guys, but I didn't usually . . ." She paused for a second, then started laughing.

"Didn't what?"

She scooted away, just enough so we weren't touching anymore, but I could see her face now. "Let's just say I got really good at putting the ax down at just the right moment."

"Oh, man . . . you evil bitch." I laughed lightly. "Was this method reserved for assholes only, or did you prey on nice guys, like Michael?"

I expected her to give me a vague smart-ass answer and end this touchy-feely conversation, but she did just the opposite.

"First of all, Michael's not a nice guy . . . he's a saint. They're a completely different breed. A guy like him would never end up with me." Her face stayed relaxed, but she seemed deep in thought and void of the usual defensive edge. "It wasn't about running over guys or manipulation. It's just . . . if you give people everything they want, then why would they need you anymore?"

Some of the weight lifted from my eyelids and I focused more clearly on her face. Finally, after all these months, Jenni Stewart made sense to me. Perfect sense. And the reasons she got along so well with Mason were clear. They had both been rejected. Not that the rest of us agents hadn't suffered the loss of loved ones, but grief had a very different effect on a person than abandonment. Mason and Stewart felt abandoned. Stewart had been abandoned in her teen years, shipped off to college early to get her out of her parents' hair, and then the radio silence when she got arrested and really needed them. Mason's mother had supposedly died in childbirth, leaving him parentless his whole life.

This was exactly why the it's-not-personal-it's-business approach had appealed to me from the very beginning of agent training. But right now, talking to Stewart, having someone know my secrets, was as comforting as having 009 and 007 Adam know.

Stewart's eyes had started to close. I shook her shoulders lightly. "Hey . . . can I ask you something?"

"Yeah?" She looked right at me, waiting.

The psychoanalytical part of my brain wouldn't shut off until I got a few more answers from her. "Why do you think it was so easy for us to . . . you know . . . hook up? Or almost hook up, until I had my emotional relapse. Then it wasn't easy at all."

She shrugged and closed her eyes again. "Because we're fucked up . . . both of us."

"So you've thought about this, too? Tried to figure it out?" I prodded, hoping she'd stay with me on this self-discovery ride.

"Yeah. We suck at being friends . . . with anyone," she said. "You pull off the act much better than I do, but it's half-assed. I watched you for two years before you started this job. You were never really close to anyone. I don't think you're an asshole or a player, either . . . You just had lots of lines you weren't willing to cross."

She was right. My friendship with Adam was probably the closest I'd gotten to having a "real" best friend. And I didn't really reveal too much to him until all the bad stuff started to happen.

Not until I got stuck in 2007.

"We suck at being friends," I repeated, grasping the concept as the words tumbled out of my mouth.

"Yep . . . and I didn't learn this from deep self-reflection or any bullshit like that. I figured it out after I read Blondie's diary." She laughed again with her eyes closed. "I really wanted to do it to you . . . get you all hot and excited and then cut you off."

If I'd had the energy, I would have shoved her off the bed. Instead, I laughed with her. "Like I said earlier: evil bitch."

"But you totally threw me off my game by trying to get me to talk. Then I had to make you stop."

I laughed even harder. "Oh, God . . . we are fucked-up . . . especially you. But seriously, that's a technique I've used many times. Kissing instead of talking . . ."

"You never told her you loved her," Stewart prompted. "Does that mean you would have been better off just being friends?"

I didn't even hesitate before answering. "I never wanted to be Holly's friend. And I did tell her I loved her. Eventually."

"And you meant it?"

I gave in to the heaviness of my eyelids and let them close. "Yeah, I meant it."

"But is it worth it?" she mumbled, sounding less coherent than she had a few seconds earlier.

I sighed, forcing back the empty feeling I'd been stuck with the past few months. It was a difficult question, because I immediately translated it to: *Is Holly worth it?* Which would obviously be a yes. Holly was worth any suffering I'd ever have to endure. But I knew Stewart wasn't asking about Holly or any one person. Just the concept. I could only imagine how much easier this job would have been had the carefree and uncommitted Jackson been the one who joined the CIA. Falling in love had ruined me. Inside and out. It made everything in my life more complicated, and I could never undo it. Ever. I could erase her memories of being with me, take myself out of the relationship over and over again, but I'd never be able to change what it did to me.

"No, it's not worth it," I answered finally. "Not for people like us."

"That's what I thought," she mumbled. "And this, my friend, is called progress."

"Meaning . . . we don't suck as much as we used to." I smiled to myself before falling asleep. Stewart was the very last person I ever thought I'd find to replace the void of not having Adam around. "Adam . . . and Mason," I muttered to her before drifting off. "I'm gonna fix it . . . even if it makes me really sick." *Or worse.* "I'll make Dr. Melvin tell me how."

JUNE 19, 2009, 10:49 P.M.

"Guess who's tailing us," Stewart whispered, without glancing behind us.

I, on the other hand, did look over my shoulder. Just for a split second. A streak of a blond ponytail stuck out from the doorway in front of a music shop on Fifth Avenue. "At least we know she's okay."

"Did you think she wouldn't be?" Stewart asked. "She's a trained agent. That has to mean something."

"I know." What I really hated, more than anything, was being so close to Holly, physically, and yet the farthest I'd been from her. Enemies. We'd never been enemies. Even strangers was better than enemies. This thought had been eating at me constantly, a virus infesting my blood and turning my insides to liquid . . . *Holly, my enemy.* I just couldn't swallow it. And even worse, Stewart, Kendrick, and I had to set our investigation aside to do some unavoidable work for Healy and Freeman all day today. Until now.

We rounded a corner, and Stewart stopped and leaned against the wall, fiddling with something on the inside of her jacket. "She stopped following us and now she's on the phone."

"How do you know—"

I was cut off by Holly's voice coming through my earpiece. "You tapped her phone?"

"Pretty nifty, huh?" Stewart said with a grin. She began walking again so we wouldn't look too suspicious.

"I'm sorry, Mom. I should have told you I quit," Holly said. "I've had so much studying to do for my summer classes."

"You haven't gotten a check from the camp for over a month," Katherine Flynn's voice came through the phone loud and clear. "When were you going to tell me?"

"I'm sorry," Holly said, frustration leaking into her voice. "Can we talk about this later?"

"When?" Katherine demanded. "It's nearly eleven. Where are you?"

"Out," Holly said firmly. "I'll be home by midnight, okay?"

The call ended abruptly. Stewart shook her head and glanced sideways at me. "I guess none of us have to deal with civilian parents. That's a complication I hadn't really thought of before."

"Lucky us," I muttered under my breath, but then I remembered

Holly's petrified face when she was standing in my apartment, waiting for me to attack her. She had begged me to let her call her mom.

Stewart was convinced that it was a code for her team to know she was in distress, but now I wasn't completely sure I agreed.

Both of us were silent the rest of the walk to NYU Medical Center. Even Stewart looked nervous about this bold move we were about to make. She started biting her nails while we rode up in the elevator.

"We can totally do this. Just remember the plan. Drop only enough information to keep him asking us for more," I whispered as my hand hovered over the doorknob to Dr. Melvin's office.

"And don't tell him that you suck at complete jumps," Stewart hissed as I knocked softly. "That's better than any weapon we point at him."

Dr. Melvin didn't answer, but light shone from underneath the door. I tried the door and it opened immediately. The first thing I saw as we walked inside the large office was the giant letters spray-painted in red across the back wall.

"Japanese," Stewart muttered. "What's it say?"

I stared closely at the symbol before answering, "Eyewall."

The word was barely out of my mouth when I heard Stewart gasp beside me. "Oh, God . . ."

The panic inside me doubled as my eyes darted to the left side of the office. Dr. Melvin lay sprawled out on the floor, eyes wide open, skin the color of a pale gray sky. *Oh, no . . . this can't be happening. He can't be . . .*

Stewart was already on the floor next to him, pressing two fingers to his neck.

"He's dead," she managed to croak out. "Melvin's dead."

CHAPTER TWENTY-ONE

The pulse of my heart . . . the blood pumping to my ears drowned out all other sounds. Stewart's mouth was moving. She was saying something to me, but I had no idea what. My gaze moved from the red writing on the wall back to the old man, cold and dead on the floor.

Finally, she kicked me in the shin and I snapped into action, closing and locking the door. "What do we do now?" I asked.

She was on her feet now, but the panic in her eyes told me she didn't know any more than I did. Thomas had been so right about me. Emotions clouded my judgment, distracted me from focusing on a task. But Stewart was by far the most levelheaded agent in our division. It took her about five more seconds of freaking out before she drew in a deep breath and started moving.

"Put these on!" A pair of latex gloves was thrust in my hands. "Put the computer back together!"

I spun around, just now noticing the pieces of metal strewn all over the floor. "Data . . . experiment data . . . that's what they took, right?"

A brief flash of Adam doing the same thing passed through my mind, but only for a split second before I returned to the horror of the present moment.

"Yeah, that's what they took." Stewart crawled under the desk beside me, feeling underneath it. "And they're CIA . . . They should know exactly how to do this without leaving a mess. And they sure as hell left a mess."

"They . . . I mean Eyewall wanted us to know they have his stuff?" I tossed components into the now-empty shell that had held the computer.

"They wanted us to know they don't agree with Dr. Melvin's theories," Stewart said firmly. "They don't morally agree."

Cloning . . . that was what Eyewall must have discovered about Dr. Melvin. But Healy had said studying cloning, figuring out how to make it real, was one of Dr. Melvin's biggest regrets. What had he called it? *A foolish boy's dream.*

"You put in the distress code already, didn't you?" I asked Stewart.

"I had to," she said reluctantly. "What else are we going to do?"

Something under the desk caught my attention. I slid on my back underneath and looked up. Stewart turned over beside me, staring at the same red writing that had caught my eye.

More Japanese.

"What does it say? I can't read Japanese."

"Death, murder," I read aloud. *"None of it can be justified unless serving the greatest purpose of all . . . preserving humanity for centuries to come. The natural state of humanity. Any other form will destroy us all."*

Silence fell between us as the words sank in, hitting way too close to home. The sound of my phone buzzing caused both of us to jump and hit our heads together.

"Yeah," I said, pressing the phone to my ear while sliding out from under the desk. I intentionally averted my eyes from Dr. Melvin's body. "It's me . . . I mean, Agent Meyer."

"Is Agent Stewart with you?" Senator Healy said.

"Yes, sir."

"Is Dr. Melvin with you?" he asked, and I could tell from the way he said those words that he most likely already knew what had happened. Maybe Eyewall had scribbled under his desk as well.

I let out a breath, trying to focus on answering his questions so maybe he could answer ours. "Yes . . . but he's . . . dead."

There was a long moment of silence, and then Healy's voice came through firm and direct. "I want you and Agent Stewart to go immediately to your father's apartment. Leave everything just as you found it and lock the door."

"No," I protested. "We'll wait here with him . . . with the body. Make sure no one else comes in."

"Jackson, please do as I ask. I've received a series of messages in the past few minutes, and one of them indicated that your father may have returned from his mission."

That was enough for me. I leaped to my feet and Stewart jumped up beside me, ready for orders. "We're leaving now," I told him, and then hung up the phone.

I gave Dr. Melvin one last glance before locking up the door. The ache inside me, the grief, had reached an inconceivable height and I had no idea how to deal with it. The only thing I knew how to do was keep going.

"Healy thinks my dad's back," I said to Stewart as we ran for the stairs, not wanting to bother with the elevator. "He seems to have known about Dr. Melvin . . . or at least suspected it."

I think both of us were holding our breath as we busted through the front door of Dad's apartment. I'd nearly blown my cover when we were forced into a few minutes of polite conversation with Henry, the doorman. And then the tortuously long elevator ride to the top floor . . .

"Dad!" I yelled as Stewart shoved past me, heading toward the kitchen.

My feet started to slow down about two seconds after walking into the living room. I could practically smell the stale emptiness of the place. Panic and grief washed over me as I stood in silence waiting for Stewart to return. I only had to glance at her face to know the answer.

"Damn it!" I said under my breath as the panic turned to intense fury. Why couldn't one freaking thing go right? I pulled out my phone and sent Healy a text.

He's not here? Then I tossed my phone across the room. It smacked into the wall, shattering the silence. I thought Stewart would be more pissed off than me, but she just sank onto the couch, bringing her knees up to her chest.

I had to do something productive or the words would keep echoing through my head . . . *Dr. Melvin's dead . . .*

The long black piano bench caught my eye. I strode across the room and flung it open, tearing through mounds of sheet music, scattering them all over the floor.

"Jackson?" Stewart said, lifting her head to look at me.

"He's left shit lying around for us before, maybe we just haven't figured out his little scavenger hunt." I was already walking down the hall toward Dad's room when I heard her sigh and then start to follow me.

There was a definite edge to my searching of Dad's closet, but Stewart skillfully ignored the reckless digging, which I really appreciated. It took about an hour to get everything out of the closet and examine it with the careful eye of a trained agent. Stewart was still looking through some pictures stuffed in a small shoe box when I called it quits.

I leaned against the wall of the now-empty closet, closing my eyes and trying to think of some amazing theory or connection between recent events, something that would help me talk to my dad. I barely noticed the sound of rumbling behind me, and then, just as my eyes opened, the floor split apart below me, literally.

"Holy shit!" I jumped out of the way of the nearly four-foot hole in the closet floor and spun around, staring at the opening. "I swear I didn't know that was there."

"What the fuck?" Stewart said, looking around my shoulder. "Did you press something or hit a trigger, maybe?"

"No, I was just leaning against the wall." I dropped down to my hands and knees, leaning into the hole. A rope ladder hung down, but I couldn't see where it led.

"What is this place? How could we have missed a crack in the floor like that? There would have to be some sign of the carpet being able to separate."

"Maybe this was for the bodyguards . . . whoever watched over me and Courtney when we were little. Like a surveillance room."

"You're forgetting that I was that person for two years," Stewart said. "Don't you think I'd know about this?"

I nodded toward the ladder, feeling the thrill of a distraction running through me. "Should we go check it out?"

Stewart bit her lip and looked out into the bedroom again. "Healy told us to wait here. He could walk in the door any second."

"Better make it fast, then," I said, then I placed a foot on the rope ladder and began to climb down. She'd follow me, I knew she would.

The area was dark and the ladder was about the length of one flight of stairs. This secret room was obviously connected to the floor below us, but was there an access door? My feet landed on what felt like carpet, and seconds later Stewart's thud came through the dark. Both of us started feeling around for a light switch. I banged my shins into a table and heard the rocking of a lamp about to tip over. I steadied it and then flipped on the light. A twin-sized bed, neatly made with a dark blue quilt, was right in front of me. The nightstand I had run into sat beside it.

The room was about half the size of my borrowed studio apartment in Kendrick's building. There was a bathroom with a shower and a very small kitchen. No microwave or TV. Just a red teakettle sitting on the stovetop.

"There's not even a smoke alarm in here," Stewart muttered. "That's totally a violation of the building code."

"I think the lack of a door is probably the biggest concern." I walked toward a bookcase and touched the record player that sat on top. Dozens of albums were neatly lined up on the lowest shelf. "Do you think a maid lived here or something . . . ?"

"Uh . . . that would be evil, considering how dangerous it is . . . no fire exit." She squatted down in front of the bookcase, eyes scanning the records. "Look at all these records. Do people still listen to records? And Hank Williams . . . Frank Sinatra . . . seriously?"

I moved the needle of the record player back into place and sat down on the carpet beside Stewart. "And the books . . . *Return to Paradise, East of Eden, The Old Man and the Sea* . . ."

"I've read that last one."

"Me, too," I said. "Everyone has, right? In school?"

Stewart shrugged and headed toward the dresser, opening the top drawer. A flash of red above my head distracted me, and I looked up at the ceiling. It was so low I could touch it if I stood on my toes. Writing in red, blue, and black ink scattered across the white surface.

"Hey, Stewart . . . look up." I stepped onto the bed so I could read better.

"I know that writing," she said, excitement filling her voice. She noticed Dad's careful handwriting at the same time I did. "Do you think he used to stay down here?"

"It's possible. Makes more sense than it being the maid's home." I tilted my head to read the sentence written directly above the pillow.

> I never think of the future, it comes soon enough.
> Albert Einstein

"Check out this one," Stewart said. Her voice had lowered almost to a whisper. Both of us had subdued considerably, as if reading these words were an invasion of Dad's privacy.

I moved my eyes to the space above her and couldn't help smiling, despite by earlier mood.

> The important thing is not to stop questioning. Curiosity has its own reasons for existing.
> Albert Einstein

"Wise words," I said, moving over to find something else to read. The longest sentence of all was written on the wall behind the bed, except it wasn't Dad's handwriting. "This one's Eileen's writing."

I recognized it from my most recent jump back to 1992 when she took notes on everything I had told her.

> Now he has departed from this strange world a little ahead of me. That means nothing. People like us, who believe in physics, know that the distinction between past, present, and future is only a stubbornly persistent illusion.
> Albert Einstein

"You know what annoys the hell out of me about that quote?" Stewart asked. I shook my head, still gazing at the words. "Einstein had no fucking clue how true that statement was. He was being hypothetical. We don't get that luxury."

"No, we don't," I agreed.

"And is there anything besides Einstein on this wall?"

My eyes dropped to the big red heart drawn under Eileen's handwriting, and then something else from Dad. I could tell Stewart was reading at the same time as me. Digging for those answers.

He felt now that he was not simply close to her, but that he did not know where he ended and she began.
Leo Tolstoy

My eyes bounced back and forth between Eileen's writing and Dad's. Imagining them down here, sitting on the bed, scribbling messages back and forth to each other, it almost felt more real than actually seeing them together in those half-jumps.

Stewart walked away from me, returning her attention to the dresser drawer she had left open. "This is such a strange place to live. You know . . . I can't imagine your dad staying anywhere but his apartment."

"Me either." I walked over to her and saw she had pulled a stack of photos from the dresser. "It's like he doesn't fit into this room, but obviously he does."

"I was thinking the same thing." She handed me a picture of Dad and me sitting at the piano. It was the same one I had seen on the mantel above the fireplace when I spent those two hours with Eileen. Stewart paused to stare at a photo of Eileen and Courtney in Central Park. "She's really pretty. It just seems so strange . . . They're your parents, but they aren't really."

"They are," I said firmly. "More so than anyone else."

I picked up a box of matches, buried under more pictures. The words BILLY'S TAVERN were printed in black across the white box. "Do you know this place?"

"No . . . never heard of it." Stewart glanced at the rope ladder and then back at me. "We should go back up."

I could see she was worried about the same thing I was: Would the floor close up again? And did anyone else know about this secret hide-out?

Only one way to find out.

When we had returned to the safety of Dad's closet, both of us started feeling around the walls for switches or triggers. "Maybe I should lean against it like I did before?"

"Go for it."

I carefully stepped over the hole and pressed my back to the wall. Nothing happened. "Well, this sucks."

Stewart frowned, her forehead wrinkling with concentration. "Try touching the wall with your hands. It's possible there's a biometric fingerprint—"

The carpet instantly began to merge the second my fingers hit the wall, cutting off Stewart's explanation. "Okay, smarty-pants . . . how'd you know that?"

"Lucky guess." She watched as the carpet sealed itself shut, leaving almost no trace of a line where the floor was split in half. "I wonder if you have to remove all the weight from the floor to get it to open. I'm sure you've never taken every single item out of your dad's closet, then touched your hands to the wall."

"Nope. Can't say that I've done that before today. But it recognized my fingerprints?"

She shrugged, looking just as frustrated as I felt with the lack of answers. The sound of the apartment door opening jolted us back to the present and we both ran down the hall so fast we nearly plowed into Senator Healy.

The grim expression he wore wasn't in the least bit encouraging. "Agent Stewart . . . Jackson . . . I'm sorry for sending you here with false hope. Unfortunately, I have some more bad news."

He gestured toward the living room couch, but neither of us moved. Stewart was holding her breath, just like me. Healy sighed and turned to face us directly. "I'm so sorry to have to tell you this, Jackson. It seems . . . well . . . it seems your father may have made a deal with Eyewall."

He's still alive. I couldn't help feeling relieved. My dad was still alive.

"What kind of deal?" Stewart asked. I could see her game face clearly plastered on.

"Agent Freeman and I have been working on this investigation for a week now," Healy said. "The EOT that we captured in Germany—Cassidy—escaped, though we thought it was impossible. Agent Freeman also confided in me about a bribe Agent Meyer had been offered several months ago."

"What?" Stewart and I both said.

The grimness returned to Healy's face, but even worse than a minute ago. "He was offered a cure . . . something that hasn't been discovered yet . . ."

"Cure?" I asked, feeling utterly confused.

Stewart glanced at me, holding my gaze for a second before whispering, "For cancer, right?"

Healy nodded slowly, confirming her theory. "Most likely he's been taken to the future . . . to help Eyewall . . ."

I felt like the wind had been knocked out of me. He wouldn't do that. He wouldn't leave me alone just to chase some idea that most likely was a trap.

"Wait . . . is that even possible?" Stewart demanded. "Wouldn't it kill him?"

"One jump won't kill him. And he isn't the first to accept a bribe," Healy said. "Treason is a threat our agency has to deal with constantly."

My head spun. This was too much to handle. What did I have left to keep me grounded to this timeline, or any, for that matter?

"Unfortunately, we can't discuss this further at the moment," Healy said. "The reason I sent the two of you here is because I knew you'd be tailed and we'd have a chance to counterattack the opposition."

"Eyewall," Stewart said. "Who's tailing us?"

"I'm not sure specifically which agents. However, our entire mission team is already chasing agents on foot. We knew Dr. Melvin's death was the kickoff event," Healy said. "The two of you are going to walk out of this building and go separate ways. Agent Parker is placed across the street, giving me updates."

"What's the exact assignment?" Stewart asked.

"Catch them," Healy said simply. "If you can keep them alive for questioning, that's preferred, but keep in mind, they may have the same plan. However, I can guarantee it won't be for very long."

My whole body was numb from shock . . . from the overwhelming sense that everything was way too big for me to handle. But the second we stepped out into the very early morning air, I saw the small, blond-haired agent hiding out behind Parker, waiting to follow him.

And I knew I'd have to be the one to chase Holly.

Stewart turned her back on me immediately and headed toward the street corner. I made brief eye contact with Parker and turned on my coms unit.

"Let me take Blondie . . . I've got her profile memorized already."

"Copy that."

Relief washed over me as Parker turned his attention and his gun to another agent. Holly's figure dissolved behind a bus and I took off on foot after her.

Her pace picked up and I almost didn't see her head for the subway steps. She froze in front of the turnstile and glanced over her shoulder, getting a full view of me. Her eyes bugged out and then she pushed the man in front of her through the gate, leaping over the turnstile in the process.

Okay . . . obviously she isn't going to surrender quietly.

I flashed a fake FBI badge to the operator and jumped the turnstile, following her. Several people screamed as Holly tore through the crowd, shoving aside bystanders, who then ended up blocking my path. But the loudest screams of all came when she jumped down onto the tracks.

"Damn it, Holly!" *This is not what I had planned. She's supposed to get scared and give up without a fight.* The last thing I wanted was for her to risk her life just to run from me.

She was safely on the other side before I had even jumped down. I hated getting on the tracks, but I did it anyway. The second my feet hit level ground again, the next train came barreling through.

I could see her about twenty feet in front of me and figured she'd get on the subway, make a plan knowing I wouldn't do anything too drastic on a crowded train. The doors opened, but she didn't get on. She ran farther through the tunnel, where there was only a few inches between her and the train. I reluctantly followed.

She moved across the narrow space with such ease, it was clear all those years of walking on balance beams came in handy. The people boarding the train had become a distant blur. The dark swallowed us both, but I could see her small frame moving forward. Then she just vanished. It took me another twenty seconds to reach the opening in the tunnel that she had dived into.

A large brown door and another staircase . . . going down. The stairs led to a dark hallway that smelled like sewage and moldy water. Her hair flew behind her and I focused my eyes on it.

At least I *tried* to, until a shoe made contact with the side of my face, throwing me against the wall. I recognized the Eyewall agent from our list of suspects. The dude reached his hands for my throat and I sprang into action, tossing him onto the hard tile floor.

I used the technique the martial arts experts had taught us in China, squeezing his neck just enough to make him pass out. I swiped his gun and ID before sprinting to catch up with Holly. My eyes still hadn't adjusted to the dark, so I was really surprised to hear the sound of her breathing, like she was close by, very close.

"Dead end," a male voice said from my right side.

Sure enough, Holly was pressed against the wall, running her hands along the surface, like she might find a door. The dude to my right lunged toward me and I knocked him out easily with a hard blow to the temple using my elbow. He stumbled back toward the wall and slumped down.

"Flynn!" the first injured man, having regained consciousness, managed to shout, but it sounded more like a dying croak. "Do it! Now."

The whites of Holly's eyes shone through the dark and she dove sideways into a door I hadn't even noticed. I leaped in after her and both of us jumped when the door slammed behind us. A loud click echoed through the near-silence. I could hear Holly breathing hard and could feel the smallness of the space. Like a tiny room.

The light from my cell phone was enough to see her face illuminated with fear. I bounced the small light around the walls and realized she had most likely led me right into this trap. That was the plan all along. Eyewall knew we'd follow . . . knew we'd go man-to-man. A sick feeling rose in my stomach. Had Stewart and Kendrick already chased their targets down? Were they trapped like me? And where were all the others . . . Parker and Freeman?

The rustle of movement forced me to shine the light on Holly again.

"Back up!" She pointed her gun at me, like she had in my apartment two nights ago, except she didn't look nearly as shaky this time.

I lifted my hands in the air and found my way to the corner farthest from her. "Guess you tricked me. Nice job."

She walked toward the door and kept one hand on the gun and one fumbling with the weird bar across the center of the door. This room was about the size of a very large walk-in closet and didn't appear to have any other exit except the one door we'd come in.

I watched as she pressed harder and harder against the bar, swearing under her breath.

"I think it's locked," I finally said, resting my back against the wall.

"No . . . no way. They'd never lock me in here with . . ." She snapped around swiftly to face me, putting her second hand back on the gun.

"Obviously, they did. For all we know, it might be a long wait. Are you seriously going to keep that gun pointed at me for hours? My arms are gonna get really tired up in the air like this."

"Yes," she said through her teeth. "I'm going to keep my gun pointed at you until I either decide to shoot you or I pass out or die."

"Okay, then," I said with a groan. "This should be a blast. Maybe you can just shoot me in the leg or something. Then we can both sit down. I'm pretty tired from that run you just took me on."

"You'd rather be shot in the leg than have your arms get a little tired?"

"You won't shoot me." I shone the light on her face again to get a good view of her expression—pissed off, as I predicted.

"Try me."

I aimed the light around every wall, one at a time, though I had already memorized the dimensions. "Well . . . based on the size of this little jail cell, if you missed the shot—"

"Oh, I won't miss."

I knew I shouldn't have been turned on by that, but I sort of was. *Commando Holly* . . . a new nickname. "Anyway . . . if you did miss . . . the bullet would bounce off these walls and there's a very good chance it would be headed your way."

She had her cell phone out now, punching in a text message that I knew for a fact couldn't be sent from underground. I waited until she glanced at me again, then I quickly whipped out my gun and the one I'd swiped from the other agent.

Her gasp was completely involuntary, as was the arm that instantly lifted to cover her head.

"See? You still haven't pulled the trigger," I said, and then I opened both pistols with my thumbs. I tucked one gun under my arm and from the other removed each bullet, one at a time. They clanked against the tile floor. Once the bullets from both guns were all on the floor, I set the guns on the floor and slid them across with enough force that they collided with Holly's tennis shoes. "Holly—"

"Agent Flynn," she snapped, still pointing her gun at me.

"Right, *Agent Flynn*. Now that I'm unarmed, I'm gonna sit down until someone comes looking for us."

She walked across the room, only a couple feet away from me now. "Take off your clothes."

Again . . . kind of a turn-on. But I forced the thought from my head, knowing this could be the setup they had intended. Holly would no doubt be able to distract me, as she had proven at Healy's ball. I kicked off my shoes and handed them to her.

"And your shorts," she said, but this time her confidence wavered just a bit.

"Seriously?"

"Yep." She tossed my shoes in a corner.

I sighed heavily and unbuckled my belt, then slipped out of my shorts, standing barefoot in boxers and a polo shirt. "This is when the door opens, right?"

I could see her roll her eyes. "Hand me your shirt, too."

"I'm totally having a middle school flashback right now." I pulled off my shirt and tossed it at her.

She waved it in the air like a flag, then picked up my shorts from the floor. Those were turned upside down until my wallet, keys, and phone tumbled to the floor. She threw the shorts at me after yanking out my belt. "You can put them back on now."

"Thanks so much, *Agent Flynn*." After my clothes were back on, I sat on the floor, in my corner.

Finally, she sat on the floor in the corner diagonal from me, relaxing a little. The gun stayed resting in her lap along with her cell phone.

"You look tired," I said. Now that my eyes had adjusted to the minimal light I could see her better.

"Sleep-deprivation training," she admitted with a heavy sigh.

"What is that, exactly?" I lifted the bottom of my shirt up to my face, wiping the sweat from my forehead.

"Regulated and monitored sleep decreasing over the course of six weeks. I'm on a strict three-hours-a-day maximum. We also take daily mental competency tests to see how we handle less sleep." She glanced wistfully at the door. "God . . . I don't get why they locked me in here with you. That was *not* the plan. There was supposed to be another door . . . an exit."

The fact that she trusted them and not me pissed me off, even though I understood why. "Do you think Agent Collins really cares what happens to you? You're not even a full agent yet. They can erase every shred of evidence. Make it look like your secretive behavior these past few months was the result of . . . I don't know . . . a crack addiction . . . and you died from a drug overdose."

"Oh, great. So, we put the guns down and you jump right to the mental games." She glared at me, then her expression turned smug. "That's preferred, actually. I'm better at reading people's real intentions than everyone else in my division."

I couldn't help laughing. "You need some better competition. I think you suck at guessing people's real intentions, otherwise you wouldn't be holding me at gunpoint. I already told you I wasn't going to hurt you, remember?"

A flicker of emotion crossed her face at the mention of that night I had caught her in my apartment. The glare returned quickly. "Yeah, because you want to recruit me. Drop the Eyewall numbers down a little bit."

"They're lying to you, Holly . . . about everything," I said, realizing my voice had suddenly become a lot more intense. "I'm not the bad guy."

"I'm not, either. How great is that? Let's make friendship bracelets and have a sleepover." She laughed, but there was no humor in it.

I took a chance and scooted across the floor until I was sitting right in front of her. She held her breath, gripping her gun tighter. "I can take you away from them. We can go anywhere you want. What happened to Adam . . . that wasn't an accident and it wasn't us, I swear."

Her eyes locked with mine, holding my gaze. "What happened to your shoulder? I saw the scar."

My fingers absentmindedly lifted to touch my right shoulder. "A bullet hit me, but it didn't go all the way through."

"I've never been shot," she said flatly. "Yet . . ."

I flinched, seeing that horrible day in her dorm room all over again. I'd never get rid of that image. "About what I said . . . ?" I pressed, because she had changed the subject so quickly on me.

She turned her head to the side, looking away from me. Obviously she wasn't going to respond to my offer. In this situation, Holly had the mental advantage over me because I was just another guy to her.

An hour ticked by without her saying a single word or even making eye contact. But I think her fight to stay awake won and she had to keep talking.

"How long have you been an agent?" she drilled.

I jolted up from my now-lying-down position as the sound of her voice cut through the silence. "Just a few months. How about you?"

Another long pause, her eyes half closed. "I started about a year ago. Adam had done some serious hacking job and got caught. He totally freaked out and told me about it because he didn't know what to do. Anyway, instead of putting him in jail, the CIA recruited him."

"Yeah, I've heard they do that."

"All they wanted him to do was basic field training and computer stuff. Nothing like what I'm doing now. He had this one training assignment, just beginner stuff, convincing a receptionist to hand over medical records. He took me along and then totally blanked and I jumped in to rescue his ass and completed the assignment for him . . . but of course—"

"They were watching?" I guessed.

She nodded, and when she spoke again her voice started to shake. "But I didn't even think about that at the time, and a few days later a man was in my kitchen, talking to my mother about a very special honors program he wanted to put me in. Complete bullshit, obviously, and I knew right then. At first I really loved the training, the assignments . . . and Agent Collins was totally cool to work for." She drew in a deep, shaky breath.

"Hol, Adam knew Tempest isn't bad . . . I saw him just before—" I froze, knowing I had just said too much.

Her face twisted with anger and I thought she might shove me away from her. "Don't talk to me like you knew him! You don't care about Adam and you don't care about me! I know exactly how this game works, probably better than you."

"I'm the one who found Dr. Melvin dead. I wonder who made that mess. Not Eyewall, right?" My voice had gotten louder and she shrank back a little. I ran my fingers through my hair, trying to calm down.

Nothing was going how it was supposed to. "I didn't mean to yell. I'm sorry."

An eerie calm had taken over her expression and she whispered, "I found him, too . . . Adam. It was the single most terrifying moment of my entire life."

"You couldn't have been there," I said. "I would have known."

"Believe me. I was there."

My stomach sank. It must have been after . . . way after. "Tell me what happened."

Her eyes focused on the wall behind me. "Another agent came to pick me up that day and we went to go get Adam. The second we walked into his house, we found him . . . He was covered in blood, I couldn't even see his face. He wasn't breathing, but his eyes were wide open, staring right at me, like he was begging me to help him, but it was too late."

I squeezed my eyes shut for a second as the pictures, the memory of seeing him, flooded my brain. Pain rolled in giant waves over me. Holly's hands had neglected her gun and were now lifting to cover her face. Her reaction startled me, but maybe this was the first time she had really talked about Adam.

Her voice was thick with tears when she started speaking again. "The guy I was with, Carter, dragged me out of there before I could do anything. He said it was protocol. I don't even remember getting in the car. We just left him there like we never saw it. And later that day, I had to sit across from his mother in the police station, while a detective questioned me. I had to lie to her face . . . say I hadn't seen him all day." She uncovered her face, revealing her tear-stained cheeks. "Do you know what the police told her?"

"What?" I whispered, even though I had already read the report a dozen times.

"They told her he fell or tripped on something." She sucked in a breath, trying to smooth her voice, but it only got more unstable. "He was murdered, and his own mother thinks it's her fault for not wrapping up the damn vacuum cord or something. I can't say a word . . . nothing. I have to keep letting her think, day after day, that she could have prevented her son's death. That maybe she even caused it . . . and I don't want to do it anymore. I don't want to do any of this. But there's no way out. I'm just going to be this person whose sole motivation for following orders is to be able to walk into my house and not see my mother bloody and lying on the floor like Adam." Her hands lifted to her face again and tears came out harder and faster.

I felt like a truck had just run over me. I reached for Holly and my arms went around her, pulling her close. It was stupid to touch her, get this close, because she didn't trust me, but none of that even crossed my mind. This was Holly, crying . . . I couldn't really think about all the invisible barriers between us now.

"I'm so sorry, Holly . . . so sorry. This should have never happened." I forced down the lump in my throat and squeezed her tighter. Her cheek pressed against my chest and her whole body shook with sobs. I moved over so I had my back to the wall, bringing Holly with me, her face buried in my shirt now.

Nothing I'd ever done with Tempest had felt this frightening. Whatever Holly had gotten herself into was far worse than my division. She was in way over her head. And it was all because of me. She squeezed me around the waist and I could feel her trying to pull herself together, to stop crying. She tilted her head upward a little and I brushed the tears from her cheeks with my thumb. My heart skipped a beat. Her mouth was so close to mine . . . *Focus! Focus on getting her away from them, convincing her to let me help. We could run away to some island that no one knows about and stay there forever.*

If I could rescue Holly from this horrible fate, that would at least be one accomplishment toward saving the world. Her fingers slowly moved from my waist to my chest, but it felt like she was holding something—a sock, maybe? I had only a half second to contemplate the item before the rag was pressed over my mouth and nose. The fumes from the poison invaded my nostrils and made everything turn black.

CHAPTER TWENTY-TWO

"Jackson . . . Jackson!" A hand smacked my cheek.

The hard floor was underneath me again, the smell of sewers returning to my nostrils, nearly causing me to gag, a thin layer of sweat forming across my forehead. I wiggled my eyes open and looked right into Kendrick's. *Kendrick . . . not Holly?*

"Don't try to sit up yet." Both her hands pressed against my chest, forcing me to stay down. "God . . . your heart is racing. What did she give you?"

I tried to recall more specifics about the scent of the chemical-covered rag Holly had smothered me with. "I don't know . . . How did you get in here?"

A high-pitched beep went off above our heads and I looked up to see a hole in the ceiling, a big chunk missing. "So that's how she got out," I said to myself.

"And it's how I got in." Kendrick pulled out a tiny handheld computer and punched in several numbers. Seconds later, the door swung open.

My wallet, keys, and phone were still lying on the floor where Holly had dumped out the contents of my pockets. I snatched the items from the floor and headed for the door.

Kendrick followed behind me as I thundered up the steps and reentered the subway tunnels. I stopped for a second when I felt her hand on my arm.

"Are you . . . are you okay?" she asked.

"Don't baby him . . . He's already spoiled and pampered."

We both turned around to see Stewart, looking slightly battered, her clothes torn and hair frazzled.

"Do you know if Holly's okay?" I asked, looking at both of them.

Stewart glared in my direction, then gave me a shove, nearly knocking me onto the tracks. "Seriously? Blondie leads you right into some kind of high-tech cave, doses you with chloroform or whatever she gave you, somehow manages to climb up the walls and knock out one of the ceiling tiles, then leaves you drooling on the floor while she escapes without a scratch . . . and you want to know if *she's* okay?"

We had just walked outside, finally breathing fresh air, and I was surprised to be hit with late morning sun. I'd been down there for hours. "I think they tricked her. She wasn't supposed to be locked in the room with me."

"Junior, I think it's time you face the truth," Stewart said.

"What do you mean?"

"Blondie's got skills," she said, lifting an eyebrow. "Way more than you ever realized."

"No . . . she's . . ." *Was everything last night just an act?* I froze in the middle of the sidewalk, piecing together this crazy puzzle. But the way she was crying . . . there was no way that was fake. It didn't mean she trusted me. Just that she used real grief to manipulate me.

None of that changed the fact that I knew Holly was scared and all she had wanted to do was survive last night. She could have killed me while I was unconscious, but she didn't.

But now wasn't the time to present this theory to Kendrick and Stewart. They both looked more than a little pissed at Holly and Eyewall. "What about everyone else? What's the mission status?"

Kendrick and Stewart exchanged a glance, then Stewart answered. "We lost two agents, killed one Eyewall chick . . . someone we hadn't been in contact with before. Freeman's holding four near the underground hospital."

"Which two agents did we lose?" I asked, feeling the weight of being out of it for several hours.

"Miller . . . Parker's partner," Kendrick said.

"And Davis," Stewart said.

I exhaled heavily, glad that I had made it out alive, but feeling guilty for the same reason. "They were outnumbered. How did they get two of us?"

"They knew exactly what we had planned. Every detail, down to who was gonna follow who. And they know all of our strengths and weaknesses," Stewart said, moving to my other side. "If Kendrick had been locked in that room that you were in, she'd have decoded the lock on the door within an hour. You, on the other hand . . ."

"Can shoot a gun really well . . . which didn't help me in that situation." We had arrived in front of our building and I figured Stewart would come in with us. "Do you think we have a mole?"

"Freeman thinks so," Stewart blurted out.

"Okay, so neither of you told me what happened to you guys," I said.

Both of them grinned. "Kendrick took Collins down in no time . . . which is seriously insane, and I'm not sure what was going through her mind. I had some dude named Strowski. We caused a little bit of a riot in the middle of a film studies class, but he wasn't too hard to catch."

I couldn't imagine Kendrick running after Agent Collins. That would be like me facing Freeman, and, well . . . actually, I had done pretty well against Freeman in another timeline, but he hadn't expected me to know any form of self-defense.

After Stewart headed for her place, Kendrick and I took the stairs in silence, but just before I opened my apartment door she started to say something. "I just . . . I wanted you to know . . . I get it . . . Holly . . . If Michael were in another agency—"

"Yeah, I figured you would." I leaned against the doorframe, thinking about my next move . . . thinking about Holly and everything I hadn't told my partner since we were experimenting yesterday morning. I straightened up the second I remembered the biggest item of all. "Hey . . . wanna go somewhere with me? I have something really cool to show you."

JUNE 20, 2009, 12:30 P.M.

"I can't believe no one knew about this," Kendrick said, spinning around to look at the hole in the floor of Dad's closet.

This time I'd gotten the idea to have Kendrick try and touch the closet wall to get it to open and it didn't work. It recognized my fingerprints, she had concluded, but not hers.

"I don't know who Dad was keeping it secret from. That's why I haven't told anyone."

She walked toward the little kitchen and stopped suddenly in front of the stove. "Do you feel that?"

"Feel what?" I walked around her so I could see her face. She had the I-just-had-a-brilliant-genius-person-discovery look.

"An electromagnetic pulse. It's so slight . . . you'd barely notice if you didn't know the warning signs."

Electromagnetic pulse . . . where had I heard that before? "What's it do?"

"I only know because it was part of my . . ." Kendrick's eyes locked with mine, a weary expression now on her face.

"Specialty training?" I guessed, shaking my head at her. Hadn't we moved past this keeping-secrets shit?

"Yeah." She gave me a sheepish grin. "I only know of a couple places that Tempest has set up an electromagnetic pulse. But I don't know exactly what it's for."

"The underground hospital," I said, suddenly remembering being trapped down there with Marshall when I did that half-jump to 1996 that one time. And that was when the answer landed right in my brain. "It keeps the EOTs from time-traveling!"

Shock filled her face. "Exactly . . . Maybe you can try it? See if you can jump?"

I focused my mind as hard as I could on a full jump. A sharp pain shot through my head, and the second I felt myself splitting apart . . . doing a half-jump . . . I pulled back, just before the room had started to fade.

I sank to my knees, clutching the sides of my head. Black and yellow spots twinkled in front me. Kendrick was on the floor next to me, resting a hand on my back. I took a few slow, deep breaths and the pain faded after a couple minutes. I stood up slowly and smiled at her. "Definitely a force field in here. It wasn't just a failed attempt. I've never had anything like that happen."

"There's one in the lab in France, too, but I have to activate it. I've turned it on a couple times just to understand the body's reaction to it. You get this short-term feeling of vertigo and then a wave of nausea. Your dad can probably deactivate this one as well," she said, flashing me another grin. "You know what this means, right?"

"Uh . . . ?"

"This little apartment is your family's personal fallout shelter."

"That's why it knew my fingerprints," I said, watching her roam around lifting up objects, inspecting everything. "But if all you need is the magnetic pulse or whatever . . . why don't they put it in more places? Why not our whole apartment upstairs?"

"Well, this room is sealed off. If the upstairs or even the entire building was secured with magnetic pulse, the EOTs could still jump out a window and time-travel that way. Or run out the door." She ran her index finger along the records on the bookshelf. "Besides, long-term exposure to EMP is dangerous."

"Dangerous? How?" *Should we even be down here?*

"A few days or even a few weeks wouldn't hurt anyone, but months or years could cause cell mutation and deformities in offspring." She lifted her head and our eyes met, both of us putting several things together.

"Those weird dudes I told you about . . . in the future . . . the bad future. They were so freaky-looking. I could see their veins through their skin." I nearly laughed out loud at the craziness of this theory. "Do you think we all turn into mutants in the future? Not us personally, but the human race?"

"What if the future that Emily showed you had so many time travelers they had to control them with EMP and then everyone started coming out deformed?" She shook her head. "No, that doesn't really make sense, because we already know the effects of EMP. They would figure it out before they let everyone give birth to mutants."

"Maybe it only takes a few mutants to destroy the world?"

"Or one mutant and the rest clones." Kendrick's serious-scientist face dissolved and she busted out laughing. "God . . . we have the most messed-up jobs ever."

She plucked a record from the shelf and handed it to me. "Let's listen to your dad's music, see if we learn anything new."

"Frank Sinatra," I said, reading the cover of the album before setting it on the player. I stretched out on the floor as "Fly Me to the Moon" began to play. "We performed this song in jazz band . . . middle school, I think."

Kendrick leaned back on her elbows, extending her legs beside mine. "What instrument did you play?"

"Saxophone." I closed my eyes, listening to the song, feeling something familiar sweep over me. "I wonder if I've ever been down here. Before yesterday, anyway."

Kendrick started to respond, but my phone rang, and when I read Parker's name, I had to answer. "Yeah?"

"Is Kendrick with you?" he asked immediately.

"Uh . . . yeah, she's with me. We were getting some stuff from my dad's place."

Kendrick froze, listening intently.

"Great. Healy wants both of you to get your asses down to the underground hospital wing," Parker said.

"Did he say why?"

"He wants you to talk to Agent Collins," Parker said, then added, "To interrogate Agent Collins. He asked for you specifically."

I hung up the phone and looked at Kendrick. "Have you ever done an interrogation before?"

"Nope. Never."

CHAPTER TWENTY-THREE

Healy stood in front of the locked door, preparing to punch in a code. He paused and glanced at me again. "Remember the techniques Agent Parker showed you . . . Give him something he wants and ask for twice as much in exchange."

I had spent a couple hours observing Parker mentally breaking down the other three EOT prisoners, trying to find out who was leading Eyewall, who called the shots, and how and when all this started. The only thing we got from the three agents was Collins . . . he called their shots. Now we needed to know who pulled his strings.

"Right . . . got it." I wiped my sweaty hands on my jeans and took a deep breath.

"He asked to speak to you. He's ready to crack," Healy said, even though I'd heard this a dozen times already today.

The door opened and I walked in alone, trying not to jump when it slammed shut. Collins sat on the tile floor, leaning his back against the wall. His arms were folded across his chest and he looked much calmer than the others had.

"Agent Meyer . . . Took them long enough to bring you in," he said in a quiet nonthreatening tone that made me even more nervous.

"I had things to do."

"Of course." He gestured toward the table in the middle of the room and we both sat down in chairs across from each other. "Since my future outside of this place is a little up in the air right now, I need to ask you something."

"Me first," I said, pointing to my chest.

"Fine."

"What's going to happen to all your other agents now that their leader is locked up?"

He smiled at me. An arrogant smirk. "We have backups, just like Tempest does."

"Right . . . because the world's going to end if you don't stop us." I rolled my eyes and waited for the sarcastic reply he'd most likely throw my way.

"Honestly, I'm not sure. The battle has gotten too big to keep track of . . . to grasp the main reason we started this fight." He leaned forward, his eyes beaming into mine, X-raying my brain. "And I really don't think I'm the only soldier feeling a little confused right now. Right, Agent Meyer?"

Okay, I officially suck at interrogating.

I decided to take the less mature route. "So . . . I heard you got beat up by a girl?"

He laughed and leaned back in his chair again. "Yes, I sure did. We knew she was with Tempest, but I honestly believed she was the brains in your partnership. The combat skills caught me off guard for a split second, which I'm sure you know is long enough."

"He's not going to kill you," I said, following the questioning plan Parker had made for me. "Healy won't kill you . . . not if you agree to help us."

"You mean tell you who my boss is?"

"Exactly." I sighed with defeat, knowing he wasn't going to tell me. Of course he wasn't going to tell me.

"Are the rumors true?" he asked, switching subjects abruptly. "I wasn't the only one to get beaten by a girl?"

"Well . . . I'm not being held prisoner by the opposition."

"'Opposition' is a very loose term, Jackson. You've been in the CIA long enough to have learned this." He stared at me again in that same intense way that made me feel like my thoughts were on trial.

"Why did you want Holly . . . Agent Flynn to be locked up with me yesterday? What was the purpose of that experiment?"

"I'm using her to get to you," he said without hesitation. "I've had questions for quite some time and the one person who was actually starting to find answers is dead . . . murdered, coincidently, and I don't doubt your division's involvement."

"Adam," I muttered under my breath.

"That's right." He leaned forward again. "Are you recording this? If I were you, I'd shut the tape off."

Something in his face, his voice, indicated that we were about to go "off the record." I turned off the tiny recording device attached to my sleeve. My pulse raced and I wasn't even sure why.

"For a long time now," he said, speaking in a low, barely audible voice, "I've been working on my own assignment. Building a team that could help me with a difficult project. And until recently I thought you were hiding the answers from me, but now I'm starting to believe you know even less than I do."

"About what?" I asked, leaning closer to Agent Collins.

"Do you know anything about my background? How I ended up in the CIA?" I shook my head. "My father was an agent . . . so was my grandfather." He reached in his pocket, removing a beaten-up wallet. An old photo slid out onto the table. "That's my grandfather . . . in 1952."

I looked down at the photo and nearly fell out of my chair. The blond-haired, middle-aged man stood next to a younger guy, maybe nineteen or twenty, with dark hair. My dad . . . Agent Collins's grand-father was in a picture with my dad . . . in 1952!

I sat there staring at the photo with my mouth hanging open. "How . . . ?"

"How is your father, a man not much older than me, in a picture with my grandfather, who died two months after this photo was taken? Kevin Meyer shouldn't have even been born when this picture was taken."

What. The. Hell? *Agent . . . you're an agent . . . think this through. Be logical.* "How do you know for sure this was taken in 1952?"

"I did a fair amount of research. Agent Silverman was my lead man on that project."

My stomach twisted, leaving me with a sick feeling. Adam . . . I needed Adam right now, more than ever. "If I look up your grandfather in the database, I'm going to find this man and that he's deceased?"

"Yes." He stared at me now, more intense than before. "This is what's kept me with Eyewall for so long. The idea that you guys are messing around with . . ."

"Time," I finished for him.

"Time."

"And you think my dad did this? He went back to 1952 and met your grandfather and took a picture with him?" Was it possible? Could he be like me? He looked right around the age he had in 1992.

"I really don't know," Agent Collins admitted, letting out a sigh.

This was the first indication or sign of stress that he'd revealed during the entire questioning. "What's going to happen to Holly? You picked her for this project and now you're here . . . ?"

"I don't know. I've done everything in my power to keep her out of anyone else's control, but now . . . it won't be easy for her." He ran his fingers through his hair—another sign of stress. "She's on her own and I'm not sure she can survive."

I had never appreciated honesty more in my life than I did right then. So much that I decided to return the favor. "I've messed around with time . . . a lot . . . but not how you think. And Holly doesn't know me, but I know her . . . or at least I used to."

He looked completely mollified. "So it is true . . . your father can—"

"Not that I'm aware of," I said. "I didn't ask to be like this. I'm still trying to figure everything out, just like you. I haven't really chosen a side, either."

Agent Collins glanced at his watch. "You've exceeded the standard time limit. They'll come in here soon to make sure I haven't attacked you."

"Right." I couldn't think straight enough to ask the questions we had left hanging.

He placed the photo of Dad and his grandfather in my hand. "Keep it . . . Find out what it means."

"Okay." I tucked the picture into my wallet and headed for the door.

"Jackson?"

"Yeah?"

"As far as Agent Flynn goes . . . be very careful. If anyone in my division suspects she's even a little less than an enemy to you, she's dead. You're not doing her any favors by surrendering and handing over your weapon."

I sucked in a breath, but made an effort to force a nod and say, "Thank you, Agent Collins."

Parker jumped up from his chair outside the door. "Dude! Why'd you turn off your communications?"

I shrugged and turned my back to him, glancing around the hall. "That was pointless. I got nothing. The guy's a brick wall."

Regardless of my proclamation that Collins had given no useful information, I still couldn't be saved from a couple hours of note-taking and dictating with Parker and Freeman. We went over the record and recordings (if we had them) of every interrogation from today and then analyzed them from multiple angles. By the time we had finished I wasn't even sure if Kendrick had left or stuck around. But it didn't take me long to find her.

Kendrick was in the lab, deep into some unknown project. The second I walked into the room, I was immediately overwhelmed by the absence of Dr. Melvin. This was his place. A room he used to create projects—like Axelle.

My entire existence revolves around this exact spot.

She removed the goggles from her face and glanced at me. "You okay?"

I shook all thoughts of Dr. Melvin from my head and focused on the newly acquired information. "Uh . . . yeah. But we need to—"

"Right," she said, catching on to my distress. "Two minutes."

It only took her one minute to finish and then we took the journey aboveground in silence, not wanting to take the chance of anyone hearing. The second we were on the sidewalk outside again, I yanked her into a crowded restaurant and started spilling the whole story.

"I don't know why he'd keep his time-traveling skills from you," Kendrick said as we walked through Central Park.

After a dinner that neither of us ate, I decided we needed to give the secret room inside Dad's apartment another look.

"Seriously, it makes so much sense now . . . even though I'd never want to trust Agent Collins. But the matches from that bar that closed fifty years ago or whatever it was . . . and the records, the books. It's almost like he wanted me to find out."

Stewart had texted us during dinner to tell us what she had found out about Billy's Tavern, and none of us knew what to think of that. She found tax records showing the bar closed in 1959.

"Yeah, I agree with you. Collins wouldn't send you on this kind of hunt if he wasn't also concerned with the same thing. Most of the present-day Eyewall agents probably don't even know about time travel. Maybe not any of them," Kendrick said. "Collins came up with this on his own time."

As we walked through a deserted part of the park, something on my far right side caught my eye. Something that sent my heart beating faster. What I saw wasn't an Eyewall agent . . . or an EOT . . . or even an adult . . . It was a little redheaded girl stumbling through the dark park, alone. I grabbed Kendrick's sleeve and pulled on it. "Oh, God . . . you won't believe this—"

"Wait . . . is that . . . ?" Kendrick asked, now looking in the same direction as me.

"Emily," I whispered.

"Is it her?" Kendrick asked again.

My eyes returned to the child, now sifting through a large trash bin. "I'm not sure. Usually she finds me . . . like she's on a mission."

Kendrick kept her eyes on me and lifted her phone to her mouth. I hadn't even seen her dial a number. "Stewart . . . meet us at Senior's place, okay?"

I walked in the direction of the little girl and could feel Kendrick following me.

"She looks smaller . . . too small," I mumbled.

"How will we know if it's her?"

The tiny head popped up from the trash bin, clutching the remains of a bagel. I couldn't see her face clearly in the dark, but neither of us needed to. The white of her eyes were visible and her trembling voice spoke in jumbled, frightened Farsi.

"Yeah, I don't think many homeless kids in New York are fluent in Farsi," Kendrick whispered.

"Not ones with pale skin and red hair, anyway." I moved closer and little Emily backed away, gripping her dirty bagel pieces. "I don't think she recognizes me."

"Emily?" Kendrick said, moving next to me.

She instantly turned around and started running.

"Emily, wait!" I called after her.

"She's not jumping," Kendrick said as we took off in her direction. "Maybe she can't. We've got to stop her, even if it means tackling her."

And tackling this frail child was exactly what Kendrick did. We didn't have a choice. The police would find her, or someone more sinister than the police. She kicked and wiggled for a minute and then gave up, tears streaking down her face.

"Speak to her in Farsi," I said to Kendrick.

I knelt down in the grass, looking her over. She was so tiny. The other versions of Emily had been thin, but this child was sickly thin. I knew Kendrick had to be worried about Emily's health, too, because she could probably feel the bones nearly poking through the little girl's skin.

"Emily, we won't hurt you, I promise," Kendrick said in Farsi. She nodded her head toward me. "Do you know him? Do you recognize him?"

Emily shook her head vigorously.

"What year did you come from?" I asked.

Emily didn't speak. Instead she lifted her hand and held up three fingers.

"Three?" I asked.

"Does she mean—"

"Three two zero zero," Emily said in Farsi.

Kendrick and I both sucked in a breath. "Damn," she muttered, releasing Emily and sinking back onto her heels.

The kid didn't miss a beat. She leaped up from the ground and started to run again, but she must have been too scared or dizzy, because seconds later she fell down on her hands and knees, panting.

I scooped her up and she didn't even fight me. Her head bobbed, like she was losing consciousness. "Do you think it's the time jump? Side effects?"

Kendrick held her wrist as we walked, pressing her fingers to it. "Her pulse is racing and she's halfway out of it . . . and look at her . . . she's skin and bones. Probably dehydration, malnutrition."

We kept walking quickly toward the path that would lead to Dad's place, our original destination, though we had no real plan.

"Kendrick?" I finally said.

"I know . . . you wanna take her to the hospital, right?"

"Yeah."

"We can't . . . I mean, we can, but Healy will find out and they'll have their own personal lab rat to study . . . or worse."

"I know, but—"

"Jackson, I know more than most doctors," she said firmly. "And she's a time traveler. She might not even be around very long."

Emily fell asleep or passed out and didn't wake up until we were safely in the soundproof confines of Dad's place.

"God . . . how long do you think she's been here?" I asked Kendrick. "If she can't jump back to the future, for some reason, maybe she's been stuck here wandering around New York for days."

"Well . . . someone hasn't fed this child in weeks," Kendrick said, her voice shaking.

I flipped on the light before setting Emily down on the couch. She stirred and started to open her eyes. With the bright light on, I could see her better now. Pieces of twigs and leaves were tangled in her hair. Her black shirt and jeans were torn. And looking at her emaciated body made me nauseous.

Kendrick returned from the bathroom with an armful of supplies. She handed me a wet washcloth and I held it up to Emily's face, but she jerked away.

"Maybe she's hungry?" I suggested. "She was digging through a garbage can."

Kendrick sat on the couch next to Emily. "Do you want something to eat? Food?" she asked in Farsi. Emily looked hesitant and then finally nodded. "Okay, then you have to let us help you. No running away . . . or leaving any other way, all right?"

Emily nodded, and more tears ran down her cheeks.

"Maybe we shouldn't bribe her like that. She's still scared."

Kendrick held up a hand to shut me up. "Get her some food."

I dug through the fridge and took out a can of Coke and a container of leftover sushi. When I returned to the living room and handed the stuff to Kendrick, she rolled her eyes at me and got up, stomping into the kitchen.

"What's wrong with Coke?" I asked when she returned. "Sushi's healthy."

"Imagine not eating for days and then stuffing your face with a bunch of sushi and carbonated beverages. She'd be puking her guts out in five minutes." Kendrick handed Emily a small container of Gatorade and half a slice of pita bread.

We watched as she nibbled the ends of the bread and then started taking bigger bites. Kendrick drilled her with questions while I tentatively wiped her face with the washcloth.

"How old are you, Emily?"

"Three thousand one hundred and ten days," she said with her mouth full.

I glanced at Kendrick, who said, "Eight . . . she's eight."

"Do you think she speaks anything besides Farsi?" I asked.

"I speak everything," Emily said in perfect English.

"Do you know what time travel is?" Kendrick asked her, holding up the bottle of Gatorade, encouraging her to drink more.

She took a long sip and nodded. "I just did it, didn't I? Dr. Ludwig said I couldn't, but he's wrong."

"Dr. Ludwig?" Kendrick and I said together.

She pulled herself upright and looked from one to the other of us. "I don't want to tell you any more."

"Okay," I said immediately. "You don't have to tell us anything, and we'll let you stay here and you can eat anything you want. That's how it works in this time period."

"In 2009," Kendrick added with a smile, "we actually feed children."

"Children?" Emily asked.

"Yeah." I held my hand up a few feet above the carpet. "You know . . . little people, like you."

"The undeveloped?" she asked, sounding less frightened than earlier, and the bread had already disappeared.

Stewart arrived before we were forced to fully describe our version of the difference between adults and kids. After Stewart's brief but shocked reaction to Emily, Kendrick took her to the bathroom for a bath. Before turning on the bathwater, she rattled off a list of items we needed from the store and ordered me and Stewart to both go. Probably so we could discuss our options for hiding this child from the CIA and mostly from Tempest.

That is, assuming no one came for her. Or came after her. I wasn't sure which it would be.

Rite Aid was pretty much the only place open at this hour. Stewart and I split up and dumped items in separate carts. Mine was filled with vitamin supplements, children's pain relievers, and electrolyte solutions. Stewart came up behind me while I was sifting through the medicine aisle.

"Should I get the gummy vitamins?" I asked Stewart.

"Those are the best." She grabbed three bottles and tossed them into the cart. "So, what are we going to do with this kid? Assuming she hasn't time-jumped herself out of there by the time we get back."

"Healy's really our only concern now." *Now that Dr. Melvin is dead.* "But I did have an interesting conversation with Agent Collins."

She looked up at me, curiosity filling her expression. "All right, you've got my attention."

I filled her in on my strange interrogation with Agent Collins and the photo of Dad and his grandfather. She looked as flustered and confused as I felt. "So . . . yeah, my dad's apparently in the future . . . and in the past with some man who died decades ago. Seriously, how fucking crazy is this gonna get before we figure out where he really is?"

Stewart was lost in thought, not really having any answer yet. The only response she gave me was, "Let's go back to the secret room later on, see if we can figure out anything else."

When we returned to Dad's place, lugging several bags full of stuff, Kendrick had tucked Emily into the bed in the guest room. Emily looked like a tiny wet rat, passed out with red hair sprawled across the pillow.

"I sedated her," Kendrick said right away. "I was afraid she might jump accidently and—"

"And maybe she should," Stewart chimed in. "Who knows what it's doing to her to stay here . . . coming from *that* year?"

"Three two zero zero," I mumbled under my breath. All of us were quiet for several seconds, absorbing the impact of *that* year. We had all wondered—everyone in Tempest—where the EOTs came from, or *when* they came from. None of us had ever considered it would be that far in the future.

Kendrick fiddled with a bag of clear liquid dangling from the side of the bed. "I had to sedate her to put in the IV as well. She's severely dehydrated. I also added a nutrition supplement that will help her gain weight rapidly."

Stewart's arms were crossed, eyebrows raised. "What are you doing, Kendrick? Are you gonna raise this kid until she's Junior's age and starts time-jumping on purpose? She could be putting us in a lot of danger. She's some kind of freakish clone of Jackson."

"Chill," I said to Stewart, holding an arm out in front of her to keep her closer to the door and farther from Emily. "We don't have to decide anything right this second."

Stewart groaned and pointed at Kendrick. "She's already decided. We both know that. She's like one of those people who rescue dying birds with their heads falling off."

Kendrick stood up, her expression completely livid. "Fine. You can wake her up and send her back outside and let her wander around eating out of garbage cans. I'm sure Emily will figure out exactly how to get back home before she dies of malnutrition or gets mugged . . . or worse."

She shoved Stewart out of the way and stormed into the hallway. I glared at Stewart and then followed Kendrick into the kitchen. She didn't even look at me . . . just leaned over a notebook on the counter, scribbling furiously. I hung back for a second, trying to muster up the courage to talk to her when she was this pissed off.

"Stewart's just letting off steam. I told her about Agent Collins tonight . . . She's got a lot on her mind," I said, finally.

Kendrick sighed and her pen stopped moving. "Yeah, I know."

Her dissolving anger gave me a little more courage. I set my hands on her shoulders and turned her around. "This is what we had to do. I don't know if it's gonna be okay or not, but keeping Emily here is the only option we have at the moment."

"She's right, you know. I *was* a kid who rescued dying birds. I probably exposed my family to a dozen diseases by dragging wild animals into the house." Her eyes met mine, searching for something. "She's worried about you, too, that your night with Agent Flynn is gonna make you do something stupid or even . . . join Eyewall."

I rubbed my eyes and felt the renewed Holly-anxiety hitting with full force. *Where is she right now? Is she okay?* "I don't think either of you get it . . . what it's like to stare at someone you once knew so well and she looks the same, has the same mannerisms, same sarcasm, and know that you're supposed to see her as a different person. Sometimes I can do it with no problem, and other times she does something that's so much like the Holly I knew, and I can't just make those feelings go away. It's not like I'm trying to be sneaky or become a double agent or whatever."

Sympathy filled her eyes. "I know. Not exactly like you know . . . but I have a pretty good idea what it's like to not be able to let go."

"Well, I'm glad we at least know not to trust you."

I jumped backward so fast I nearly tripped. Stewart stood in front of the refrigerator, arms folded across her chest, glaring at me.

"I better go check on Emily," Kendrick muttered, leaving us alone.

"Look—" I started to say.

Stewart pressed her hands over her ears the second I looked at her. "Not now, Junior. You've given me way too much shit to deal with already tonight. Let me absorb one thing before I have to figure out how to keep you from getting yourself killed by a pint-sized, barely out of high school agent . . . Can you just do the fingerprint thing so I can go down and check out the fallout shelter . . . alone?" She added that last word firmly, and I knew this was not the time to argue.

After I opened the closet floor for her, I returned to the guest room and sat down on the small couch next to Kendrick, who was back to scribbling in her notebook, using a slanted shorthand that was nearly impossible for anyone to read.

"I always assumed that Emily and I would meet when I'm, like, forty or something. Past August of 2009 when I first met her. I never imagined it'd be *before* that date," I said, trying to read over Kendrick's shoulder.

"Do you want to know something really strange?" Kendrick asked, closing her notebook.

I laughed. "You mean something else strange?"

"She has your fingerprints. No two people have the same prints," she said. "I checked it, like, twenty times, running it through the computer program. I've never heard of anything like this."

I stared at Emily, my mouth practically hanging open. "It's like she doesn't even have her own identity."

"And she's a girl and doesn't even look like you . . . except the eyes." Kendrick's gaze was fixated on the side of my face and she lowered her voice. "What did they do to make her? I can't even fathom it and I can understand quite a bit when it comes to science and technology."

I watched Emily's chest move up and down taking tiny little-kid breaths, her lips moving, forming words without any sound. "It's not like she's a robot. A person is a person, right?"

The question was too ambiguous for Kendrick to answer. I knew that, but I asked anyway. Finally, she stood up and walked toward the door. "I think we should stay here tonight. Changing her surroundings might be a little traumatic."

"Agreed," I said, tearing my eyes from Emily to glance at Kendrick leaning against the doorframe. "What about Michael?"

She shook her head and her eyes filled with tears. "I told him . . . I told him we were leaving tonight. For France."

"But—"

"I already said good-bye, Jackson," she said firmly, pulling herself together. "I just can't . . . He's everything . . . everything I lost when my parents and Carson were killed . . . and I'm gonna lose him, too, if I'm not careful . . . It'll happen, won't it?"

I remembered how much I appreciated Agent Collins's honesty when he admitted Holly was in grave danger, and I knew Kendrick needed the same from me.

"Yes, it'll happen."

She sucked in a breath and then nodded slowly. It killed me to watch this happening, like it had for me. Her heart just shattering into a million pieces, way too many for anyone to be able to put it back together. She was ruined. Just like me.

My feet moved across the room without any conscious thought and I wrapped my arms around her. She only stiffened for a second before breaking down and crying into my shirt.

"I'm not going to come back," she said. "I can't go back to him . . . It's too risky."

I squeezed her tighter and said the only words I could offer, "We'll help . . . me and Stewart. We'll come up with a cover . . . get his name out of the database and off any radar. I'll use time travel if I have to."

She laughed through her tears and gave me one last squeeze before letting go. "Thank you."

"We're in this together now, right?" I joked. "Now that we've broken nearly every CIA rule."

She gave me a half smile. "I really need to take a shower. Will you keep an eye on the little one?"

"No problem."

I got the sense that even Kendrick wasn't sure Emily was on our side. And yet, like me, she had trouble seeing past the child in her. Good or evil, she was still just a little kid.

CHAPTER TWENTY-FOUR

Last night, I fought to stay awake. Around five in the morning, I dozed off for a little while and woke up to the sound of pages turning frantically. I figured it was Kendrick writing more notes, but then I saw her stretched out across the end of the bed, sound asleep. Stewart was sprawled out on the floor, also asleep. Her laptop rested in front of her, still turned on.

That was when I saw Emily, sitting cross-legged on the bed, eyes zipping over Kendrick's notebook pages. I walked slowly toward her and tugged the notebook off her lap. She jumped and glanced up at me with big eyes, before sliding back until she ran into the headboard and couldn't get any farther away.

"It's okay," I said, sitting down by Kendrick's feet. "I'm not gonna hurt you. None of us will."

She pointed to the numbers written across the top of the notebook. "Is that right?"

"You mean the year? 2009?" She nodded. "Yes, that's right."

This seemed to stun her too much for her to look scared again. My eyes traveled to the needle lying on the bed. The needle connected to the IV that should have been connected to her hand. She caught me staring at it and picked it up, placing it in my hand.

"That solution has impurities. I can smell them," she whispered.

At first I thought that statement was a little weird, but then I thought about it, like, what would I think if I went back two hundred years and someone handed me a glass of water? I'd smell impurities. Notice things that people from that year wouldn't think twice about.

"Are you hungry? I can make you something to eat," I said, hoping this would get me on her good side. I got a tiny little nod. "Great. Let's go to the kitchen."

She snatched the notebook out of my hands and climbed off the bed, following close behind me. Kendrick had dressed her in one of my T-shirts and it hung down to her knees.

The notebook was clutched to her chest, with a death grip I knew better than to test. But she let me steer her toward the table and she sat in the chair I pointed to.

She nibbled on more pita bread and Gatorade while I sat across from her. When both her hands were occupied, I took a chance and stole the notebook back. She dropped the bread and reached for the spiral end, catching her fingers between the wires. The look on her face was so desperate, I released the notebook immediately.

"I just . . . don't understand," she said. "I need to read something . . . data. I like to read data."

The way she explained it, you'd think I'd taken her mother away or something. Suddenly, I had an idea to provide Emily with some concrete evidence. I opened the junk drawer to the right of the kitchen sink and riffled through it, tossing random items onto the counter until I found a black ink pad, half dried-up but still usable. I grabbed a plain white sheet of paper and the ink, setting it down in front of us. Slowly, I pressed my thumb in the ink and then against the paper, leaving a black fingerprint. I slid the ink pad toward Emily and she stared at me for a long moment before lifting her hand. "It won't hurt you, I promise."

She nodded and made her own mark next to mine. I watched carefully as she leaned forward, practically touching her nose to the page. I gave her the small magnifying glass attached to my pocketknife to help with the examination. "It's . . . it's the same . . . We're the same."

"Yes." Another idea came to me, and I ran from the kitchen to retrieve my bag and lockbox. I showed Emily how it read my fingerprint and then opened, revealing my journal and Holly's diary along with some other personal items. She repeated the same move—opening the top and then closing it again—at least ten times. Then she reached her hands out to touch my face, almost like Eileen had done that one time. We were nose to nose for several seconds before she finally whispered, "But you look different?"

"I know . . . I don't understand it, either. Actually, we were hoping you might know something."

She sank back into her chair, looking less afraid, less tentative. "You're not like them . . . They hate that you're not like them." She swallowed hard, eyes meeting mine. "They hate that I might be like you."

I could only assume she was talking about the EOTs, about me being more emotional, more human. And someone must have told her, maybe out of anger, that she was acting like me . . . the person who shared her fingerprints. Her identity, in a way.

Emily pointed to the notebook again. "Can I read it, please?"

"It doesn't belong to me, so maybe we should wait until after Lily gets up?"

"She has two names?" Emily asked. "You called her something else last night."

"Kendrick is her last name." I paused for a second before asking, "Do you have a last name?"

"No . . . only numbers." She eyed the refrigerator wistfully. "Do you have chickens?"

"Uh . . . not in there . . . not live ones, anyway."

"I had a chicken. He lived with me, but he got sick and died." She looked down at her hands and sighed. "He was the last one."

"The last one?"

"Extinction?" she said, as if talking to someone much younger than herself. "Dead species?"

"There's no chickens in the future?" I asked.

Curiosity filled her expression, leaving no room for the fear from earlier. "No . . . but won't everything die out eventually?"

"I don't know . . . will it?"

"How old are you? How many names do you have?" she drilled.

"I'm nineteen . . . years . . . as in three hundred and sixty-five days times nineteen years."

She picked up the bread and started eating again, but I didn't miss the tiny roll of her eyes. "A year is three hundred sixty-four and one-quarter days. And where I'm from, time movers record their age in days. Year of birth is nonessential."

"Nonessential? Do all eight-year-olds say 'nonessential' where you're from?"

"I don't know. I've never met any others my age." She shrugged. "If you have chickens, then you have eggs?"

"Yeah . . ." *Why? Do they worship chickens in the future?* "Do you want me to make you some eggs for breakfast? Or are you planning on raising a chicken farm in this apartment to keep the species from dying out? Is that the mission that brought you here?" I asked.

Then she did something I hadn't expected . . . she laughed. "You can't raise chickens in here. Where would I take them for a walk?"

"Central Park?" I suggested before getting up to pull the egg carton out of the fridge.

Emily followed me and examined each egg carefully before letting me crack it into the bowl. "They look exactly the same . . . All those years and it won't change."

A few minutes later, we both had plates full of scrambled eggs and Emily was practically inhaling them. I hoped Kendrick would approve of this food choice for her. If not . . . well, it was too late now.

"When did you meet me, before? How old was I?" she asked.

"You were eleven the last time I saw you." I rolled my eyes at the patronizing look she had just given me. "You do the math and figure out how many days that is."

"I like math," she said. "We don't call it math, but I read about that in history data."

"What do you call it?"

"Either logics or number tech . . . sometimes origins and angles." Her feet swung back and forth, not even close to touching the floor. "'Tech' is short for 'technology.'"

"Yeah, I figured that." I took a deep breath before plunging into the lecture I knew I needed to give her. "Emily, you're gonna have to be careful with what you tell us. It doesn't mean you can't answer any questions, but some information can cause more harm than good. Does that make sense?"

"I understand," she said, nodding. "I shouldn't have told you about the chickens, right?"

"I'm not sure. It doesn't really bother me, but I've seen more than Lily or Jenni . . . I've time-traveled. So it's different for me. You can tell me a little more than them, but not everything, okay?"

"Because we're the same." She smiled, looking up at me. "I always wanted to meet you. Everything I heard was bad, but I just knew you weren't . . . You couldn't be, or they wouldn't have used you to make me."

So she knew how it had happened. She knew more than I did about it. What a weight for a child to carry. And to be told one thing and decide on her own that she didn't agree, at such a young age . . . that level of freethinking was unbelievable.

I held up my thumb with the ink still on it. "Yes, we're the same."

Kendrick came jogging into the kitchen, looking half asleep, half frantic. She stopped when she saw us and tightened the tie of her bathrobe. "Thank God . . . I saw the IV line had been pulled . . . You're eating eggs?"

"She asked for them . . . I wasn't going to say no. Emily's got a chicken obsession."

Emily giggled again and Kendrick looked at both of us and shook her head. "Eggs are fine. Anything she wants is fine." She squatted down in front of the little girl, looking her over carefully. "You look so much better already. You've got some color back and your cheeks aren't as sunk in."

It was Stewart's turn to come stumbling in, sleepy-eyed. "She does look better. Don't forget, we have gummy vitamins."

I gave Stewart a little smile, knowing that was as good as an apology for her outburst last night. A peace offering. I grabbed a bottle of vitamins and fished around for two. "Look, I think this one's supposed to be a chicken."

Emily laughed again and examined the little gummies resting in my palm. "Those look just like micro-meals—" She stopped abruptly and glanced at me, her eyes growing bigger. "Sorry. I'm not supposed to talk about that stuff."

Stewart held up a small Gap bag and removed a blond-haired doll. "I found this last night . . . you know . . . *downstairs*. There's a dress and another outfit that would probably fit the mini-time traveler."

I took the doll from Stewart and stared at it for a long minute. "This was Courtney's. Lily . . . that's her name."

Kendrick stood beside me, touching the doll's dress. "It's an American Girl doll. I had this one, too. Obviously, I'd picked the one with my name."

A tiny black mark on the plastic arm caught my eye and I started laughing. "I strapped her to a Lego mine full of dynamite once and then wrote Courtney a ransom note."

Kendrick snatched the doll from my hands and handed it to Emily. "Keep Lily away from Jackson, would you?"

She took Emily into the bedroom to give her some real clothes and left Stewart and me alone in the kitchen. "Is that all you found, *downstairs*?"

"Yeah." She stared at me for a long, uncomfortable minute. "I think Collins was right . . . about being careful not to be too *accommodating* to Agent Flynn . . ."

I let out a frustrated breath. "I figured you'd agree with that."

"Would you just let me finish?" she snapped. I immediately nodded, waiting for her to continue. "It's about Holly . . . I checked up on her yesterday, like I said I would . . . and when I said she was fine . . . when I texted you yesterday . . . I may have left out a few details."

My stomach started doing double flip-flops. "Like what?"

"Let's just say . . . I think you should keep an eye on her . . . from a distance . . . not interference, or you're both dead."

Regret was written all over her face, but I didn't know if she regretted not telling me sooner or caving and telling me now. Either way,

I was grateful that we had become close enough for her to go against her better judgment for my benefit. "Thanks, I owe you."

"Uh . . . yeah, you do." She glanced at her watch. "I tapped her phone again. Blondie should be at the NYU library later this afternoon and you should be there . . . regardless of what's going on with this freaky clone kid." She shook her head in disbelief. "I don't know why . . . but it feels like everything's connected . . . Holly, Agent Collins having that picture, Emily, your dad and his MIA status, Marshall gone, too. I can't put my finger on it, but any second now, it's just going to snap together somehow."

"We'll figure it out," I said, putting an arm around her, squeezing her shoulders.

CHAPTER TWENTY-FIVE

After spending most of the day doing my assignments and covering for Kendrick so she could stay with Emily, I wasn't able to look for Holly until evening. I checked the NYU library for Holly like Stewart had suggested. I saw the back of her head as soon as I entered the section where she always sat, according to the reports. But Agent Carter's voice stopped me before I could get any closer. I pulled my baseball cap farther down over my eyes and dove behind a shelf.

My phone vibrated and I quickly read the text from Stewart: *Is she there?*

Yeah, but so is Carter.

Damn. Take him out if you can. Only if he's alone.

Stewart texted me seconds later, before I had a chance to reply to the last message: *I'll head your way now. Let me know if Carter leaves the building and I'll take care of him.*

"You've got two strikes, Flynn . . . don't screw up tonight," Carter said.

Tonight? What was happening tonight? Another mission?

"I've got the computer robot dude monitoring me. I don't see why you need to be here," Holly snapped.

I peered through the tiny space between the top of the books and the shelf. Holly had a laptop open in front of her and books and papers strewn all over the entire six-person table. She and Carter had their backs to me, his chair right next to Holly's. "And I heard you got a D on your last calculus exam. If you're really nice to me, maybe I'll tutor you."

I had to fight off the disgusted groan I so badly wanted to let out.

"I'm only allowed to sleep three hours a night. How do you expect me to pass any test?"

I sent another text to Stewart: *Have you ever done sleep-deprivation training?*

Yeah. It's hell.

Agent Carter leaned closer and Holly's entire body stiffened. The reaction didn't just make me angry, this time . . . it worried me. A lot. Agent Collins had warned me life would be bad for her, but Stewart hadn't said anything about Carter this morning.

This must be what she had been keeping from me.

Holly furiously typed something on her computer and then turned back to the notebook in front of her.

"I'll tell you what, Flynn," Carter said, resting a hand on her shoulder. "You do something for me, and I'll let you off for the night."

Oh, no . . . no way. I nearly jumped out from behind the shelf, but a short blond woman breezed past me and walked toward their table.

Katherine Flynn.

"Mom!"

"Holly . . . I've been looking for you, calling. Finally the girl in the room next to yours told me you might be here." Katherine moved her eyes to Carter and then back to Holly.

"This is Patrick," Holly said mechanically. "We have a class together."

"Nice to meet you," Carter said, then he stood up and winked at Holly. "Don't fall asleep studying again. The librarian might start thinking you don't have a place to live."

He waved good-bye and left them, heading toward the exit door. I was following him before I even realized it. Anger pumping through every ounce of my blood. I nearly laughed out loud when he turned down a deserted street.

Too easy.

"Agent Carter . . . long time, no see," I called.

He spun around immediately and narrowed his eyes at me. "Have you guys executed Collins yet? How about the others?"

"Nope," I said before lunging for his waist. Today I was fearless, mostly because I had a spare injection of the drug I was supposed to have used on Collins last night if he tried anything while we were alone together. One toss to the ground and I had him stabbed with the needle, eyes rolling in the back of his head. I dragged him off to the side and threw a couple garbage bags in front, to hide him a little. He'd be out for twelve to fourteen hours. At least. I texted Stewart, letting her know his location, as I walked back into the library.

When I returned to my hiding spot behind the bookshelf, Holly was typing quickly on her laptop again, while Katherine waited impatiently. I decided to step out a little farther and get a closer look.

"I'm sorry I haven't talked to you in forever . . . things are so busy," Holly said.

"Just come with me and get some dinner. You look terrible. How much weight have you lost?" Katherine slid into the chair Carter had just abandoned and began riffling through her purse. "I brought vitamins, to help you sleep and keep you from getting those bad colds."

Holly did look terrible. Beyond exhausted, and haunted by dark circles under her eyes. She usually had a nice tan, but her skin was paler than I'd ever seen it, like she hadn't been out in the sun for a while. The conditions of our recent dark underground entrapment hadn't allowed me to see her clearly.

"I have to stay here . . . I got a D on my last calc test." Holly's voice shook a little.

Katherine didn't miss that. She put her hands on her daughter's face and examined her carefully. "Please, honey . . . just tell me what's going on with you. Is it Adam? I think you need to talk to someone. You're making yourself sick."

Holly drew in a deep breath and nodded. "Okay, I'll talk to someone . . . a counselor or therapist. You're right, I need help."

Apparently agent training could also be used to soothe worried mothers.

Katherine leaned forward and hugged her, so tight. "Thank you. Give me your room key and I'll get some groceries to put in your fridge."

"Sure," Holly said, but she didn't let go. "I'm sorry . . . I just . . . I'm sorry."

"Don't apologize, sweetheart, just take care of yourself. Promise?"

"I promise," she said, then whispered, "I love you, Mom."

"I love you, too." Katherine stood up and ran her hand over Holly's ponytail. "I just wish you could have waited until September to start school. It's so much for you to stress about." She sighed and tried to smile. "Anyway, I'm coming back to check on you tomorrow, all right?"

"Okay," Holly said, handing over her spare room key.

The second Katherine had exited the building, Holly put her head down, burying her face in her arms on the table. I saw her body shaking before I heard her crying. I stood there for ten agonizing minutes, watching her cry and fighting the urge to walk over there.

Eventually she stopped shaking and stopped making any sounds. Stewart had said I could attempt to question her if she was alone. I moved closer and tapped her lightly on the shoulder, preparing to run if she looked up, but she didn't. A loud *BEEP, BEEP, BEEP* rang from the computer. I nearly jumped out of my skin. Holly didn't even flinch. I knelt down in front of it and saw the long chat that must have been going on the whole time Holly had been sitting here.

That was the test. She had to keep answering questions all night long to prove she had stayed awake.

7:08 P.M. SLEEP MONITOR: *How many individuals reside on your block?*

I took about thirty seconds to review the residents of Holly's neighborhood and then quickly typed:

7:09 P.M. AGENT FLYNN: *28*

I slid a chair over, placing it in front of the computer. Holly's breaths were long and deep now, and I hated the idea of waking her, knowing she was beyond exhausted. But maybe I wouldn't have to and could help her keep out of trouble, keep from getting another strike against her.

The beeping had stopped and I scrolled back through the previous questions to get an idea of what it might ask next. This was honestly the most ridiculous exercise ever:

6:58 P.M. SLEEP MONITOR: *Name something you've recently learned about a team member.*
7:00 P.M. AGENT FLYNN: *Agent Carter can't keep his hands to himself.*
6:48 P.M. SLEEP MONITOR: *Name something you've learned recently about your organization.*
6:50 P.M. AGENT FLYNN: *Apparently, sexual harassment laws don't apply to the CIA.*

It took a minute or two for the shock of her candid answers to wear off, then I snapped into agent mode, analyzing the situation. From what it looked like, the questions came every ten minutes, so she probably had ten minutes to answer them. The phone was next to start making noise. Even though it was on vibrate, the whole table buzzed and I snatched it up quickly before she woke up. Text message from Brian. Great.

Hey sexy, where u been?

I checked for Holly's deep breathing, my fingers itching to type a reply.

Regretting losing my virginity to a guy with a 2 inch penis. I quickly deleted the message before sending it and instead wrote, *Busy. School . . . stuff.*

Wanna talk?

I rolled my eyes. Of course he just had to be nice. *Bastard.* But really, how could I be jealous of Brian when I knew she couldn't really tell him what was wrong. She didn't have anyone to talk to. I had Stewart and Kendrick. But Holly was truly alone.

I sent a quick reply to Brian just in case her phone was being monitored, too: *Tomorrow?*

Cool ☺

Another question popped up on the screen and I set the phone down to respond before the beeping started up again. It was an easy question asking about the people in her current surroundings. I answered it in about thirty seconds and then slipped the notebook out from underneath Holly's arms. Her arms thudded against the table and I held my breath, waiting for her to jump up. But she just mumbled something incoherent and then started to snore quietly.

The ink had smeared a little on the page, probably from her tears, but I could still read the essay she had been attempting to write for her required Freshman English course. I vaguely remember doing this exact same assignment: WHO AM I?

Great topic for a CIA agent.

I'm not sure I can answer this question, but I'll try. Every time I think about a proper response, my mind drifts to other questions, like who I used to be, who I want to be, and only sometimes can I bear to think about who I am right now. Five years ago, I was the little freshman girl who took pity on a tall skinny boy, way too nice to stand up for himself. I yanked a very inappropriate sign off his back, right in the middle of the cafeteria on our first day of high school. From that point on, we were best friends. I never doubted my loyalty to David, but getting older makes it hard to tell who to be loyal to. Five years ago, it was crystal clear. Black and white. Now, it's so much more complicated.

Three years ago, I still hugged my mother. I'd tell her I loved her and the weird thing is, she already knew. I didn't need to say it then, but now, she might not be sure and I should tell her. But I haven't for a long time. Two years ago, I was the girl who studied obsessively for the SATs, saved every penny, and dreamed of living in New York, being on my own and loving every minute of it. I craved the freedom and endless possibilities. I wasn't afraid of the unknown. I hated ordinary.

Now, I wake up every morning as the girl who only has one goal: Survive today. Make it out alive and everything will be okay. But lately, I'm wondering why I should keep doing it. Keep surviving. So I can spend another day afraid of not making it? Thinking about how much worse tomorrow will be?

There's so much uncertainty that I think I've stopped feeling things, like how warm the sun is at noon, the smell of freshly brewed coffee, the scent of my mother's perfume—something I've remembered forever. Until now.

I always thought life burst from every direction after a person has a brush with death, or when they feel it coming. The world is supposed to come alive and make you want to stay so badly you'll do anything. But it just keeps getting darker and I can't see colors anymore. Everything looks, smells, and feels . . . gray.

And I'm so tired, I could sleep forever.

That's who I am now. Someone who just wants to sleep and never wake up. But I can't because I have to rewrite this essay since I could never tell anyone this much about me. Or this little. Depends on how you look at it.

I stared at her notebook page long after I had finished reading. My chest physically ached when I drew in a breath. Everything made sense and seemed more terrible all at once. Whoever had planned this twist of events, this new path Holly's life had taken, whoever decided to put her in Eyewall as a method to torture me—maybe Thomas—knew exactly what they were doing. Unlike Holly, I had several reasons to get up in the morning, to face the day, whatever might come with it. Keeping her alive . . . that was my biggest reason for a long time. And Dad, being his only family. Now there was Stewart and Kendrick . . . and Emily.

Whoever made this plan needed me to have someone . . . several someones. All this time, I had thought it was just the opposite. That everything was being taken from me until I had nothing left. That needing someone made this job so much harder.

All along, I'd been devastated that Holly didn't know me, didn't know how much I loved her, but now that didn't matter. Not even a little bit. It only matter that I knew. That I *know*. If Holly was in my position and had loved someone and let that person go, she'd have something to write about. She would be someone with a good reason to keep going.

After answering another question on Holly's laptop, I laid my head on my arm, right next to her, and drew in a deep breath, recognizing her scent immediately. Her mouth had opened, and every time she took a breath she inhaled pieces of loose hair. I gently moved her hair off her face and rested my fingertips on her cheek.

I hated reading the desperate, depressing words she had written, but at the same time, it made me realize that Holly would always be Holly.

Stewart had been wrong about this . . . It wasn't the fact that she looked the same as my Holly that made it confusing to me. It had nothing to do with appearance. You could take everything from her, change her entire life, and I think, deep down, she'd still have the same soul. The one that belonged to *my Holly*. Just like Emily, who had been surrounded by people telling her I was bad, that she'd never want to be like me, and something inside of her resisted that. She could be wherever and whenever and she'd always be Emily.

And the 009 Holly I had left . . . if she had died when Thomas threw her off that roof, she would have died knowing I loved her, but more importantly, knowing she could love someone that much.

There are worse things than death.

She didn't even need to know how I felt. Ever. Telling her I loved her would just be about me. She would have to take that journey on her own. With me, with someone else . . . Maybe she had moved a little in that direction tonight, with her mom.

That didn't mean I'd forget my mission to help her or that I'd forget about what Agent Carter had said to her, what she wrote in her answers about him. No—I still wanted to break him into a million pieces.

I picked up her calculus book and the unfinished worksheet lying next to the book. And then I started completing her homework, one assignment at a time.

Around ten, Stewart called me. "I just did something really stupid . . . really, really stupid."

Oh, God. "What?"

"Gave Healy truth serum," she croaked, panic already flooding her voice.

"Why?" I asked, and then lowered my voice to a whisper. "What for?"

"I don't know how much time I have to explain, so you're gonna have to do this quick."

I could hear cars zipping by in the background. She must have been outside running.

"You need to do a half-jump to . . . October twentieth . . . 1952."

"Huh?"

"Just do it, Junior! You owe me, remember," she pleaded. "It's about your dad. Remember Bill's Tavern?"

I listened to her describe the street and the exact corner I needed to be on and then hung up the phone. I had no idea if I was capable of jumping this far back, even with a half-jump, but I had to try.

1952 . . . this should be interesting. But just before I managed my half-jump, I felt my cell phone go off. *Too late now . . . I'm already half gone.*

CHAPTER TWENTY-SIX

The jump had been more disorienting than ever. The city was amazing in this year. To see it, to feel it . . . how had I not done this before, just for the experience? I found Bill's Tavern after walking a few blocks, but going inside was a different story. Since it was only a half-jump and I wouldn't change anything or truly harm someone, I didn't feel guilty at all about the jacket I swiped from a picnic table after an old man had set it down and then bent over to tie his shoe.

As usual the half-jump dulled the sensation of cold but my very modern T-shirt wouldn't help me fit in. I zipped the jacket up to my neck and tried to pull the bottom of my jeans over my shoes, so they wouldn't stand out too much. The rest of me seemed okay for 1952.

But the second I saw the dark-haired guy walk out of Bill's Tavern, I no longer cared about fitting in. I wanted answers. Now.

Right here, in the middle of the sidewalk, strolling comfortably under the midday sun, was my dad. A very young version of him. Younger than I'd ever seen in real life.

I kept my feet as quiet as possible, trotting behind him to keep up with his much more purposeful steps. He knew where he was going. He wasn't a lost time traveler. Or was he? He had an old worn navy-blue jacket on over his khaki dress pants and wore black dress shoes. His hair was parted and combed to one side.

He walked about three more blocks before turning into an alley between two buildings. He slowed up a little and then suddenly snapped around quickly, drawing a gun and pointing it at me. "Hands up!"

I lifted them quickly in the air, stunned to see his face up close. "Wait—"

"Why are you following me?" he demanded, taking two steps closer to me.

He looked me over briefly and his face faltered a little, giving away his surprise. "Who the hell are you?"

The gun was tucked away immediately.

"Uh . . . Jackson."

Dad's face revealed mild panic. "Sorry . . . but you shouldn't sneak up on people like that." He patted the back of his pants, where the gun had been stowed. "It's not even loaded, so don't go calling the heat."

"I . . . I won't." *Whatever that means?*

"If you had my job, you'd do the same thing. The phrase 'don't kill the messenger' doesn't seem to be widely known. I've got guys going ape on me every day. Can't just stand there defenseless."

"You're Kevin, right?" I croaked. "Kevin Meyer?"

He narrowed his eyes at me. "Do I know you?"

"Um . . . maybe . . . from *somewhere*," I said, then remembered that none of this mattered. *It's a half-jump.* I just needed to know how he got here. "Actually, I might know you . . . We just haven't met yet."

His hands lifted to his face and he groaned. "Oh, God . . . this isn't happening again. Where the fuck is Melvin when this shit goes on?"

"Dr. Melvin?" I asked.

Dad laughed, looking way more freaked out and threatened than I did. "I wouldn't exactly call him a doctor. That would require medical school. Considering he's seventeen."

It could be *the* Dr. Melvin . . . that would be about right. "Does he study you . . . or help you time-travel? What year did you come from?" I asked.

He stared at me blankly and then finally said, barely above a whisper, "Is that why I keep running into them . . . you . . . people like you? They don't think I belong here? Or that I'm hiding out like Superman or something?"

"Are you . . . hiding your abilities?"

"No," he said firmly. "I don't have any time-traveling powers."

For some reason, I believed him. "Well . . . then you've been displaced . . . one of them dragged you here and—"

"Them? Why not you or your people?" he asked.

Definite interrogation question. *Has he been trained?* "We don't all work for the same side . . . at least I don't think we do."

"I haven't been dragged anywhere," he said with a defensive edge. "If that's why I keep getting cornered in dark alleys by fellows from the future, then maybe you can just give them a message for me: This is my home. I don't have any information about future events. Nothing."

"This is your home *now*," I pressed, just to clarify. "Like, you'd rather stay here than whatever year you came from?"

He threw his hands up in the air. "Damn! When will this end? I. Live. *Here*." He enunciated each word slowly. "I'll take you to my mother's house right now. It was her mother's house before that. We have documents . . . This is my father's jacket. He died in World War II . . . My younger brother Gabe is home right now. We have the same blood type, test us . . . whatever it takes to make this end."

Oh. My. God. He said it . . . in 1992, to Eileen . . . and I didn't get it . . . didn't get the meaning.

If I lay here and close my eyes, it almost feels like . . . like I could be anywhere.

Anywhere? Like forty years in the past?

I had never heard my heart beat so fast. Ever. "So, you were born in—"

"1934."

My back crashed into the wall behind me as I leaned against it for support. He hadn't been brought here by an EOT or another time traveler. He'd been brought . . . to the future . . . to the 1990s, probably. I clutched my chest, gasping for air. He had no family alive . . . no one . . . He had a secret room with all the things that reminded him of what he had left. Frank Sinatra . . . record players . . . old books.

He belonged here. In this year. "Damn . . . how in the world . . . I just . . ."

"So, you believe me?" Dad asked.

"Are you . . . are you even in the CIA yet? Does the CIA exist in 1952?" I blurted out.

His eyes darted side to side, checking for people strolling by. "I'm still training. And I don't know how you got this information, but I swear to God I'll find you if it gets out."

I looked at him, finally catching my breath. "So, you did this job before anything happened. It makes sense when Melvin said you got in on your own merit."

His forehead wrinkled. "I've been training in secret intelligence and espionage since I was twelve years old. A little boarding school in D.C. called Dunston Academy . . . ever heard of it?" I shook my head and he continued seeming very proud to have information that I didn't have. "We're handpicked from all across the country in grade school. Of course, the prestigious academic-prep-school reputation is just a cover. We do fieldwork from year two on, and by graduation we've all done international missions and college-graduate-level courses . . . fluency in eight foreign languages in six years. My father was a Dunston graduate as well. I never knew what he did or what the school represented until two years after he died. Until I was accepted and given his old dorm room. Well . . . me and Melvin, anyway."

All I could do was stare at him . . . *my dad* . . . maybe a few months younger than me right now . . . and yet he was beyond amazing. A true secret agent . . . and his father before him . . . "Wait . . . so your dad died when you were just a kid?"

"I was ten. He died in France . . . fighting Hitler . . . or so I've been told," he said bitterly, leaning against the wall next to me.

"I'm sorry . . . and you have a brother?"

"Gabe . . . he's four years younger than me." He pulled a cigarette from his shirt pocket and offered it to me. I shook my head and watched as he removed a box of matches from Bill's Tavern and lit his cigarette, taking a long drag. I'd never seen my dad smoke before. Ever.

"So, who were these other guys . . . the ones who came to see you before me?"

He flicked the ashes onto the gravel of the alley and kept his eyes straight ahead on the building in front of us. "A gentleman who looked a little like you . . . a cute red-haired girl—"

"Blue or green eyes?" I drilled.

"Blue. I assumed the little girl was a special child . . . off her rocker . . . but now I'm not so sure," he said, pausing to smoke some more. "And a tall colored man . . . bald head."

"Marshall."

"Didn't get a name from him." He turned his eyes on me. "Actually, you're the first to give me a name . . . and you look a hell of a lot more surprised to see me than the others. I got the feeling they had had the same conversation with me a dozen times before."

"What did they want?"

He dropped the cigarette onto the gravel and smashed it with his black boot. "To take me back . . . where I came from."

"But you came from here," I said, understanding his frustration earlier. He had started to doubt his own story, maybe.

"Right . . . it all started when I found those pictures of the Russian man and his family. I swear on every Bible in this state that those pictures were dated twenty years ago, but the man was here, in Billy's place, having a drink, looking exactly the same. Melvin's a forensic genius . . . he said it himself." He took a deep breath looking at me desperately. "If I hadn't figured that out . . . they'd probably be off my back, right? I started something I never wanted to start, and now I'm stuck with it. And who the hell do I tell this to? I'll be shipped off by the men in white coats faster than you can say Joe DiMaggio."

You're gonna be shipped off somewhere . . . that's for sure. I could feel myself fading. This jump was so far back, I'd never be able to stay long. "I'm leaving now."

"What? Why?" he asked, eyes darting around again.

I looked at my hands, and the transparency made my head spin. "It's not by choice . . . but I'll see you again . . . for sure."

Blackness swept over me, leaving Dad alone in that alley. Smoking. In 1952.

CHAPTER TWENTY-SEVEN

JUNE 21, 2009, 10:20 P.M.

I could feel the table underneath me. My sweaty forehead pressed to it. The present day, time, *year,* were very slow in coming back to me. My phone vibrated from my pocket again. I fumbled around trying to retrieve it before attempting to lift my head. When I saw the glow of the light, I realized my surroundings had become dark. Like someone had turned the lights out in the library. I should have gone somewhere safer to do this half-jump, knowing I'd be leaving my body behind in 2009. Behind and vulnerable to attack. *Idiot.*

I blinked several times before reading the text . . . an address. An old apartment building a few blocks away.

"I knew it! The second I saw the two of you at Healy's ball. Double agents never get away with it for long. She should have known better."

My heart pounded, the rush of adrenaline giving me the strength to lift my head. Agent Carter stood in the nearly dark library, several feet away, holding out his gun.

Wait . . . Agent Carter?

"Thought your little injection trick would work on me, huh?" His vicious grin shone through the dark. "Just like Flynn . . . don't have the balls to go for the kill."

My eyes darted around the room and I realized Holly was still sleeping beside me, but starting to stir, turning her head from side to side. My gaze dropped to the floor a little ways from my feet.

I leaped up from the chair and raced toward the body lying on the carpet. "Freeman!"

What the hell is he doing here?

The nausea and grief rushed over me in one giant wave. His eyes were *open.* Open. How long was I out in the half-jump? Couldn't have been more than a couple minutes?

Oh, God . . . not Freeman, too.

"Carter! What the hell is going on? What happened to the lights?"

I barely glanced back at the table and saw Holly sitting up, trying to focus her eyes in the dark.

"You tell me, Flynn. How long have you been working for Tempest?" Carter sneered, walking closer to Holly.

Her eyes were huge and she sucked in a quick breath. "I don't . . . I'm not—"

"It's a rhetorical question. I already know the answer."

"You idiot! Is this what you spend all your time thinking about? Seriously," Holly snapped.

I tried to grasp on to some kind of a plan to get me and Holly out of this situation, but so much was running through my head at once. Like the fact that my dad should be as old as Dr. Melvin right now. And Freeman lying dead at my feet. And who sent the text message . . . the address? Were Marshall or Dad back? Would they come looking for me if I didn't show up soon? And then there was time travel . . . kicking my ass again.

I zoomed in on Holly's face, which was filled with panic despite the anger dripping from her last words. *Play your part,* Stewart had told me.

So I did. "I think there's only one idiot in this room, and it's not Agent Carter," I said to Holly.

She stood up fast, drawing her gun and pointing it at me. Just as I thought she would. "Tell him . . . tell him I don't work for Tempest!"

I glanced at Carter and said, "She doesn't work for Tempest."

He smirked at me. "Uh-huh."

"Think about it, Agent Carter." I moved closer to Holly with a few slow steps. Her gun lifted a little as she ground her teeth together. "Just a few carefully placed situations, and I've turned an agency against one of their own. And I didn't have to do anything. No messy cleaning up, no bodies to hide or cover stories to create."

Holly's mouth literally hung open. "You're such a liar."

"So, you *are* a double agent?" Carter asked her.

"No!"

"Then shoot him," he said. "Shoot him, and this conversation will be over."

The pounding in my heart echoed into my ears, making Carter sound far away. I didn't know what I was more afraid of—Holly shooting me, or Holly *not* shooting me.

"Do it, Flynn!" Carter repeated. "If you're working for Tempest, they'll kill you if you shoot their precious Agent Meyer. But if you do it . . . I'll say it was me."

Holly's eyes locked with mine and the hatred poured from her to me. She lowered her gun, just a tiny bit, aiming it at my knee.

"Not the leg, Flynn," Carter said. "Head or chest . . . you pick."

She took a deep breath, tapping her finger against the trigger. Adrenaline rushed through my veins, giving me the energy to make a move. I dove for her legs, grabbing her around the knees, causing the gun to fire into the air.

I sucked in a breath as we tumbled to the floor, and the stray bullet shattered a glass light next to us. I wrestled the gun from Holly's hand and immediately stood and backed away, pointing it at her.

Carter laughed, this booming sound following the drop of silence we had had after Holly's gun had fired. "This is fun. Not much of a hostage, Agent Meyer. You think we can't spare a trainee or two . . . or a dozen?"

"It might not be your decision to make," I said, reminding him that I was also now armed.

Carter laughed again, shaking his head as he walked closer to Holly and ignored me. "And here I was truly impressed, Flynn . . . Collins's little wing girl had actually learned some skills. But unfortunately, that's just not true. You're worthless, Flynn . . . worthless and easy . . . very *easy*."

"Fucking asshole," Holly said, staring daggers at him.

She looked pissed, but I could see her trembling . . . see the brand-new wave of fear that swept over her when he said the word "easy."

"You know that little game we play in our division?" Carter said, taunting her further. "The point system?"

"Cut the bullshit, Carter," Holly said. "I know the point system . . . and I know what you're going to tell me. So, which is worth more? Turning in a double agent or killing a weak trainee?"

"You know what got me the most points so far?" A sly grin spread across his face. "Nailing a virgin spy. Apparently it's off the charts . . . easiest points I ever got."

All the color drained from Holly's face at the same time that blood rushed to mine as I strung all Carter's statements together. *It wasn't Brian.* She never even said they were together . . . I just assumed.

"Poor Flynn, your best friend's dead . . . need a shoulder to cry on . . . how about a few drinks, too," he said, reaching out to touch her hair. She shrank back from him. "It couldn't have been any easier. And I think I'll probably go with the dead double agent . . . just to put my rank up top as it should be."

Blood pumped through me fast, obscuring any apprehension I may have had. *He's gonna kill her.*

The decision was both difficult and easy. In a millisecond, the gun I stole from Holly went from aiming at her to firing right at Agent Carter's chest. He fell as fast as he had been shot, a puzzled expression frozen on his face.

He didn't think I'd do it. *He's been studying me.* My arms, my legs . . . everything shook. Holly gasped and then looked up at me, a horrified look I'd probably never forget.

Ever.

Play your part, or someone else will assume the same thing Carter had assumed. I grabbed her and pressed the gun to her temple, and the shock and numbness that followed, killing Agent Carter, seeing Freeman dead, was almost welcome. I didn't know if anyone else was here, listening in and waiting for me to show some compassion toward Holly so they'd know exactly what to do with her. I couldn't let that be my fault, no matter how much I hated being the villain. "We're getting out of here, and if you try to run, I'll find you. I have methods of hunting people down that you'd never be able to prevent."

There were no tears from Holly this time, there was no anger.

Nothing. She walked slowly, a step or two in front of me, as I held her gun to her back, but low enough so no one would see once we got outside. "Where are you taking me?"

I didn't answer her, because I wasn't exactly sure where this place was. My fingers gripped her upper arm as I steered her toward the address from my phone.

Both of us acted the part of agents once we were outside in the warm night air, eyes darting around every corner, studying the scene. My pace picked up, forcing Holly forward fast as my toes hit her heels. When I reached the back door to the old building, I tightened my hold on her, letting the gun return to her temple. The door was slightly cracked, so I pushed it open with my foot, not wanting to risk an escape from Holly by using my hands.

We walked into a nearly dark hallway. The dirty wood floor, chipped, cracked, and peeling, creaked under our weight. The musty smell was so thick, I had to breathe through my mouth. My shoulder brushed up against the wall and I felt a large photograph there start to peel off. I stopped to examine it and nearly dropped the gun, seeing the image personified along with an entire row of photos.

It was me . . . and me.

The first image was a version of me strolling down the sidewalk on Ninety-second Street wearing jeans and long-sleeve blue polo shirt. I loosened my hold on Holly's arm, practically pressing my nose to the wall. The next image was the same version of me but two strides closer to my destination . . . and just behind him, turned around, facing the other direction, was another me . . . one with his arm in a sling and a bruise streaked down the side of his face . . . and a tear in the knee of his jeans from climbing around a rooftop at a hotel in Martha's Vinyard.

These were the surveillance photos from March 15, 2009. From the street-corner camera Adam had told me to check. The photos that had mysteriously vanished.

And there it was, plain as day. Proof that I had done a Thomas-jump. Two versions of me in the same photo . . . But then what happened to him . . . to me . . . the other me?

I saw the cell, much like a jail cell at the very end of the hallway, before I could tell what was in it.

Rusty metal bars ran from floor to ceiling. I squinted into the almost-empty space, trying to make out the shadow of a person in the corner.

"Oh, my God . . . is that—?" Holly whispered under her breath.

My arms fell to my sides as I stared in disbelief. "Holy shit . . ."

A haunted, dirt-covered, unshaven, and in-great-need-of-a-haircut version of me huddled in the corner of the cell, head leaning against the wall, eyes closed, knees pulled up to his chest.

There was no World C. Just like Eileen had suspected. I really, truly erased me and 009 Holly in the most permanent way possible. A new kind of grief swept over me. All this time I think some tiny part of my brain had hoped that I could jump back to World A . . . someday. Even if it never worked out, I wanted the choice, and yet some part of me must have known that I'd debate going back . . . cheating on my promise to myself. Now here I am still in World A, not World C. But the World A I knew and left is completely gone.

I couldn't tear my eyes away from this version of me, even when I heard shuffling feet behind me. But some part of my brain remembered my cover . . . my plan. I quickly grabbed Holly again, keeping her hostage so she wouldn't run or become someone else's hostage.

"Agent Freeman led you here after all." Healy . . . Healy was behind me . . . and I still couldn't turn around.

"How . . . I mean . . . who . . . ?" My mouth was so dry, I could barely form words.

"How are there two versions of you? And it's not a half-jump?" Healy said, moving beside me.

A dim light turned on above our heads. The other me in the cell stirred, his forehead wrinkling from the light, but he didn't wake up.

"You can let her go," Healy said to me. "She works for us."

My stomach plummeted and I peeled my eyes from the other me and turned around, dragging Holly with me. "Us?"

"Yes . . . us."

Oh . . . damn. I glanced down at Holly, who looked slightly re-lieved after seeing Healy.

"Relax, Jackson," Healy said. "I know what you're thinking."

"That I'm screwed," I spat.

"Now, *that* . . . is up to you," Healy said. "Tell me how it's possible that you are here, on this side of the cell, and over there, inside it."

The shaking in my legs returned as his words and the pictures sank in . . . *complete jump*.

Healy nodded as if he could read my thoughts. "Yes, that's right. On March fifteenth, 2009, you landed here from a few months earlier under the impression that you had created a new timeline. But tell me, Jackson, when you left the date August sixteenth, 2009, what was your goal? What did you feel you *needed* to do?"

Erase me and Holly. But I didn't say that out loud. My grip loosened on Holly, but I kept my gun pressed into her side.

"You don't have to say it," Healy said. "I already know. And we knew the second you arrived and then had to scramble to hide the other version of you."

Normally I would have thought his reference to "we" meant Tem-pest. Now I wasn't so sure. Now that Dr. Melvin was dead and Dad and Marshall just happened to be missing. "Why didn't you just tell me? I could have gone back if it wasn't supposed to be like that."

Holly's eyes darted from me to Healy as if to say, *What the hell are you guys talking about?*

"You couldn't have gone back." Healy shook his head. "We wanted the boy who could *truly* jump through time, but you weren't ready to have that knowledge. Not all at once."

Holly gasped beside me and I waited a second to see if she knew something or was piecing ideas together.

"So, you and Dr. Melvin and Marshall and my dad knew I could do Thomas-jumps . . . *complete jumps*?" I had a strong desire to turn my gun on Healy.

Healy snapped his finger and an Eyewall agent I recognized from the ball appeared. "Take Agent Flynn to the other room . . . She's been held under gunpoint long enough . . . fooled by Agent Meyer . . . manipulated."

The agent pulled her by the arm away from me, and I didn't resist because her glare shot right through my heart. He led her carefully down a separate hallway, asking her if she was okay.

Healy began speaking again the second Holly and her companion were out of sight. "The first night I spoke with you, I knew that you wouldn't risk time travel for the sake of your job. You've always been a stubborn, self-involved, irrational *child*. And the training had changed you . . . which would have been helpful to our agency—"

"Oh, yeah? Which agency is that?" My anger had thickened. I could feel the tension building between us, the threat of something worse to come.

Healy turned his back to me and ran his hand along the wall under the photos, leaving me waiting on purpose. I had a gun in one hand and no backup whatsoever. Quickly, I snuck a hand in my pocket and called Stewart's number, leaving it on, hoping she'd figure out where I was.

"There is no Tempest, Jackson. Not in the future, anyway." Healy snapped around to face me. "I've taken over this division and I've been using it as a method of testing the capabilities of agents under unique circumstances. For example, we tested your father . . . his emotional stability when it came to serving the government. He chose your sister over his job . . . over you. And on a whim . . . something irrational and unproven . . . just like that, he was sold."

"Where is he?" I said, grinding my teeth together.

"Exactly where I said . . . the future . . . working for Eyewall." Healy's eyes narrowed and he stepped closer to me. "We have no idea what to do with you, son. So much power, so much ability, but you've broken every rule. Lied. Turned against your own agents. And you don't even care, do you? All the people you've hurt, the damage to the future you alone could save . . . and none of it matters to you?"

I sucked in a breath, squeezing my free hand into a fist. "A lot of things matter to me."

His eyebrows lifted. "Yes, and I've used all of them on you, trying to force you to practice, to hone your ability and be able to use it freely. When I found out about your connection with Holly Flynn and Adam Silverman, I altered their lives, certain that you'd realize the power time travel can hold."

My gun dropped to my side. "You . . . you did that? Put Holly and Adam in the CIA?"

"I have a partner who performs the alterations for me . . . a job I had hoped to eventually give you."

"Thomas," I said under my breath.

"No, Jackson. Not Thomas."

Healy stepped even closer, his gray hair and sweater-vest such a contrast to the intimidating power he held. "Why didn't you do it? After Mason? One short complete jump and you could have saved him. I was sure you would. Then I decided to send Agent Flynn to riffle through your belongings . . . let you in on Adam's death, and she hated you after that . . . and still, you didn't change it."

I clutched my chest with one hand. Sweat trickled down my forehead, my arm, making my fingers slide from the trigger of Holly's gun. "You did . . . all that?"

"Yes," he said firmly. "And I'll keep doing it until you understand what your responsibility is to this world." His expression turned from stern to livid in two seconds flat. "You have no idea, do you? The timelines . . . what you've worried about all along . . . you've made one alternate universe. One other timeline. That's it. That's all there is. For anyone. None of the others can do that and you probably will never do it again. You may travel to that other timeline, but it's just a parallel world. The power to change anything and everything is right at your fingertips and you have no desire to follow anything that resembles orders."

I was sinking in quicksand . . . fast and without air. Eileen had been right about the alternate timeline, about giving me a way out. "Wait . . . who's been sending me the stuff . . . the diary? You said I erased it."

"Also me," Healy snapped. "Your father had a record of it on his memory card from the future and we replicated it. Her handwriting, everything."

"Did you kill Dr. Melvin?"

Healy's quick movement was completely unexpected. He moved like a blur around me, and in one breath my back slammed against the metal bars and Holly's gun was pressed to my head, his fingers curled around the front of my shirt. "Are you listening to a word I'm saying, son? I've been to the future . . . I came from the future . . . and if you don't control yourself, it's going to crumble to bits . . . literally."

I sucked in a breath, staring right into his eyes. "I saw it . . . all of it . . . Emily . . ."

He looked at me, anger turning to desperation. "I'm trying to fix it, Jackson. And you aren't helping. You're supposed to help. Agent Kendrick is supposed to help."

"Help with what?" I'd never been so completely lost and unsure in my entire life.

"Your father," he croaked. "We need him . . . someone needs to get him. He's been captured . . . kidnapped."

The gun clanked against the floor and Healy stumbled back away from me. I couldn't keep up with his shift in emotions. It was almost like he was under some spell and fighting his way out. "Why is this other me here?" I asked pointing at my other self. "Why did you keep him here?"

"To show you," he said as creases popped up all over his forehead. "And if you don't help . . . the EOTs will use him to answer a question."

"What?"

The EOTs, Tempest, Eyewall . . . *who belonged to who, and what did any of them really do?*

Healy sank to his knees, looking so shaken I thought he might be having a heart attack. "A paradox theory we have yet to test."

It hit me hard. All at once. "Shoot him, a younger me, and see if I'm still alive."

Healy's eyes grew to the size of golf balls. "Yes. And they're coming.

Now. The rest of Eyewall. They don't know everything, but they know to kill the prisoner."

He's insane. No, he's manipulating me . . . a trick. But why?

"What's wrong with you?" I asked, kicking one of his legs to try to startle him back to normal.

His hand lifted to touch something behind his ear. The expression on his face turned to absolute horror. So much so that I found myself leaning over, looking behind his ear. A shiny silver circle the size of a dime seemed to be buried or implanted under his skin.

"They got me . . ." he whispered. "Mind control."

"Mind control?"

Those people in the perfect future . . . walking around . . . nothing bad ever happened. Did someone control their minds somehow? My head spun. This was way above my comprehension level. And yet, I found myself kneeling in front of Healy and letting him grip my shirt again.

"You have to get him . . . they're coming. Now."

"I can't jump to the future!" I said desperately. "I don't even know the year!"

"The girl knows."

"Holly?"

He shook his head, closing his eyes for a moment. "The little one. She escaped . . . somehow . . . I don't understand . . ."

"Oh, no," I groaned. "She's here? Emily's here?"

I didn't wait for his answer. I jumped up from the floor and ran in the direction Holly had been led to earlier. I opened the first door on the right and walked into what looked like a conference room. Bright lights filled the room.

The first face I saw was Mason Sterling . . . *Mason*. Looking just the same as the last time I'd seen him. I gasped out loud and then saw the person standing next to him. I stopped breathing. Forgot what I was supposed to say or do.

"Courtney . . . ? How . . . ?" She looked just like she had that time I'd seen her in Central Park. Fourteen, probably. I walked right up to her, placing my hands on her shoulders. The last time I saw her, she was taking her last breaths, and now . . . now she was so very much alive . . . again. "Courtney . . . I can't believe this . . ."

"Oh, man . . . this just gets weirder and weirder," she said, studying my face, which I was sure looked so much older than the last me she had seen.

"Jackson, I'm sorry . . . I didn't know . . ."

I turned my head in the direction of the little voice, which was so pleading and tear-filled. *Emily.* She was little and thin just like the version I had seen this morning. "What are you doing here? When is it for you?"

I squatted down in front of her. "It's the same day, I think . . . I read your journal and I thought . . . and then I heard you were here . . ."

The lockbox . . . our matching fingerprints . . . Emily had access to it while I was in the library with Holly. She must have read all the things I wanted to fix with Thomas-jumps . . . something she most likely could perform better than me.

"Fuck!" Mason said, throwing his hands up in the air. "I'm dead, right? This sucks! Completely sucks. I knew it . . . the second you looked at me like I should be transparent and glowing. Even she looked at me like that." He pointed to someone over my right shoulder.

I glanced around the room again. Holly had her back pressed into the corner. "Where's the dude that brought you in here?" I asked her.

"Oh, no . . . you don't get to ask me a question. Seriously! What the hell is going on?"

"We have to rescue my dad from the future," Courtney said to Holly.

"How did you—?"

"I told her he was missing. I think she can help us," Emily said, then her face filled with panic. "I didn't know where he was before . . . I swear, Jackson. I'd never keep that from you."

"Okay," I said slowly, standing up. "Do you think me and Courtney will be too much for you? How far are we talking about?"

Emily chewed on her bottom lip. "Close to where I came from."

I swallowed hard and realized Courtney was right next to me, studying my face again. "Oh, my God . . . you look so different . . . but not really."

My hands rested on top of hers. "I can't believe you're here . . . I've gone to see you, but it's different. It didn't change anything."

"So, who's going to kill me?" she said, attempting sarcasm, but I didn't miss the tremble in her voice. "Come on, Jackson . . . I'm getting the seeing-a-ghost feeling from you, too."

I just stared at her, unable to speak.

Finally, she rolled her eyes and shrugged. "It's all right. I'm here now. Just like this dude over here." She pointed a finger at Mason. "At least we don't have another version of ourselves to be imprisoned."

Grief and panic took over, and I knew everyone was waiting in silence. Only Courtney didn't know her outcome. The rest of us knew exactly what would happen. And how much had Emily told her? Seriously. What was she thinking? "Right . . . you're here now," was all I could say.

The sense of urgency returned. "Emily, can we do it? Can we jump that far? Without killing ourselves?"

She nodded her little head, the red braid swinging back and forth. Kendrick or Stewart must have fixed her hair. A pang of longing hit me . . . wanting to have my teammates here to help me through this. "Courtney can do it . . . she can jump. I just showed her once and she did it, but she can't go—"

"Backwards," Courtney finished for her.

The opposite of me.

"Hey, if you guys are going on some rescue mission, I want in on it," Mason said.

From the corner of my eye, I saw Holly creeping toward the door. "Mason! Stop her! She works for Eyewall . . . the opposition."

Mason pulled out his gun and pointed it at her. "That's good, because Healy said they're coming here, and we need a hostage."

"Exactly," I said, avoiding eye contact with Holly.

Emily gave me a puzzled look, but didn't ask. "Mason can help us . . . He'll be fine . . . I know he can handle it."

"How do you know that?" I asked Emily.

"I'm already dead, man. Can't get much worse than that."

"You're not dead—" I started to say, but the door burst open and several agents poured in. I recognized most of them from our recent study of Eyewall.

"Flynn?" one of them said, looking at Holly in shock.

I grabbed her by the arm and removed my own gun. One arm curled around her neck and the other held her at gunpoint again. "Stop right there. We've got a room full of hostages," I spat at one of the agents. From the corner of my eye, I saw Mason grab Courtney and hold a gun to her head. She gasped convincingly, which was probably real, because I doubt Courtney had ever had contact with any kind of firearm.

"Innocent children," Mason added, nodding toward Emily.

There were about six of them, all with weapons drawn. We only had a second to make a decision. I saw Mason pick up Emily with one arm and slide behind me. Courtney's hand curled around my shoulder and Emily gripped my other shoulder.

"You can do it . . . She'll be fine," Emily whispered.

Holly . . . and she wasn't telling me to let go of her. She wanted me to bring her. If I didn't, they'd kill her the second we vanished.

Somehow, I had to keep it from affecting her mind. Dad survived going forty years in the future. But three two zero zero was a hell of a lot more than forty years.

"Don't kill Meyer . . . or the little kid," a new voice said, calling out orders from behind the others. Just then I saw the person attached to the voice push through the door and my eyebrows raised seeing Agent Collins, who should have been locked up underground. "Hold your fire, agents."

"Collins!" Holly said, hope rising in her voice.

Agent Collins's gaze locked with mine, like he was trying to converse silently. He gave me a slight nod when I tightened my hold on Holly, as if saying I should take her . . . maybe?

"Agent Meyer is holding some valuable hostages in here," Collins said. "Let's take a minute and find out what he wants . . . follow the protocol like all of you have been taught."

His eyes locked with mine again, beaming out a sense of urgency that wasn't reflected in his voice.

"It's the same place," Emily whispered, probably sensing Collins's message. "The place I took you before . . . in the future."

She must have read that in my journal, too. Damn fingerprint clone . . . and *damn, not that place*. I could feel Emily starting to pull us there and I knew she was right. I could do this if I wanted to, and all along I thought my focus was always on the date or the time, but really it was the senses . . . smell, feel, weight of the distance . . . I remembered it because I'd already been there.

But it was also possible this might kill us. This might be the last time I'd ever see Holly, and I was holding her at gunpoint.

Quickly, I spun her around and wrapped my arms tight around her, despite her resistance. I buried my face in her hair, breathing her in, as if closeness might hand over some of my abilities. Something that would keep her alive.

"I'm sorry," I whispered, with my mouth pressed against her ear.

Then everything turned black.

When I opened my eyes again, some part of me knew this wasn't reality . . . it wasn't real, but more dreamlike. I was standing alone on a sidewalk, my arm in a sling, pain shooting through it. A second later, the sidewalk vanished and my feet landed on a doorstep. Holly's house. Before I could allow myself to contemplate the significance of this location, this day, the door flew open.

Am I dreaming or dead? Dead . . . ugh. A definite possibility. I lifted my eyes and saw her . . . *Holly*. Smiling and tan. Her hair was down and she had on a yellow dress.

What's happening? What is this?

"You're early?" she said.

I opened my mouth to answer, but she threw her arms around my neck, standing on her toes. "Holly . . . ?"

She let go and stepped back quickly. "Oh, God . . . I'm sorry, did I hurt you?"

I couldn't do anything except shake my head as she ushered me inside her living room and closed the door.

"You should sit down," she said, nudging me toward the couch. "All that pain medicine is probably making you loopy."

"Yeah . . . probably."

She sat next to me, lifting my good arm around her shoulders. "I'm so glad you came over. My mom was already freaking out about this weekend and she'd kill me if I left the house again."

I lifted my hand to feel my shoulder, the source of the pain running down my arm. "I got shot?"

This definitely wasn't real. The portal to this world had been erased forever.

Holly's eyes widened and she rested a hand on my cheek. "Yes . . . Are you okay? You seem totally out of it. Maybe you need to sleep."

This was like the Ghost of Christmas Past or something . . . my life if I hadn't said good-bye to her.

She was still scrutinizing my face, but I smiled a little and she relaxed. My good hand moved through her hair and then she leaned closer, light blue eyes locking with mine. I could read her like an open book. Like she trusted me completely.

And then she kissed me.

The sling instantly disappeared from my arm and Holly's mouth was on mine, hands in my hair, on my face.

It was so good . . . so amazingly perfect, I could feel tears stinging my eyes. Death . . . heaven . . . hell . . . a dream . . . I didn't give a shit. *I'll take it. Whatever it is.*

"I love you," I mumbled into her hair. "I love you . . . I really, really love you."

She laughed and moved her head back so she could see my face. "Does it get easier if you say it more often?"

"Not sure," I whispered, closing my eyes and kissing her neck all over. "I love you . . . I love—"

"Okay," she said laughing harder. "I believe you."

I stared at her face for a long moment and then dove into kissing her again . . . it was all lips and tongue and teeth and Holly . . . my Holly exactly as I remembered.

My eyes flew open and I froze, feeling the presence of someone else in the room. The pain returned to my arm and everywhere else and I nearly yelled out loud when I saw the person standing behind the couch.

Me.

The unshaven, insane-looking version of myself. Suddenly my limbs felt disconnected, as if I'd lost control of them, and I could feel *his* movement, *his* intentions.

"No!" I yelled, but I wasn't sure if it was for me or the other *me*.

The gun appeared out of nowhere, bullet exploding from the barrel so fast and hard into Holly. The booming sound echoed in tune with my loud holler.

I felt Holly's body go limp against mine, the red blood blending with her yellow dress and turning bright orange. The other me dropped the gun, staring down at his hand as if it had acted on its own. I realized I was doing the same thing, not knowing which one of us had made this happen.

CHAPTER TWENTY-EIGHT

"Jackson! Dude, snap out of it!" A hand slapped me across the face.

I shot up fast. "Holly!"

"Over there, man," Mason said, pointing to Holly, who was standing five feet away, looking completely freaked.

I jumped up and raced over to Holly, grabbing her arms and pushing up her sleeves. Her skin was pale and unflawed. She snatched her arms away, but turned her head enough so I could see her ears were perfectly free of oozing blood. I did the same thing with Courtney, and she just watched me curiously, but didn't ask any questions.

"I thought you guys were nuts, when you talked about time travel. I thought Adam was literally insane . . . and now . . ." Holly stuttered.

I looked around for the first time. "Now . . . we're in the weird subway station and those genetically mutated, faceless dudes are up there ready to jump our asses."

"What?" Mason, Courtney, and Holly said together.

"How long was I out?" I asked Mason.

"Five minutes. So, what about the faceless dudes?"

"Emily?" I said, hoping she knew something more than the date. "I thought my dad would be here and we'd just grab him and go back."

She shook her head, looking slightly panicked. "I think I know where he is . . ."

"Let's go," Courtney said, pointing toward the steps.

"What? Not gonna hold me at gunpoint anymore?" Holly said, following behind me.

The contrast between this girl and the one I had just been dreaming about was so huge. The reminder of what she had been to me, before, made this kidnapping so much harder.

"It's not like you can go anywhere."

I shook my head and headed up the steps. A throbbing pain had started just behind my temples and I had no energy to argue with Holly or keep up some act of playing the enemy.

Mason and Courtney reached the outside first, and I heard their reaction before I saw the horrible, crumbled city for a second time.

"Holy shit," Mason said, turning around slowly.

"Oh, my God," Courtney muttered. "This is . . . it's New York?"

The dust swirled through the air, just as I remembered. The demolished and half-intact buildings surrounded us.

"A Vortex," Mason muttered, catching my attention.

"You know about that?" I asked him. He didn't bother to answer. Obviously he knew about it. He probably read the same data Kendrick was able to get her hands on.

"We should leave," Holly said. "How are we supposed to find anything here? It's like a needle in a haystack."

Courtney looked at me, her eyes filling with tears. "Maybe she's right, Jackson? What if there's no way to get Dad back . . . what if it's too late?"

I coughed and then gripped my ribs as pain shot through them. "Emily says she might . . . know where . . . to go."

"Who is this kid, Jackson? Some kind of genius psychic child? And why does she look like your sister?" Mason asked, as he pointed his gun in every direction, waiting for the unknown attack that might come at any time.

"She's not psychic . . . she's from this year." I swallowed hard and glanced at Courtney again, and then Holly. "And she looks like my sister because . . . we're sort of . . . DNA twins . . . kind of."

Courtney and Holly both looked confused, but Mason spun around, pointing his gun at me and Emily. "That kid is a clone? Of you?" He glanced over his shoulder at Courtney, then back at me. "How do we know *you're* not a clone . . . and the real Jackson was the one locked in that cell?"

My head throbbed even harder. I rubbed my forehead with my fingertips. "Cut it out, Mason, we don't have time for this."

Courtney crossed her arms, eyes narrowing at me, as she stepped closer to Mason. "I don't even know what you're supposed to look like at nineteen . . . I've got nothing to compare it to."

Holly moved closer to Courtney at the same time Emily pressed herself against my side.

"I really wish someone wouldn't have swiped my gun," Holly said, staring me down harder than Courtney.

Mason reached down toward his shoe and lifted the leg of his jeans, pulling out a gun and passing it over Courtney to Holly. "I try to keep a spare, just in case."

"Thanks," she said, staring at it like she couldn't believe a Tempest agent had offered her something useful. She turned it over in her hands before pointing it at me. "This is just like mine."

"Um . . . I think you guys are forgetting that we might be your only way back," I said.

Emily tugged at my shirt, and when I looked down, she was pointing into the distance . . . the faceless, creepy dudes. Four of them, running toward us.

Mason, Holly, and Courtney all turned around at the same time.

"Oh, damn," Holly said.

"What the hell are those things?" Mason said.

"I don't know, but maybe we should . . . run," Courtney said.

All five of us took off running. Eventually I snatched Emily up and carried her as we kicked up more dirt in our eyes.

"Turn right!" Emily shouted.

To the surprise of us both, Mason, who now led our group, followed directions. "I'm calling a temporary truce," he shouted at me from over his shoulder.

The stabbing pain in my head had moved to the rest of my body and every step was agonizing. Courtney had at least two inches on Holly and passed her, leaving me to jog beside her, Emily's weight in my arms slowing me down.

The fallen city seemed to dissolve and a hill of brownish green grass stood right in front of us. What part of New York was this? A small remnant of Central Park?

"What now?" Mason asked.

"Other side of the hill," Emily instructed.

The sky opened just then and rain started pouring down. *We made it rain?* Courtney let out an ear-piercing scream, causing my head to snap quickly in her direction, every muscle strained.

The faceless dudes . . . right in front of us . . . at the bottom of the hill. "Let's go!" I shouted to Mason.

One of the men lunged for Courtney, but just as I pulled out my gun, she vanished into thin air. My heart beat fast as I set Emily down and spun around in a circle. "What the—"

"How the hell?" Mason said.

The faceless men had paused for a few seconds, just as perplexed as the rest of us. Then, poof . . . Courtney was at my side again, clutching her chest and breathing hard. "Oh, my God . . . oh, my God . . ."

Mason took the distraction as an opportunity and fired at the attacker closest to him. The man fell to the ground at Holly's feet and she screeched and jumped back as if he were diseased. I couldn't blame her—they were pretty freaky-looking.

"They don't have weapons," Emily said as the three remaining men stared us down. "They're rejects who escaped . . . They don't have anything."

I shook my head, not letting myself process anything except the fact that we could shoot them. Holly, Mason, and I all stood ready, guns pointed, waiting for one of them to move.

One dude glanced at the man to his right and then, just like that, they vanished. The first one popped up right behind Courtney. I dove toward her and fell on my face as she vanished before the man could lay a finger on her. I sucked in half a breath and she was right back again, next to Holly, eyes wide, looking like she had no idea what she had just done. Holly took the opportunity to kick the stunned man in the stomach, while Mason shot another one right in the head.

The two remaining men finally stopped, holding their hands up in the air. "Let's get out of here!" one of them shouted to the other.

They were like a pack of wild wolves. No goals or direction, just reckless, aimless fighting until they knew they couldn't win. Nothing like the EOTs. The man closest to Mason nodded, but just as we held our breaths, waiting for a reaction, he vanished and ended up right behind Mason.

"Mason!" I shouted, heading closer to him.

The man jumped on his back, getting his hands around Mason's gun. It fired aimlessly into the sky and Courtney and Holly dropped down onto the grass immediately. The dude's elbow contacted Mason's temple hard. The gun was free and in the hands of these weird-ass attackers.

I couldn't get a clear shot, not with Mason in the way. The man aimed at Courtney, who instantly disappeared again. I didn't even have a millisecond to contemplate how she kept doing that and why I hadn't thought about jumping, too, because the man was now about to fire at Emily. I dove forward, grabbing her around the waist and pulling both of us to the ground. I heard the shot as we fell, then a second one just after. My eyes barely opened to see Holly shoot the man square in the chest with perfect aim. I squinted through the black spots of my horrible headache and saw a window of space between Mason and the remaining man, who looked like he was about to flee.

I shot him right in the back and he fell, mid-run. Holly, Mason, and Courtney all sank to the now-wet grass, breathing hard, as Emily and I sat up again.

Holly kept staring at the gun in her hand, then back at the man she had shot. I had a feeling she was thinking the same thing as me . . . four people . . . all dead. In a matter of minutes.

"Hey," I said, glancing at her, "thanks . . . it was a great shot and he would have hit me the second time."

"Yeah, he would have," Mason answered.

"Courtney?" I said finally, looking at my sister. "What the hell were you doing? How did you jump? I couldn't focus on anything here."

She shook her head, eyes wide. "You'll never believe me . . . Maybe I'm just going crazy."

"I think we're all losing our minds. That's what it feels like, anyway," Holly said, squeezing the rain from her ponytail.

"Maybe," Courtney concluded. "But it was like . . . I knew what they were gonna do a second before they did it."

The pain hit me again and I squeezed my eyes shut, wincing. "Should we go . . . up the hill or whatever . . . ?"

"Jackson? Are you okay?" Courtney asked.

"If that's even the real Jackson," Mason reminded her as he stood up.

We all managed to stand. As soon as we reached the hilltop, I could see figures way in the distance, running toward us. Not the faceless men, but people with hair . . . different-colored hair. There wasn't much else I could make out.

"Jackson!" Courtney said, grabbing my arm. "I think it's Dad!"

All of us took off running and we could see the three people moving closer, shouting something at us. "What?" I yelled back.

Several small houses rested at the bottom of the hill between a sea of trees that didn't fit into the dirty, demolished world we had just run through. I could even make out a stream or a creek in the distance, behind the houses.

Suddenly the three people stopped running. Just froze right in the grass as we ran closer. One of them looked young . . . a guy maybe my age, with dark hair, long and tied in a ponytail, and a woman with red hair and almost the exact same face as Cassidy . . . and Dad . . . really the real Dad . . . in a real jump . . . not a half-jump.

Dad's eyes locked with mine as we stood in front of them, panting and leaning over. It was then that I realized how horrified all of them looked. Complete defeat written on their faces.

"Dad? What is it?" I asked between breaths.

He opened his mouth to speak, and then his eyes drifted to my far right. "Oh, my God . . . Jackson, what did you do?" His legs shook and I thought he might fall over, then the look he gave me, as he tore his eyes from Courtney, was something I'd never forget, pure gratefulness and grief all at the same time. "Courtney . . . oh, my God . . . I can't . . . It's impossible . . ."

He hadn't come here to save her . . . to reverse anything, because that wasn't possible. I knew he wouldn't have done that. He'd never have let himself get trapped like that.

I stood up straight again, watching Dad stumble over to Courtney, looking her over and then opening his arms. She fell right into them, hugging him tight around the waist. "I'm so glad you're okay, Daddy."

"Sweetheart . . . I missed you . . . so much . . ." Everyone heard the crack in his voice and saw the tears streaming down his face. But I don't think he cared.

Emily was the first to speak and break through the reunion. "I'm sorry for bringing her . . . I just . . . Jackson said he wanted to fix it, and . . . I'm sorry."

Emily's words hung in the air as everyone watched Dad, gripping Courtney like she was a lifeline. Mason looked like he was fighting his own emotional battle. But a minute later he snapped into action, the agent coming to life again. "Agent Meyer . . . Courtney and I are a little worried about the cloned kid and, well . . . we think Jackson's a clone, too?"

Dad lifted his head immediately and Courtney wiped the tears from his face with her sleeve. "You think Jackson's a clone?" Dad asked Courtney specifically.

"Don't clones look like the person they're made from?"

"Not exactly . . . not always," the redheaded woman spoke up. "Although I do look almost identical to Experiment 787."

"Otherwise known as Cassidy," Dad said, nodding at me and Mason.

The younger guy stepped toward Emily with a tiny flashlight in his hand. "We can settle this right now."

Emily backed right into me as if she knew what was coming.

"Don't touch her," I warned the guy approaching with his crazy laser-beam thing.

"It's all right," Dad said, looking me right in the eyes.

Emily's entire body stiffened, but she didn't protest. The beam shone into her eyes and the guy pulled what looked like a tiny computer from his pocket and read aloud. "Experiment 1029 . . . Emily. D.O.B. July fourth, 3192. Death date unknown."

"Clone," the woman said. "One of Ludwig's."

He turned the laser beam on me and quickly read, eyebrows lifting. "Experiment Axelle, Product B . . . Jackson . . . D.O.B. June twentieth 1990. Death date . . . unknown."

"Axelle!" Mason said, his mouth hanging open.

Dad shook his head. "Jackson's not a clone. Axelle was an experiment with a surrogate mother—"

"I know what Axelle is," Mason snapped. "I just thought . . . well, I didn't know it was him . . . that's all."

"I'm only half of it," I said. "Courtney's the other half . . . I guess Product A?"

The young guy with the laser beam headed straight toward Courtney, but Dad stopped him and pointed at Holly. Holly's eyes grew large and she began to back away, but she stopped eventually, letting him flash the thing at her.

The guy shook his head, forehead creasing as he read his computer. "All it says is she has the DNA of a known Eyewall agent . . . enrolled in the year 2008."

Shock filled Dad's face despite his gift for composed agent faces. Holly was taking it all in, moving closer to me, looking hard at Dad's expression.

"Dad, did you know that I did a complete jump? Right before I joined Tempest officially?"

His eyes widened, but it wasn't total shock. It was as if several pieces had snapped together. "Wow . . . the chances were so slight that I never wanted to worry you with it. Honestly, even Dr. Melvin was scrambling to figure it all out. Especially the timeline issue."

"Well, that is a whole different subject," I said bitterly, then I took a deep breath before adding, "Dr. Melvin's dead . . . and Freeman."

"And me," Mason said, raising his hand in the air. "I'm dead, too."

Dad looked shaken, but I didn't think he knew what to say. It was Holly who spoke up next.

"That's it, isn't it?" she said, forming some conclusion that she had obviously been working through her mind in the last several minutes . . . something she hadn't let us in on yet. She grabbed my wrist and turned me around. "You did some voodoo time-traveling trick. You knew me before. That day I saw you in the bookstore, with Brian . . . you acted so weird. I should have known something was up then, but of course I never would have guessed *this*."

"Holly?" I said, trying to shake her hand from my arm. She was practically off in her own world and I understood where the excitement, the energy, came from. This whole jump-to-the-future thing was major brain overload, and people like us, trained agents, we lived for answers to the endless questions. I tried to catch her eye, get her to really look at me. "Hol, listen—"

"God . . . it's practically genius, what you can do. Blow your cover with me, and then, poof! Time-travel back a few hours and erase the screwup. No wonder they freaked out about you. Collins would have had me move in with you and propose if he could have, just to get more information. That's how much you baffled them."

I rested my hands on her shoulders and shook her a little. "Holly! Look at me."

She did meet my eyes for a split second, and then her gaze drifted to my wrist. I felt my body stiffen when I saw what she was staring at. I leaned closer, examining the blue and black streaks etched across my skin. My heart pounded so loud, I couldn't hear if she said anything to me. I glanced over my shoulder and quickly tugged the sleeve of my sweatshirt over my wrist.

Eileen had said the side effects would be instant. Maybe they were and I'd ignored them . . . my head throbbing uncontrollably. But things were happening then, too many things to pay attention to pain.

"Dad, can we just go home?" Courtney asked, tears trembling in her voice. "I don't understand all this experiment stuff, but let's just go home and then you can tell me everything."

Holly was still staring at my wrist, then back at me. I dropped my arms to my sides, grateful that nobody else had seen the bruises. This wasn't the time to add more drama.

"Wait . . . am I going to be dead if we go back?" Mason asked. "I'm working through the paradox theories and time-travel basics, but it's not coming out right."

Dad let go of Courtney and moved closer to the younger guy and the redheaded woman. They all exchanged a few looks, and then the woman spoke first. "You can't go back . . . We tried to stop you from entering, but it was too late."

"Entering what?" Mason and I asked at the same time.

"We call it Misfit Island," the younger guy said. "Like that Christmas movie *The Island of Misfit Toys* . . . except we're misfit time jumpers." He laughed a nervous laugh, and then turned it into a cough when he realized no one else had even cracked a smile.

Mason looked up at the sky, which was spinning around in a circle. "What is it? Some kind of a force field?"

"Yes," the red-haired woman said.

Her words didn't even sink in with me. I had always been able to go back home . . . except when I was stuck in 2007 . . . but I was so far beyond that mental block now. There had to be a way, otherwise why would Healy even send me here to get Dad?

"And an electromagnetic pulse," Dad said, his eyes filling with worry and sympathy. "Every day, I hoped you wouldn't come here and try to find me. I told them there was no way Jackson would attempt anything that risky after everything he'd been through."

I was barely listening to Dad. The pain in my head had reached a climactic peak and I wanted to figure this out before I passed out. "We got here—if we jumped to this place, then we can leave. Somehow we got through the—"

"Try it," the woman snapped at me. "Walk toward the bottom of the hill."

Mason and I were both striding across the grass at the exact same moment. Suddenly a shock ran though my body, paralyzing every muscle. I knew I was falling, but I had no control over it. I tried to force myself forward instead of backward. I ended up flat on my back about twenty feet from the spot that had paralyzed me.

Mason was right next to me, sitting up and looking just as confused as I felt. Neither of us had felt the force field tossing us backward. We stood up slowly and I stared at Dad, desperate for him to fix this, to tell me there was another way.

Mason pointed a finger at Emily. "You did this! You tricked us into coming here, didn't you?"

Emily burst into tears. "No, no, I didn't know . . . I promise."

I rested a hand on her shoulder, trying to offer comfort. I didn't know if she had done this on purpose, but either way, she was just a little kid.

"I'm sorry, Jackson . . . I messed everything up," Emily said.

My eyes traveled from Courtney to Mason to Holly, absorbing their shock and mine at the same time. Trapped.

"You were tricked into coming here," the redheaded woman said, as if reading my thoughts. "Just like the rest of us . . . It's what they do with time travelers who don't conform, don't offer the agency anything or try to make their alterations. We can guess when a new one is coming based on the weather, and we try to stop them using any means possible, but it almost never works."

The grass and the houses and the stream swirled in front of me. Healy . . . he tricked me . . . used all my weaknesses against me. Dad, Holly, Adam . . . The tears in Courtney's eyes and the ones I knew Holly was fighting to keep hidden hit me right in the gut.

This was my fault. I should have found Stewart, and talked it through. She wouldn't have let me screw up like this. The hopelessness swept over me and I closed my eyes, forcing my mind back to 2009.

Please work . . . please work.

The sharpest pain I had ever felt hit me right between the eyes. I fell to my knees, every muscle in my body shaking violently. My breath came out in loud and effort-filled gasps.

"Jackson!" Dad said, running over to me. He looked up at the redheaded woman with panic as he pushed up my sleeves, revealing the bruises. *Just like Cassidy . . . and the EOT in the basement of the Plaza.*

I threw an arm across my ribs, clutching them to relieve the pain. Holly stood next to me, hands covering her mouth. My eyes locked with hers and there was something there . . . something I hadn't seen from this Holly. Something that stole my breath and made me forget everything else. Like a magnet, I pulled her closer with my eyes. One step inside my world . . . the one that had included me and her.

Just keep looking at me like that and I'll be okay. My hand brushed across the side of my face and I was mildly aware of the sticky substance between my fingers. I waved my hand in front of my face, breaking my eye contact with Holly and letting the cold draft of reality blow in.

"Oh, no," Dad moaned. "Oh, no, Jackson . . . is it too late?"

"No," the redheaded woman said firmly. "Blake . . . go . . . get help!"

Blake? The ponytail kid?

"Mason, go with him," Dad shouted.

The world was already fading before me . . . losing all of its clarity. The redheaded lady's hair and face blurred and blended with Dad's. Courtney was right beside him, panic written all over her face, but all I could see was the recognition. Just like I had known, when she had slipped away from me so many years ago, I knew she felt this. The pain faded, and in this case I knew that wasn't a good sign. But I welcomed it, so much. *Just let it be quick . . . let me close my eyes and just sleep . . .*

The sound of Courtney sobbing gave me a brief, five-second electric shock to the heart. I felt the pain again for several seconds and then it drifted. As I focused all my attention on Courtney's face, I wondered if this was what she had fought, this exhausting battle to hold on, when letting go was so much easier. Would she fight it all over again? Would she feel the emptiness that I had felt when she died? I wished I had told Dad or Adam or my Holly what had happened to me . . . I knew it was real . . . it had to be.

I had written a poem . . . in 2009 . . . not intentionally, more like subconscious thoughts that had vomited themselves onto my computer and then into the hands of an overly dramatic teacher. Voices echoed around me, from a distant tunnel, as I recalled those words I wrote about Courtney in another life . . . as another person,

> I shared a womb with someone . . . does that mean we shared a soul?
> Maybe half my soul is buried, deep under the ground, and I'll never get it back.
> I'm cold when it isn't. I hear storms that aren't there. There's space in me I can't fill.
> Empty. Cold. Storms. And then I smell the carpet, hear deep breaths that aren't mine.
> When I open my eyes, she's still gone.

But I didn't feel like that anymore . . . I was whole again. Because of Holly. And now she was here with me. Somehow, she had managed to pull my arm out of my sweatshirt and had the sleeve pressed against my ear, trying to stop the bleeding. Was I sitting up or lying down?

Sitting . . . sort of. I felt my body swaying, falling into her, our foreheads crashing together as she attempted to hold me up. Images flashed through my head at high speed, but I saw each and every one of them: Courtney and me in the snow on Christmas Eve . . . me, standing over Courtney's casket, squeezing my eyes shut, not letting myself see her for more than half a second . . . me and Dad tipping the sailboat on purpose, splashing Courtney with ocean water . . . and Holly, kissing me that first time . . . *the very first time* . . . I could taste her, smell her, feel her arms around me still. Holly asleep in my bed, the two of us breathing in rhythm. Different but always in sync.

I shook my head, zooming in on her face, the one right in front of me and not the one etched in my memories. This was the last image I wanted to see. Not the grief and panic on Dad's, Courtney's, and Emily's faces. Holly . . . *just Holly.*

"We have to get him inside!" someone shouted.

"If his brain was bleeding he'd be screaming from the pressure." Another voice, one I didn't know.

"Let him go," someone said, leaning over Holly.

I felt my hand lifting up to touch her face, or at least that was what I wanted it to do. My forehead still rested against hers. *This is it . . . this is all I get.* Her eyes were closed now and it made me feel the world around me again. I didn't want that pain. Not ever.

"Hol?" I whispered, not sure if any sound had actually come out. "Look at me."

She opened her eyes and I started seeing two of her, but relief washed over me in an instant. My head slumped over, leaning against her shoulder. I couldn't hold it up . . . only a few more seconds and I'd fall over completely. My face made contact with the side of her neck as I succeeded in turning my head. "Hol?"

"What?" she whispered back, as if I were about to tell her some great escape plan before dying.

"Don't give up . . . It's worth it, I swear. You're worth it, Holly. I was wrong before . . . so wrong."

And finally, I let my eyes close. The hot, wet tears that splashed the side of my neck were the last sensation I felt.

Holly's tears. Maybe she was just overwhelmed by the moment, or maybe she truly felt my words . . . heard the truth behind them and knew that she *had* someone. She wasn't alone.

Someone was prying us apart and the desperate fight for life sprang up again. My fingers curled around the back of her neck and I whispered, as loud as I possibly could, "I love you."

Then my back hit the grass and I stared up at the clouds, my body relaxing, *shutting down.* I struggled against the darkness, trying to sit up and being pushed back down. I opened my mouth, but no sound came out.

The echoing voices turned to silence . . . and I was being sucked into a black tunnel . . . maybe forever . . .

Acknowledgments

I have to keep this much, *much* shorter than the *Tempest* acknowledgments. I won't get away with another five pages of thanking people.

Tempest Launch Event on January 21, 2012

First off, I want to thank all my family and friends, my community—the super-awesome Champaign-Urbana, Illinois—for following my journey from the beginning and being there for the release of *Tempest*. Also, Betsy Su and the Champaign Public Library for hosting my launch event and making it such an amazing day. Suzie Townsend, for being there. My editor, Brendan Deneen, for wishing he could be there.

Also Beth Revis, Megan Miranda, Maureen Lipinski, and Carrie Ryan for joining me on January 17, 2012—the official *Tempest* release day—at Books of Wonder in New York City.

St. Martin's Press/Thomas Dunne Books/Macmillan Folks

Those with big offices make big dreams come true—Tom Dunne, Matthew Shear, Anne Marie Tallberg, and Pete Wolverton.

Two amazing ladies who have worked hard to get *Tempest* out in the world and are so fun to hang out with—Brittney Kleinfelter and Eileen Rothschild.

The guy I pester almost daily for marketing and social media advice and who answers all my questions with patience and humor—Joe Goldschein. It's been so fun to work with you!

Nicole Sohl—for all your behind-the-scenes work.

Also publicity folks—Rachel Ekstrom and Jessica Preeg.

And last, but not least, the guy behind the curtain who sees all my writing way, way before the final version and still believes in me—my editor, Brendan Deneen—someone I can tell just about anything to and know that he won't lose faith in my ability to finish this trilogy, and make it the awesome series he and I both envisioned way back in April 2010.

Other Equally Important People in Smaller Groups

The amazing UK folks at Macmillan Children's—Sally Opiant and Ruth Kristin Nelson and the amazing Nelson Literary Agency crew. Alltimes.

Writer friends and inspiring authors—Roni Loren, Kari Olson, John Green, Veronica Roth, Courtney Summer, Ally Carter, Erika O'Rourke, Kody Keplinger.

Vortex cover models—Mark Perini and Scarlett Benchley, thanks for bringing Jackson and Holly to life.

The Perfect 10, my amazing teen panel, teamTEENauthor, all the book bloggers.

Librarians everywhere, YALSA, and ALA—amazing organizations that get books into people's hands for the sole purpose of helping others fall in love with reading.

And superspecial thanks to Every. Single. Fan for your support, reviews, and honest thoughtful words. You are the ones who have truly kept my butt in the writing chair and made words continue to appear on the page. I hope this sequel is everything you wanted it to be. I have thought of every one of you as I poured my energy into creating this story.

Turn the page for a sneak peek at
the next book in the Tempest series

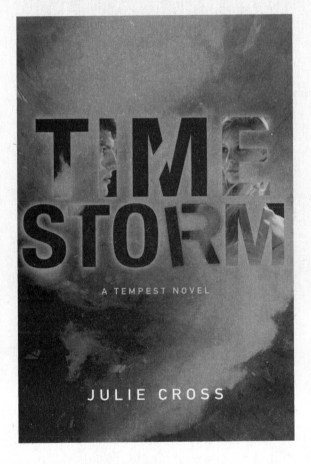

TIME
STORM

A TEMPEST NOVEL

JULIE CROSS

Available February 2014

CHAPTER ONE

I stood in front of the cell staring at . . . well . . . staring at *me*. The caged, unshaven, animal version of me. The way he looked, not at me, but through me, brought on the sudden self-awareness that I probably hadn't survived the bleeding brain or whatever the hell happened to me when I jumped into the future. My eyes dropped to my arms as I lifted a hand toward my face. Transparent. I was transparent.

A magnetic force seemed to pulse in the space between the two versions of myself, pulling us together. Footsteps echoed from behind me and I jumped out of the way as Senator Healy stalked right up to the cell, opening the door and somehow cutting off whatever force had been dragging me forward. The other me stood up slowly, shakily, bruises marring his face and legs.

"Senator Healy!" I tried to croak, not hearing a sound outside of my own mind.

"Come on, son. Let's get you out of here," Healy said, his voice gentle, barely above a whisper. It reminded me of the way he had spoken to me while I had hung my head over a sink after watching Mason get blown to pieces. Even just thinking about what happened still made me feel nauseous.

The other me shuffled closer, leaning heavily on Healy for support as if his legs weren't used to walking. The urge to somehow unzip him and crawl inside so I could be seen and heard intensified. I had to find a way! Somehow I just knew that I was dying. And then the old warehouse dissolved and pain shot through every inch of my body.

"He can't breathe! We've got to do something!"

A truck.

A truck sat on my chest and every ounce of energy I had was devoted to shoving it away. Air. I needed air. Nothing would enter. Nothing would exit.

"His lungs are full of fluid! Open him up!" someone shouted.

And I felt the stab to my chest, skin splitting open and my ribs cracking. I had to get out of here. People aren't supposed to feel these things.

"Pulse is fading and then coming again . . . I can't get it steady," a woman's voice spoke right next to my ear.

"He's jumping," someone said.

Silence followed for a full five seconds, then I heard Dad's voice, in my other ear, sounding more terrified than I've ever heard him in my life. "Jackson, just stay here . . . please."

But I couldn't. There was no way to control it.

"Are you all right, son?" Healy said to the other me, hand clutching his shoulder.

The other me had sunk to his knees with a loud crack as his knee-caps made contact with the hard floor. He clutched his chest, a look of panic in his eyes and then raised his shirt. A faint line appeared slowly down the center of his chest, blood trickling from the wound.

Which one of us is dying? I thought it was me. He's not in the future. How can he feel what is happening to me?

A gunshot rang from right behind me, breaking my concentration. Healy fell to the ground, blood oozing from his head. Eyes wide open.

"What the . . . ?" the other me said, staring at Healy's body. Then he looked up, right at me. Or through me.

"Who . . . who are you?" he stuttered, still on his knees, attempting to stand.

Was he talking to me? No, he was talking to whoever had just shot Healy. But for some reason I couldn't make my body turn around to see who it was. I needed to breathe air. To feel my heart beat again.

"I'm the only one with enough guts to do this," the deep voice boomed from behind me.

Chief Marshall. I didn't have to look.

"Do what?" the other me said, his eyes wide.

Using all my willpower, I forced my body to start to move. The gun fired again. Not just once, but three times. I heard myself scream inside my head . . . heard the other me's scream cut off as he slumped to the ground.

Thump . . . thump . . . thump.

My heart gave three quick beats as I finally turned, just in time to see Chief Marshall vanish.

CHAPTER TWO

DAY 5

"He's waking up."

"Jackson? Can you hear me?"

I found my hands and brought them to my face, rubbing the sleep from my eyes. The room came into focus—white walls, a few gray cabinets, a table beside the bed. The bed had metal rails and white sheets that covered my legs. It looked a lot like a hospital room in 2009. Maybe this wasn't the future after all?

Dad and Courtney stood at the foot of the bed, watching like they'd been staring at me for weeks and I had finally moved.

"Chief Marshall," I managed to say, looking at Dad. "He killed me." I took a breath, slowly letting the scene fall into place in my head so I could articulate it. "The other me. He killed the other me. And then Healy. He killed Healy."

My heart raced, causing a searing pain to rip through my chest like it was being split open all over again. "Healy told me before . . . he said that he had someone doing his time travel changes for him, someone doing the alterations like putting Holly and Adam in the CIA! He did that, Dad. But he said it's not Thomas. It's Marshall! I *know* it is. He vanished right in front of me. He can time travel!"

Dad's eyes widened, but not because of what I'd just revealed, but because of the loud beeping on the monitor beside me. "Jackson, I need you to calm down. Breathe . . . focus on the present for the moment and then we'll figure out what you saw or *think* you saw."

"I know I saw it . . ." The pain in my chest elevated, shutting me up. I relaxed back into the pillow, closing my eyes briefly, breathing as slowly and deeply as possible without aggravating my pain. After a couple minutes, the monitor stopped beeping and Dad let out a sigh of relief.

"Good, very good."

I opened my eyes again. "Where are we? Did we make it back?"

Dad shook his head and patted my foot over the covers. "It's still the same place. Same year."

My heart sped up as I touched the back of my head, feeling a large bandage behind my ear. Then I remembered my dream, or was it a half jump? My fingers fumbled around, moving toward my chest. I drew in a deep breath and felt the tightness of stitched skin pulling apart. There was another bandage horizontally placed between my sternum and left armpit.

"I'm not dead?" I looked up at Dad and Courtney who were both standing still as statues. "Obviously, I'm not dead . . . I just . . . I thought I was."

Before they could respond, a man with light brown hair and a striking resemblance to Thomas walked into the room, followed by a red-haired woman. I remembered her welcoming us here with Dad, just before my almost-death.

The man held up his hands as if in surrender. "I know, we look alike, but don't worry, my name isn't Thomas and I'm not a clone either."

Courtney laughed and my eyes bounced to her and then back to Dad, who seemed at ease, not worried at all about these strangers.

I sighed with relief.

"I'm Grayson and this is Lonnie." He nodded toward the redheaded woman. "You met her five days ago."

"Five days." I could hardly wrap my head around the idea that I'd lost that much time. More details about how we'd ended up here hit me all at once. I tried to sit up too quickly and was instantly knocked back down as pain shot through my head and chest. "Holly . . . Emily . . . Mason . . . are they—"

"They're all fine," Dad said.

"Except for the being stuck here part," Courtney added.

After holding a stethoscope to my chest briefly, Grayson held up a giant syringe with a long needle. "Pain medication. I wanted you to wake up first and see how your heart and lungs were functioning."

He plunged the needle into my IV. "You're going to experience some drowsiness in about five minutes. Luckily, you guys got trapped on an island with a doctor who's practiced medicine in two different centuries. I used a combination of new technology and old school methods to relieve the pressure in your skull and stop the bleeding as well as saving your collapsed lung."

"Wow . . . so I was pretty messed up?"

No one said a word for several long seconds but I could see it all over their faces. I really *had* almost died.

Dad gripped the rail at the foot of the bed with both hands and looked me in the eye. "Grayson says you'll be good as new in a few days."

The pain in my head and chest reached an almost unbearable level and I tuned out until Grayson, Dad, and Lonnie left the room to get supplies and talk about me behind my back.

Courtney walked closer and sat beside me on the bed. "I really, really hate you for scaring me like that. And Dad, he's been in hell for the past five days."

I moved my hand closer to Courtney's and squeezed her fingers tight. "I'm sorry."

Tears spilled from her eyes but she started laughing at the same time, wiping her cheeks quickly. "God, this is so weird. I still can't get over how old you are and how old I'm not. And this thing with Holly. She's not saying much but we all heard you. Loud and clear."

The fogginess of the drugs started to set in, but not enough that I didn't feel a sudden sense of alarm. What had I said to Holly?

Oh right.

I love you.

I looked down at my hand, now covering my sister's. "I thought . . . I thought it was you," I lied.

Courtney's eyes widened. "Seriously? You were saying goodbye?"

A knot formed in the pit of my stomach. "Yeah, something like that."

I wasn't quite swept under by the pain meds yet, but I closed my eyes anyway, pretending until it really happened so we could end this conversation.

When I woke from my drug-induced sleep, Courtney was gone and Holly sat in a chair beside my bed, knees pulled up to her chest, arms wrapped tight around her legs. Her eyes were focused on the monitor to my right, but she blinked rapidly and yawned.

I didn't speak at first because my mind was so groggy I had to remind myself which Holly this was. What had we done together? How did she feel about me?

It came back in an instant. Agent Holly. The one who saw her best friend Adam lying dead on the floor in a puddle of blood. The one who thought I'd killed him. The Holly who wrote that terrible letter about herself, about the hopelessness of her life now and how survival—self-preservation—were the only reasons she had to get up in the morning.

The ache of these revelations hit me like a punch in the stomach.

"Hey," she said, noticing I had woken up.

"Hey." I suddenly felt very insecure about the state of my personal hygiene and the fact that I had tubes and wires coming out of *way* too many body parts. "Where is everybody else?"

"It's the middle of the night." Holly yawned. "We've been taking turns watching the heart monitors, switching the bags of fluids. Stuff like that."

My eyes carefully avoided hers. "Well, that answers my question about whether or not you've decided to continue working for Eyewall."

"Nobody's enemies here. What's the point?" Holly sighed and gave me a tight smile. "This is awkward, isn't it?"

I finally looked at her and knew in an instant that I was going to lie, just like I had with Courtney. Not because I smelled bad and looked like hell, but because I couldn't imagine being in Holly's position: having someone tell you that another version of you was *in love* with this person you sort of hate. A person that held you at gunpoint and dragged you into the future.

Everything that had happened since I left August of 2009 trying to save the other version of Holly had created a hell on Earth for this version of Holly. She had had no choice about any aspect of her life from the point that Adam had first asked her to help with a CIA mission. This time around, I was determined to make damn sure she got to choose who she fell in love with, if anyone at all. From now on, Holly would be in full control in the course of her life.

Eyewall had her boxed in with no way out and I wasn't about to do the same thing to her. Not after getting her trapped here. I still couldn't believe, after all my efforts to keep Holly safe, she'd ended up working for 2009 Eyewall, a division of the CIA that seemed determined to take down my own division, Tempest. And Eyewall hadn't exactly been a pleasant work environment for Holly. I hated to think about being the reason she was stuck here, but at the same time, I couldn't forget what had happened when I "held her hostage" before the jump to the future. Her own people, her own division, had been poised to write her off without a second thought.

"I know what you think," I said to Holly, making a quick decision.

Her eyebrows lifted as if to ask if I also had mind-reading abilities in addition to time travel powers. "What I think is . . . that you know me a little better than I know you. And I'm not sure how I feel about that. How would you feel?"

"I don't know." I rubbed my face with my hands. "About what I said, Courtney filled me in and honestly, I thought it was her. You have to realize, I hadn't seen my sister in years, and then she's here and I'm dying."

"So you were trying to tell Courtney you loved her before you died?" Holly clarified.

My eyes froze on hers, unwavering as I forced my pupils to stay normal-sized. "Yes."

"But you did know me, things I don't have any memory of, because of time travel, right?" She looked so focused, so incredibly on task that it occurred to me for the first time that Holly probably made a fantastic CIA agent. A lot better than I would have if I didn't have superpowers.

Now for the cover story.

"Adam," I said forcing calm. "Adam was my best friend. We were working together on time travel stuff. He was also your friend, so obviously I knew you then, too."

"But you didn't know I was an agent, did you?" she asked, drilling me as if I were 100 percent healthy and not at all in danger of heart failure or whatever.

"That kinda shocked me," I admitted because it lined up perfectly with my cover story. "Which I'm sure you noticed."

I could tell she was deep in thought, reviewing those memories, but after a few seconds she nodded. "Yeah, I noticed."

The back of my throat felt like sandpaper and I coughed a few times before asking Holly if there was water or anything to drink. She jumped from her chair and opened a cabinet, pulling out this flat, round water bottle. When she unscrewed the cap, a rubber straw popped out.

"Weird." I looked it over carefully before taking several big gulps. It hurt like hell, but I was too thirsty to care. "What's it like out there, anyway?"

Holly took the bottle from my hands and set it on the table before sitting down next to me again. "It's so odd, seriously. There's a few cabins and some tents, and a building with all this weird-ass technology and supplies. It's like they want us to stay alive, but also not be all that comfortable. Mason thinks they're watching us constantly. Most of the area isn't all that future-like considering the year."

"If we're being watched, why don't they just kill us?" I asked, regretting my choice of words immediately. "Sorry, that wasn't the positive thinking I had been trying to display."

Holly laughed. "Believe me, that was the first thought to go through my head. But I think Mason could be right. We're in some kind of guinea pig maze. Like a social experiment or something."

"How many people are here?"

"Mason, Courtney, Emily, your dad, me," Holly rattled off. "Grayson, Lonnie, Sasha, and Blake."

"Making friends?"

Holly rolled her eyes. "Yeah, it's just like summer camp."

"I've met Lonnie and Grayson. I have no idea who Sasha is," I assessed. "Blake? Why does that name sound familiar?"

"The guy with the ponytail," she said, reminding me that I'd already met him. "He's our age. They've been here awhile, you know?"

"How long?"

"Almost two years," Holly said.

Our eyes met again and we sat in silence, letting the gravity of two years sink in slowly. If there was a way out of here, they would have found it by now.

But did it even really matter to me how long we were stuck here? I had Courtney, Dad, and Holly with me. Three people I loved more than anything else.

Could I secretly be happy in this place?

I had a feeling if I brought this up with anyone else, I'd be in need of more medical attention. Or maybe they'd excuse it and label the behavior as one of the weird things that happens to people after they almost die.